Mar

Henry III. King of France and Poland: His Court and Times

Vol. III

SALZWASSER
VERLAG

Martha Walker Freer

Henry III. King of France and Poland: His Court and Times

Vol. III

Reprint of the original, first published in 1858.

1st Edition 2023 | ISBN: 978-3-37513-886-8

Verlag (Publisher): Salzwasser Verlag GmbH, Zeilweg 44, 60439 Frankfurt, Deutschland
Vertretungsberechtigt (Authorized to represent): E. Roepke, Zeilweg 44, 60439 Frankfurt, Deutschland
Druck (Print): Books on Demand GmbH, In de Tarpen 42, 22848 Norderstedt, Deutschland

HENRY III.

KING OF FRANCE AND POLAND:

HIS COURT AND TIMES.

FROM NUMEROUS UNPUBLISHED SOURCES,

INCLUDING MS. DOCUMENTS IN THE BIBLIOTHÈQUE IMPÉRIALE,
AND THE ARCHIVES OF FRANCE AND ITALY, ETC.

BY

MARTHA WALKER FREER,

AUTHOR OF
"THE LIFE OF MARGUERITE D'ANGOULÊME,"
"ELIZABETH DE VALOIS AND THE COURT OF PHILIP II."
&c. &c.

Lilia non laborant neque nent.

IN THREE VOLUMES.
VOL. III.

LONDON:
HURST AND BLACKETT, PUBLISHERS,
SUCCESSORS TO HENRY COLBURN,
13, GREAT MARLBOROUGH STREET.
1858.

CONTENTS OF VOLUME III.

BOOK V.—(*continued.*)

CHAPTER II.

1585—1587.

CHAPTER III.

1587—1588.

CHAPTER IV.

1588.

BOOK VI.

CHAPTER I.

1588.

CHAPTER II.

1588.

CHAPTER III.

1588—1589.

CHAPTER IV.

1589.

BOOK V.

(*Continued.*)

HENRY III. KING OF FRANCE:

HIS COURT AND TIMES.

CHAPTER II.

1585—1587.

King Henry presents the edict of Nemours to his parliament—His comments thereon—Departure of the Flemish ambassage—Interview of king Henry with the presidents of the parliament and the provost of Paris—Bull of excommunication against Henri king of Navarre—Preparations of the Calvinists for the war—The king of Navarre—Enthusiasm of his subjects—The League des Seize—Its constitution and influence—Nicholas Poulain—Correspondences of the king—He makes overtures to the duc and duchesse de Nevers—Defeat of Condé—His flight to England—Deportment of the duc de Guise—He departs from Paris for Nancy—His farewell interview with king Henry—Puts himself at the head of his army—Commencement of the campaign—Envoys from the German States arrive in Paris—Interview with the king—Negotiations of Catherine de Medici—Conferences of St. Bris—The duchesse de Montpensier—Progress of the League—Plots to seize the person of the king—Funeral oration of Mary Stuart—The duc de Mayenne—Joins his sister madame de Montpensier in a conspiracy against the royal person—Death of the comtesse de Bouchage—Marriage of the duc d'Epernon—Entry into the realm of the German levies—Tumults in Paris—Battle of Coutras.

Not content with having extorted so humiliating a treaty from the necessity of their sovereign, the princes of Lorraine and their adherents insisted that Henry should present the edict to his parliament, and give renewed sanction to the treaty of Nemours, by personally commanding the registration of the decree. The cardinals de Bourbon and de Guise arrived in Paris to be present at the ceremonial. Catherine, however, dissatisfied with herself, with the treaty, and with all the world, retired to Chenonceau. The health of the queen was now much broken; and the vigour of her once iron constitution yielded before the anxieties of her position, and her mortification at beholding her long-tried counsels superseded by those of Epernon and his partisans. She was much tormented with gout, which assailed her alternately in her arms, feet, and stomach; moreover, the queen had caught a violent cold during her protracted negotiations with the duc de Guise, an accident which at first threatened her with an attack of pleurisy. Both the favourites repaired to Paris, to give their royal master the benefit of their support at this season. The dissensions between them, however, neutralized the pleasure which their presence might have conferred on their royal master. The duc de Joyeuse obediently went out to meet his rival on his return from Nemours, but no greeting passed between the two, and for several days "the dukes" refused to speak to each other, until the king pathetically implored them to be united and at peace.[1] The treaty recently concluded seems to have been their subject of contention at this season. The duc de Joyeuse, a warm partisan of Lorraine, maintained its necessity and legality; while Epernon inveighed against its clauses, and predicted, as afterwards became apparent, that the convention of Nemours was a first step towards the downfall of the royal dynasty

[1] "Les ducs se morguèrent deux jours un grant regret de leur maître, qui en jeta maintes larmes les voyant ainsi divisés. Ils se parlent maintenant, mais dans leur âmes ils ne se veulent pas du bien."—Lettre de Louis Cardinal de Guise au Duc de Nevers. MS. Bibl. Imp. Béth. vol. 8866, p. 67. 17 Janvier, 1586.

of Valois. The revolution in affairs at court, however, had diminished the arrogance of Epernon. Formerly the duke's assurance had been so inordinate, that often he permitted princes of the blood to address him bareheaded, whilst he himself remained covered. The change in the favourite's deportment gave rise to the saying, "that Epernon had never before known where to seek his hat, but that now he had fortunately found it!" The duc de Joyeuse had never assumed such overbearing airs; and his extreme suavity of manner offered a notable contrast to the blustering of his rival, who was now often ironically honoured by the courtiers with the appellation of Monseigneur le premier Mignon.

On the 7th day of July the king proceeded to the Chambers, to cause the registration of the obnoxious treaty wrung from him. The senators had been commanded to assume their robes of ceremony; and never was the royal cortége more brilliant than on the day when Henry met his parliament to announce the degradation of Henri de Navarre, and to proclaim a bloody crusade against his subjects of the south, defaulters from the orthodox faith. The king looked pale and harassed; his words were few after he took his seat on the throne, and with a gesture of the hand he directed the chancellor to explain the purport of the edict to the Chambers. On leaving the Palais some feeble cheers were uttered for the king and the edict. Henry, however, took no notice of these plaudits, but sat still with compressed lips. He bitterly felt his humiliation; but he possessed neither energy nor ability to free himself from the yoke. In thus coercing their sovereign, the duc de Guise and his colleagues forgot the one trait of unflinching vindictiveness at the root of the king's character; for long his majesty's animosity might slumber, but its awakening carried terror and vengeance signal as his endurance had been passive.

"Mark well, mon oncle," said Henry, on descending from his coach in the courtyard of the Louvre, "against my conscience, but most cordially, I gave my edict of pacification of Poitiers to the Huguenots of my realm. To-day I have revoked this said edict to the tranquillizing, as you say, of my conscience, but most reluctantly, because I foresee that this said revocation will entail the ruin of my realm!" The duc de Nevers, who being still at Rome, was enlightened by the keen comment of Sixtus V. on passing events, wrote to the cardinal de Bourbon in language of unmeasured condemnation of the terms wrested from the sovereign. "Monseigneur, you must excuse me if I show you that the duc de Guise has gone far beyond the things which we had previously agreed. It was indeed a great fault to treat the king as an enemy, and to impose conditions injurious to the royal dignity. You actually forgot that you were the subjects of the king, and proceeded to treat with him as if you yourselves were sovereigns, or, at least, deputies sent by some potent prince! I fear me, monseigneur, that the king's motives, in making such concessions, have not been those of clement forbearance, or of zeal for the faith. The edict which his majesty has just presented to the parliament terrifies me; he therein sanctions the taking up of arms, the appropriation of the public treasure, and every other of your past acts of hostility. Believe me, monseigneur, the king has not spoken as he thinks; and the command he has promulgated to others to forget the late occurrences, is to himself as a secret bond never to forgive, but to make you all repent your deeds on the first opportunity.[1] I conjure you, there-

[1] "Cependant il ne paroit que le roi approuve la sainte Ligue, ni qu'il y adhère sincèrement. On ne doute point que ce ne soit de belles apparences pour tirer de l'argent, et que lorsqu'il en sera venu à bout, il changera de conduite: le temps le decouvrira!"—Lettres de Busbecq.

fore, submit yourself now, and restrain the ardour of MM. de Guise, and try that your future deportment be such that you may hereafter obtain, if possible, the free pardon of your sovereign."[1] This wise though unpalatable counsel was not heeded; indeed, the popular agitation was such in all the great cities, inflamed by the seditious orations of the clergy, that now the most unconditional reconciliation with the king, and the abandonment of the League by the great chieftains, could alone have restored the royal authority, or have neutralized the evil already perpetrated.

The day after his progress to the Chambers the king gave final audience to the Flemish deputies, whose arrival had so fatally precipitated the measures of the duc de Guise. The king informed them briefly "that he had as great a complaint as their countrymen against the king of Spain, who aided the pernicious designs of MM. de Guise; nevertheless, on account of the condition of the kingdom, he could not then afford the protection they demanded." His majesty promised to aid the States as far as lay in his power, and to recommend their cause to the protection of the king of Navarre and of the queen of England.[2] He then took a cordial farewell of the deputies, and proceeded to give audience to the two chief presidents of the parliament of Paris, the prévôt des Marchands, the dean of Notre Dame, and the cardinal de Guise—all these personages having been summoned to the Louvre by command. "It gives me satisfaction," began his majesty, "to have been able to follow the good advice which you united in giving me to revoke my edict of Poitiers. I acknowledge that I have had difficulty in reconciling myself to this step; not because I am less zealous for the faith than any one of you, but because I believed

[1] Mém. de Nevers, tome i. p. 670.
[2] De Thou.

that insuperable obstacles would beset any other design. The die, however, is now cast; and I have reason to believe that, with the help and succour of so many enlightened personages, I may hope to bring the pending war to a happy conclusion. Nevertheless, to undertake this war with any hope of success, I must have three large armies: one army will remain with me, a second I shall despatch into Guyenne, and the third must advance to the German frontier to arrest the advance of mercenary troops; for whatever you may be pleased to believe and to assert, it is certain that these Germans, summoned by M. de Condé, are already advancing into our country. These matters, messieurs, must be met and provided for immediately, before the enemy is at our doors. I repeat, it is against my judgment that this war has been begun; nevertheless, I am resolved to spare neither pains, nor exertions, nor cost, to bring it to a happy conclusion. It is just, however, that, as you did not choose to be guided by the wisdom of your sovereign when he advised you to maintain the edicts, you should aid him in providing for this said war. I have throughout acted on your desires and responsibility; but it is not my intention to bear alone the burden of this war!" Henry paused; then addressing the first president of the parliament of Paris, he said: "M. le Premier, I commend your zeal and that of your colleagues, who, you tell me, so very highly approve the revocation of the edict, and have so earnestly exhorted me to defend the faith. I have, however, to remark to you that war is not made without adequate funds to meet its expenses; therefore you will apprize your said colleagues that so long as the war continues it will be useless for them to pester me for the restoration of their salaries, which the necessity of the times has caused to be curtailed. As for you, M. le Prévôt, you will have the goodness to assemble my loyal burghers of Paris, and say to them, that as the revocation of the edict has also given them such unfeigned pleasure, I trust that they will not object to furnish me with the sum of 200,000 gold crowns. I have caused a careful computation to be made, and I find that the war will cost on an average 400,000 crowns a month. You perceive, monseigneur de Guise," continued Henry, angrily addressing the cardinal, "that I am making arrangements to enter quickly on your war, and that with my own contribution I have raised money for its exigencies for the space of one month. It rests with the clergy to afford the remaining funds. I do not intend to ruin my royal domain, nor yet to await the consent of the pope. This war is a religious war; therefore I shall have no scruples of conscience in availing myself of the revenues of the church. It is chiefly owing to the clamour of the clergy that this war has been agitated; it is a holy war, and therefore it shall be maintained at the expense of the church!" The king then waved his hand in token of dismissal. The personages were mute with astonishment at a speech so angry and sarcastic. One of the presidents presently asked permission to reply. Henry rose, and exclaimed vehemently, "Messieurs! not one word—I do not want to hear your useless and stupid speeches; but I desire to witness your deeds!" His majesty then abruptly quitted the saloon.[1]

The irritation demonstrated by Henry produced great and visible disquietude: nevertheless, ultimately the impression was adverse to the royal cause. It led people to overrate the influence of the princes of Lorraine, which had compelled their sovereign to an undertaking avowedly so distasteful. The true power of the crown was prostrate, despite the ebullition of temper wherewith his majesty essayed to veil his defeat.

[1] De Thou, liv. lxxxi., p. 335.

For a time the people pitied; then they began to scorn and to defy the authority which had suffered such outrage. The inconsistency of Henry's demeanour increased this contempt; and it is lamentable to read of the pitiful imbecility which could induce the king, the day following his indignant protest, to sally forth from the Louvre at the head of a disorderly troop, and to parade the streets of the capital playing with a cup-and-ball. This exhibition of himself Henry was not ashamed to repeat on several occasions; indeed, for some weeks his majesty wore a *bilboquet* at his girdle; and from Epernon to the meanest page of the wardrobe, all the courtiers followed the example of their royal master, and practised assiduously until they became expert players.[1]

The arrival of the duc de Guise in Paris compelled the king for the moment to lay aside his follies. The duke entered Paris in the guise of a conqueror. The streets were decorated; and a vast concourse of people thronged on the roads for more than a league beyond the gates of the capital to hail their orthodox champion. None of the personages appertaining to the royal household, however, rode out to greet the duke, "but," says the cardinal de Guise, "what was better still, he had a throng of nobles, citizens, and churchmen." The duke's cavalcade numbered between six and seven hundred horsemen. On entering the capital Guise proceeded to his hôtel, where he was received by the duc de Mayenne, and by the duchesses de Guise, de Montpensier, and de Retz. The following day the duke went to the Louvre to make his obeisance to king Henry. He was accompanied by the princes of his house, by two hundred cavaliers, and by a guard of honour, which had been assigned for the safe keeping of his person by the treaty of Nemours. The duke

[1] Journal de Henri III. L'Etoile, année 1585-7.

advanced to the dais, and bending the knee, raised the king's hand to his lips. Henry received this homage with grave dignity; and after exchanging a few words in public, he signed to his potent subject to follow him to his cabinet. There the two conferred for some short time; and when they emerged the duke accompanied the king to hear vespers in the chapel de l'hôtel de Bourbon. "The king," says the cardinal de Guise, "gave and continued to give M. my elder brother cordial greeting."[1] The presence of the duke, nevertheless, acted as an extinguisher on the royal festivities. Henry, therefore, commenced a course of penance and fasting for his past sins, as his majesty said, of such extraordinary rigour that the pope was presently compelled to send a special envoy into France to admonish him to desist. "The king," writes the imperial ambassador, "has given himself over to such strange acts of devotion that every one fears his health and life will be the sacrifice, or that he will become completely superstitious and credulous." Probably one of the secret causes of Henry's retreat was to rid himself of the presence of the duc de Guise whom he hated and feared, and by whom he dreaded to be compelled into making fresh concessions.

The king of Navarre, during these transactions, published a declaration, in which he set forth in eloquent language the injustice of the recent edict, and the interested motives of the princes of Lorraine. The perturbation of Henri's mind had been such when he heard of the signature of the treaty of Nemours that, it is said, in one night the half of his *moustache* turned grey. With the utmost spirit and decision, however, Henri prepared for the deadly combat offered by his ambitious foes. He sent to demand succours from all the Pro-

[1] MS. Bibl. Imp. F. de Béth. vol. 8866. Lettre du Cardinal de Guise à M. de Nevers.

testant princes of Europe, especially from Elizabeth queen of England and the palatine Casimir; and before the end of August he had concluded a league with the duc de Montmorency and Condé. He next sent a private missive to the king to remonstrate on the gross injustice of the design to exclude him from the succession; and offered to march to the rescue of his majesty, and to put down the intolerable tyranny of MM. de Guise. The duc de Montmorency, moreover, addressed a letter to the cardinal de Bourbon, and warned him not to fall into the snare laid by the enemies of his house.

One more overture was ostentatiously volunteered by the Catholic party to achieve the conversion of the reprobate and jest-loving Henri de Navarre preparatory to the promulgation of a papal excommunication and interdict, which was to inaugurate the coming war, and to justify the summary seizure of Béarn, the stronghold of Calvinism. The pope, though he had stoutly maintained the royal prerogative when Henry found himself beleaguered by rebels, yet when his Holiness was summoned in the name of the king and of the Catholic League to fulminate the church's anathema against heresy, Sixtus believed himself bound to comply. Previously, however, the cardinal de Lenoncourt, M. d'Angennes, Brulart, secretary of state, and Cueuilly, one of the factious ecclesiastics of Paris, proceeded to Nérac to confer with the king of Navarre. Henri heard them patiently, and replied by refusing to change his religion. De Lenoncourt then, to gain time, proposed an interview between queen Catherine and the king of Navarre at Champigny, to which the latter assented, provided that the duc de Guise laid down arms, and the royal generals in the south suspended their operations. The envoys then requested the king to postpone the advance of the German levies until after this interview with the queen—those mercenary troops being already on the march under the baron de Dhona, lieutenant of prince Casimir. This request Henri likewise declined; and the deputies took leave of the king greatly exasperated, and having obtained none of their demands. The bull of excommunication and interdict was therefore published about the middle of the month of September, 1585.[1] It commenced by stating that the functions of his sacred office compelled his Holiness to draw the apostolic sword against two sons of wrath, Henri de Bourbon, *ci-devant* king of Navarre, and Henri de Bourbon, prince de Condé. The document then in the usual form absolved their subjects from their allegiance; declared the princes anathematized, deprived of their possessions, rank, and dignities, and especially proclaimed them incompetent to succeed to the crown of France.

The king of Navarre showed himself not less valiant with his pen than with his sword. Almost immediately a manifesto was issued in the name of the excommunicated princes, and boldly affixed to the public edifices in Rome. The king there retorted on Sixtus the term, "heretic," "anathematized," and challenged him to submit his own doctrines and conduct to the scrutiny of a general council. "The kings my royal ancestors have in days of yore chastised such officious blunder-makers as M. St. Sixte, *soi-disant* pope of Rome, whenever they notably transgressed the bounds of justice and right, as, with the help of God and of all Christian princes, I hope to do."[2] Sixtus was convulsed with

[1] "Déclaration de notre St. Pere Sixte V. à l'encontre de Henri de Bourbon soi-disant roi de Navarre, et de Henri semblablement de Bourbon prétendu prince de Condé, hérétiques, contre leurs postérités et successeurs."—Archives Curieuses, tome ii. Goldast: Monarchie de l'Empire, p. 124.

[2] Journal de Henri III. De Thou. Hotman: Brutum Fulmen Sixtus V. adversus Henricum.

fury when he read this manifesto, and offered large rewards for the apprehension of the "insolent apostate" who had presumed so to sully the precincts of the holy city. The search was made in vain; Henri's loyal coadjutor escaped the inflictions of papal revenge. The powerful mind of Sixtus, however, involuntarily rendered homage to genius, even when its weapons assailed his dignity and infallibility; and the same impulse which caused him to eulogize Elizabeth queen of England and to desire her friendship, impelled the pontiff generously to predict the eventual triumph of the king of Navarre over his foes.

The contest which had menaced France ever since the accession of Henry III. now commenced in earnest. The character of the three Henrys, each the chieftain of a faction, was as diverse as the causes they individually defended. The king, luxurious, facile, sarcastic, and vindictive; the duc de Guise, a warrior by descent, chivalrous, skilled in diplomacy, ambitious, and dauntless; the king of Navarre, able, insinuating, alike ready with a jest or a tear, inconstant in friendship, and of surprising activity and resource—such were the combatants about to vindicate their respective feuds. The liberal opinions professed by the king of Navarre fascinated many; and but for the brand of heresy, France undoubtedly would have hailed the Béarnnois as chief and leader of her armies. The mind of Henri de Navarre harmonized with his wiry and nervous frame; perpetually in motion, perpetually excited, now interchanging coarse jests with his brave Gascons, or brandishing *bons mots* with his nobles, Henri was never at rest. He had no vocation for study or meditation; the dry scholastic harangues of his churchmen wearied him; his religion was his badge, not his paraclete; his nature was essentially social and jovial. The business and glory of Henri's life was warfare; his genial temper and kind heart shone amid the stirring scenes and pathetic incidents of camp life: his recreation he found at the feet of Corisandre d'Andouins, Gabrielle d'Estrées, or in the smiles of that beauty whose bright eyes held enthralled for the moment the valiant heart of the king of Navarre..

In Paris, meanwhile, that most seditious confederation, termed La Ligue des Seize, was at this time organizing—the bulwark in reality of the designs of Guise and his patron king Philip; for the provincial associations not eventually absorbed into this Parisian league soon fell to pieces. Its originator is said to have been one M. de Roche-Blond, an opulent burgess, who, being moved by the calamities and irreligion of the times, resolved to oppose an antidote, and, perchance, a barrier, to the universal corruption. For this purpose he first consulted with Prévost, his parish priest, the turbulent curé of St. Severin. The curé of St. Benoît, Mathieu Boucher, was, by the advice of Prévost, next taken into the counsels of the *soi-disant* reformers. A small council was then organized of these parsons, to which were added the names of de Lannoy, Acarie, a counsellor, and of two needy advocates named Menager and Crucé. The sittings of the secret society were holden in the College de Fortet, afterwards called the cradle of the League, or in the Sorbonne, in the chamber of Boucher. A further number of persons soon joined the society, which in a few weeks numbered about twenty persons, "all prudent, zealous for the faith, and enemies of kingly tyranny." Five individuals out of this number were next elected to watch over and report every event that happened in the sixteen sections into which the city of Paris was then divided.[1] These

[1] Hence the name of the confederation, "the League of the Seize quartiers de la ville et fauxbourgs d'icelles."—Hist. de la Ligue. Cayet: Chronologie Novennaire. De Thou. Davila.

individuals were Crucé, Chapelle, Louchart, and Bussé. The strictest subordination existed; none of the members of the club being permitted to associate at pleasure with other persons, but were compelled previously to apply for a licence from the council. Every member took an oath of fidelity and secrecy, and swore to bring as many recruits to the cause as his influence, wealth, or persuasion rendered possible. On stated evenings the society met to receive reports, issue directions, and concert measures. When the cabal had been thus far organized, the members, with Roche-Blond at their head, offered their aid and services to the duc de Guise to work for the common weal; and principally to insure the succession of a Catholic prince, in case his majesty should demise without leaving heirs male. The League des Seize, through the intervention of the princes of Lorraine, therefore put itself into communication with the clergy of the capital, but so secretly that the spies and agents of Villequier and others of the royal ministers could never surprise the members in conclave. These men, therefore, disaffected, and for the most part agitators for their own sordid interests, prowled stealthily over the capital, laying snares for all, practising on the consciences of the weak and credulous, and entrapping others by most scandalous machinations and threats of betrayal to the authorities. The chief stronghold of the League was the confessionals of the capital. There the fanatic priesthood raged, denounced, and terrified their penitents by pictures of the temporal and eternal pains decreed against the upholders of heresy. Every crime, they said, became venal which aided in purging the land from its curse; every hostile deed brought down on its perpetrator the blessing of the Most High, and would be more efficacious hereafter for the weal of the soul than the most lavish outpourings of the treasury of the saints, the key of which, in the hands of the supreme pontiff, turned only at the ring of mundane gold. The people, therefore, were invited to help themselves liberally and to take no stint of heretic blood.

The princes of Lorraine, meanwhile, selected three inhabitants of Paris, the sieurs de Meneville, Conrard, and Beauregard, as their medium of intercourse with the League des Seize: all communications were to be addressed through these individuals until MM. de Guise deemed it politic to treat in person with their adherents. The duchesse de Montpensier, nevertheless, openly embarked with zeal in the association, which she aided with money, and by the many and various secret advices which her rank enabled her to glean. Since the decease of her husband[1] madame de Montpensier had spent her leisure in dabbling in all imaginable conspiracies likely to assuage her hate for the sovereign, and to advance the interests of her brothers. Her wealth, which was enormous, gained her followers and influence, riveted by the versatility of her accomplishments and by her ability. No arts did the duchess despise to win adherents. Her moods were as variable: some individuals she would persuade and fascinate with tender blandishments; others she would inflame by the vehemence of her declamation; while the philosophical she equally propitiated by discussing the sophistry of the schools, soaring in hardy dogma above the most sceptical of cynics. Her tongue lashed pitilessly, while her pen indited the bitterest of satires. Another qualification madame de Montpensier possessed, and which she often exercised to the confusion of the prodigals of the court; —she excelled in the art of arithmetic, and could detect almost at a glance any flaw or deception in the financial statements promulgated by the authority of

[1] Louis duc de Montpensier died at his superb palace at Champigny September 23, 1582.

the sovereign. Her step-son, the duc de Montpensier, a young man distinguished by no particular abilities, suffered himself also at this period to be influenced by the overwhelming energy of the duchess.

The League des Seize, after the publication of the treaty of Nemours, was reinforced by many important adherents. Amongst these, however, came a traitor to the cause, whose revelations, if Henry and his ministers had possessed common prudence, energy, and decision, ought to have brought these agitators to condign punishment. Early in the year 1585, Nicholas Poulain, lieutenant of the provost of l'Isle de France, was induced by the emissaries of the League to join the association. Poulain's qualifications were many, his situation was important, and he was endowed with personal courage, resource, and resolution. His admission into the councils of the League, therefore, was speedily effected. The first work assigned to Poulain was the purchase of arms to the amount of 6,000 francs; a task of difficulty and peril to most men, as a recent edict had forbidden the armourers of Paris to sell weapons without taking a written acknowledgment from the purchaser. This mission Poulain executed under cover of his office, and caused the weapons, as they were purchased, to be conveyed during the night and stowed in apartments in the hôtels de Guise, Montpensier, and other abodes of the malcontents. Poulain, however, soon after his initiation, beheld with astonishment and misgivings the extensive intelligence possessed by the Seize throughout every class of the capital. Half of the superior officers of La Chambre des Comptes had been suborned by their comrade Marteau de la Chapelle, one of the five original founders of the association; many members of the high court of parliament enrolled themselves at the private exhortation of the president Neuilly; while the master of the Mint, Roland, and many advocates of the Cour des Aydes, followed the same pernicious example. Agents were actively engaged in canvassing for the League amongst the guilds and trade-unions of the capital. The ferrymen and watermen of the Seine, to a man, gave in their adhesion; as did also the pork-butchers, the horse-dealers, and the hardware venders of Paris. All these classes, during the years 1585 and 1586, took the oath of secrecy, obedience, and fidelity to the leaders of the great League for "the defence of the faith betrayed by the criminal partiality demonstrated by the king their sovereign lord for the king of Navarre and for his favourites!" The duc de Guise regulated, encouraged, reprimanded, and trained these bands of factious demagogues, fondly hoping that the possession of Paris would give him the much-coveted diadem at the decease of the king: yet so cautiously did the duke proceed, that he is not seriously compromised in the subsequent revelations made by Nicholas Poulain.

During the autumn months of the year 1585 the king made some faint efforts to conciliate several personages whom his inconsistency and levity had alienated. He wrote urgent letters to the queen his mother, praying her majesty to return to Paris, and thanking her in grateful language for the services which she had rendered to the state at Epernay and Nemours.[1] Catherine, as soon as she was able to travel, returned to Paris; nevertheless, the same partial alienation continued to exist between the queen and her son. The king, prompted by Epernon, distrusted his mother; while Catherine, unaccustomed to have her *dicta* submitted for the approval of a third party, steadily refused to attend the council or even to

1 Lettre de Henri III. à la Reyne sa Mère. MS. Bibl. Imp. Béth. 8874, fol. 360.

enter the Louvre. Some letters also passed between the king and his sister Marguerite, who, perceiving a war to be again inevitable, and wearying of her position of sufferance at the court of Nérac, suddenly took the resolve to retire to Agen, one of her dowry towns, and there to hold herself independent equally of her husband and her brother. The inhabitants of Agen received their countess with due enthusiasm; but there also Marguerite's want of restraint and decorum alienated her adherents.

The king next addressed the duchesse de Nevers in most cordial fashion; for Henry was sensible how much he owed to the scruples and sage counsels of the duke her husband, and was very sincerely desirous of a reconciliation with the duchess. A sense of contempt must have pervaded the mind of madame de Nevers as she perused this familiar and even coaxing epistle, and remembered the insult to which she had been subjected by the king in his undisciplined resentment.

HENRY III. KING OF FRANCE TO MADAME LA DUCHESSE DE NEVERS.

Ma Cousine,—Having found an opportunity to write to you, you have me hopelessly on your hands; not, however, to trouble your repose, but to assure you that the affection I bore you before you quitted Paris has not diminished: on the contrary, it has gathered strength; so that as long as I live I vow to bear you all honour and love, and to demean myself as your very faithful relative and good friend. And this, ma cousine, I swear to you by the Styx, the inviolable oath of the gods! In all sincerity, however, I pray you to believe my words, and to remember me sometimes.

Adieu, ma bonne cousine, I am yours entirely; and say the same to M. de Nevers, as you will both soon experience. Return hither soon; for it is not seemly that you should both be absent (from Paris) for so long a period. I kiss your hand, ma cousine, a thousand times. HENRY.[1]

[1] Henri III. à Madame la Duchesse de Nevers. Bibl. Imp. Béth. 8704, fol. 365. MS.

The king also wrote to the duc de Nevers, praying him to remain faithful to the royal cause, and promised to bestow upon him one of the first vacant governments. The duke had sent an Italian retainer, the sieur de Cabriani, to the court to negotiate some matters with the king. This Cabriani wrote to the duchesse de Nevers to request her influence in persuading her husband still to remain aloof from the League: "Madame, if ever you wished to convince the king and the queen that you have loved them, now is your opportunity by using your influence over monseigneur your husband, to whom his majesty has despatched Montclar, exempt' of his guard, to explain at length his intentions and desires to monseigneur."[1] Henry offered the duc de Nevers the government of Picardy—that centre of the League. A governor of less reputed orthodoxy would have been unceremoniously rejected by the Picardians; but the king felt confidence that, although the latter might be permitted by Nevers to cabal, any armed demonstration would be rigidly suppressed. These propositions being highly acceptable to the duke, he returned to court on taking leave of the pope, and proved of great assistance to his sovereign in moderating and balancing the designs of the duc de Guise. The king also partially reconciled himself to the cardinal de Bourbon, whose professions of loyal deference Henry accepted; while his majesty feigned to acquiesce in the prelate's interpretation of the laws relative to the royal succession. Overtures of renewed friendship were also successfully made by the king to the duc de Retz, who, on the elevation of "the dukes," had indignantly resigned his offices in the household of the sovereign.

The duc de Mayenne, meantime, entered Guyenne

1 Le Sieur de Cabriani, agent du Duc de Nevers, à Madame la Duchesse de Nevers. MS. Bibl. Imp. Béth. 8877, fol. 12.

with the troops of the League, and formed a junction with the maréchal de Matignon. The latter was a faithful servant of the crown, and a great enemy of the princes of Lorraine. Matignon, therefore, in pursuance of secret instructions which he had received from court, suggested, as was supposed, by Epernon, traversed in every way the designs of Mayenne. The duc de Montmorency, Chatillon, and Lesdiguières held Languedoc; while the latter, in the course of a few days, captured all the most important places in Dauphiny. Condé, meantime, was not idle; the exigencies of the times, and the perils with which the decree of proscription menaced the faith, had effaced his differences with the king of Navarre, and had once more united the two as faithful brothers-in-arms. Condé, therefore, issued from his trusty refuge of St. Jean, and marched to besiege Brouage. Whilst before this place, Condé received advices of an insurrection in Angers, the garrison of which rose and murdered their governor. The citadel, where the mutineers retired, was immediately besieged by a small division of royal troops under Brissac. Condé, thereupon, withdrew a portion of his army from before Brouage, and resolved to raise the siege of the citadel, and by the aid of the rebels to seize the town of Angers. The prince, however, lost eleven days in issuing instructions and gathering levies; therefore, when he arrived before Angers, the place had capitulated to the duc de Joyeuse, who had been hastily sent by the king to put down the revolt. On attempting to retire back again into the Pays d'Aunis, Condé found himself entangled by the army under Joyeuse, which lay in wait for him on the banks of the Loire; while lower down, on the opposite side of the river, another detachment, encamped close to Saumur, threatened to cut to pieces the gallant little army of the prince, even did it escape this first peril. Thus entrapped on all sides, Condé, resolving not to afford the enemy the *prestige* of a victory, disbanded his troops, and after exhorting each man to escape singly across the river as opportunity afforded, and join his companions in arms before Brouage, he himself fled in disguise to Avranches, from whence he embarked for Jersey. Condé afterwards proceeded to England, where the result of his conference with Elizabeth was his triumphant return to the port of La Rochelle, which had been partially blockaded by the royal fleet, with ten vessels and the sum of 50,000 crowns, sent by the queen as a gift to the king of Navarre.[1] No further enterprises were essayed during the remainder of the year 1585; the duc de Mayenne retired into winter quarters in Angers, while Matignon withdrew to Bordeaux.

The duc de Guise during these transactions was quietly concerting his future designs, and providing funds for the vigorous prosecution of the war. For this purpose he mortgaged several of his lands,[2] and with the moneys thus raised continued his private levies in Germany. His demeanour towards the king was respectful, and even deferential. During the winter of 1585, the banquets and entertainments at the hôtel de Guise were numerous. It has been conjectured that at this season, Guise, having obtained the desired edict for the total proscription of heresy, could he have trusted the king, and have relied on his sincerity and on the faithful execution of the treaty of Nemours, never would have tampered in those enterprises which occasioned such deplorable calamity. The wily cunning of the king, and the ironical cordiality of his tone,[3] justly

[1] De Thou, liv. lxxxi. Davila: Hist. de la Ligue.

[2] "On reduit Guise par la pauvreté. Il vient d'engager sa meilleure terre de 25,000 livres de revenues."—Dépêches de l'Ambassadeur de Savoie. Archives de Turin—Michelet: La Ligue.

[3] "Le roy est vindicatif et dissimulé."—Dépêches Inédites de l'Ambassadeur de Savoie. Archives de Turin—Michelet: La Ligue. "Je

inspired the duke with distrust. Besides, the conduct and language of Epernon were offensive and menacing as ever; and the latter was imprudent enough to declare, "that in his judgment the king ought never to pardon the enterprises of MM. de Guise, and the concessions exacted by them at Châlons." The evident decline of the favour of Joyeuse was deemed by the duke another ominous indication of the king's ill-will. It was true that the duc de Joyeuse had been gratified with the command of the army sent to the midland provinces, but yet that dignity had been bestowed upon him rather as a general well approved by the League, than as a mark of royal favour. A cloud at this season evidently enveloped the able mind of Guise, whatever might be its origin. Perhaps it may have been an irresistible presentiment of future woe, such as has ofttimes weighed upon and temporarily paralyzed the most aspiring intellects on the eve of great and perilous enterprises. "The king now refuses to consult the queen his mother, whom he suspects; the friends of Guise are uneasy, and the duke goes no longer to the Louvre, except at the head of 300 gentlemen," writes the ambassador of Savoy at this period.[1] The duke, however, continued assiduously to visit and confer with the municipal authorities of the capital. He also frequented the house of madame de Sauve, who still preserved that extraordinary beauty which had formerly caused Henry III., Henri de Navarre, and Condé to contend as rivals for her favours. The duke seldom presented himself at the council, at which the most indecorous scenes of strife were of frequent occurrence. Edicts had been issued for the confiscation of

crois qu'on verra bientost éclater ce que le roi couve au fonds de l'âme, le dédain qu'il porte dans sa poitrine."—Ibid.

[1] "Guise va toujours à pied au milieu de ses gentilhommes à cheval, 20 Fevrier, 1586."—Ibid.

all property, lands, and lordships appertaining to the king of Navarre and to Condé; and under this decree Henry appropriated the revenues of the duchy of Vendôme. Envoys were, during the winter, despatched to Rome to petition his Holiness to sanction the permanent alienation of certain church lands appertaining to vacant benefices which it was proposed to suppress; and to ask the assent of Sixtus V. to the succour of 100,000 gold crowns, which the Gallican church had at length offered to pay monthly, for a limited period, in aid of the costs of the war.

Whilst these preparations were in progress for the renewal of the campaign in the spring of 1586, intelligence reached Paris that the Protestant princes of Germany had deputed certain noble personages to proceed to the court of France, and mediate between the king and his subjects of the reformed faith. This step was thought to be a justifiable interference by the princes, especially as meantime they arrested the march of the great army preparing to invade France under the banner of the king of Navarre. The most violent Leaguers of the council, nevertheless, insisted that the advance of these ambassadors should be forbidden, as, the king having given his royal word to proscribe heresy, war, they said, was therefore inevitable. The proposal, which was still persisted in by Henry, that the queen-mother should again proceed into Guyenne to confer with her son-in-law, likewise gave infinite offence to the duc de Guise. "It is not in accord with your majesty's engagements to treat for a peace, or even for a suspension of arms; if the king of Navarre sees the right and abjures his heresy, still your majesty must receive his tardy submission with arms in your hand!" "Mon cousin," responded Henry, drily, "I greatly dread that in your zeal to destroy *le prêche*, you will abolish the mass."

The campaign of 1586 had been opened by the capture of some small places in Guyenne by Mayenne, who wrote bitter complaints to the government respecting the impediments thrown in his way, and the little zeal displayed by the officers of the crown to furnish him with supplies. Matignon, meanwhile, laid siege to the fortress of Castonel, and sent a summons to Mayenne to request him to advance into the neighbourhood of Bordeaux, as the king of Navarre at the head of a gallant army menaced that important city. The destination of Henri was not, however, to assault Bordeaux; he steadily advanced and compelled Matignon to raise the siege of Castonel, and pursued him to the confines of Poitou. The chagrin which the duc de Guise experienced at this check, and at the want of zeal displayed by the king, determined the duke to quit Paris at the commencement of May to place himself at the head of the army of Champagne, then encamped in the environs of Châlons to oppose the progress of the German troops when they entered France. Moreover, the king affected to treat the war as one peculiarly of private interests; and in the financial demands which his majesty made to his parliaments, he generally introduced the name of the duke as the cause and originator of the unwelcome pecuniary demand. Hence these edicts were popularly termed *Edits Guisards.* The exhibition of this petty spleen injured the royal *prestige;* it rendered more conspicuous the degradation of the throne; while the emissaries of the Paris Leaguers failed not to draw unfavourable deductions relative to Henry's orthodoxy, and of his private desire that the heretic king of Navarre should be hailed as heir-presumptive. It is a remarkable coincidence that the fall of Henry III., who had commenced his public career as the exterminator of the Calvinists and the instigator of the massacre of Paris, should have been principally hastened by a suspicion that he regarded with undue favour that religion which he had then so bitterly persecuted.

The duc de Guise, therefore, took leave of the king on the 28th day of May. It is possible that the duke's departure from the capital may have been as much dictated by prudent foresight as by military ardour. A brief reaction seems to have then set in for the king; for the rigid levy of taxes, and the contributions demanded for the carrying on of the war, had thrown a temporary unpopularity on the League. Edicts innumerable instituting new offices, which were immediately sold to the highest bidder, were daily presented to the chambers, with an intimation that either that method of raising money must be sanctioned, or another expedient devised by the members. A tumult in the streets of Paris, in which a cry of "Vive Guise!" had been promptly suppressed, served to encourage the hopes of the royal adherents. Epernon even boldly suggested to his master to arrest the duke, and cause him to be imprisoned at Vincennes, and volunteered himself to execute the warrant. Amidst these dangers Guise moved calmly and loftily; and, doubtless, one cause which contributed to the impunity with which he continued to thwart and defy his sovereign was his power of self-concentration and support, which never required the solace of sympathy from another. This rare faculty enabled the duke at this period to treat with comparative indifference the dubious support of Catherine de Medici and the neglect of Philip II.—who, absorbed by the conduct of affairs in the Low Countries, and by the preparations in the port of Lisbon for his Invincible Armada, left his allies very much at this period to their own resources, delivered, as he now was, from apprehension of French intervention to disturb the operations of Farnese, his viceroy in Flanders. On taking leave of the king, Guise said, "I perceive that my enemies, sire, even during your majesty's life, may wrest from me my honour, and perhaps my life. I will, however, take care to demonstrate to them previously the incredible misfortunes such a project will entail. Sire! one hundred years hence the rankling of such a wound shall be felt!"[1] Bold words were these, full of ominous menace and foresight. The duc de Guise proceeded to Joinville; from thence he repaired to Nancy to confer with the duc de Lorraine; afterwards he journeyed to Châlons, the head quarters of his army, where many valiant soldiers impatiently awaited the advent of their chief.

As soon as Guise had quitted Paris, the king, listless and relieved from a scrutiny which he had found intolerable, hastened to take recreation after his own peculiar fashion in the monastery of Capuchins, in which he shut himself up for a whole week, seeing no one excepting Epernon and Villequier. The king then removed to Vincennes for change of air, and to visit his protégés the Geronomite monks. During his sojourn at the castle his majesty condescended to partake of the repasts served to the monks in their refectory, and at the conclusion of the meal he frequently read a homily, or addressed them on some edifying subject; for the king was an apt speaker, and ofttimes seasoned his discourses with pungent sarcasm.

Henry returned to Paris to meet the chambers, in order to present twenty-seven financial mandates for the levy of supplies for the war. After having accomplished this distasteful task, Henry repaired to Olinville, leaving the factious senate to exhaust itself in vain protests and recriminations with the clergy on these perpetually recurring extortions. A monarch of spirit and judgment would have seized the opportunity of these dissensions to build up again his authority, and have

[1] Archives de Turin, quoted by M. Michelet: La Ligue.

compelled the malcontents to acknowledge some law and court of supreme appeal; the king, however, preferred the luxury of his palace, and the ignoble post of arbiter of the squabbles of his favourites.

The campaign, during these transactions, had opened with vigour and promise. Seven powerful armies took the field. The duc de Guise commanded the army of Champagne; the duc de Mayenne and Matignon that sent into Guyenne; the duc d'Aumale held Picardy; the duc de Joyeuse the midland provinces and Auvergne; the duc d'Epernon was created governor of Provence, and had the command of that district conferred upon him. For the maintenance of this vast military force during the year 1586 and 1587, Paris furnished 200,000 crowns—a sum which, by some mismanagement, dwindled away in the space of eight days. The clergy contributed 500,000 crowns, and the king the sum of 40,000 crowns from his privy purse. There were besides the moneys raised by the sale of state offices, that contributed by voluntary subscription and the donations of the opulent chieftains of the League.

To oppose this force, the king of Navarre and Condé led to the field an army consisting of choice soldiers—veterans long in the service of the Protestant confederation; while the duc de Montmorency, Châtillon, and Lesdiguières garrisoned the whole of Languedoc. An immense host of German mercenaries hovered on the frontiers, whose junction would enable the Protestants to meet almost on equal terms the armies arrayed for their destruction by the Christian king. The name of "*reiter*" created throughout France a feeling of shuddering terror; the ferocious violence, barbarism, and rapacity of these troops were woes under which the realm had too frequently suffered.

Notwithstanding these formidable demonstrations, the year passed without any military enterprise of consequence; the duc de Guise alone turned his arms against the principality of Sedan and captured some small forts. During these his enterprises on the territory of the duc de Bouillon, the deputies sent by the German princes entered Paris. Henry was at Plombières taking a course of mineral waters, when notice of the arrival of the princes was transmitted to him. He reluctantly returned to St. Germain to grant them audience; as his majesty indignantly contemplated their proposed interference with the internal condition of his realm. He therefore greeted the deputies with cold haughtiness, after having uncourteously detained them so long in Paris that the two chief ambassadors, the comtes de Montbelliard and Isembourg, returned to Germany, believing their dignity to be compromised. The harangue was made to the king by Helmstad, the envoy of duke Casimir. The orator sharply reproached the king for his repeated and faithless violation of his royal word; he exhorted him to restore peace to his realm by banishing the factious from his councils, and by calling the king of Navarre to his aid, offering, in the name of the princes of Protestant Germany, to interdict the levy of troops for the invasion of his realm, provided that they were suffered to mediate between the belligerents. Henry made a most acrid reply, telling the princes "that he was king, and could govern France without their interference or suggestions." He then terminated the audience, and retired, well satisfied at the spirit and vigour with which he had repelled, as his majesty termed it, "a second servitude." During the night, however, passages in the speech addressed to him by Helmstad occurred to the king, which put his majesty into such a furious rage that he sprang from his bed, and taking a slip of paper he wrote, "that whoever had dared to say that by revoking his Edict of Pacification given at Poitiers he had violated his word and honour, was a fool, a liar, and a slanderer;" then rousing the chamberlain-in-waiting, he desired him forthwith to proceed to the abode of the ambassadors and read them that message. The envoys were residing close at hand at Poissy; they immediately rose from their beds to receive the royal communication. The effect of such a message may be divined: a silence of some moments ensued, for the ambassadors scarcely knew how to reply. They at length contented themselves by demanding that a copy of the message might be left. This request was refused by the royal emissary, who said "that he had been instructed to read the message, but not to deposit the writing." The following morning the deputies quitted Paris without deeming it requisite to take leave of the king, or previously to communicate with his ministers.[1]

This ignominious repulse of their well-meant intentions exasperated the German princes, and the greatest alacrity henceforth was displayed to embody troops for the service of the king of Navarre; so that in a few months a prodigious army of *reiters* had gathered on the frontiers, waiting only for the signal to swarm over the fair eastern provinces of France.

The king's next enterprise was to make an attempt to prevail on the duc de Guise and the chieftains of the League to disarm, offering them amnesty, honours, and guarantees of his faith and of his zeal for religion. The precise points of the accommodation proposed by the king are not on record; nevertheless the royal concessions must have been ample, as the chieftains repaired to Orcamp, an abbey appertaining to the cardinal de Guise, to consider his majesty's propositions. After a brief discussion they were rejected by the duc de Guise, who insisted on the execution, *pure et*

1 De Thou, liv. lxxxi. L'Estoile: Journal de Henri III. Dupleix. Mathieu: Hist. de Henri III.

simple, of the treaty of Nemours.[1] At the same time that Henry forwarded these proposals to the duke, he intimated to the queen-mother that he was informed her presence in the capital occasioned much cabal and disaffection, and he therefore prayed her majesty to take her departure for Chenonceau, and there to repose until it was considered expedient for her to repair into Guyenne to meet the king of Navarre.[2] Catherine, though aware that her departure had been decreed by Epernon, nevertheless complied without remonstrance. The Leaguers, as her majesty anticipated, however, immediately raised a clamour that Catherine's orthodoxy was the cause of her loss of influence with the king her son; and this ill-advised step exercised an adverse effect on the conferences of Orcamp. Catherine had greatly obliged the princes of Lorraine; and the downfall of her power they deemed the herald of the ascendency of Epernon, and consequently of the Huguenot faction.

Some three weeks after thus offending his mother, the king wrote to request her to repair to confer with the king of Navarre, and make a last effort to win him to renounce Calvinism. A long and most wearisome negotiation ensued between the agents of the queen and the king of Navarre relative to the place of interview, and the precautions to be used to secure the safety of both parties. The king of Navarre desired that Catherine should confide in his honour and cross the Loire; the queen insisted that Henri might trust her word, and repair to Champigny. Henri refused the latter proposal unless the army under Mayenne was recalled; the queen then protested that she would not stir a step from Chenonceau until her son-in-law agreed to a truce

[1] "Résolutions de ceux du Parti de la Ligue assemblés à Orcamp."—MSS. du Chancélier Séguier, Bibl. Imp. vol. 1495. De Thou: Journal de Henri III.

[2] "Le roi ne consulte plus sa mère."—Archives de Turin—Michelet.

pending the conference.[1] In this recriminatory style the negotiation continued until the middle of December, 1586, when a compromise was effected, and the queen advanced to Poitiers, while the king of Navarre repaired to Jarnac. Catherine was attended by the ducs de Montpensier and Nevers, by the maréchal de Biron, and MM. de Rambouillet and de Lansac. The only lady of honour in her suite was Catherine de Bourbon, abbess of Soissons,[2] aunt of the king of Navarre. The amazement, and perhaps disappointment of the cavaliers of the court of Navarre was intense. Hitherto the queen-mother had come amongst them attended by a troop of beautiful maidens, whose allurements had often proved more powerful to persuade than the fluent sophistry of their mistress. Now Catherine presented herself, attended by a grave abbess considerably past the prime of life, whose prayers had been asked for the better enlightenment of her reprobate nephew. The queen proceeded from Poitiers to the castle of St. Bris, a league from Cognac, to meet the king of Navarre. The latter came, attended by Turenne and Caumont de la Force, and by his chancellor du Ferier. The first two interviews passed absolutely in recriminations, the queen reproaching her son-in-law for his stubbornness, his conjugal infidelities, and his apostasy. Henri took Catherine's objurgations patiently, and replied aptly to the charge of contumacy. Before the third interview the king of Navarre wisely sent Turenne to the queen, in the hope that her majesty feeling less excitement while conversing with the viscount, might enter upon the propositions for the discussion of which they had met. Catherine, accordingly, commissioned Turenne to impart to his master that she was there to

1 Lettre de M. de Pibrac au Cardinal d'Este touchant les Négotiations de la Reyne Mère. MS, Bibl. Imp. Dupuy, p. 500.

2 Daughter of Charles duc de Vendôme and Françoise d'Alençon.

say, "that the king saw no other means of restoring peace to the realm and satisfying MM. de Guise, except by the king of Navarre changing his religion, which consequently the king peremptorily commanded him to do." When the viscount brought this message Henri was setting out for St. Bris. His first impulse was to return to Pau, but eventually he repaired to the interview. He found the queen anxiously awaiting the result of her communication. Henri commenced by positively declining to change his faith, and in an address of some length represented to her majesty the impracticability of the step she proposed. "But, mon fils, think of the ruin and disquietudes you are seeking to impose upon yourself!" "Madame, I strive to endure them patiently and virtuously," rejoined Henri. "And for what?" asked the duc de Nevers; "your majesty has not power to levy a tax even in La Rochelle!" Catherine then dexterously proposed that a truce of one year should be concluded between the belligerents, during which period the exercise of the reformed ritual was to be totally prohibited on condition that the States-general were convoked finally to legislate on the controversy. This proposition Henri sturdily rejected. He said that a general council, and not the States, must legislate in affairs of religion. Besides, during the present condition of the realm, and the ascendency of MM. de Lorraine, the States would not be permitted the free exercise of their functions. After some further parley the royal negotiators separated in high displeasure; Catherine, however, agreeing to send a message to the king to ask for conditions more in accord with the sentiments of her son-in-law and his party.[1] The queen then retired to Fontenay,

[1] Lettre de M. de Pibrac à M. d'Este touchant les Négotiations de la Reyne Mère. Bibl. Imp. MS. Dupuy, p. 500. Henry's admonition to his brother-in-law the king of Navarre somewhat resembled that of

and from thence to Niort, with the understanding that she was to have a final interview with the king of Navarre after the return of Rambouillet. The latter, however, brought so ambiguous an answer from the king as to leave the plenipotentiaries exactly where they were. The king of Navarre, therefore, excused himself from visiting the queen, who had been summoned back to Paris by her son, and deputed Turenne in his stead. A long and irritable interview ensued; the queen became much excited, and several times vehemently exclaimed, "there should be but one faith in the realm, and that the king her son would find abundant resources to make the king of Navarre repent his contumacy." "As for the matter of one religion, madame, we have no objection to urge, provided that it be our own," retorted Turenne. The duc de Nevers, who assiduously attended the queen, then asked, "whether the king of Navarre was so bound by his alliance with the German princes, that he could no longer treat with the king?" The viscount replied, "that the foreign army was entirely at the disposal of the king of Navarre, who, if the king gave the invitation, would bring these soldiers to the rescue of his majesty!" After this interview the conferences were suddenly suspended, as Catherine hastily returned to Paris, in consequence of some dangerous cabals being there discovered connected with the return of the duc de Mayenne. Henry seems to have had no hesitation in summoning again his mother, after having before coolly requested her to depart. The king never appears to have contemplated the possibility that any of the individuals whom he

the duchesse de la Force to her daughters-in-law, who were determined Calvinists, when during the reign of Louis XIV. they were exhorted to recant, "Mais, mesdames, je ne conçois pas les façons que vous faites pour moi, je crois tout ce que je veux!"

treated so unceremoniously could harbour resentment, or retaliate his injurious usage.

The duc de Mayenne had returned from the south in a mood not calculated to improve the aspect of the king's affairs in the city of Paris. He had achieved no military success in Guyenne; and his period of command had been embittered by the steady opposition of his colleague the maréchal de Matignon. The duke's last exploit before resigning his command had been to carry off mademoiselle de Caumont,[1] a great heiress, whom he desired to marry to his son the comte de Sommerive. As the young lady was a Protestant, a subject of the king of Navarre, and, moreover, affianced to the prince de Carency, this abduction excited the greatest clamour. The duke alleged, in excuse, that she had been, when a child, betrothed to his son with the assent of her mother, who was the widow of the maréchal de St. André—a lady, however, whose subsequent marriages and eccentric conduct had brought her into much disrepute. Anne de Caumont proved herself to be a worthy representative of her valiant race; and refused the suit of the comte de Sommerive with such determination, appealing to the king for rescue from the custody of the duchesse de Mayenne, that eventually the duke was compelled to restore her to her kindred. The young prince de Carency subsequently falling in a duel against the son of the maréchal de Biron while maintaining his claim to the hand of his wealthy *fiancée*, Anne showed such constancy to his memory as immediately to transfer herself and her possessions to his brother and heir,[2] whom she married,

[1] Anne de Caumont de la Force, posthumous daughter of Geoffrey de Caumont and Marguerite de Lustrac, widow of the maréchal de St. André, marquise de Lustrac; born in 1574.

[2] Henri de Pereuse d'Escars, prince de Carency: the marriage took place 1587. The prince de Carency dying in 1590, his wealthy widow

to guard against further misadventure, at the expiration of her period of mourning.

The presence of Mayenne in the capital was the signal for renewed agitation. The council des Seize immediately waited upon the duke in the hôtel de St. Denis at ten o'clock at night, to impart the condition of the city and to promise him devotion. The leaders of the Seize, meantime, too precipitate in their measures, had prematurely roused the animosity of the people against their rulers. It was all that the most influential members of the League could do to prevent the populace from breaking out into open sedition. Schemes had been concocted and approved for the seizure of the principal state edifices of the capital, all of which Crucé communicated to the duc de Mayenne. The Louvre was to be taken by the help of barricades in the adjacent streets, formed of barrels filled with earth and bound together by chains. The person of the king was to be seized and his guards murdered, as well as the chancellor Cheverny, the first president, the attorney-general le Guesle, and other obnoxious persons of minor note. Possession was to be gained of the arsenal by means of an artizan employed therein, who had agreed to open the gates to an armed mob. It was industriously circulated that the duc de Guise had pledged his word that in three years heresy should be extirpated from the realm; but to enable the duke to execute his designs it was necessary for the people to restrain the evident desire of the king to favour the Huguenots. One Ameline, a zealous Leaguer, was accredited by the Paris League to confer with the provincial confederations. This man was presented with 3,000 crowns and with two horses to fulfil his mission, and set out on his journey during the con-

espoused François d'Orléans, comte de St. Paul, son of the duc de Longueville.

ferences at St. Bris. A plot was likewise concocted to seize the town of Boulogne, as, in case the military successes of the king of Navarre might render it desirable to call in the aid of the duke of Parma, a Spanish reinforcement might be landed at that port. Measures were actually taken to execute this scheme, by means of traitorous intelligences in Boulogue, with such skill and foresight that doubtless the town would have fallen into the hands of the duc d'Aumale, nominally the royal general commanding in Picardy, had not Nicholas Poulain betrayed the plot to Cheverny. "I reflected well," says Poulain, "on the nature of these most damnable enterprises, and decided that they were concocted, not for the public good, but to deprive the king of his crown by means of the populace of Paris, and to give it to those of Lorraine; and that religion was merely a pretence and a blind to cover such treasonable plots!" The government being forewarned quietly frustrated the design, the reality of which was rendered palpable by the sudden and unexpected advance of Aumale to within three leagues of Boulogne. The panic occasioned by this revelation had caused the king to summon back his mother, as the tacit connivance of the duc de Mayenne in the plot could not be disputed. Nevertheless, the king did not feel strong enough to arrest or to command the duke's absence from the capital; he therefore designed "to negotiate."

The king, however, dealt the League a blow in return by confiscating the temporalities of the cardinal de Pellvé,[1] whose intrigues at Rome had long been a

[1] Bishop of Amiens, archbishop of Sens in 1563, cardinal in 1570, and archbishop of Rheims in 1589; one of the most fiery of the Leaguers and upholders of the canons of Trent. The cardinal died in Paris at the hôtel de Sens, in 1594, of grief and rage at the capitulation of Paris to Henri IV.

source of tribulation to the government; but whom his majesty dared not recall.

The Christmas of 1586 passed gloomily at St. Germain, where the king had retired. The position of affairs dispirited his favourites, while Henry beheld little hope of a return to the peaceful luxury of the earlier years of his reign. Foreign nations began now to scoff at the power of France; distracted by civil war, it was felt that the energy of the nation must be concentrated on home affairs if it were hoped ever to revive the ancient glory of the realm of St. Louis. This mortifying fact was daily brought under the king's notice by the despatches of his foreign residents. The queen of England boldly put Mary Stuart, dowager of France, on her trial for participation in the regicidal plots of the English Leaguers, and signed the sentence which condemned the widow of Francis II. to perish by the axe of the executioner. Henry sent the able and virtuous Pomponne de Bellièvre to remonstrate with Elizabeth, and to beseech her to spare the life of a queen his near kinswoman. His majesty proposed to become responsible for the future actions of his sister-in-law; while the duc de Guise offered to send one of his sons as a hostage for Mary's abstinence from hostile demonstrations against Elizabeth. "For how much will all these fine professions and guarantees serve when I shall have been assassinated?" gloomily asked Elizabeth. "My ministers see in them no surety for the safety of my person! I have determined, therefore, to do all that is requisite to preserve my life. Your master, nevertheless, may be assured of my moderation and equity in this affair, as in all others in which his majesty may be concerned!"[1] Mary, therefore, was led to execution,[2] and the news

[1] De Thou, liv. lxxxvi.

[2] February 8th, 1587.

of her death reached the king on the first day of March, 1587. Henry passionately bewailed her untimely end; and so far from having encouraged Elizabeth to proceed to this extremity, as it has been alleged, numberless secret despatches are extant (some in cypher) in which he instructs his ambassadors at the court of London to exert all the influence of France in Mary's behalf, short of breaking with the English queen. Elizabeth, however, was aware of this reservation: she knew also that fear of her alliance with the king of Navarre and the French Calvinists was a barrier opposed against the liberation of the unhappy queen of Scots, more to be relied upon than the strong walls of Mary's prison fortress. To solace his grief Henry commanded a solemn *requiem* for the deceased queen in the cathedral of Notre Dame. The king was present at the service, accompanied by the two queens and the court. The duc de Guise arrived in Paris for the ceremony, but remained only twenty-four hours; the duchesse de Montpensier and other members of the house of Lorraine mustered in force, making parade of the most extravagant grief. The archbishop of Bourges preached the funeral oration, and did not lose the opportunity of pronouncing a panegyric on the house of Lorraine, all the members of which, he said, like the illustrious martyr deceased, were ready to lay down their lives for the holy Roman faith. He alluded to the duc de Guise and his brother Mayenne, whom he termed "*deux foudres de guerre.*" This discourse greatly displeased the king, who summoned the preacher, and after reprimanding him for his audacity in thus alluding to princes under ban of the royal displeasure, he ordered the passages in question to be suppressed before the publication of the oration.

The disaffection of the duchesse de Montpensier seemed to receive fresh impetus from this event. Her malice and intrigue redoubled; and her denunciations against the king, whom she accused of complicity in the death of her cousin-german Mary Stuart, at length incurred the censure of the duc de Guise. A few weeks previously to the reception of the intelligence of the decease of the queen of Scots, though after Mary's sentence of decapitation had been recorded, the duchess and her allies of the League formed a daring project to seize the king on his return to the Louvre from his annual visit to the Foire de St. Germain, which was to be followed by an assault on the Louvre, the Bastille, and the arsenal, as previously concerted. This project was imparted to the duc de Mayenne, who gave it his unqualified aid and approval. The temporary regency of Catherine the conspirators afterwards determined to proclaim, pending the settlement of the question relative to the succession. This plot was carefully concealed from the duc de Guise, who was known to be of opinion that a popular rising was at this period premature; besides, the duke still clung to the belief that Henry would of himself eventually make the concessions desired, when he beheld his realm inextricably involved in a war from which no other issue was apparent. The duchesse de Montpensier, in pursuance of her design, purchased a house in the Rue St. Antoine, in which the king's intended captors were to lie in ambuscade. His majesty after his capture was to be conducted into a little turret chamber, near the belfry tower of the adjacent church of St. Antoine, where for a few hours he was to be vigilantly guarded pending the decision of the Seize relative to his destination. This plot was privately revealed by Poulain, who denounced it, as before, to Cheverny. The king at first insisted upon the arrest of madame de Montpensier, of Mayenne, and of all concerned. The queen-mother, however, procured the rejection of this vigorous measure by observing that no testimony would be forthcoming, excepting that of the informer Poulain, to sanction the detention of such illustrious personages. Henry, therefore, determined to do nothing, but simply to abstain from visiting the Foire de St. Germain; though, under pretext of securing the tranquillity of Paris during that popular revel, he caused the bridges of St. Cloud to be occupied, and commanded the advance of troops to St. Denis. The king also changed the commandants in all the edifices whose seizure had been menaced. The Louvre was garrisoned, and the drawbridge raised. To test the truth of Poulain's statement, Henry next persuaded the duc d'Epernon to repair in his stead to the Foire de St. Germain and ascertain the temper of the people. Epernon complied, to his cost; he was received with execrations by the people, and finally had great difficulty in extricating himself from the throng.

Affairs continued in this condition for several days, during which the duc de Mayenne kept his chamber, perceiving by the unwonted precautions displayed that the plot had transpired; and being greatly in dread lest the king, having so fair an opportunity for retaliation, should seize it by ordering his arrest and that of his *aide-de-camp* Bassompierre. He first determined to withdraw privately from Paris; but being dissuaded from such a step by his sister, the duke had recourse to queen Catherine. He therefore privately waited upon her majesty, and assuring her that he had had no share in the recent plot against the royal person, which he affected to treat as apocryphal, he asked Catherine to obtain for him permission to retire to his government. The treachery of Poulain never seems to have been suspected by his colleagues; the nerve and address of the former are almost without parallel. Poulain regularly took his seat at the council-table of the League, and there listened, surrounded by a gang of desperate men—each of whom would have buried his dagger in the betrayer's body on the most remote suspicion of treachery—to creep away in the dead of the night to the hôtel of Cheverny, and impart to the ear of that minister the resolutions agreed upon. The secret was faithfully kept both by the chancellor and his royal master. Unfortunately, however, Henry only partially believed, and never applied his power to crush these formidable cabals. His mother, according to her custom, advised negotiation, caution, and a forbearance which might eventually bring back many to their allegiance. Henry, therefore, had the weakness to grant Mayenne the desired permission to leave Paris; only, when the duke came to take leave, the king said, "Ah! M. de Mayenne, is it true that you seriously intend to abandon your beloved League and your faithful Leaguers of Paris?" De Thou states that when the duke had proceeded to some little distance from the capital, he turned round, thanking God for his escape from so perilous a predicament; and with knitted brow surveyed the capital, uttering a tremendous oath never more to expose his life to such risks from the vengeance of a tyrant, or the fury of a ferocious populace. When the duc de Guise was informed of this contemplated enterprise, he gave vent to a transport of passion, and despatched his agent Maineville with a message to the chief members of the council des Seize, importing "that he marvelled how they presumed to doubt his word after he had promised to avail himself of their aid at the suitable moment; therefore, for the future they might manage their own affairs as they liked; as for himself, he would have nothing more to do with their concerns." The duke also addressed very sharp reproofs to his sister madame de Montpensier, and sarcastically asked her how she had proposed to proceed having once got the king into the turret-chamber of St. Antoine?

The duc de Mayenne, feeling that he had compromised himself by giving his sanction to so crude and ill-concerted an enterprise, withdrew to his government of Burgundy without visiting the camp of his brother. The chieftains of Paris made many humble apologies to the duc de Guise, acknowledged their folly, which they prayed him to overlook, and in testimony of their contrition, they presented his envoy Maineville with a massive gold chain, and sent the duke a contribution of 300 gold crowns for the prosecution of the war.

The imbecility of the king naturally gave courage to his opponents. A dangerous plot came to light, and the king was persuaded to dissemble and connive at the escape of its authors. The consequence was, that by some Henry was represented as utterly enervated by his excesses, and so conscience-smitten at his past indifference for the maintenance of religion as to be reduced to the last stage of mental and physical debility. By others the sovereign was declared to be so daunted by the genius, the fortune, and the ambition of his subjects of Lorraine that, feeling convinced of their eventual triumph, his present leniency was prompted by the hope of making better conditions after his compulsory abdication. Henry, however, was content to crouch as long as humility might stave off the necessity for vigorous energy and self-denial, and while the mediations of queen Catherine offered a prospect of delusive tranquillity; but urged beyond that point, no promptings of religion, humanity, or justice sufficed to restrain the fierce vindictiveness with which he rose at last to dash from his path every opposing obstacle. The king, at this period, smiled and congratulated the duc de Guise on the efficient condition of his army. Whenever a member of the Seize entered the Louvre, the significant irony and oppressive condescensions of the king kept their recipient in a constant fever of anxiety lest, on leaving the presence, a company of the royal guard might not be without ready to convey him to the torture vaults of the Conciergerie. Henry's *empressements* at this period infuriated the duchesse de Montpensier. Between Catherine and her royal son, however, the greatest discord continued to reign. The individual whom the queen most loved throughout her life had been her son Henry; on him her proudest maternal aspirings had been riveted, and he had for years rewarded her affection by devoted homage. On his accession Catherine had hailed her own supremacy; and this expectation had for many years been realized, until the ambition of the "dukes," and the consequent torpor of the king, snatched from the hand of the queen-mother not only her traditional influence, but caused her to witness the usurpation of the entire functions of the crown. Catherine's spirit rose to avenge and arrest these assumptions, and to win back her power. Having vainly tried to rouse the king from his apathy, she threw herself into the opposing faction with all the energy inspired by fidelity to her religion, her resentments, her hate of Henri de Navarre, and her proud partiality for her eldest grandson, the son of the duc de Lorraine and her daughter Claude.

After the departure of the duc de Mayenne, the court assumed the most lugubrious mourning for the comtesse de Bouchage, the consort of the brother of the duc de Joyeuse. The countess, who was the sister of the duc d'Epernon,[1] was a lady of eminent piety, and whose brief life was spent in works of charity and self-denial. Madame de Bouchage was only twenty years old, but appalled at the impiety of the court she had

[1] Catherine de la Valette. She married Henri de Joyeuse, comte de Bouchage, in 1581. Madame de Bouchage left one daughter, Henriette Catherine, eventually the heiress of the potent house of Joyeuse.

taken refuge in a life of virtual seclusion. She nursed the sick in the hospitals of Paris; and often rose from her bed to visit the dying sufferers whose pains her charity and benevolence had assuaged. Henry bore madame de Bouchage the most intense veneration, and sometimes knelt to kiss the hem of her robe. Often after she had affectionately admonished him to reform his life, the king was known to weep convulsively and retire to his oratory, where he remained in seclusion for hours. The countess was buried in the church of the Franciscans; her loss was so mourned by her husband, who imitated her life of piety and contemplation, that during the following month[1] he entered a Capuchin monastery, where he eventually took monastic vows. Nevertheless the count, on succeeding to the dignity of his elder brother the duc de Joyeuse, made some further figure in the world.

Henry allotted a period of eleven days for the outward mourning of her whom he termed "the greatest saint in his dominions," when the aspect of the court was changed for the magnificent nuptial festivities attending the marriage of the brother of madame de Bouchage, the duc d'Epernon, with Marguerite de Foix, heiress of the house of Candale. The feud between Epernon and the princes of Lorraine had caused the relinquishment of the design he once entertained of espousing the youngest sister of queen Louise; while the prevalent report that the king contemplated the alliance of his favourite with the sister of the king of Navarre was deemed a rumour so dangerous in the present temper of the Parisian populace, that Henry resolved to give it most effectual contradiction by uniting the duke to another lady. Marguerite de Foix was

[1] On the following 4th of September, 1587, the count took the name of le Père Ange.

the grand-daughter of the constable de Montmorency,[1] and therefore allied to the most potent houses in the realm. She had been brought up by her aunt Diane de France, duchesse de Montmorency, who loved her as a daughter, and highly disapproved of her alliance with Epernon; for the hand of the young countess had been sought by several foreign princes whose suit the king summarily rejected. Marguerite herself seems not to have been averse to her marriage with the duc d'Epernon; at any rate she afterwards made him a devoted and affectionate wife, and exulted in the prowess and spirit of her husband. The marriage was celebrated with little pomp in the chapel of Vincennes, on Sunday, August 23rd, 1587. The bridal pair on the following Sunday offered a magnificent ball to the king and the two queens, Catherine and Louise, in the hôtel de Montmorency—a palace, part of the rich possessions of the bride. The king danced with the young duchess, and treated her with royal honours. His majesty was attired in a dress beset with strings of jewels, and was frizzed, perfumed, and beruffed in the most approved fashion of his court. At his girdle, however, the king wore a scourge, his chaplet of death-heads, and a rosary having a multitude of little effigies of saints in gold hanging therefrom. The superstition of Louis XI. was more respectable than that of Henry III., when the former on any emergency pulled off his hat and gravely prostrated himself before the leaden images of Notre Dame with which it was adorned. The royal gift to the bride was a pearl necklace of the value of 100,000 crowns.

The galas as well as the fasts of the court were,

[1] The countess was the daughter of Henri de Foix, count of Caudale Captal de Buch, and of Marie de Montmorency, eldest daughter of the constable Anne.

however, suspended by the intelligence of the descent of the army of Germans on the frontiers of Champagne. Onwards they came, spreading desolation, famine, and pestilence. Neither age nor sex was respected by these fierce marauders; by sword and by fire they opened for themselves a highway, and swarmed down on the fertile country adjacent to the river Loire. The famous march of the duc de Deux Pont from the Rhine into Guyenne, in 1568, was the exploit attempted by the baron de Dhona, the lieutenant-in-chief of the palatine Casimir. The army consisted of 16,000 Swiss troops, 5,000 *reiters*, and a body of 6,000 cavalry. The duc de Bouillon, moreover, brought into the field 2,000 troops and a squadron of light cavalry 1,800 strong. In the south the king of Navarre made a review of his troops—a small but gallant army, well equipped, and burning with zeal for their master's cause, and for the reformed faith, proscribed and banished, with its upholders, from the land. The prince de Condé and his younger brother the comte de Soissons, the duc de la Tremouille (now after the marriage of his sister to Condé[1] a renegade from the League), Turenne, and a crowd of chieftains, brought gallant reinforcements, and joined their banners to the noble standard of Bourbon-Albret. The greatest activity and enthusiasm everywhere prevailed; mothers exhorted their sons to conquer for the faith or to die on the battle-field; young girls sold their trinkets, and some even gave their hair, to buy equipments of war for their lovers and brothers. The Béarnnois ladies brought their jewels to the treasury; the chieftains mortgaged their lands; all united in the desperate struggle

[1] Charlotte Catherine de la Tremouille, daughter of Louis duc de la Tremouille and of Jeanne de Montmorency, espoused the prince of Condé at Taillebourg March 16, 1586. Her brother Claude, duc de la Tremouille, married Elizabeth de Nassau, daughter of the prince of Orange, and was the father of the countess of Derby.

for liberty and their faith. Henri wept tears of joy as he witnessed the enthusiastic loyalty of his brave Béarnnois. The plan of campaign contemplated by the king of Navarre was first to throw reinforcements into his strongholds of Gascony, and in those places contiguous to the Spanish frontier: then at the head of his army to follow the course of the river Dordogne and effect a junction with the German troops in Burgundy, and offer battle to the generals of the League.

The king was thrown into the greatest agitation of mind when he learned the advance of the German mercenaries. The uproar and panic in the capital increased his majesty's solicitudes. One of the preachers of Paris ascended the pulpit in the church of St. Séverin, and delivered an address filled with menace and treason. The leaders of the Seize, concluding that the king would issue orders for the arrest of this ecclesiastic, awaited the decree to excite a popular commotion. Henry, by the advice of his mother, refrained from this measure; nevertheless, a report was spread that the king intended to have the preacher seized and drowned during the night in the Seine. A tumultuous assemblage, therefore, gathered round the house of one Hatte, a demagogue, where Crucé and other Leaguers awaited any overt act taken by the government to punish the orator. Henry, the following morning, assembled his council. The chancellor and the duc d'Epernon advised the king to vindicate his authority, to arrest the rioters, and to cause an inquiry to be made into the turbulent demonstrations of the preceding night. Villequier, however, demeaned himself with insolent arrogance, and protested that the people of Paris were loyal, and never really meant any enterprise hostile to the royal authority. Cheverny insisted; having during the night received a warning from

Poulain to hold himself on his guard; whereupon Villequier, who had partially pledged himself to the Lorraine faction, exclaimed sneeringly, "Well, the panics of M. le chancélier will not hinder me from draining my three cups as usual to-night!" In the evening the streets were again blocked by tumultuous bands, which, on the appearance of a detachment of archers, sent to disperse the mob and arrest its leaders, flew to arms and commenced a fight. The people tore up the pavement and hurled the stones through the windows of houses appertaining to persons obnoxious to the League. Boucher, one of the turbulent *curés,* meantime ran to the Palais and caused the tocsin to be rung. At this ominous sound crowds of people swarmed from the obscure streets and alleys of the capital and joined the fray. The mob shouted seditious speeches under the very windows of the Louvre, and clamoured for the heads of Henri de Navarre and Epernon. The tumult was fast ripening into an insurrection, when the king, daunted by the representations of his mother, actually consented to recall his troops; whereupon the people dispersed in triumph. After this exhibition of weakness, the royal authority fell into such contempt that the leaders of the Seize often took upon themselves to annul or alter the royal mandates issued to promote the tranquillity of the capital. As the king's progress through the streets of Paris was attended with peril, the duc d'Epernon organized at this period the famous band *des Quarante-cinq,* for the security of the royal person. The men were distinguished for their tall stature and great strength; they were Gascon gentlemen, of no political bias, though most inclined to revere the military prowess of the king of Navarre, with whose valiant deeds they were familiar. The troop was commanded by M. de Lognac, a bold, needy, and unscrupulous adventurer.

The duc de Guise, on the advance of the Germans, marched to Bar-sur-Aube to watch and, if possible, intercept their progress; while the duc de Lorraine, at the head of 5000 troops, encamped on the confines of his duchy, waiting for the permission of the king to enter France. The duc de Joyeuse, meantime, asked and obtained the command of the division sent against the king of Navarre, to pursue his army and to prevent his return into Guyenne, after relieving the garrisons of Béarn, and consequently to hinder his junction with the mercenary army. The favour of Joyeuse had fallen, and he now possessed little influence with his royal master. The retreat of his brother M. de Bouchage had greatly affected the duke, and he vainly tried to induce the former to leave the monastery and mingle again with the world. The taunts of the duc d'Epernon cut him to the quick, while the king often jested on the insignificant services which he had as yet rendered. The duke, therefore, resolved to signalize himself by some eminent deed, or to die in the attempt. At the commencement of the autumn Joyeuse took the field, and traversing the Anjoumois he entered Perigord. In his army were the duc de Mercœur and many noble cavaliers, who sought under his auspices to distinguish themselves by a glorious campaign. The duke, therefore, determined to arrest the passage of the king of Navarre across the river Drogue, and drew up his army in battle array on the plain half a league from Coutras.

The king of Navarre readily accepted the combat. He made an eloquent harangue, encouraging his troops from an eminence in the midst of his camp. Henri stood surrounded by a martial throng, men whose names recalled the triumphs inaugurated by the genius and courage of Coligny and of Jeanne d'Albret. The duc de Joyeuse, on the contrary, had no experience in arms; his officers were young and hot headed, impatient of control, and unable to stand the shock of the steady and well-disciplined battalions of their opponents. On the termination of Henri's address, the troops to a man prostrated themselves and engaged in supplication to the God of battles to give them victory. Their movements were narrowly watched by Joyeuse. "Look!" exclaimed he eagerly to his aide-de-camp M. de Lavardin, "look! the Huguenot traitors are already beaten; they prostrate themselves!—they tremble!" "Do not be deceived, monseigneur; I know these said Huguenots; they are pleased now to appear down in the mouth and sanctified, but when we come to the charge we shall find them devils, and of lion courage!"

Between seven and eight o'clock on the following morning the armies formed into battle array. A suspense of an hour's duration ensued, during which the Huguenot soldiers again engaged in prayer. The king of Navarre disposed his men with consummate skill.—He gave the command of the left wing to the comte de Soissons, and that of the right to Condé; the king himself led the centre, and Turenne the cavalry, forming a corps-de-reserve. The duc de Joyeuse commenced the conflict by opening with his artillery on Condé's division. Lavardin and Montigny next advanced at the head of a troop of horse 800 strong. This force was opposed by Turenne; but such was the impetuosity of its charge, that the Huguenot light cavalry gave way on all sides, while Turenne was unhorsed and slightly wounded. During this preparatory skirmish, the main body of the Huguenot army remained firm, and ready for the attack. Joyeuse perceiving the retreat of the enemy's cavalry, and imagining that the victory was already won, suddenly gave the signal for a general onslaught, and himself led the attack. The shock was severe, the soldiers on both sides performing gallant deeds of prowess. The king of Navarre and

Condé led with irresistible courage and vigour. The combat lasted only three-quarters of an hour, at the expiration of which brief period the royal army was broken and dispersed, and the battle-field strewn with the bodies of its most gallant chieftains.[1] The duc de Joyeuse valiantly distinguished himself, and was three times unhorsed. Towards the conclusion of the conflict, after his infantry was dispersed, and flying on all sides, the marquis de St. Luc rode up to the duke and asked what were his designs in this emergency. Joyeuse replied in a voice broken and tremulous, "*De mourir après cecy, et ne vivre plus, M. de St. Luc!*" Though bleeding and exhausted from his wounds, Joyeuse made a last attempt to rally his army; he was, however, again unhorsed, and taken prisoner by two Huguenot troopers, who shot him in cold blood, notwithstanding that the duke offered them a ransom of 300,000 crowns to spare his life. The marquis de St. Luc yielded himself a prisoner to Condé, after having first defeated the latter in single combat, during which he dealt him so severe a blow in the side that the prince never recovered the injury. The brother of Joyeuse was killed, and also the comtes de Suze and d'Aubigeoux, and numbers of other illustrious personages. "This victory," says a contemporary, "was the most complete and extraordinary that had ever been gained; for at nine o'clock in the morning the armies had scarcely struck a blow, while at ten o'clock not a single man of the army of M. de Joyeuse held arms in hand, they all being in flight or prostrate on the battle-field. The cavalry was first routed, then the infantry was defeated, and broken by the regiment called that of the king of Navarre." The royal army lost 2,000 men, including 400 officers and nobles, and all its baggage, artillery,

[1] Relation de la Bataille de Coutras, Octobre, 1587. Archives Curieuses, 1st serie. De Thou. Dupleix. Mathieu. Davila.

and standards. The loss of the Huguenots was computed at 30 men killed and 100 wounded; they likewise captured 3,000 prisoners, and valiantly pursued their foes for three hours after the termination of the combat.

The king of Navarre, thus master of the field, commanded a muster of the victorious army, and returned thanks to God for this signal and speedy triumph. He then commanded the interment of the slain and the transport of the wounded into the adjacent towns and hamlets, directing that the greatest care should be bestowed to insure their recovery. He next burned the camp of the duc de Joyeuse, and commanded that the prisoners of war should be paraded before the army. The king publicly enjoined the greatest moderation on their captors. To some valiant officers Henri generously restored their liberty by himself engaging to pay their ransom. The king then entered the town of Coutras to take repose after his victory.

The bodies of the duc de Joyeuse and his brother, meantime, had been transported to Coutras and deposited on a table in the lower hall of the house where the king of Navarre was to dine. Henri, when informed of this circumstance, entered the hall; he shed tears while viewing the body of Joyeuse, and put back with his own hand the long locks of fair hair, all dabbled in blood, which streamed over the face of the deceased. He then caused the bodies to be reverently covered and gave them in charge to Turenne, who was nearly related to the duc de Joyeuse, commanding him to cause them to be embalmed and transported to Paris, or wherever the king might command.

Thus terminated the battle of Coutras, a signal triumph of the Huguenot arms. Had this victory been followed by the march of the army to join its German allies, the League probably, defeated on the battle-field and broken by dissensions, must have fallen; while the power of "*le Béarnnois*"—as Catherine called her son-in-law—thus confirmed and his rights acknowledged, the princes of Lorraine would have found no other resource than submission to the dynasty they had intrigued to supplant.

The charms of the comtesse de Guiche, however, indemnified Guise for the loss of the fight at Coutras. The king of Navarre forsook his valiant army and folded the banner of Albret, to lay at the feet of the fair Corisandre the ensigns and spoils of the vanquished.

CHAPTER III.

1587—1588.

Departure of Henry III. for the camp at Gien—Campaign of 1587—Return of the king to Paris—His reception—Dissensions between the duc d'Epernon and the archbishop of Lyons and M. de Villeroy—Death of the prince de Condé—Arrest of his widow—Articles of Nancy are rejected by the king—Cabals of the house of Lorraine—Henry forbids the advance of the duc de Guise to Paris—Mission of Bellièvre—Guise disregards the royal mandate—Entry into Paris—Interview with queen Catherine—Exasperation of the king—Guise is conducted to the Louvre by the queen-mother—Henry resolves upon the assassination of the duke—Interview between the king and the duc de Guise—He is suffered to leave the Louvre owing to the interposition of queen Catherine—His second interview with the king in the garden of the Tuileries—Henry commands domiciliary visits to be made in the disaffected quarters of the capital—Agitation in Paris.

THE repeated insults which the king had received from the Parisian populace, and the mutinous deportment of the authorities, rendered it imperative that Henry should now either notably assert his power by bringing the rebels to punishment, or manifest his displeasure by withdrawing from the capital. The secretary of state Villeroy and the duc d'Epernon proposed that the king should first retire to St. Germain, and then proceed to place himself at the head of his army—a measure which they averred would awe the spirit of insubordination rife in the capital. To the surprise of the council Henry accepted this proposition; and, moreover, to the great discomfiture of the Seize, he commenced the most vigorous preparations for the campaign. The invasion of the German army seems to have awakened a martial glow in the bosom of the king; it was against the combined forces of Coligny and the marquis of Baden that Henry at the battle of Moncontour had gained that military repute which at this period alone redeemed his reputation from utter obloquy. The *prestige* of his early victories Henry now burned to renew. Accordingly, about three days before the fight at Coutras, the king quitted his capital and repaired to the camp at Gien. His army consisted of 8,000 cavalry and a body of 18,000 infantry, half being French levies and the rest German. During the royal absence the regency was intrusted to Catherine to the contentment of the citizens of Paris, with whom the queen-mother was still popular.

The duc de Guise, meantime, continued to follow and harass the Germans. The duc de Bouillon held the rank of lieutenant for the king of Navarre in the confederated army, pending the arrival of the prince de Conty, brother of Condé. Châtillon led the French infantry: Dohna commanded in chief as lieutenant of prince Casimir.[1] Lorraine was ravaged by these mercenaries; their advance was attended with rapine and insubordination. The army, composed of soldiers of diverse races, refused obedience to its officers, not one of whom was of rank sufficiently elevated to claim command over the whole. The Swiss troops contended with the German landsknechts, and the French soldiers in the battalions of Bouillon and Châtillon hated both. For more than a week these fierce bands hovered in the neighbourhood of Bassigny; dread and suspense hung over all; churches were desecrated, tombs rifled,

[1] Davila, liv. viii. De Thou, liv. lxxxvii. Dupleix: Hist. de France.

and villages fired, and the monasteries mulcted or utterly despoiled. The generals in command followed the bidding of their savage mercenaries, and discipline was set at defiance. The vineyards of Champagne and Beausse, however, slew hundreds of these marauders; while the pillage of the contents of the adjacent wine vaults afforded the foraging parties from Guise's army numerous victories over the enemy. After an ineffectual attempt to seize the town of La Charité, the German soldiery poured into the valley of the Seine and encamped between Châtillon and Montargis. The duc de Guise followed, reinforced by detachments brought by the ducs de Mayenne and d'Elbœuf, who each took command in his army, and encamped at Courtenay, so as to place his army between Paris and the invaders. It was the duke's policy to preserve the capital from violence and rapine; he desired that Paris and its League should shine as the model and emulation of all the provincial associations. The disposition of its citizens was well known to him; factious, self-loving, insolent, and inconstant, the duke apprehended lest, on the first stroke of calamity or peril, the Parisians might altogether repudiate their League and shelter themselves under the legitimate protection of the throne.

The murmurs, meantime, in the confederated camp daily augmented; though wine was abundant, provisions were scarce. The soldiers, likewise, reproached Dhona and their chieftains for having, as they averred, deluded them into the realm under the pretext that the king of France tacitly approved of their juncture with the king of Navarre, while his majesty instead had taken the field to oppose their advance.[1] They

[1] De Thou, liv. lxxxvii. Mém. de Jacques Pape, Seigneur de St. Auban. Dupleix. Cheverny. Davila: MSS. Bibl. Imp.—Number-

also justly complained that the king of Navarre had failed in his promise to place himself at the head of their legions as soon as they should have penetrated to the Loire. The glorious intelligence of the victory of Coutras even increased the disaffection; for with it came the news that Henri, having partially disbanded his army, had retreated into Béarn, instead of marching to give them the *rendezvous*. This grave oversight, which the capacity and energy of the king of Navarre could never retrieve, occasioned the sanguinary campaigns of seven subsequent years; the consequent dictatorship of the duc de Guise, and the overthrow of the dynasty of Valois. After the battle of Coutras not a single impediment lay in the way to prevent the junction of the Huguenot army with its German confederates;—that union effected, one of the largest armies ever assembled on the soil of France, led by ardent and able generals, would have been enrolled under the banner of Bourbon. Money was plentiful from the liberal contributions of the Protestant powers; an English fleet lay in the harbour of La Rochelle laden with ammunition of war; while Montmorency in the south, master of fertile Languedoc and Dauphiny, offered plentiful supplies to the Huguenot camp. A spirit of misgiving, and probably of distrust, must for the moment have oppressed the valiant heart of the king of Navarre, when, regardless of these advantages and the interests of the Protestant cause, he took leave of his victorious army to kneel at the footstool of his fair Corisandre; and to indite to Henry III. that humble letter of condolence for the decease of Joyeuse, and of excuse for the triumph of his arms at Coutras.

less manuscripts on this campaign, all confirmatory of the narrations of the historians quoted.

A conflict ensued at Vimory between the confederates and the duc de Guise, which, as it terminated in the partial defeat of the former, still more disheartened the allies. The quarters of the baron de Dhona on the 28th day of October were in the little town of Vimory, while his army encamped in its vicinity. In the dead of the night the ducs de Guise and de Mayenne surprised the enemy, and a hand-to-hand fight ensued in the long straggling street of Vimory. Mayenne and the baron de Dhona personally engaged in single combat; and the conflict ended in the evacuation of the place by the allies with the loss of 200 men, the baggage of the army, and the symbols of its commander. Dhona, on his side, captured the *guidon* of the duc de Mayenne and the standards of the royal army; also a number of prisoners.[1] The allies then marched upon Château Landon, which was assaulted, pillaged, and burned; their army then proceeded to Malesherbes, where it encamped.[2]

The king, meanwhile, guarded the passages of the Loire. His head-quarters were at Gien. His majesty was accompanied by the ducs de Nevers and Epernon, and by other nobles of the court. His equipage was sumptuous; and the luxury of the camp greatly diminished the regrets which Henry might feel at leaving his palaces and embarking in the vicissitudes of war. The duc de Nevers was Henry's chief counsellor, and by his directions the fords and the banks of the river from La Charité to Orléans were fortified, and strong entrenchments thrown up at the points most liable to be assailed. Henry had scarcely joined his army when news reached him of the battle of Coutras and the decease of Joyeuse. The king's grief was at first vehe-

[1] De Thou. D'Aubigné: Hist. Universelle.
[2] Ibid.

ment; but his concern became greatly modified when Epernon observed to his royal master that Joyeuse, had he survived, would certainly have become a stanch supporter of the League, as his relations with Guise were of the most devoted nature; while the nobles who fell in the fight had almost without exception declared themselves adherents of the same cause—so that his majesty, therefore, had fewer partisans of the duke to contend against. The king, nevertheless, refused to admit the envoy of the king of Navarre, or to receive his letter; while he gave orders that the body of the duc de Joyeuse should be deposited with great pomp in one of the churches of the capital, until his funeral obsequies could be suitably solemnized. The king also wrote to Lavardin, late aide-de-camp to the deceased duke. His letter is full of condolence, and of regrets for the loss of Joyeuse and of the day at Coutras. The king desires that the fragment of the duke's army should join M. de Malicorne, who commanded a division in Guyenne, or the force under the duc d'Aumale in Picardy.'[1] As Guise had predicted, the news of this defeat depressed the zeal of the Paris Leaguers. Catherine wept, and publicly exclaimed that for twenty-five years the realm had not experienced so woful a calamity. She therefore addressed letters to the duc de Nevers, imploring him to shield her son the king from a like misfortune; and stated her opinion that his majesty ought not personally to be allowed to engage in battle. Her majesty entered into an argument to prove that though Henry might not be actually engaged in the fight, yet it would still be said, in case of a successful result, "the king has gained a battle; and hence, mon cousin, the king will have the credit so necessary

[1] Henri III. à M. de Lavardin: Bibl. Imp. MS.—Portef. Lancelot cotté, Louis XII. et Henri III., fol. 373.

to him without the personal risk." Catherine then dilates on the loyal and peaceful demeanour of the Parisians; and the assertion which she makes is not to be contradicted, that when under her sway their animosities were lulled, while the queen's dexterity of diction and manner allayed much factious opposition.[1] In Paris Catherine was always popular; her affability, magnificence, and especially her independence of private partialities, endeared her to the people. One of Catherine's maxims, however, was always to adjust her policy so that it might ebb and flow with the tide of public opinion; and few possessed characters supple enough to analyze and acquire a similar element of popularity.

After the conflict of Vimory the duc de Guise retreated to Montereau, and the duc de Mayenne retired into his government of Burgundy. This march roused the king's suspicion that Guise intended to garrison Paris and leave the burden of the war on his shoulders. Accordingly his majesty despatched Joachim seigneur de Dinteville to inquire the cause of the duke's retreat from the province of Beausse, where his presence was so necessary; also, the reason wherefore the duc de Mayenne withdrew, and the duc d'Aumale declined to join the royal army? Guise received the royal messenger with profound deference, and while condescending to explain that he retreated to afford his troops rest and refreshment before following the confederated army into the open plains of Beausse, where a pitched battle would be imminent, he nevertheless persisted in his march to Etampes.[2] Whether this retreat was a preconcerted plan or not, it were difficult to decide; it is certain, however, that envoys from the League

[1] MS. Bibl. Imp. Beth. No. 1. La Reyne Mère à M. le Duc de Nevers.

[2] Davila, lib. viii.

des Seize secretly waited upon the duke during his sojourn at Etampes to propose to him to seize the person of the king; while they were ready to arrest the members of Henry's council of state in the capital, and the presidents of the parliament of Paris, precisely in the way which was afterwards adopted. Louchard, the principal envoy, then informed the duke that the brother of the duc d'Aumale was then in the capital, and waited but his assent to declare himself the leader of the enterprise. The duc de Guise was too prudent openly to lend his sanction to such premature projects, especially when their conduct was to be committed to the discretion of so young a man as the chevalier d'Aumale, and to a cabal of turbulent citizens. Although the duc d'Aumale was openly a zealous supporter of the League, the duc de Guise distrusted him; his consort was that fascinating Marie d'Elbœuf whose sprightly charms had all but won the crown of France, and it was known that she greatly disapproved of her husband's opposition to his sovereign. The duchesse d'Aumale, moreover, was suspected upon several occasions of having furnished to the king those intelligences which had enabled him to defeat the designs of the League. The duc de Guise, therefore, replied, "that the time was not yet come for so overt a proceeding as that suggested by the Seize; he therefore desired to postpone the execution of their proposed design, but thanked them for so notable an evidence of their good-will."[1] Such was the encouraging answer made by Guise to this treasonable proposition: the intoxication of power must then indeed have bewildered that mind once so chivalrous. The duke, however, deluded himself with the subterfuge that all these rebellious plottings were not personally directed against the sovereign, except in so far as they might serve to compel

[1] Maimbourg: Hist. de la Ligue. Cayet: Chronologie Novennaire. Davila, lib. viii.

the king to proscribe heresy, and to recognise an orthodox successor. This achieved, the king's loyal subjects would afterwards unite in a hearty support of his throne.

The retreat of the king of Navarre into Béarn produced another outbreak of mutiny in the camp of the confederates, despite the presence of the prince of Conty, who had now joined their army. The Swiss levies, exasperated at receiving no pay; and pricked in their consciences at the hostile attitude they had assumed against the sovereign of France, in whose armies their forefathers had gloriously fought, took the resolution of sending deputies to Henry to explain the causes which had induced their entrance into his kingdom. This step once resolved upon, the disorganization and consequent disbandment of the confederate army became merely an event of time. The Swiss deputies found king Henry at Bonneval; he received them sternly, and declared that he was about to send an ambassador to the Cantons to complain of their illegal enrolment, and to demand that exemplary chastisement might be inflicted on every man concerned in this invasion of his realm. The deputies were then dismissed and conducted into the presence of the duc de Nevers, who addressed them in a long harangue, half menace, half persuasion. The duke then once more led them before the king. On one of the deputies observing that, in obeying the summons of the king of Navarre, they had been induced to believe that they were at the same time serving his majesty's cause against the usurpations of certain of his subjects, Henry stopped the speaker by wrathfully observing, "Well! you now see me alive, and know that I am commanding in my army to oppose yours; you will therefore be inexcusable if you remain longer amongst those whom I esteem my enemies. You have nothing for it, therefore, but to decamp from my realm, according as M. de Nevers has proposed; else, be assured, I will avenge myself on every one of you, and through the government even of your own Cantons."[1] The Swiss, therefore, withdrew from the army of the confederates, and, in reply to the clamorous reproaches of Dhona and the allied chieftains, promised only not to depart from the realm until they had previously communicated with the king of Navarre. The efficiency of the army was, nevertheless, destroyed; divisions ensued between the officers, while their troops gave themselves over to the wildest excesses of rapine and violence. The duc de Guise attentively watched the progress of this anarchy, and organized a second expedition like that at Vimory, in which he obtained a signal victory over the enemy. On the 24th of November Dhona established himself at Auneau, a small town in the district of Beausse. The castle, however, resisted the attempts of the confederates for its capture; while the governor sent to advertise M. de Guise that the garrison would sally out and support him if he deemed it advisable to assail the place. The duke accepted the suggestion, and at midnight the gate of the town was opened to admit a detachment of French infantry, while Guise advanced and enveloped the town with a body of 3,000 cavalry. A desperate conflict ensued, in which the enemy was driven out of Auneau with great slaughter and the loss of the treasure and baggage. Dhona fought his way inch by inch to the gate of the town, and escaped being cut down by extraordinary good fortune. The fugitives, as they passed the royal camp at Gien, were pursued by the duc d'Epernon, who slaughtered many; while such was the panic, that a battalion of landsknechts 1,200 strong laid

1. Députation des Suisses au Roi—De Thou, liv. lxxxvii. Journal de Henri III. Pasquier, liv. xi.

down arms and surrendered to a party of twenty-five of the royal arquebusiers.[1] The rout of the Germans was complete; they lost 2,000 men, their treasure, all that remained of their baggage, their horses and mules of burden, and nine standards. Dhona, nevertheless, being afterwards joined by the Swiss troops, who deemed their honour compromised by this sudden defeat, boldly drew up his army in battle array; but as no further molestation was offered, the allies, being distrustful of the fidelity of the Swiss, retreated to Château Landon in the greatest confusion and disarray. The duc de Guise, meantime, sent la Châtre to the camp of Gien to notify his victory of Auneau to the king, and to lay at his majesty's feet the captured standards of the enemy. Henry gave a cold reception to the envoy, and omitted to present him with the customary gratuity. The king could not fail to perceive how greatly these triumphs over the confederated army would augment the popularity of the duc de Guise at the expense of the royal *prestige*. Nevertheless, Henry, from some unexplained cause, never himself attempted to attack the enemy, though his army trebled in numbers that of the duc de Guise. His mania for negotiation, imbibed from the queen-mother, and his hatred of action, caused Henry to neglect this opportunity of rendering himself the equal of the duc de Guise in military renown.

Guise, meantime, arrived at the camp of Gien to pay his respects to his royal master. On his route the duke took the opportunity of attacking the outposts of the Germans, and dispersed several of their detachments. His supercilious scrutiny of the royal army, and his popularity amongst the men, still further increased the king's umbrage. Henry's displeasure reached the

[1] Pasquier. Vie du Duc d'Epernon—Giraud.

climax of indignation when he heard of the exultant reception which the intelligence of the conflict at Auneau obtained in Paris. The pulpits resounded with eulogiums on the gallant achievements at Vimory and Auneau; nor did several of the preachers scruple to proclaim that while "Saul had killed his thousands, David had slain his tens of thousands." Multitudes nightly assembled beneath the windows of the hôtel of madame de Montpensier singing hymns in praise of her brother; and exalting his renown above that of the most famous heroes of antiquity.

The king, therefore, resolved to arrest the exploits of his rival by himself concluding a prompt accommodation with the chieftains of the Swiss and German levies. To Epernon he intrusted this negotiation, as the duc de Nevers had fallen from his horse and fractured his thighbone below the suture of a severe wound which he received at Moncontour. A long and dangerous illness ensued, as the duke's old wound opened afresh; he was, therefore, compelled to take leave of the king and retire to his castle in the Rhetellois—an illness which might so far be termed fortunate as it prevented him from sharing in the frightful tragedies of the ensuing year.

The king, therefore, of his own accord and will, despatched the sieur de Caumont to offer a free passage home to the German and Swiss levies—a pardon for any subject of France who had joined in their invasion, provided that such individuals conformed to the orthodox faith; or to those who adhered to the reformed tenets, a license to quit the realm in safety, after first disposing of their lands and offices. The sole condition imposed by the king was, that the army should relinquish into the hands of his majesty's commissioner their standards; or that the chieftains should promise, upon oath, never more to bear arms against the king of France or the emperor Rodolph.[1] This last stipulation was added because the emperor had caused his displeasure to be notified to prince Casimir and other of the Protestant chieftains of Germany, for having permitted levies for the invasion of France to be made within their respective dominions, and recommended their recall. To give greater effect to these propositions, the duc d'Epernon pursued the unfortunate confederates with a detachment of cavalry, and followed them into the Pays de Morvent, a district between the rivers Dheune and Saône, cutting off stragglers and harassing their rear. This country was barren, and famine soon prevailed in their camp; the roads, moreover, were so impassable that frequently their cavalry was compelled to ride in file. Under these circumstances the confederates, after a brief parley, accepted the stipulations sent them by the king, but preferred to surrender their standards to giving their word to refrain from making future war on the empire, or on the realm of France. The treaty was concluded at Lency in the Maçonnais. The comte de Châtillon, however, refused to be comprehended in the accommodation; the duc de Bouillon retired to Geneva; while the prince de Conty succeeded in fighting his way through the county of Maine, and eventually joined the king of Navarre. The baron de Dhona and the other confederated chieftains, Germans and Swiss, visited the duc d'Epernon at Marcigny le Nonnain to take leave. The duke entertained them at a magnificent banquet, the carousing after which lasted several days.[2] The army then set forth again to meet with fresh perils, though declared the "faithful and well-beloved of king Henry." The duc de Guise and the marquis de Pont pursued it

[1] De Thou, liv. lxxxvii. Davila. Pasquier. Dupleix. Aubigné.

[2] Mezeray: Grande Histoire, Vie de Henri III. Bouchet: Généalogie de Coligni—La Retraite de M. de Châtillon.

through Franche Comté, putting all to the sword; the soldiers of the League committing dreadful atrocities to avenge, as they declared, the sack of the duchy of Lorraine and the county of Beausse. The stipulation concluded by the king was regarded by Guise as null and void; and soon his emissaries caused it to be bruited that Epernon had negotiated the convention with the confederates, whose extermination had been so happily begun by Guise, on purpose that they might at a future day enter France in support of Henri of Navarre. The king, meantime, manifested the most apathetic indifference respecting the victories of Vimory and Auneau, and the sentiments of the duc de Guise; he gave him no thanks, nor proffered him reward. The duke. therefore, in high dudgeon, retired to Nancy, where he had convoked a second family conclave. From all the Catholic princes of Europe, Guise, however, received the most flattering ovations. Philip II. wrote him an autograph letter, in which he lauded the duke's zeal, orthodoxy, and prowess. The duke of Parma sent a suit of armour exquisitely inlaid, having the words "*Il n'appartient qu'à Henri de Lorraine de se dire Chef de Guerre,*" engraven on the helmet—a eulogium the more exalted from the high military repute of the donor.[1] Sixtus V. presented the duc de Guise with a consecrated sword. Catherine de Medici caused the duke's already brimming cup of elation to overflow by the refinement of her adulation on the "high deeds with which Christendom resounded."

Flattered by so many tributes to his valour and conduct, the duc de Guise not unnaturally wished to obtain some avowal and testimony of his royal master's

[1] Journal de Henri III. There was also a report which greatly disquieted the king, that the duc de Guise had paid a visit in disguise to Rome, where he had remained three days, discovering himself to no one but to the cardinal de Pellvé.

approbation, the more especially as Henry had given commands that a medal should be struck with his own effigy, in honour "of the defeat of the reiters." The decease of the duc de Joyeuse left two posts of high preferment vacant—the office of lord high admiral and that of governor of Normandy. The governments of Angoulême, Saintonge, and the Pays d'Aunis were, moreover, vacant by the decease at Coutras of the only son of the maréchal de Bellegarde, one of Henry's early favourites. The duke, however, asked nothing for himself, but sent to pray his majesty to confer the post of admiral on the comte de Brissac, who throughout the campaign against the reiters had acted as his aide-de-camp. He also asked for governments for three persons, his partisans. Henry at first seemed inclined to grant the duke's prayer, and even entered into various details and stipulations with Brissac. Suddenly, however, without consulting Catherine or any member of his council, the king bestowed at one time all these posts on the duc d'Epernon, who thus, besides his palace appointments, beheld himself high admiral, colonel-general of infantry, governor of Provence, Normandy, Saintonge, Pays d'Aunis, and Angoulême! It is difficult to imagine an infatuation so dense as that which seems at the most critical periods of his reign to have deluded the unhappy prince. The duc d'Epernon, nevertheless, showed as little prudence in submitting to be thus invested with the highest offices in the realm, the varied duties of which he could not discharge even had his services or his hereditary rank given him the semblance of a claim to a monopoly so flagrant.

Henry, meanwhile, relieved from the monotony of a camp life, advanced with his army to within a few leagues of Paris, where he arrived December 23rd, 1587. The most magnificent entry into his capital, from whence he had so ignominiously departed, awaited Henry by the intervention of queen Catherine, who frequently speculated advantageously on her son's foible for pompous display. The two queens and the duchesse d'Epernon proceeded as far as Lagny to meet his majesty, whose health had greatly improved under the discipline of a camp life. At the gates of the capital Henry was received by the parliament, the municipality, and the foreign ambassadors. His reception was enthusiastic, and once more the royal ears drank in the welcome sounds of applause from the mutinous citizens of Paris. "*On lui a crié, Noël! jamais roi ne fut plus chéri!*" ironically wrote Pasquier.[1] Henry proceeded to the Louvre, where his first care was to order the due solemnization of the obsequies of the duc de Joyeuse. This ceremony took place in the church of the Augustinians with the utmost splendour, and with the *appareil* appertaining to a prince of royal blood. Madame de Joyeuse caused daily services to be performed in the church of the Franciscan monastery during the remainder of the month, at which she assisted in state, clad in mourning robes, and attended by the princess Christine of Lorraine, grand-daughter of queen Catherine, and by the duchesses de Montpensier and Nemours.[2] The cardinal de Bourbon manifested the most vehement grief; he wept over the bier of Joyeuse, and loudly expressed the desire "that his miserable nephew Henri de Navarre reposed beneath the pall, rather than that most gallant champion of orthodoxy Joyeuse!" When the words of the witless old prelate were repeated to the king, Henry shrugged his shoulders

[1] Lettres de Pasquier, tome ii.

[2] L'Ordre que fut tenu au Service Quarantin que fait Madame de Joyeuse en l'Eglise et Monastere des Cordeliers de Paris. MSS. Bibl. Imp.—Dupuy, 324, fol. 207.

and exclaimed, "A speech worthy of that poor drivelling simpleton!"[1] During the invasion of the German reiters, the cardinal de Bourbon, forgotten for the moment as a political personage, had returned to the tranquil round of his ecclesiastical duties, diversified by the friendly interchange of visits with the queen-mother, to whom he was sincerely attached. The cardinal used to acknowledge that one of his highest recreations was to discourse of past events and personages with Catherine. The reminiscences of these two colleagues and actors in the most momentous events of the sixteenth century must have indeed possessed surpassing interest.

Henry kept the festival of Christmas with great solemnity. On New Year's day he held a chapter of knights of St. Esprit, which was followed by a sumptuous banquet and revel. The popularity of the king proved of very brief duration, the immediate cause of fresh agitation being threefold—first, the partial retirement of queen Catherine de Medici from the councils of her son; secondly, the threat which the king was heard on more than one occasion to utter relative to the castigation which he had still in reserve for his lieges of Paris; and thirdly, the arrogant conduct of Epernon, and his quarrel with the two most influential members of the council, Villeroy and the archbishop of Lyons. Ever since the partial revolt of the governor of Lyons, Mandelot, the most unsparing warfare existed between Epernon and Villeroy, whose conduct on that occasion, in preferring the interests of his son to the prosperity of his sovereign, Epernon pronounced scandalous and treasonable. Thus having a grievance fraught with mutual vituperation, it required little additional excitement to bring matters to a condition of open warfare between

[1] Journal de Henri III.

the astute secretary and the favourite. During one of the last councils which Henry held at St. Aignan before his return to the Louvre, Villeroy advised the king to devote a surplus sum of money arising from the sale of some of the dower lands of the late queen of Scots, situated in Poitou, to enable the provost of Paris to raise a military band for the better defence of the capital. Epernon violently opposed the measure, doubtless believing that the king could apply his money more advantageously than by giving it into the hands of personages whose *liaison* with the princes of Lorraine was notorious. Villeroy persisted; when Epernon rose in a furious rage and accused the secretary of embezzling and perverting the royal finances, and even so far forgot himself as to call Villeroy "a scoundrel who deserved to be driven from office by the spurs of his majesty's guards." Villeroy was leaning on the back of the chair in which Henry sat. The king hastily rose, and, confronting his secretary, commanded him not to reply; he then gave the same command to Epernon, and broke up the council.[1] The outrageous and unfounded words of Epernon rankled in the mind of Villeroy, who could obtain no redress; and after Henry's safe return to Paris, he gave himself entirely over to the faction of the Guisards, who made the downfall of the favourite one of the clauses of their charter. A similar act of inexcusable folly alienated the archbishop of Lyons—a scene which occurred during Henry's Christmas festivities after his return from the camp. Espinac, who was a busy and eloquent churchman, of acute ability but depraved life, was one day discoursing in the court circle upon the claims of the king of Navarre to the succession. The archbishop ended by declaring that the Béarnnois was unworthy in every respect to aspire

[1] Mém. de Villeroy. Journal de Henri III.

to so exalted a dignity. The duc d'Epernon rudely contradicted the assertion: "And pray inform me, monseigneur," said he, "if such is the case, how a prelate who is accused, like yourself, of incest, one who has also been convicted of simony, of debauchery, and excessive prodigality, can dare to retain the purple?" Espinac retorted in terms if possible of more gross vituperation; but the king, as usual, laughed, and with his accustomed *inconsequence* declined to interfere.[1] But Epernon soon found to his cost that he had provoked the attack of a swarm of hornets in assailing the witty and irascible prelate. Libels, pasquinades, and caricatures hemmed in the duke wherever he turned. Words acrid as wormwood fell from the pen of the prelate in his pitiless dissection of the faults and foibles of the duke. The worst, however, was that the king came in for a share of these aspersions; and of such malignity were they, that, says a writer, "the Furies must have inspired the pen and lighted the inditer with their lurid torch." Henry and his minion were again likened to Gaveston and Edward II. king of England, and parallels innumerable were collected, all tending to the overwhelming discredit of the parties satirized. The fiery and indomitable spirit of the archbishop of Lyons greatly delighted madame de Montpensier, and an intimate alliance was forthwith cemented between this turbulent pair.

The news of the decease of the prince of Condé, combined with the suspicious circumstances connected with his death, served for a few days to divert public attention from the broils of the Louvre, which Espinac pronounced the "most disreputable abode in Paris." On Thursday, the 3rd of March, 1588, at St. Jean, the

[1] De Thou, liv. xc. "Jusqu'à ce moment Espinac n'avoit paru prendre aucun part décisif. Il se déclara alors pour la Ligue. On croit qu'il engagea le duc de Guise à précipiter l'exécution de ses projets."

prince was suddenly seized with colic and convulsions, about an hour and a half after supper. The most violent agony followed, the unfortunate prince crying aloud for relief and even death to ease him from his torments. He continued in the same condition until Saturday, when insensibility supervened, and during the afternoon he expired.[1] The symptoms were those of poison of the most virulent description, a suspicion rendered a matter of certainty by the *post mortem* examination of the body. A fugitive page named Belcastel was implicated; also Brillaud, a favourite equerry in the service of Condé, who was arrested on the charge of having furnished horses on the evening of the prince's demise for the evasion of Belcastel and of two servants supposed also to be concerned in the crime. Brillaud being put to the torture, his revelations were followed by the arrest of the princess de Condé, Charlotte de la Tremouille, whose marriage with the prince had only been solemnized during the spring of 1586. The motive which, it was alleged, had induced the wife of Condé to perpetrate this foul assassination was, that being guilty of a criminal intrigue with the king of Navarre, the princess, finding herself three months advanced in pregnancy, poisoned her husband to avoid the disgrace and penalty of exposure. The page Belcastel was declared by others to have been the object of the abandoned inclinations of the princess.[2] In this century crimes were so commonly perpetrated by the highest personages, that even the atrocious accusation levelled against madame de Condé occupies a subordinate rank in the ghastly catalogue; nevertheless, antecedent cir-

[1] All the details of this death and subsequent prosecution are to be found, MSS. de Béthune Bibl. Imp., vol. clxxxvi.

[2] MS. de Brienne, Bibl. Imp., tome clxxxvi. Archives Curieuses, 1er série. Hist. du Maréchal de Matignon, liv. ii. Mém. de la Ligue, tome ii. p. 304.

cumstances attest strongly in favour of the innocence of the princess. The union of Condé with mademoiselle de la Tremouille had been on both sides what is commonly termed a "love match." The marriage was strongly opposed by the duchesse de la Tremouille, whose liberal politics were not conciliated by the fact that it was a prince of the blood who made suit for the hand of her daughter. For long, therefore, mademoiselle de la Tremouille was interdicted by her mother and brother from holding communication with Condé, and was detained in a kind of captivity in her brother's strong fort of Taillebourg. On the breaking out of the war after the treaty of Nemours, mademoiselle de la Tremouille sent Condé secret intelligence which resulted in the capture of her brother's stronghold of Taillebourg; and this triumph, combined with the honour of becoming brother-in-law to a prince of the blood, induced the duc de la Tremouille on reflection to abandon the interests of the League, and unite with the king of Navarre in resisting the edict of Nemours, which had been dictated alone by the princes of Guise. The marriage between Condé and mademoiselle de la Tremouille was solemnized on the return of Condé from England in 1586; and from that time the princess had resided at St. Jean d'Angely, still apparently retaining all her enthusiasm and affection for her gallant husband.[1]

These facts, however, did not alter the decision of the judges appointed to investigate the crime. They condemned the page Belcastel and Brillaud to be torn in pieces by horses, and their remains consumed by fire; and the princess de Condé to be put to the torture preparatory to the infliction of the capital punishment of decapitation. The princess pleaded her pregnancy,

[1] De Thou: Hist. de son Temps.

and appealed to the parliament of Paris and to the council of state. Her first plea being admitted, the sentence was suspended, and she was incarcerated in a small chamber of the citadel of St. Jean d'Angely, access to her presence being granted only to two ladies, mesdames de Brisembourg and Ste. Mêsme, who were likewise appointed to be present, and to attest the *accouchement* of the princess. Madame de Condé entered her prison chamber on the eleventh day of July, and on the first day of the month of September following she gave birth to a prince. The birth of this son saved the life of the princess; the judges of the criminal court of St. Jean d'Angely respected the mother of Condé. Still the princess did not regain her liberty, though her little daughter Eleanore was restored to her, and she was permitted to associate with the ladies of her household as usual. For seven dreary years the princess remained at St. Jean; her ignominious and, to all appearance, unjust sentence suspended over her head. When Henri IV. had established his right to the throne of France, the princess de Condé petitioned for the abrogation of her sentence; the depositions were examined by commissioners appointed by the parliament of Paris, who pronounced them untenable, and annulled the sentence, and commanded all the documents connected with the cause to be burned.[1]

The premature decease of the valiant and conscientious Condé produced immense sensation throughout France. The king of Navarre wept, and exclaimed, "that he had lost his right arm." The duc de Guise sincerely mourned the catastrophe, or at least appeared to do so, he having been intimately associated with the prince during the earlier years of his life. Moreover, the death of Condé by poison suggested stirring and

[1] Archives Curieuses, 1er série; edited by Messrs. Danjou and Cimber.

not very pleasant reflections for the chief of the League, a subject, and not of the blood royal. As for the king, he was too much occupied with the cabals of the capital and the task of satisfying his favourites, to have leisure to think even of his personal pleasures. The state of public feeling seemed daily growing more hostile; nothing that his majesty did, in the opinion of his subjects of Paris, proceeded from righteous and legitimate motives; while every public act of merit, grace, or valour was due to the Guises. It was a fixed idea with the Parisian people that Henry, with Epernon, intrigued, bribed, and caballed to support the claims of the king of Navarre; and that in league with the latter his majesty meditated some terrible retaliation on his orthodox capital.

Meanwhile, whilst Henry vacillated—one day a saint, the next a despot or a voluptuary, the second scene of the great drama of the League was being enacted at Nancy, the capital of the duchy of Lorraine. The members of the conclave there convened by Guise were the ducs de Lorraine, Mayenne, Aumale, Elbœuf, Mercœur, and the marquis de Pont. Fresh resolutions were embodied, the most audacious ever presented by subjects to sovereign. The great war of extermination upon which they had entered languished; the defeat of Coutras, the hostile attitude of Montmorency, and the overthrow of the army of Germans, had brought the campaign, as it were, to a conclusion. The king, glad of a reprieve, spent his time in paltry and querulous negotiations with individuals, and seemed well inclined to allow the treaty of Nemours to remain a mere form. Accordingly, the following articles and demands were drawn up for presentation to the king, and signed by the princes of Lorraine during the month of January, 1588:—"That king Henry should be challenged to give open countenance to the holy and orthodox League; that his majesty should be required to remove from all charges and offices the enemies of the commonwealth and the supporters of heresy, the which personages will be named at a convenient opportunity. That he shall accept the holy canons of Trent, and cause such to be generally recognised throughout the realm. That Chambers of Inquisition be established in every large and populous town throughout France, and that the ecclesiastics selected as judges in those courts shall be foreigners. That the clergy may be authorized to redeem all church lands alienated or confiscated, on paying the value to the present occupiers. His majesty, moreover, was required to cede a certain number of towns to the League, and grant permission for the construction therein of citadels. That a decree shall be promulgated commanding the sale by auction of lands and tenements appertaining to heretics; moreover, that all persons suspected from the year 1560 of favouring heresy, though they might not have gone the length of apostatizing, shall contribute a third of their revenues for the support of the war. That the king's orthodox subjects shall be mulcted only to the limit of a tenth of their revenue until the happy proscription of heresy. Finally, that his majesty shall maintain an army on the frontiers of Lorraine to repulse any future invasion of reiters."[1]

These infamous articles the duc de Guise sent to the king, so low had reverence for the royal authority fallen. Henry, thereupon, commenced a cavilling correspondence with the duc de Guise, which lasted for several months, on the names of the personages whom the latter thought fit to designate "as enemies of the commonwealth and the faith!" and, as if to repel the injurious doubt that perchance Epernon might be classed

[1] Les Articles dressés par la Ligue de Nanci en 1588, et rejettés par le Roi Henri III.—Bibl. Imp. MSS. de Gaignières, 788.

in that category, his majesty despatched the duke to take the oaths of high-admiral before the chambers. Epernon was presented by an eloquent advocate of the name of Marion, who, in his harangue, lauded the duke, whom he termed a bulwark of the faith, sent as the antidote to repair the evils perpetrated by the late amiral de Coligny. Marion concluded his oration by a piece of fulsome adulation to the king, whom he termed "le saint des saints."

On quitting Nancy the duc de Guise proceeded to Soissons to support his cousin the duc d'Aumale in Picardy in case the king should return a negative to the request made by Aumale that his majesty would be pleased to institute him as lieutenant over that province, the government of which he had held only as the *locum tenens* of the prince of Condé. Henry returned an ungracious refusal, and actually gave the government to Epernon, making the fourth command which he had bestowed on his favourite within the space of three months. The clamour, however, became so great at this nomination that the duc d'Epernon in a few days prudently resigned the office, which Henry then bestowed, as he had promised, on the duc de Nevers. As the illness of the latter precluded him from service, the duc d'Aumale continued temporarily in supreme command over the province—a convenient mode of adjusting the difficulty, but one infinitely subversive of the royal power of veto.

In Paris the fury of the Leaguers, after the publication of the articles of Nancy, demonstrated itself in all manner of plots and tumults.* A second conspiracy was organized to seize the person of the king and compel him to sign the above articles during the revels of the carnival, which was again betrayed by Nicholas Poulain, who outwardly demonstrated the fiercest hatred for the court. This zeal secured his life in his perilous calling of informer; for the Seize, in their blind animosity, cared not to scrutinize too closely the motives of such demonstration. The cause, meantime, had received a great accession of strength by the arrival of eight able and prudent officers from the camp of the duc de Guise, in deference to the earnest request of Crucé and other leaders of the Seize; who lived in constant apprehension that the long-suffering of the king might at length be exhausted, and that he would avenge their repeated and malignant cabals. Had Henry been left to the guidance of Epernon, all the members of the Seize would soon have been lodged in the dungeons of the Châtelet; but it suited the tone of the king's mind to believe those counsellors who persisted in asserting that their intrigues were exaggerated, and that the peril was not so great as represented. Villequier, moreover, threw discredit on the reality of the plots said to be in agitation by the League; while Catherine maintained that no danger existed, and that, provided her son enforced the clauses of the treaty of Nemours, the duc de Guise was his humble and devoted servant. "You have only, monsieur, the testimony of this Poulain, who may have purposes of his own to serve by the invention of these terrible conspiracies; had not you pledged your royal word, it would be well to denounce him to those whom he maligns." So hard was it for Catherine to believe that the duc de Guise harboured designs hostile to her offspring. In the month of April, the League numbered 20,000 men in Paris alone; the chieftains, therefore, believed it time to act, and to secure themselves from the vengeance of their outraged sovereign. A conspiracy was again concocted to seize the Louvre on the 21st day of April, 1588, to massacre the royal guards and the duc d'Epernon, to proclaim the regency of the queen-mother, and to invite the duc de Guise immediately to the capital, under the title of lieutenant-governor of the realm. No sooner had the mind of Poulain grasped all the details of the plot than he hastened to the palace, and under the pretext of soliciting the king, relative to a petition which with great wiliness he had presented the day before at Henry's public audience, he requested to be admitted into the royal presence. He was not then suffered to see the king; but M. d'O and Pierre Paul Tosinghi, a new counsellor introduced by Epernon, in whom Henry reposed much confidence, were empowered to receive Poulain's communication.[1] The Louvre, therefore, was placed in a state of defence; and during the following day Henry caused large quantities of arms, cuirasses, and gunpowder to be publicly transported from the arsenal to the palace; while the gates of the town were secured, and messengers held in readiness to communicate with the Swiss guards encamped in the vicinity of the capital. His majesty, moreover, departed early on the morning of the 21st from the Louvre for St. Germain. Previously, he admitted Poulain to an interview in the presence of Epernon, d'O, Tosinghi, and the comte de Guiche. His majesty subjected Poulain to a severe cross-examination, but failed to induce him to falter in a single assertion.[2] The king, before his departure, sent to the duchesse de Montpensier an order to quit the capital, as he was well informed of her treasonable and factious proceedings. The duchess ridiculed the mandate, and insolently returned for answer that, far from being his majesty's opponent, as he erroneously imagined, she was exerting her best ability to obtain for him the third crown which appeared in the royal device.[3] The duc de Guise, meantime, atten-

[1] Procès Verbal du nommé Nicholas Poulain, Lieutenant de la Prévôsté de l'Isle de France. Davila: Journal de Henri III.

[2] Ibid.

[3] Henry's device was three crowns—two of which were represented as

tive to the events in the capital, advanced to Gonisse, and announced his resolve to enter the capital and justify himself in the opinion of his king and sovereign, particularly relative to the alleged enterprise of the 21st of April; and to aid his majesty in putting down the treasonable plots said to be concocted for the seizure of the royal person. At the same time madame de Montpensier went to Catherine, and requested her assent to the arrival of the duke. The queen declined to give this permission; for the condition of affairs, and the menaces of her son, began seriously to rouse her apprehension. There is no doubt, however, that the good wishes and tacit approval of Catherine were given to the duc de Guise. Her majesty hated Epernon and abhorred the king of Navarre; she deprecated the misgovernment of her son the king, and the lavish prodigalities which impoverished the realm, and would gladly have seen the existing government annihilated. In her old age Catherine was growing devout, and real zeal for religion mingled with her grievances and her designs to secure the throne for her grandson. The agitation, therefore, that was likely to obviate these evils could not be displeasing to her majesty. There was, however, a wide difference in the result contemplated by Catherine and by the duc de Guise: the queen meant a coercion which would place the government more absolutely at her disposal, to be followed by the nomination of an orthodox successor to the throne; Guise intended a skilful and daring appropriation, in due time, of the diadem.

The rumour of the duke's intended visit to the capital renewed Henry's panics. He returned to Paris, after taking a tender farewell of the duc d'Epernon,

being on earth, the third was suspended from an azure cloud—to signify that his majesty already held two crowns, those of France and Poland; while the third, the heavenly crown, was still in reserve for him.

who was proceeding to his government of Normandy, and despatched M. de Bellièvre to Soissons for the express purpose of requesting the duke to abstain from visiting the court. He desired his envoy to say to Guise that his majesty had never doubted his loyalty, and discredited the reports current to his disadvantage.[1] Bellièvre was also to inform the duke that M. d'Epernon had departed to take possession of his new government of Normandy. Catherine, however, had a word to say to the envoy before he departed. Though she had refused directly to grant the request of the duchesse de Montpensier, she yet made it so apparent to Bellièvre that she desired the presence of Guise in Paris, during the absence of Epernon, that the former departed on his mission with the intention of neutralizing, by his significant manner and gestures, the words which the command of his sovereign compelled him to pronounce. The duc de Guise replied, "that his majesty's message was an implied reproof which deeply wounded his honour; nevertheless, he would obey, provided the king promised that no harm or damage should happen to the loyal citizens of Paris, whose lives had been endangered by the aspersions of the king's counsellors and by their zeal for their faith."[2] Bellièvre promised to do all in his power to obtain such guarantees, and took leave of the duke, engaging to write or to return to Soissons within the space of three days. During the conference a messenger arrived from the Seize, bringing alarming reports of the hostile disposition evinced by the king, who, it was reported, intended to seize the ten principal leaders of the League, including the president de Neuilly, Crucé,

[1] Chronologie Novennaire, tome i. Mathieu: Hist. de Henri III., liv. viii. Amplifications des Particularités qui se passèrent à Paris lorsque M. de Guise s'en empara, et que le Roi en sortit. Mém. de la Ligue, p. 318; edit. de l'Abbé Goujat. Davila, lib. ix. et seq.

and the curé Boucher, and hang them summarily from the battlements of the Louvre. The duke was therefore emphatically admonished and implored to appear in Paris, when such enterprises must be relinquished. From his sister, madame de Montpensier, the duke likewise received urgent solicitations; and probably the secret assurance of Catherine's support, did he venture on the bold deed of disregarding the commands of his sovereign and repairing to Paris. It has been a subject of much controversy, whether the duc de Guise on deciding upon this latter step, contemplated or had actually taken measures to bring about, at this particular period, the revolution which ensued; or whether he was not himself surprised at the vastness of the consequences resulting therefrom. The probabilities are, that Guise went to Paris animated by the design of seizing supreme authority with the aid of the queen-mother, intending to enforce the articles of Nancy, and to compel the king to proclaim him lieutenant-general of the realm, with the powers possessed by his father during the reign of Francis II. Confident in his popularity and oblivious of the temper of his sovereign—who was capable of avenging himself, either by the most remorseless treachery, or by an act of abject humiliation, such as might awaken a sentiment of compassion and perhaps of returning loyalty—the duke committed the error of repairing to Paris, unaccompanied by a *cortège* sufficiently imposing to insure his own safety if menaced, or powerful enough to restrain the imprudent enthusiasm of his adherents. Nevertheless, though Guise was, as it were, betrayed into his eventual triumph, he knew how to profit by it: summoning to his aid his natural endowments of decision and daring sagacity, and possessing those important adjuncts to popular success—a handsome person, courtly grace of manner, and fluent eloquence, he firmly grasped the position which, despite his denials, had been the aim of his career since the year 1586. Bellièvre, meantime, had reported the conditions of the duke's obedience to his majesty, who promptly acceded. Important financial negotiations relative to the pay of the Swiss troops[1] being then pending, the king desired Bellièvre to despatch a courier to the duke, instead of himself repairing again to Soissons. The packet was intrusted to a courier, who, upon demanding twenty-five crowns to defray the costs of his journey, met with a flat refusal from the clerk of the treasury, acting, it is believed, on a suggestion from the queen-mother. The courier, therefore, sent the despatch by the ordinary post, which in those days was not renowned for celerity. A second communication was also thus forwarded to its destination. The king, moreover, to obviate any possible mistake, despatched the comte de Guiche and Benoise, his private secretary, to interdict again the duke's approach.

The mode in which Bellièvre's despatch was transmitted signified little, except that it enabled the duke positively to assert that he had never received the mandate; for at midnight on the very day the envoy returned to Paris Guise precipitately quitted Soissons for Mortrives, at which place he arrived at eight o'clock in the morning of Monday, May 9th. He then entered St. Denis, where he dined and baited the horses belonging to the escort of eight persons which attended him. The duke then fearlessly traversed the camp of the Swiss troops, and entered Paris[2]

[1] The Swiss were encamped at St. Denis, and threatened to mutiny if the arrears of their pay were not forthcoming.

[2] "Le duc," says Mathieu, "qui avait l'âme atteite d'une cuisante fièvre, ne trouve l'appetit ni plaisir qu'en propre gout. Il veut voire le Louvre ou mourir par les chemins : il monte à cheval avec huit gentilshommes sur les neuf heures du soir, laisse le cardinal son frère, et le

by the Porte St. Martin at midday. He rode enveloped in a huge cloak, hiding his face in its folds until he reached the Rue St. Denis, when he cast the mantle from him and boldly showed himself. His destination was the palace of queen Catherine, the hôtel de Soissons.

The queen, on this eventful Monday, was reposing on a couch, upon which she now spent the greater part of the day, on account of her increasing infirmities. She was attended by the duchesse de Montpensier, now publicly called by the king madame la Boiteuse, and by the duchesse d'Usez, whose wit greatly enlivened her majesty's solitude. At the window of the saloon, which looked into the street, stood Catherine's favourite dwarf Majosky, who was entertaining his mistress by jests and gibes at the expense of the people passing. Suddenly Majosky called out that M. de Guise was alighting from his horse at the portal of the palace. Catherine reprimanded the dwarf for lying, and threatened to send for the governor of the jesters to administer a sound whipping. Majosky, nevertheless, nothing daunted, again screamed out that M. de Guise was now entering the hôtel, a fact which the confusion and vivas without confirmed.[1] Catherine rose from the couch, pale and terrified. Presently the duke entered, and bowing obsequiously kissed her majesty's hand. For a second the words faltered on the lips of Catherine. At length she faintly bade the duke welcome; "though, monseigneur, the pleasure would have been tenfold more vivid at any other period than this; also, had you obeyed the command of your sovereign!" "The queen," says de Thou, "received the duke with perfect amity." A conference

prince de Joinville son fils à Soissons, et prie l'archevêque de Lyons de le suivre le lendemain matin."—Liv. viii.

[1] Histoire de la Journée des Barricades—MS. Recueil de Moisy Bibl Imp.

then ensued; the queen first despatching Luigi Davila, her gentleman usher, to summon the comte de Guiche, whom she desired to charge with the errand of imparting to the king the arrival of the duke, and to invite his majesty to repair to the hôtel de Soissons.

The news reached the Louvre before the arrival of Catherine's messenger; the streets of Paris swarmed already with multitudes of eager inquirers, and shouts of "Vive Guise!" "Vive le Pilier de l'Eglise!" reached the cabinet in which Henry was at the time holding council with Villequier, d'Ornano,[1] and Cheverny. The king was at first greatly overpowered, and leaning on the table, covered his face with his hands; it was a terrible defiance and contempt, the very security which had induced the duc de Guise to venture unattended into the capital of the monarch whom he had so repeatedly braved. "M. de Guise, you perceive, has ventured to defy my commands. If you were in my position, what course should you adopt?" at length asked his majesty. "Sire!" rejoined the comte d'Ornano, "do you esteem the duke your friend or your foe?" Henry replied by an expressive gesture. "If your majesty will issue the command, I will bring you the head of the duc de Guise, or secure his person." "Merci! mon ami!" said Henry; "I trust to provide other means." Henry then rose, his eyes sparkling, and his face suffused with fury. At this moment the comte de Guiche, Bellièvre, and the abbé d'Elbêne entered the apartment, the latter being the bosom friend of the duc d'Epernon. The comte de Guiche delivered the message with which he had been charged by the queen. The king uttered a passionate negative to the proposal that he should repair to the hôtel de Soissons, and demanded how the count presumed to mention such a

[1] Alphonse d'Ornano, son of Sampietro Ornano, a famous Corsican adventurer. Ornano died in 1610, at the age of sixty-two years.

proposition. Guiche replied that her majesty the queen-mother only waited his royal commands; and wished to know whether she should therefore bring the duke to the Louvre.[1] Henry paused irresolute; the abbé d'Elbêne and Ornano, detecting the fierce impulse which actuated the king's mind, approached, and boldly advised his majesty to receive the duke in that very cabinet, and cause him to be assassinated on the spot, as the just retribution for his rebellion and disobedience. "Sire!" exclaimed the abbé d'Elbêne, "Percutiam pastorem et dispergentur oves!" The counsel seemed pleasing to the king, who thereupon fell into a fit of musing. A few minutes thus elapsed, when Henry approached the window of the apartment which opened on the gardens of the Louvre, and throwing it back, he leaned out and said, addressing Villequier and the comte de Guiche, "Go, return to the queen my mother, and say that, as her majesty will condescend to take the trouble of conducting hither M. de Guise, that I pray her to repair with him to the chamber of the queen my wife." The count was further instructed to desire the queen to defer the duke's arrival at the Louvre as long as possible. Henry next despatched

[1] Another relation is as follows:—"Un domestique de Villeroy soudain lui dit à l'oreille, 'M. de Guise est arrivé : je l'ai vu descendre chez la reyne mère. Villeroy se leve, et va au Louvre ; trouve le roy dans son cabinet, qui n'en scavoit rien, et n'avoit lors auprès de lui que le sieur du Halde, l'un de ses premiers valets-de-chambre. Et voyant arriver le sieur de Villeroy à heure indue, comme tout estonné lui demande, 'Qu'y a't il, M. de Villeroy? Sortez, du Halde!' 'Sire,' dit Villeroy, 'M. de Guise est arrivé; j'ai cru qu'il estoit important au service de votre majesté de l'en advertir.' 'Il est arrivé?' dit le roy, 'comment le savez vous?' 'Un gentilhomme de mes amis me l'a dit, et l'avoir vu mettre pied à terre chez la reyne votre mère.' 'Il est venu!' dit encore le roy; puis contre sa coutume jura, disant. 'Par la mort Dieu! il en mourra! Où est logé le colonel Alphonse? (Ornano).' 'En la Rue St. Honoré,' dit le sieur de Villeroy. 'Envoyez le querir,' dit le roy, 'et qu'on lui dit qu'il s'en vienne soudain parler à moi!'"—Relation de la Mort de MM. de Guise.

d'Elbêne to summon to his presence Lognac, captain of the formidable Quarante-cinq, with five of his men. When they entered the presence, his majesty abruptly asked them, "whether they would obey implicitly whatever command he might give them?" They replied, "Yea, sire, to the letter, and without scruple!" Henry then desired Lognac to post himself in a closet in the apartment used as a place for private audiences, next to the bed-chamber of queen Louise. The king then ordered his body-guard to draw up in the hall of the Louvre as on occasions of ceremony, while Crillon ranged the Swiss guards, consisting of 200 picked soldiers, in lines extending from the portal of the palace to the gate of the drawbridge.[1] During these preparations, which the king made without reference to the counsellors present, Henry never once mentioned the name of the duke. At length Bellièvre and Villequier humbly represented, "that it was not reasonable to suppose that M. de Guise, if actuated by hostile intentions, would have intruded into Paris; and that doubtless the result of his visit would be agreeable to his majesty, and beneficial to his affairs. Finally, they besought the king to moderate his indignation; for the death of Guise would excite a commotion most dangerous, as the forces of the League in Paris were now too formidable to be thus provoked." On hearing such language from his minister Villequier, who had lately bragged of the loyal condition of the capital, and maintained that no real disaffection existed, an angry retort burst from the royal lips; and with withering sarcasm of tone the king again commanded Villequier to proceed to the palace of the queen-mother and bid M. de Guise welcome in his name, and announce that he waited to

[1] Mathieu, liv. viii. Davila, liv. ix. Amplifications des Particularités que se passèrent à Paris Mai, 1588. Archives Curieuses, 1er série. MSS. Bibl. Imp.—Dupuy, 661, 662.

receive his homage. Henry then opened the door of his cabinet, and said to the usher-in-waiting, "Descend and note who arrives with M. de Guise. He must enter the queen's chamber alone, as her majesty finds herself indisposed, and has not left her bed." It was to ensure the isolation of the duke that Henry had commanded his reception in the chamber of his sick wife; for queen Louise was then recovering from a slight attack of a malady which ultimately terminated in dropsy. The vivid nature of Henry's fury when roused may be appreciated, when he could thus plan the remorseless assassination of a prince, the near kinsman of his consort, at the very foot of her bed.

Queen Catherine and the duc de Guise at length set forth for the Louvre. The queen was borne in an open sedan, followed by a second conveying the princess Christine of Lorraine and madame d'Usez. The duke walked by the side of her majesty's chair, erect, bareheaded, with a smile on his lips, as with princely courtesy of manner he acknowledged the plaudits of the citizens. The streets were crowded with people, who, with joy almost delirious in its manifestations, hailed the presence of the great duke as a deliverer from undefined perils. They cried, "Vive Guise!" and pressed around the duke, some saluting him, some kissing the hem of his robe, some touching him with their rosaries, all blessing his advent. Young girls, as he passed along, scattered flowers on his path; the fairest and most noble ladies waved their handkerchiefs, and wished him God speed. In the Rue St. Honoré a young girl, Louise de l'Hopital de Vitry,[1] stood prominently forward, and, taking off her mask as the *cortège* approached, waved it, exclaiming, "Gracious prince, as thou art now here we can have nothing to dread." The features of

[1] D'Aubigné: Hist. Universelle. Satyre Menippée, tome ii. p. 86.

the duke expressed the emotion he felt at this reception; he waved his hat, and a vivid colour rose to his face. The sedan of the queen meantime moved slowly along, the hand of the duke resting on its door. Catherine sat looking grave, but making no demonstration whatever; it was, however, observed, that she was attentively noticing events. Perhaps the delusion was then dissipated, that this great and overwhelming popularity had been intrigued for and won by Guise, to be alone exercised for the elevation of the young son of the deceased duchesse de Lorraine to the throne of his maternal ancestors. As the *cortège* approached the Louvre, the clamour became more overpowering; the duke then pausing a moment exclaimed, "Messieurs! messieurs! c'est assez, c'est trop! Criez, Vive le roy!"[1]

An aspect of ominous gloom and silence surrounded the Louvre. The queen was visibly disturbed, and when she perceived the Swiss guards drawn up within the inner court, she expressed a wish to enter the palace by a private door opening into the racket-court. This, however, the duke prevented by handing her majesty from her chair, and leading her through the lines of soldiers, whom he saluted as he passed. The sight of the stern and resolute countenance of Crillon, the officer in command, seems suddenly to have aroused the duc de Guise to a sense of his imprudence, and of the extreme peril of his position after he had passed the drawbridge of the Louvre. He turned pale, and

[1] Amplification des Particularités. Davila, lib. ix. When Sixtus V. heard of the arrival of the duke in Paris, he exclaimed—"O le téméraire! O l'imprudent, d'aller ainsi se mettre entre les mains d'un prince qu'il a si vivement outragé!" On learning, however, that the king had received the duke, the contemptuous observation of his holiness was, "O, le lâche prince! O, le pauvre prince! d'avoir ainsi laissé échapper l'occasion de se défaire d'un homme qui semble né pour le perdre!"

for an instant paused, but quickly shaking off the feeling he continued his progress. Catherine, however, surveyed, with foreboding, the evident preparations for their reception, and the body-guard under arms. Her majesty was conducted to the bed-chamber of queen Louise, according to Henry's command, followed by the princess Christine and the duchesse d'Usez, and accompanied by the duc de Guise. Queen Louise was in bed, attended by one lady, who, on the entrance of the queen-mother, withdrew. Catherine took a seat by the couch of her daughter-in-law, whose face was pallid, and her manner nervous. Presently the young queen began to address Catherine in low and rapid tones. The duc de Guise, after making obeisance to the queen, retired into the embrasure of a window of the apartment, and commenced a conversation with the princess Christine.

The king, meantime, was in the adjoining apartment with Villequier, the comte de la Guiche, and Bellièvre, who had followed his majesty, still hoping to induce him to relent. Lognac and his five Gascons had duly taken their position where the king directed. Henry angrily repulsed the remonstrances and prayers of his ministers, though, nevertheless, they seemed to make impression, and declared that Guise should not live to brave him again, but that he would cause him to be shot and his head severed from his body, and placed on a pike in front of the Louvre before the expiration of another hour. Henry then gave Lognac the signal, upon hearing which he was to rush into the queen's chamber, and do just execution on the rebel. He then took a key from his girdle, and opening a private door close to the tester of the queen's bed, he entered the apartment.[1]

[1] Mathieu: Vie de Henri III. Vie de Louise de Lorraine—Dreux de Radier et Brantôme. Davila, liv. ix.

On the click of the key in the lock, the duc de Guise advanced; he then bowed profoundly before his majesty, almost touching the floor with his knee. "What brings you here? I ordered you not to come!" said Henry, in angry tones. "Sire, I come to confide in your majesty's equity and justice; I pray your majesty to have confidence in my loyal fidelity. I am here to offer my humble services to aid your majesty in suppressing the cabals and tumults of this capital!" The king replied, that M. de Guise spoke falsely, and that he was well aware he was the cause and author of all the troubles and commotions; that he guided at will all the princes of Lorraine, and especially the ducs de Lorraine and de Mayenne, whom he led about by the muzzle like bulls; and that he was now resolved to prove to them that he was their king, and insisted upon their obedience! The duke undauntedly replied that, "he was his majesty's faithful subject; and it would be seen that he carried a sharp blade to avenge himself on his calumniators! He should not have presented himself, had he been plainly told that his majesty commanded him to stay away."[1] Henry now had worked himself up into a frenzy of exasperation; he, therefore, called Bellièvre from the adjacent chamber, and asked him, "whether he had not commanded him to forbid the presence of M. de Guise in the capital?" Bellièvre was about to reply, but the king suddenly stopped him with the manner of one who, having made up his mind to some course of action, needed not confirmation on the point, but, again addressing the duke, he asked him, "whether he had duly received and read the last amiable letters sent him by madame de Montpensier?" These letters had been intercepted

[1] MS. Bibl. Imp. Baluze, 4 Lettres sur les Barricades. Amplifications des Particularités qui se passèrent à Paris. Hist. de la Journée des Barricades. Mém. de la Ligue, tome xi.

by the royal agents; and afterwards, according to the timid policy then in the ascendant, had been sealed up again and forwarded to their destination. Catherine, at this point, rose and approached the king; versed in interpreting her son's looks, and divining that some great catastrophe must have been determined, to explain the energy of the king's language and manner, she deemed it time to interpose. The king, therefore, very reluctantly followed the queen-mother to the embrasure of a window, when the queen entreated her son to refrain from any rash demonstration, and told him of the scene she had witnessed in the streets of the capital, and that any precipitate vengeance would ruin the royal cause. The duchesse d'Usez approached at a sign from the queen, and likewise confirmed the statement relative to the popular excitement.[1] The duc de Guise, whilst this conversation was going on, stood by the bed of queen Louise and began to converse. Suddenly, however—whether upon a hint given by the queen (which is probable), that some terrible manifestation of royal wrath awaited him—the duke approached the king, and craved permission to retire, as the hour of his majesty's public repast was drawing near, and as he was himself fatigued with his journey. Henry hesitated, but Catherine promptly gave the permission sought. The king then stopped the duke, and attempted to pass his mother, but Catherine steadily laid her hand on her son's arm, and continued to address him until the duc de Guise had accomplished his retreat. She then expatiated in general terms on the folly and treachery of a design to slay an enemy who had entered the palace unarmed, and who had all Paris for his *garde-du-corps*; and finally, Catherine's arguments, as usual, prevailed, and she obtained her son's promise

[1] Mathieu: Hist. de Henri III. Davila, liv. ix.

that he would sanction no act of violence, but, on the contrary, grant a second audience to the duke, during the following day, in her garden at the Tuileries.

The duc de Guise retired to his hôtel, escorted by several thousand persons of condition and by a mob of rabble. At the hôtel de Guise, Rue de Chaulne, he was received by madame de Montpensier. His stormy interview with the king had made great impression on the mind of the duke; he perceived that Henry's irritation was excessive, and divined what, but for the presence and intervention of the queen-mother, might have been his fate. Sooner or later all whom the king hated had fallen beneath the ban of his wrath—Lignerolles, Coligny, Bussy d'Amboise, and his sister the queen of Navarre, besides numbers of persons of less note. Forewarned, the duc de Guise adopted the measures which he believed alone compatible with his safety. Before nightfall, therefore, he had accepted the offers of service made by above 400 cavaliers; he granted audience to the council of the League, and gave orders that guards should be kept in every ward of the city, ready to repel a surprise; while, during the night, a large quantity of muskets and arms of various kinds were introduced into his hôtel. At the Louvre similar preparations were in progress; strong pickets were posted in the adjacent streets; the Swiss remained under arms throughout the night. The same precautionary measures were adopted at Catherine's palace, whither her majesty returned at dusk, escorted by a detachment of Swiss. All was distrust, confusion, and anarchy. The sanguinary counsels of the two Italian adventurers,[1] whom he had recently patronised, infuriated the king; while the temporizing and vacillating policy recommended by Villequier and Cheverny

[1] Ornano and Elbêne.

harassed the mind of the unfortunate prince, until at intervals he wept in the very helplessness of his anguish and distrust. At midnight, the spy Nicholas Poulain was introduced by Henry's command. Anxious to learn the effect of the duke's arrival, the king put the question; Poulain replied, that the presence of M. de Guise had revived the spirits of the faction. "But," said the king, "M. de Guise denies all knowledge or share in these conspiracies, and holds them to be fables!" "Sire!" replied Poulain, "this very night the Seize meet at the house of La Chapelle. It will be easy for your majesty to seize the members during their session. I for my part desire nothing better than to remain here a hostage for the truth of my words."[1]

The following morning the duc de Guise repaired very early to the Louvre, followed by a suite of 400 gentlemen, armed with pistols under their cloaks. He proceeded first to visit queen Louise, and then waited until the king left his chamber to attend mass in the chapel de Bourbon. On returning to the palace, he found that the queen-mother had arrived. She greeted the duke cordially, and courteously observed that "she hailed his presence, as she doubted not that he would aid the king in restoring tranquillity to his province of Picardy, and to the capital."[2] "Madame," replied the duke, sternly, "I have no influence in Picardy; besides, the affairs of that province are not those which require the most prompt alleviation; it is as if a man, covered with ulcers, bestowed all his solicitude on healing a tiny blister on his finger. M. de Lyons will render good account of Picardy." The duke then asked the king whether he would permit the archbishop of Lyons and

[1] Procès Verbal de Nicholas Poulain.

[2] Hist. de la Journée des Barricades. MS. Recueil Historique. F. de Thoisy, tome iii. in fol. Bibl. Imp.

the cardinal de Bourbon, whom he had left at Soissons, to enter Paris? "Certes, mon cousin," answered Henry, carelessly, "he who loves the master tolerates his dogs!"[1]

During the day the guards at the Louvre were increased, and a proclamation issued, commanding all mendicants, venders of street wares, and itinerant players to decamp from the capital. Simultaneously the great gates of the hôtel de Guise were barred, and ingress into the mansion only permitted by the wicket. During the afternoon the duc de Guise repaired to the Tuileries to confer with the king. He was there received by the queen-mother, who lavished her most winning and pleasant sophistries to smooth the way for the approaching conference. Henry arrived, attended by M. d'O, "that renegade and infidel," as the duke termed him. His majesty appeared splendidly arrayed, but his countenance was gloomy and careworn. The trio then commenced a promenade on the terrace, the queen-mother walking in the midst. The conference was opened by Henry, who again questioned the duke severely on his disobedience of his command in coming to the capital. The duke denied upon oath that he had received command to abstain; nor had he even seen a despatch on the subject from Bellièvre. Guise next commenced a long and elaborate address, in which he vindicated his taking up of arms, the treaty of Nemours, and the articles of Nancy. He demanded the reception of these articles, the recognition of the council of Trent, the abolition of the concordat of Francis I., the exile of Epernon and the favourites, and the reformation of the government on principles just, economical, and orthodox. Finally, he pronounced a most flattering eulogium on the genius and the tried

[1] MS. Histoire de la Journée des Barricades. Recueil de Thoisy.

abilities of the queen-mother. Henry replied to some of these propositions; others he prudently left without comment. He said that he was willing to arm for the extirpation of the Huguenots, and that no prince hated and persecuted sectaries more than himself; yet the plots and machinations of the League were highly offensive to him, and subversive of the royal dignity—nor would he longer submit to be coerced. As for the duc d'Epernon, he had proved himself valiant, able, and prudent; he was the son of a Catholic father, and sprang from a house which had always deserved well from the sovereign. His majesty declared that he was not inclined to deviate from the practice of his predecessors, who honoured whom they would, regardless of dictation. Neither had he ever received pernicious counsels from Epernon. As for the house of Lorraine, his majesty said that he had ever favoured it; but that all offices and dignities could not be bestowed upon one family. That, as for the treaty of Nemours, he was minded to maintain it; but that the people must consequently be burdened with taxes to support large standing armies. Those who cried out most seditiously against the existing imposts were the individuals who, against his own will and experience, had forced him into this war; therefore, that he was brought to bear the blame of a fault that was not his; and not only had his government been defamed, but his person conspired against. He was, however, aware that the citizens of Paris had little share in the said outrages; therefore he had come to the resolve, immediately to purge the city from all strangers and foreigners; but that before he had recourse to force, he intended to appeal to the loyalty and patriotism of his good people of Paris.[1] The king then informed the duke that an

[1] Davila, liv. ix. MS. Relation de la Journée des Barricades. His-

edict, directing all strangers, foreigners, and visitors then resident in Paris to leave the capital within twenty-four hours, would be promulgated; and that domiciliary visits from district to district would take place on the morrow, to insure the literal and punctual execution of the mandate. The prévôt des marchands and the sheriffs of Paris having, meantime, arrived at the Tuileries, in obedience to a summons they had received, the king, in the presence of the duc de Guise, commanded them diligently on the morrow to search houses, and to dismiss all new comers who had settled in the capital, unless they should satisfactorily account for their residence; and that no distinction of persons was to be made.[1] The provost La Perreuse commended the resolve, and promised to serve his majesty faithfully. The duc de Guise also declared that the king had done well, and likewise promised to aid in the exact execution of the edict. Henry and the duke, therefore, took leave of each other on apparently amicable terms. His majesty returned to the Louvre to sign his edict; he then appointed Villequier and M. d'O to superintend its execution, and to witness the departure of "the agitators of his capital."

The strangers and agitators of the capital, however, were precisely those persons who had resolved not to depart; they were the dependents of the chieftains in league, and for the time being the leaders, orators, and rulers of the Parisian democracy. Moreover, this turbulent throng interposed as a shield to defend the burgesses from the wrath of their offended sovereign, and the flippant but dangerous menaces of the favourites. Accordingly, during the night of Tuesday, May 11th, the clubs within the various wards of the city were in

toire très véritable de ce qui est advenu à Paris, par St. Yon, Echevin de Paris et Ligueur.

[1] Ibid.

active communication, and emissaries passed to and from the hôtel de Guise. A determined resistance was organized against the domiciliary visits announced by the king. The pen of madame de Montpensier was put into requisition, and before dawn placards were distributed through the city stating that his majesty intended to hang or decapitate all the popular leaders and curés of the capital; that their arrest was to be effected during the following day; and that the headsmen were already waiting for the victims in the Hôtel de Ville. The person of the duc de Guise was declared to be in the greatest peril; and the approaching triumph of Calvinism and of the king of Navarre predicted.

At the Louvre, also, anxious debates were holden throughout the night. The arrest of Guise, the military occupation of Paris, and the temporary suspension of the charter of the municipality, were the important topics of conference. If the king had acted as boldly and to the purpose as he opined, all might still have been well. At this period the capital lay at the feet of the king, and a few severe and vigorous measures would have subjugated the factious. The duc de Guise alone in Paris, unsupported by the princes his kinsmen, and as yet comparatively unprotected by the city levies, was at the mercy of his offended sovereign. In the arsenal Henry had twenty field-pieces; in the Hôtel de Ville were two hundred small cannons and falconets. Six thousand Swiss troops lay encamped in the vicinity of St. Denis, and the royal *gardes de corps*, under the brave Crillon, were well disciplined and loyal. Moreover, the duc de Guise evidently showed indications of desiring a reconciliation with the king. Catherine de Medici, indignant and alarmed by the impending rebellion, began to show less solicitude for the prospective rights of her grandson; and to act with that dexterous ability, for which she was renowned, in support of the crown of her son. Madame de Montpensier perceived the change which had dawned on the mind of her royal mistress, and warned her brother that, unless he hastened any measures he might contemplate, he would find himself opposed by the ability and influence of the queen-mother—a power far more dreaded than that of the king.

All these advantages were defeated by the pusillanimity of Henry and his ministers. They undertook great enterprises; but failing in the courage and constancy requisite to insure success, thereby revealed their own weakness, and suggested to their foes those daring exploits which ended in the defeat, shame, and disaster of all concerned.

CHAPTER IV.

1588.

Seditious demonstrations are made against the execution of the royal edict—Resolution taken to garrison Paris and enforce obedience—Entry of the Swiss troops and the French *gardes de corps* under Crillon and the maréchal de Biron—La Journée des Barricades—Negotiations of queen Catherine with the duc de Guise—Flight of the king from Paris—Catherine assumes the conduct of affairs in the capital—Deportment and measures of the duc de Guise—Attitude of the queen—She maintains her authority—Exultation of the duchesse de Montpensier—Madame de Guise and the cardinal de Bourbon arrive in Paris.

The day had scarcely dawned, on the morning of Wednesday, May 12th, when the Prévôt des Marchands and his staff, the sheriffs, MM. de Villequier and d'O, set out on their domiciliary investigations. As they proceeded along the streets, the people pelted them with stones; while the obstacles and obstinate resistance which they met with, on entering suspected houses, soon convinced his majesty's envoys that their mission was a fruitless one unsupported by a military escort. After making some statistical inquiries and jotting down a few notes, Villequier and his colleague returned to the Louvre and reported to the king the failure of his experiment, adding "that the people declared their resolve to do nothing to aid in the expulsion of their defenders." Henry, though the hour was early, had heard mass and was receiving the morning salutations of the court in the queen's audience chamber. His chagrin and displeasure were palpably evinced; moreover, when the duc de Guise appeared Henry turned away his head and refused to accept his greeting. The duke took this rebuff with admirable patience, seated himself on a coffer, and addressed his discourse to Bellièvre. When the king left to hold a privy council, to remedy, if possible, the ominous condition of affairs, he passed without inviting Guise to attend him. The duke, therefore, haughtily withdrew to his hôtel, scorning to obtrude his advice or to assert the privilege of his peerage.[1]

The session in the privy council chamber was tempestuous: it was, nevertheless, deemed expedient by all his majesty's advisers to vindicate the royal authority, though the mode to be adopted was angrily debated. At length it was agreed, as a first step, to garrison Paris; and after having taken military possession of the principal avenues of the city, to enforce the edict for the exodus of the factious bands of adventurers swarming in the capital. The king, therefore, commanded the maréchal de Biron to proceed to the camp of the Swiss, and lead certain divisions into Paris by daybreak the following morning. M. d'O, at the same time, received orders to introduce the French regiments of the royal guard, also encamped outside the city.[2] The men forming the usual garrison of the Louvre were to be mustered; also the archers and gentlemen-at-arms, and forbidden to quit the precincts of the palace. These precautions were well and skilfully taken, only the decision came too late. Had like vigorous measures been adopted before the late ignominious departure of the king for his camp at Gien, the royal power would pro-

[1] Histoire de la Journée des Barricades. MS. Bibl. Imp. F. de Thoisy, tome iii. in fol.

[2] Davila, liv. ix. De Thou, liv. xc. Dupleix.

bably have been restored. After the council broke up, mandates were sent to the captains and colonels of the city wards to collect their bands and to occupy certain positions indicated. To explain this unusual muster M. d'O was sent by the king to confer with the provost and sheriffs, and to enforce, if necessary, his majesty's command. Some objection being raised as to the imprudence of this measure, which, it was stated, would inflame the populace, M. d'O arrogantly clenched the argument by observing, "Par la mort Dieu, messieurs! I am not here to listen to your objections. I have his majesty's command; and this time he will make himself be obeyed!"[1] The muster, therefore, was called during the afternoon: the companies, however, were not posted in their proper localities; for instance, the men of St. Honoré were stationed on the Petit Pont, and those appertaining to the latter district on the Place de Grève. D'O stationed eleven bands in the cemetery Des Innocents. He afterwards harangued the men, and declared that the king reserved them for special service, which would be unfolded on the arrival of M. de Beauvais Nangis, the officer appointed to command them. The telling out and distribution of these guards created great commotion in the city: the partisans of Guise artfully inflamed the excitement by distributing seditious placards calling upon the people to rise and defend themselves. Throughout the night the streets of Paris swarmed with excited and threatening groups, eagerly discussing the struggle which every individual felt to be imminent. The Rue de Chaume, Quartier Ste. Avoye, in which stood the hôtel de Guise, was thronged; crowds gathered before the wide gloomy façade of the palace of the popular hero, speculating on the duke's probable intentions and conduct at this

[1] Histoire très véritable de ce qui est advenu à Paris Mai, 1588, par St. Yon, Echevin de Paris.

crisis. All, however, was silent; the duke made no response to the plaudits;[1] the gates were strongly barred; the windows defended by plates of iron; and, excepting that occasionally an individual glided through the narrow wicket, no sign of sympathy with those without was discernible.

At four o'clock in the morning the roll of drums and the shrill sound of the fifes and clarions of the Swiss troops were heard. The soldiers entered at the Porte St. Honoré, led by the maréchal de Biron on horseback. Three French companies followed, led by Crillon.[2] The troops marched in battle array, with colours flying and matches lighted; their numbers altogether amounted to between 2000 and 3000 men. Biron distributed his men in the following manner: 900 Swiss he posted in the cemetery Des Innocents, which commanded the Rue St. Honoré; M. d'O occupied the Pont au Change; du Gast the Pont St. Michel; the guard of the gate of the Louvre towards the Rue St. Thomas was committed to M. de l'Archant and to a company of French *corps des gardes* exclusively. Companies were placed on the Place de Grève so as to command the Hôtel de Ville; also, on the Marché Neuf and the Place du Châtelet. The Places Maubert and St. Antoine, however, by a grave oversight were left unoccupied. These districts lay the nearest to the hôtel de Guise; they swarmed with disaffected persons, and were of the utmost importance for the command of the city. The maréchal de Biron and M. de Dinteville, occupied the Marché Neuf. Had the king's troops seized the streets in the neigh-

[1] "Je dormois quand tout commença," said the duc de Guise in his letter to king Henry. An author states that the duke appeared at a window clad in a white satin *robe-de-chamore*, and innocently asked "Eh! que fait on donc?" on hearing the noise of the tumult.

[2] Davila, liv. ix.

bourhood of the Bastille and the hôtel de Guise, also the Rues St. Denis and St. Martin—in these days the main avenues of the city—the menaced insurrection might easily have been suppressed. The Swiss soldiers and the captains of their companies received strict orders to assail none, but to maintain themselves on the defensive;[1] if attacked, even then they were not to fire on the people without direct orders from Biron, or from the Louvre through one of his majesty's *aides-de-camp*.

The people, meanwhile, gathered, surveying the extraordinary preparations for the garrison of their city with feelings of mingled astonishment and rage. The shops were closed; in many districts the tocsin was rung, and hundreds of armed citizens emerged from their houses at the sound of that well-known signal of sedition. Biron caused it to be proclaimed to the vast concourse of people which gathered on the Marché Neuf to survey the battalions of Swiss, that the sole object of his majesty was to cause his capital to be evacuated by all strangers and seditious persons; and that the king granted his subjects of Paris permission to take up arms, provided that they remained within their houses, and used them only for the defence of themselves and their families. The members and chieftains of the Seize, however, were industriously inflaming the populace;[2] Brissac, Bois-Dauphin, Chamois, La Chapelle, and other zealous partisans of Guise and the League, headed tumultuous bands of rabble, and, demonstrating

[1] The soldiers were expressly forbidden to take provision without payment, to pilfer, or to fire on the people. Davila.

[2] Crucé hired two young lads to rouse the inhabitants of the Quartier St. Jacques from their beds by frantic cries: "Aux armes! le fils de Coligny est au Faubourg St. Germain avec ses Huguenots!" "Le peuple s'echappe," says the historian Mathieu; "l'artisan quitte ses outils, le marchand ses trafics, l'université les livres, les avocats leurs cornettes, les présidents mettent la main aux hallebardes; on n'entend que cris epouvantables, que plaintes etrangères, que regrets, et dépits!"

a better knowledge of street tactics than the royal generals, they took possession of the Rues St. Martin and St. Denis, thus securing a communication with the factious on both banks of the river.

Catherine, during these preliminaries, quitted at daybreak the hôtel de Soissons, and repaired to the Louvre for the safety of her royal person, and the better counselling of the king her son. As Catherine stepped into her chair, she despatched her gentleman-usher, Luigi Davila, to the hôtel de Guise, with a message inquiring after the health of the duke, and explaining the cause of the military occupation of the capital. Davila made his way through the streets in the grey light of early dawn, and arrived safely at the hôtel de Guise. After some discussion he was admitted through the wicket. In the court, which was the largest attached to any private hôtel in Paris, he beheld two rows of gentlemen armed, and in the midst stood the duc de Guise. Around lay piles of arms of all descriptions; the shutters of the lower apartments were barricaded and defended by bags of sand, or by casks lashed together. The retainers of the duke were also under arms. The duc de Guise advanced to receive the royal message, and taking Davila by the hand he condescendingly led him apart into the garden at the back of the palace. The queen's envoy then perceived (as it was intended he should do), that the lower apartments of the palace were filled with armed men. Guise listened with great respect to Catherine's message, and returned a deferential reply. Davila was then reconducted through the wicket to make the best of his way to the Louvre, a progress of no small peril.[1] Shouts of arm! arm! and the clangour of the tocsin ringing in every parish, now resounded throughout the streets. Stones, offal, and mud, were showered on the

[1] Davila, liv. ix.

soldiers, who, obedient to their orders, stood rigidly to arms, making no retaliation. Seditious placards were borne about the city, with every other symbol of approaching insurrection. Davila was admitted to the royal closet on his arrival at the Louvre, in which he found the king, queen Catherine, Cheverny, Ornano, Bellièvre, and others. He minutely related what he had seen, the aspect of the hôtel de Guise, and the words of the duke; also the menacing attitude of the people. By the advice of the queen, Henry despatched his secretary Benoise to Crillon, commanding him to advance with the troops under his command, and take possession of the Rues St. Martin, St. Denis, St. Antoine, and the Place Maubert. The order came too late. The students of the university under Bois Dauphin,[1] the watermen from the Quai de Grève, and a troop of rabble, opposed the advance of Crillon and the French guards thus tardily sent to occupy the Place Maubert, which lay between the city and the university. A parley ensued, for the royal orders continued to prohibit a charge on the insurgents. Meantime fresh bodies of people rushed into the Place by the Rue du Pavée, and after a brief interval, Crillon beheld the rise, as if by magic, of the first barricade which ushered in that mode of street warfare, which since has become the especial favourite of the Parisian populace. The Place Maubert was nearly surrounded by collegiate edifices; other barricades were there rapidly built up with barrels filled with earth, logs, and flag-stones, which the people tore up from the cloisters and courts of various adjacent colleges. Chains were also stretched across the streets opening from the square, while the great bell of the parish church of St. Martin gave forth its sullen toll. Crillon then attempted to retreat, but

[1] Urban de Laval de Bois Dauphin, who was created a marshal of France by the duc de Mayenne in 1593.

found himself intercepted in the rear by Brissac with a great body of insurgents gathered from the Faubourg St. Germain. Again barricades were built up along the streets at the distance of thirty paces; women brought the furniture of their houses, and aided in the construction of these defences. Crillon, therefore, presently found himself unable to advance or to retreat; his communication with Biron and d'O was ignominiously cut off, and his soldiers exposed to the mocking gibes of the triumphant populace.[1]

Along the Rue St. Denis barricades were reared; the people of St. Eustache and Montmartre gâthered, led by M. St. Paul, an officer devoted to the princes of Lorraine, and taking possession of the streets in the neighbourhood of the cemetery Des Innocents, completely blockaded the Swiss troops posted there by Biron. The city resounded with cries of "Alarme! alarme, les Huguenots!" Crucé and other leaders of the Seize went from barricade to barricade, exhorting the citizens to lose their lives in defence of their liberty and their faith. Chains were stretched across the Rue Notre Dame; and strong barricades constructed at the mouth of all the streets communicating with the positions seized by the royal troops. M. d'O, nevertheless, succeeded in occupying the Hôtel de Ville and the Place de Grève. He also despatched an aide-de-camp to the palace, to represent to the king the dangers to which his troops were exposed, hemmed in by furious mobs, and requested permission to attack the insurgents. The answer returned was a decided negative, accompanied by an order, however, to hold firmly the sites captured.[2]

[1] Hist. très véritable de ce qui est advenu en la Ville de Paris Mai, 1588. Archives Curieuses, 1er série.

[2] Davila, liv. ix. De Thou, liv. ix. Particularités de ce qui se passèrent à Paris Mai, 1588. Journal de Henri III. Hist. de la Journée des Barricades. MS. Bibl. Imp. F. de Thoisy.

By nine o'clock, therefore, the streets were completely fortified, each barricade being defended by men armed with muskets, swords, clubs, and determined to shed their blood to the last drop in ridding Paris of "her invaders."

Henry, meanwhile, remained in his private cabinet at the Louvre, apparently little disturbed by the turmoil raging without. Between seven and eight in the morning the president Tambonneau, colonel of the city bands, arrived at the palace, and being admitted to the presence of the king, entreated his majesty to command his troops to evacuate Paris. Henry sternly refused, and dismissed the president. The duc de Guise soon afterwards despatched his secretary to the hôtel of the chancellor, to demand whether the king's military demonstration was directed against his person. Cheverny answered by an emphatic, Non! and exhorted the duke to refrain from showing himself in the city. The treacherous and unstable character of the king was so dreaded by the duke, who remembered his narrow escape from assassination on the previous Monday, that he prevailed upon the archbishop of Lyons, who had arrived in Paris on the preceding evening, to repair into the royal presence, under pretence of paying his respects, and report his majesty's language and demeanour. The step which Henry had taken in calling in the Swiss and the regiments of his *gardes de corps* was so unexpected, that had the enterprise been conducted with vigour and ability, Paris must have been disarmed. The duc de Guise momentarily expected arrest; and during a few hours subsequent to the appearance of the troops, the leaders of the Seize, disconcerted and doubtful of the support which an attempt at a general rising might receive from their fellow-citizens, hesitated as to the measures most expedient to pursue. The king now appeared to be in earnest, and Catherine de Medici was no longer to be implicitly trusted. The inaction of the soldiers, the want of strategic skill displayed in the occupation of the city, and the confusion which ensued from the arrival of orders and counter-orders from the Louvre, soon reassured the malcontents. "Ah! these soldiers are puppets—mummies encased in iron; they will do no harm. They dare not charge us!" exclaimed Crucé, contemptuously, as with his own hands he helped to build the first barricade which defended the *embouchure* of the Rue St. Aubry.

The archbishop of Lyons called on his road to the Louvre at Catherine's hôtel, to secure, if possible, her majesty's co-operation in the remonstrances he was preparing to offer. The queen, however, had departed at daybreak for the Louvre. The archbishop proceeded thither, and was admitted to an audience by their majesties between the hours of nine and ten in the morning. In the name of the duc de Guise, Espinac implored the king to command his troops to quit the capital: "Sire, it is, in the present temper of the populace, as playing at dice for your crown!" "Monseigneur, I will be obeyed; and to-day I will show that I, the king, am master and lord over these said rebel Parisians!" retorted Henry, angrily. The archbishop then hastily retired from the presence: the tone and manner of the king admitted no further expostulation. So menacing, indeed, did the prelate deem the attitude of the king, that when he had passed the wicket of the Louvre, he hurried to the adjacent house of a friend, and there borrowing a mule he rode at great speed to the hôtel de Guise; and after recounting the scene at the palace, ended by assuring the duke, "that he was minded to live, or rather, as it seemed to him, to die, his true friend and partisan." A more august ambassage next waited on the king. The parliament of Paris deputed the presidents Brisson and Seguier to admonish his majesty that in consequence of the unusual introduction of troops into Paris all business was suspended, the shops closed, and the thoroughfares blockaded; the high court, therefore, humbly prayed his majesty to advise on the evil. Henry returned a courteous answer, and replied by despatching instructions to M. de Villequier to perambulate the principal streets of the capital, with his staff, to proclaim the pacific intents of the government towards the citizens, and to command the resumption of business. Villequier made the attempt enjoined on him, but was soon compelled to return to the Hôtel de Ville, not being permitted to pass the barricades in the adjacent streets. Henry also condescended to inform the presidents that the reason of his demonstration was, "that having been ill obeyed by the citizens in the orders which he had issued for the departure of all strangers from the capital, he had resolved to enforce his edict."[1]

The king next despatched M. de Bellièvre to the duc de Guise to reassure him that no hostile intent was harboured against his person, and to suggest that the duke should quit Paris immediately upon receiving satisfactory pledges for his own safety, and for that of his immediate adherents. Guise received this communication in the presence of the archbishop of Lyons and of the bishop of Nevers, who had just arrived at the hôtel, escorted by a body of retainers. He demanded leisure to deliberate and to confer with his partisans. He said that he was aware that it was the king's desire and intent to commit him a prisoner to the Bastille, and to inflict the punishment of death on some of his most zealous adherents; but that if his majesty still persisted in the resolve, such blood would be spilled as would afterwards appal the king's mind

[1] Histoire de la Journée des Barricades. MS. Bibl. Imp. F. de Thoisy.

to reflect thereon; that, as for himself, he was determined not to approach the Bastille except by his own free-will.[1] Already Guise descried his approaching triumph, and duly appreciated the weak and timorous spirit of the king. Bellièvre was compelled to return to the Louvre with this reply; the duke, however, positively pledged his word not to leave the street in which his hôtel was situated, unless at the express command of the king. Henry appeared highly indignant at this response, and again took counsel whether the arrest of the duke might not yet be effected, so utter was his disbelief that the citizens of Paris would dare to assail his troops. Between the hours of eleven and twelve, certain spies, who had been sent out by Catherine, returned with the alarming intelligence that the Rue St. Honoré was impassable, and that his majesty's troops were everywhere completely enveloped and hemmed in by barricades. A great shout and acclamations of "*Vive Guise!*" close to the Louvre alarmed the king, and sending to investigate the cause, Henry was informed that a barricade had been built close to his chapel de Bourbon, under the very windows of his palace. "These said barricades," says a contemporary,[2] "were solid, strong, and impassable. It has been calculated that if the citizens had left the doors of their abodes open, 100,000 men could not have taken the city, defended and barricaded as it then was. The barricades were constructed of heavy beams and barrels filled with sand and paving-stones." The Spanish ambassador declared that the strength of the defences was amazing; and that the city of Paris had

[1] "Le duc a dit que quant à l'envoyer à la Bastille, il n'y entreroit jamais que de sa propre volonté."—MS. Bibl. Imp. F. de Thoisy.

[2] MS. Hist. de la Journée des Barricades. F. de Thoisy. Davila: "A jour enseigna aux Parisiens le vray moyen de se fortifier châcun en son quartier."—Ibid.

concentrated for the occasion the spirit and energy of two hundred towns. About twelve o'clock the duc de Guise quitted his hôtel for the first time during that eventful day, and paraded the street in which it was situated with the archbishop of Lyons. The street was filled with people, who greeted Guise with shouts of applause: "Some," says de Thou, "regarding their hero with fear, others with lively admiration, and a few with indignation." From time to time messengers arrived and presented despatches to the duke from the leaders of the insurgents; Guise read the missives on the spot, and returned verbal replies. The pusillanimity of the government roused the daring energy of the duke. From this period his indecision ceased; and being about, as he believed, soon to hold the king a captive in his Louvre, he was resolved to avail himself of the opportunity and obtain in a few hours the concessions comprehended in the articles of Nemours and Nancy, without further effusion of blood or the risk of a third campaign. "At twelve o'clock on this most disastrous day," writes de Thou, "I walked through the streets in the neighbourhood of the Louvre and the hôtel de Guise. The Louvre I found deserted; a sombre desolation reigned around the palace. With grief in my heart I proceeded to the hôtel de Guise. The duke was promenading with his friends. I detected in the eye and in the erect demeanour of the duke confidence, satisfaction, and security. He evidently now was no longer solicitous concerning his own safety, but rather, as I judged, was concerting the way to shield his reputation and to give a good colour to the conspiracy by eventually delivering the troops of the king from the fury and insults of the populace."

Meanwhile, some powder and arms sent from the arsenal for the Swiss regiments stationed in the Cimetière des Innocents were intercepted; also the rations of bread and wine for the soldiers. The barricade defending the entrance of the Rue St. Honoré had been reared within twenty yards of the gate of the cemetery. Thither the food destined for the Swiss was carried and devoured before the longing eyes of the men, who had tasted no meal since their nocturnal march from St. Denis. Some friend of one Cossin, a captain of the Swiss guard, shouted from the barricade an inquiry as to how he felt himself. Cossin replied that the prévôt des marchands had deceived the king when he told his majesty that 30,000 of the citizens would rise to defend the royal cause; for he now understood that thirty of the people were for the king and the thousand for M. de Guise![1]

Brissac, after a conference with the duc de Guise, proceeded with a small party of insurgents and seized the fort of the Petit Châtelet, overpowering and turning out the royal garrison. A furious assault was also made on the detachments of the French gardes de corps posted on the Pont St. Michel. Missiles were showered from the adjacent houses, and the people rushed from the barricades and attacked the soldiers, uttering savage cries of *"à bas Chastillon et les Huguenots! Vive Guise!"* The soldiers, assailed on all sides, offered no resistance, and suffered themselves to be disarmed, when they were commanded not to stir for their lives. On the Marché Neuf a similar skirmish took place, in which about thirty-nine Swiss soldiers were killed. The troops were driven from the place by a furious discharge of musketry, and by showers of stones, which rained upon them on every side. The Swiss laid down their arms, and took refuge, some in the *abattoirs* of the Marché, others in private houses. The majority, driven from the square, approached the barricade upon

[1] MS. Hist. de la Journée des Barricades.

the Pont Notre Dame, through which the soldiers were to be allowed to pass, when an insurgent, a tailor by trade, was accidentally shot dead. A cry being raised that the Swiss had committed the deed, the barricade was closed, and a volley of musketry discharged upon the soldiers, who fled back to the Marché Neuf, from which they had just been expelled. The unfortunate Swiss then fell on their knees and implored mercy, which was granted.[1] The Swiss in the Cimetière des Innocents likewise surrendered their arms and submitted to the people. "In short," says a contemporary,[2] "they had no alternative to save their lives, being so enclosed and hemmed in by barricades that it was then impossible for any of the king's troops to extricate themselves, unless, like mice, they could have burrowed underground."

The panic in the Louvre became great, as messenger after messenger brought intelligence of the spread of the insurrection. Many great ladies of the court fled to the palace for protection, others sought safety with madame de Montpensier—a refuge deemed even more secure. When Catherine was informed of the attack on the king's troops, she rose and earnestly entreated her son to show himself on horseback to the people, and command their dispersion on their allegiance. Henry peremptorily declined, not, however, from personal cowardice—for when roused from his apathy the heroic spirit of his grandfather Francis I. occasionally showed itself—but because he deemed such appeal, if unsuccessful, as likely to subvert even the remnant of authority left to him. The king, therefore, sent the maré-

[1] "C'étoit horreur de voir les Suisses jetter les armes bas, tomber les uns sur les autres, fuir de tous côtés, navréz de coups de pierres que les femmes jettoient dès fenêstres ; et levant les mains au ciel crioient, 'France, France, Chrétiens nous!'"—Particularités de ce qui est advenu à Paris Mai, 1588.

[2] Ibid. Hist. des Barricades. MS.

chals d'Aumont and de Biron to expostulate with the leaders at the most strongly defended barricades. The marshals departed on their mission, but failed to obtain a hearing, and were saluted with a volley of stones and musketry.[1] On their return to the Louvre the king received their relation with mingled rage and apprehension. When Biron informed Catherine of the disarming of the troops, and of their perilous siege between barricades manned by the most resolute defenders of the League, the tears flowed down her cheeks. The young queen Louise, terrified by the fierce denunciations which issued from the lips of her royal husband against all of the blood and lineage of Lorraine, was carried in a swoon to her chamber. The cavaliers, whom in the days of his power and luxury Henry had pampered and preferred to the veteran statesmen of his father's reign, increased the panic by their bluster and officious interference. The king moved amongst the affrighted groups with a countenance pale and defiant as he listened to the shouts and tumult which approached nearer and nearer to the Louvre. Sometimes Henry issued a mandate for the defence of the palace, at others he incoherently commanded that couriers should be despatched to summon back "his gallant son" the duc d'Epernon. Catherine at length, after a period of meditation, said resolutely, "M. de Biron, proceed to the duc de Guise, and command him, in the king's name, to suppress the tumult and deliver his majesty's troops." Bitter as was the humiliation, there was no other resource; the interposition and good-will of Guise were now absolutely requisite to preserve the

1 "A quoy ledit de Biron, d'Aumont, et d'O, répondirent n'avoir charge d'entendre leurs remonstrances; ausquels aussi tot fut dit par toute la compagnie qu'ils eussent à se retirer s'ils ne voulaient se voir tailler en pièces; ce qu'ils firent soudain, voyant tous les harquebusiers les coucher en joue."—Hist. très véritable de ce qui est advenu à Paris Mai, 1588.

abode of the sovereign of France from assault; and to save the lives of the most obnoxious of his courtiers. It was about three o'clock in the afternoon when Biron departed on his errand. He obtained a safe passage through the streets and admittance at the hôtel de Guise, when he announced that he was bound on a special errand from the king to monseigneur de Guise. The marshal was received by the duke with grave courtesy. In reply to the command sent him by the king, the duke coldly said, "that he could not restrain the people, who were infuriated by misgovernment and the follies of the sovereign." "Monsieur, what is it that I hear?" exclaimed Biron. "You perceive, monsieur," retorted the duke, "that I have no share in this insurrection; I have never stirred from my abode, though much solicited to do so. This is the result of the deliberations of the fine council of the king. It is that rascal d'O, who has led his majesty into such error. I am persuaded that you must disapprove of such proceedings. M. d'O is not of our calibre. He dares to say that I consort with the porters and pickpockets of the capital! Let all, however, be assured that whenever I catch this said d'O, I will cause him to be flogged by those said porters and pickpockets from the Porte St. Antoine to that of St. Jacques."[1] Some further discourse was exchanged, the duke for long pretending to decline taking part in the insurrection. He had, however, waited in triumph for this proud moment when, as the deliverer of his sovereign, the defender of the people, and the protector of the Swiss and French soldiers, still crouching in abject terror amid the barricades, he might be hailed as lord paramount by all, the captain and lawgiver whose patriotism had saved the crown, secured the orthodox faith, and confirmed the

[1] MS. Hist. des Barricades. F. de Thoisy, Bibl. Imp.

liberties of the people. Guise at length feigned to yield to the expostulations of the maréchal de Biron. His preparations for his progress were ostentatiously simple. He threw a cloak over his white satin *pourpoint,* and took a small truncheon, in shape like a marshal's *bâton,* in his hand. The duke was followed by two pages; one carried his sword, the other his shield. Four gentlemen on horseback attended the duke, without other arms than a drawn sword, which they carried on their shoulders.[1] The duc de Guise and Biron proceeded first to the Place de Grève. The poor Swiss were there on their knees disarmed, and exposed to the greatest peril from the savage assaults of the populace. The appearance of the duke was hailed with delirious joy. Paris resounded with acclamations, the barriers fell before him, and his colours and device floated over many a barricade. The women from the windows and balconies cheered him as he passed. "Messieurs, arrêtez! vous me ruinez; criez, Vive le roy!" exclaimed the duke, with affected moderation, when before the Hôtel de Ville. A passage was opened for the progress of the duke, who rode into the centre of the Place, and addressing the people, prayed them to let the Swiss depart, as God had been so merciful to them as to defend their lives, families, liberty, and religion. The words were received with acclamations and loud cheers; the soldiers were permitted to rise, and march in file through the barricade in the direction of the Porte St. Martin, by which they were ordered on the instant to quit the capital. So gracious and princely was the aspect and demeanour of the duc de Guise that the soldiers joined in the cheers with which he was greeted. The duke then proceeded to rescue the other portions of the besieged garrison. As he passed the Pont Notre

[1] F. de Thoisy. Bibl. Imp. Davila. De Thou. Dupleix. Mém. de la Ligue.

Dame, he admiringly surveyed the huge barricades which blocked up the entrance to the Marché Neuf, and the order and soldierly deportment of their defenders. "Mes amis, you have evinced marvellous skill and valour!" exclaimed the duke to some of the insurgents, as he passed the barrier. "Monseigneur, before your arrival we were feeble as flies, but your presence has inspired us all with the courage of lions to defend our faith and our liberties."[1] The Swiss troops in the Marché Neuf were in a piteous plight; many were lying prostrate with bleeding wounds, some reciting their prayers, others loudly imploring mercy. Stones were continually being hurled from the windows of the houses amidst this fainting and famished band. When Guise rode forward, accompanied by Biron and Bellièvre, a clamour arose — "*Bon duc de Guise, ah! sauvez nous! bonne France!*" The duke turned towards Biron and said, with a sigh, "He who is the cause of this misery ought to allay it." "True, monseigneur, evil be on the head of him who counselled it. I obeyed the king in conducting these hither." The duke then commanded that liberty might be given to the troops to depart; and also that M. de Dinteville, their commander, who had found shelter in a house, should receive no further molestation. The duke and his companions next repaired to the Pont St. Michel to release Crillon and his companies of household guards. He directed St. Paul to conduct these troops safely to the Louvre, and to restore their arms. St. Paul thereupon preceded the troops and the bands of Swiss guards which had been rescued on the Marché Neuf, brandishing a cane. One of the Swiss soldiers addressed St. Paul as "monseigneur." "What!" exclaimed he, with a laugh, "you who, when M. de Guise arrived at the

[1] MS. Bibl. Imp. Hist. des Barricades. F. de Thoisy. Recueil Historique. MS. Dupuy, 661, 662, Bibl. Imp.

Louvre, refused to salute him, and since, when he has presented himself, refrain from showing him respect, now call me 'monseigneur' who am only his poor and humble servant!"

Paris was now in the hands of the duc de Guise and the Seize. The king's troops had evacuated the city, beaten and pursued from the Porte St. Martin to their camp. The Louvre was defended merely by the ordinary guard, and by the wounded and broken-spirited detachments of Swiss, led thither by the colonel St. Paul. The council of the Seize now put itself in open communication with the hôtel de Guise, the barricades were reinforced and strengthened, cannon were placed before the Hôtel de Ville and at the gates of the town, and the hostile factions prepared to take ample advantage of their victory.

Queen Catherine, meantime, confident in her powers of negotiation, and relying on her influence over the duke, resolved to proceed to the hôtel de Guise, and there hold conference. Soon after the departure of the maréchal de Biron, therefore, she sent Luigi Davila to demand passage from the leaders of the sedition through the streets of Paris to the Rue de Chaumes. Bois Dauphin and Crucé gave audience to her majesty's envoy; they abruptly refused to allow passage to the queen's coach, but consented to permit her sedan to pass the barricades. This insolent reply greatly irritated Catherine; nevertheless she resolved to attempt the journey, feeling little apprehension for her personal safety. About five o'clock in the afternoon, therefore, her majesty set out, attended by the secretary of state Pinart, and by two other gentlemen of her household. The queen sat erect in her sedan with a calm and fearless countenance, from time to time boldly rising to survey the barriers and the aspect of the streets. Her progress was tedious. When her majesty arrived at a barricade, she waited whilst passage was made for her sedan. During this interval she put pertinent questions with the greatest coolness to individuals of the mob of insurgents around. The queen's sedan was detained until the opening thus made was again blockaded. Two hours were consumed in this progress; at length the queen arrived safely before the hôtel de Guise.[1]

The duke had just returned from his progress through the streets of Paris, when a still greater triumph awaited him in the arrival of the mother of his sovereign as a suppliant before the portal of his palace. Having been previously informed by his emissaries of Catherine's progress, the duke waited at the entrance of the mansion to hand her majesty from her sedan. The duke, though his demeanour was more than usually humble and deferential, commenced, as soon as he saw the queen, to make bitter expostulation on the folly of the counsels which had resulted in so notable an insurrection. "Madame, the citizens of Paris have never before been coerced by a garrison. The people will not submit to it; they believe that his majesty intends to take the lives of many of his Catholic subjects, and my own especially. Madame, the wit of man combined cannot remedy that which has unhappily this day been perpetrated. I have, nevertheless, done all in my power to allay the tumult and to reassure the citizens!" The queen replied, "that his majesty wished nothing but to purge Paris from strange and turbulent factions; that the king had caused his guards to enter Paris, himself intending to make search. That the people had taken arms rashly, urged by these said turbulent demagogues; but she trusted, when the truth was known, that every one would depart to his home peacefully." This conversation took place in the court of

[1] Davila, liv. ix. Hist. de la Journée des Barricades. MS. Bibl. Imp F. de Thoisy.

the hôtel, openly, and so as to be heard by all present. The queen then signified to the duke her desire to converse privately with him; they, therefore, retired together and entered a cabinet. The queen then angrily reproached the duc de Guise for the events which had happened. The duke replied, "that he had no share in promoting the insurrection, which had happened suddenly on the ill-advised resolution adopted by his majesty of taking military possession of the city; and that, far from having provided for his own safety, as he should have done could he have foreseen the emergency, his hôtel had been totally destitute of arms and defences. That his friend M. de Grand Rue had even lent him a cuirass." Catherine retaliated by reproaching the duke with his inopportune presence in Paris against the command of the king. Guise again denied that M. de Bellièvre had forbidden his approach in the name of the king; nor did he even scruple to recall to her majesty the fact, of which she now appeared to be oblivious, of certain significant hints, given in her name by Bellièvre, of the advantage which might possibly arise from his presence in the capital during the absence of Epernon. Catherine then tried to waive further discussion, by commanding the duke to cause the instant submission of the revolted city, adding, "that his majesty and herself would hold him responsible for all future disturbances." Guise coldly replied, "that he knew the king's designs, and that it was his majesty's resolve to destroy certain eminent personages of his realm, and himself among the number; that he hated all who had presumed to oppose his favourites, and question the claims of Henri le Béarnnois; therefore, it was necessary that he should look well to his own safety. He would not, therefore, permit the people to lay down arms, unless the king accepted the articles of Nancy, and gave good and trusty guarantees." He then proceeded to demand that "the king should declare him lieutenant-general of the realm, the letters-patent to be modelled on those granted by Francis II. to his father François second, duc de Guise; that the States-general should be convoked to settle the question of the succession, his majesty, as the queen knew, not having any chance of posterity. That the *soi-disant* king of Navarre should be immediately proclaimed incapable of inheriting royal honours; that the taxes should be lessened; that Epernon, and his brother M. de la Valette, the maréchals de Retz and Biron, M. d'O, and 'the adventurer' Ornano, be banished from court, with the loss of their offices and honours; that the king should dismiss his guard of les Quarante-cinq, and forbid members to return to court; that Crillon should be deprived of his office of commandant of the king's household guards; that Villequier should be deposed from his office of governor of Paris, and that post bestowed upon the comte de Brissac. That the war against the heretics should be diligently prosecuted." The duke further demanded the government of Picardy for the duc d'Aumale; that of Lyons for the duc de Nemours; and that of Normandy for the duc d'Elbœuf. Six towns were to be yielded to the lords of the League. The post of admiral was to be given to the duc de Mayenne; and the *bâton*, vacant by the proposed demission of Biron, to be bestowed upon M. de la Chastre, the duke's most confidential adherent.[1]

Catherine listened with intense indignation to these demands; anger sparkled in her eyes as she sharply demanded, "What will the people of France think, or the princes of Europe believe, if the king should concede such preposterous and shameful articles? Is it your intent, monseigneur, to take the crown from the head

[1] Davila. De Thou. Dupleix: Hist. de la Journée des Barricades. MS. Bibl. Imp.

of the king my son!" "Madame, I ask no office nor promotion for myself. The medicine may be bitter, but it will be a salutary one in the end." Catherine in vain reasoned with the duke, and condescended to remonstrate, and even threatened. Guise firmly declined to make concession whatever, adding, "that since the king had at last revealed his hostile intentions and his hate towards himself, he was resolved either to lose his life or to secure the dominance of the orthodox faith, and the safety and dignities of the house of Lorraine.[1]

Catherine was compelled to return with this response. It was quite dark when her majesty re-entered her sedan. She took leave of the duke, promising to return and renew the conference early on the morrow, after Guise had peremptorily declined to present himself at the Louvre.

During the night diligent watch was kept by the city militia in all districts not defended by barricades. At muster hour the prévôt des marchands gave the watchword, as usual, in the name of the king. The city bands, however, refused to accept it, and sent a deputation to ask it from the duc de Guise. During the night the duke passed several times on horseback through the streets, while his emissaries diligently inflamed the resentment of the people against their sovereign, bestowing the most extravagant eulogiums on their master. No one slept; all waited for and dreaded the probable events of the morrow. From the period of the visit of the queen to the hôtel de Guise the duke threw off dissimulation, and openly assumed the conduct of the insurrection. The duchesse de Montpensier and the chevalier d'Aumale were the only members of the family of Lorraine then present in the capital. The

[1] Ibid. Mathieu: Hist. de Henri III.

activity of the duchess was unparalleled; she harangued and entertained the captains of the League in her hôtel; wrote their proclamations, and concocted their libels. Her beauty and the fierce energy of her gestures and words inspired the adherents of Lorraine; while her daring personal courage permitted none but cravens to shrink from perils so boldly incurred by herself.

Within the Louvre, on the contrary, all was despondency and terror. The king, with his mother, Villeroy, Cheverny, Villequier, d'O, Rambouillet, Pinart, d'Ornano, and the abbé d'Elbène, held council throughout the night. In the ante-room the gentlemen in waiting kept watch, with drawn swords and pistols, to defend their master, in case the Louvre was suddenly assaulted. The drawbridge of the palace was raised, and sentinels were posted by Crillon so as to descry the smallest tumult or gathering in the streets adjacent to the palace. The courtyard was filled with troops, all under arms, and without in the tennis-court and the Cour de Bourbon, the Swiss regiment of the guards, rescued during the afternoon by the duc de Guise from the fury of the populace, was stationed. It was doubted, however, whether these troops would engage in actual combat against their benefactor, as they now termed the duc de Guise. The apartment of the young queen was likewise carefully guarded. Louise passed the night weeping with her ladies, and praying for the prompt dispersion of the enemies of her lord the king. The princess Christine of Lorraine remained with queen Louise; the former displayed no symptoms of fear, and was suspected of praying rather for the success of her cousin of Guise, which she had been told was greatly to benefit her brother, than in deprecation of the wrath of Heaven in behalf of her uncle king Henry—*le fainéant*—which ignominious epithet had been often heard on the lips of the spirited young princess. The proposals made by Guise to queen Catherine were hotly debated. The king steadily vowed that he never would assent to conditions so infamous; that if the duc de Guise had indeed usurped the royal power, it was not for him to make terms and share that which was his own. The chancellor Cheverny, M. de Villeroy, and de Villequier, —all more or less secret partisans of the League—exhorted their royal master to accept the articles proposed by Guise, which they said would tranquillize not only Paris, but the realm of France, and secure a Roman Catholic successor to the crown of Charlemagne. It was observed that the eyes of the king were fixed with malignant steadiness for some moments on these perfidious advisers; his majesty, however, made no observation, except to reiterate his determination to yield to none of these demands. Henry was supported in his resolve by M. d'O, the abbé d'Elbène, Rambouillet, and the comte d'Ornano. The queen suspended her decision until she had again visited the hôtel de Guise, as her majesty said "she had good hope that M. de Guise, on reflection, would modify his conditions." D'O then tendered the resignation of his office as chamberlain and colonel of the guard, which Henry ordered him to retain. The comte d'Ornano then implored his majesty to bestow upon him the post of commandant of the Bastille, promising to maintain that important fortress at any risk or cost. Henry had the weakness to refuse his sanction to a measure which, he erroneously said, was likely to increase the irritation of his lieges of Paris. The pangs of hunger were added to the weariness of suspense which the trembling inmates of the Louvre had to endure during this eventful night of the 13th of May. So great had been the panic during the day, that no stock of provisions had been amassed in the palace for the consumption of the household; and during the night any attempt to pass the barricades, which completely cut off the Louvre from the city of Paris, would have been death to any bold enough to make the experiment.

At dawn the tumults re-commenced; alarming reports were spread over the capital that the king intended to send again for his troops, and especially for artillery, and for a regiment remarkable for its steady discipline, called the regiment de Picardie. It was likewise reported that one Rapin had been sent by the king to confer on this matter with the first president de Harlay. Brissac, therefore, repaired to the abode of the president to investigate the truth of the rumour, and to attempt to win over to their cause so influential a personage as the first magistrate in the realm. "Monsieur," said Brissac, flippantly, "the king says that you are good for nothing neither on sea nor on land; I am therefore sent here to ask whether you might not be worth something to us on the pavée?" No persuasion, however, could induce de Harlay to enter into relations with the Seize; the king, he said, he would alone obey, and that, at whatever cost, to the very letter. Brissac under a feigned anxiety for his safety, but in reality to keep the president under *surveillance,* offered to build a barricade before his house, and to place a guard at the back of his residence. De Harlay drily refused to accept any protection from the duc de Guise.[1] Thus baffled, Brissac departed, being summoned hastily to quell a tumultuous rising of the students of the university, who threatened to march upon the Louvre and seize the person of the king, incited thereto by one Péginard, a fanatic doctor in theology. These students armed themselves with poniards and swords, and decorated their caps with a white cross. The Seize, meanwhile, pursued their de-

1 Cayet: Chronologie Novennaire. De Thou, liv. xc.

liberations in the Hôtel de Ville, having ejected Henry's faithful prévôt des marchands and his municipal staff.

Amongst those individuals most surprised at the result of the Journée des Barricades was the duc de Guise himself. True though it was that the duke had contributed to bring about the events of that memorable day by his intrigues, his disaffection, and his bribery, yet he neither foresaw nor had precisely organized the rising. So greatly was he astonished and terrified by the magnitude of his peril, that from dawn until eleven o'clock in the morning, had the king's ministers possessed either courage or enterprise, his arrest might easily have been achieved. The cardinal error committed by the government was the attempt to seize Paris before they had secured the person of the duke. The citizens fought and rallied round their hero, whose life the League proclaimed to be menaced. Guise then imprudently suffered the enthusiasm of the people, his own ambition, and the violent exhortations of madame de Montpensier, to overpower his judgment. He greedily accepted the position of mediator, rescued the royal troops, assumed the power of dictator, angered the queen, and committed himself irretrievably by the arrogance of his demands to Catherine, and by his treasonable asseverations, that the acceptance of those terms alone should disarm the citizens or rescue the crown from violence. On the morning of May 14th, 1588, the duke arose, the arbiter of his sovereign's destiny, and apparently possessing every facility to grasp the sceptre falling from the faltering hand of the king; yet from this period the real difficulties of the duke commenced. No precautionary measures had been taken to consummate the victory so daringly won; there was no organized scheme, and therefore no defined object for the insurgents to attain. Every one adopted his own crude notions concerning the general welfare—confusion and insubordination were the inevitable results. The ducs de Mayenne and d'Aumale, the most able princes of the house of Lorraine, were absent—the one in Burgundy, the other in Picardy; with the exception, therefore, of Brissac, the duke stood alone in Paris, unsupported by his powerful kindred. His adherents—those who had provoked the contest and won for the duke his perilous eminence—were for the most part individuals of dissolute life and no family influence—impoverished, and therefore reckless; or they were gloomy fanatics—men of less than average ability, the business of whose existence seemed to consist in predicting calamity and in gloating over every indication of the royal incapacity. The duke had no disciplined troops to restore order in the city or to repress excesses. Dazzled with the altitude which he had now attained, he forgot that, if the sovereign escaped from his present dictation, the half of his power vanished. The city was barricaded to prevent the advance of the troops; but it never seems to have entered into the mind of the duc de Guise and his sapient council of the Seize, until too late, that it was possible for the king to withdraw and join his army, although access to the Louvre was denied to the soldiers.

Early during the morning of Friday, May 14th, the royal family sent an envoy to the Hôtel de Ville to demand that the barricades might be removed to enable them to attend mass in La Sainte Chapelle. An answer was returned that a way should be opened for their majesties to proceed on foot, if such was their desire. Henry thereupon indignantly declined to quit the Louvre; but Catherine and her daughter-in-law, queen Louise, proceeded in sedans to the Palais. "The queen-mother," says a chronicler, "assumed a smiling deportment, and appeared by no means scared like the young queen at the lawless condition of the capital." On the return of the queen a second council was holden: advices had been conveyed to the king of the meditated assault on the Louvre by the students of the university; also, that it had been proposed at the Hôtel de Ville to send out a body of insurgents to cut off retreat from the Louvre by the open country which then extended behind the new Palais des Tuileries. The appearance of M. d'Amville with a squadron of sixty horse at the Porte St. Honoré, whose advance had been some time previously commanded by the king, had renewed the tumult in the city. The inhabitants of the district flew to their barricades and sounded the tocsin, so that after a brief parley d'Amville was compelled to retire.[1]

Henry, therefore, whose long-suffering was now quite exhausted, resolved no longer to delay the execution of a resolve, which he had privately formed from the commencement of the insurrection, and announced to the council his intention to quit the capital whilst it remained in his power so to do. The majority of the ministers approved this measure; but Catherine vehemently opposed it—or, probably, feigned so to do—and insisted, as she had ever done, that Guise, when convinced of his majesty's sincerity in the matter of religion, was not to be dreaded. "Yesterday, when I visited monseigneur de Guise," said the queen, "he meditated not the hostile designs which you now attribute to him, but appeared, on the contrary, desirous to conciliate. I will proceed again and visit him, with the assurance that, at my request, he will suppress this tumult." The king, nevertheless, persisted in his

[1] Particularités qui se passèrent à Paris Mai, 1588. Archives Curieuses. Hist. de la Journée des Barricades. MS. Bibl. Imp. F. de Thoisy. Mathieu.

resolve to quit Paris, "a city which had subjected him to cruel contumely." This resolution has been branded as cowardly and unworthy of the majesty of the throne. Henry, it is averred, ought never to have abandoned his capital, or have consented to an ignominious flight before the treasonable enterprises of one of his subjects. Nevertheless, the unfortunate monarch seems to have chosen the lesser of the evils impending over him: had the king remained in the capital, the morrow would have found him a prisoner in the hands of the duc de Guise, and compelled, at the clamorous demand of an infuriated mob, to ratify every article the former chose to present. The oversight was great, on the part of the rebels, to have left the gate unguarded, which communicated with the gardens of the Tuileries—a palace then partly without the walls of the city; but that very night it had been determined by the Seize to blockade every avenue leading from the Louvre. It was time for Henry to withdraw from a position of peril and degradation; and, judging by the language used by the duc de Guise in the circular letter which he wrote during this day and sent off by hundreds to his adherents in the provinces, the king's resolve came not a moment too soon. "Admonish our friends," says the duke in this document, "to come hither with the greatest speed, bringing horses, arms, and baggage. I have defeated the Swiss, cut to pieces the greater part of the king's guard, and I now hold the *Louvre so closely besieged that you may be certain I will render good account of all whom it may contain.* This, our victory, is so complete that its renown will endure for ever!"[1]

It is difficult to assign a motive for Catherine's opposition to the departure of her son; if, indeed, her

[1] Mém. de la Ligue, tome ii. p. 313.

objections, as is most probable, were not feigned on purpose to facilitate his escape by casting some uncertainty as to the eventual proceedings of his majesty, who, it was notorious, had hitherto, on occasions of peril, acted entirely on his mother's counsel. The king gave his mother, in the presence of the council, unlimited authority to treat with the duke, and to arrive at some agreement, if possible, during their pending interview. Catherine boldly engaged to bring back the duke to the Louvre, and departed on her mission between midday and one o'clock, promising to give the king timely information if she found that Guise remained inflexible, or did she detect that any great enterprise was meditated against his person. Their majesties also conferred during a brief interval apart.

The progress of the queen to the hôtel de Guise was tedious as before. Catherine demeaned herself with the same affability, and was greeted with respect. As she was passing through one of the barricades a man approached, and stooping under pretext of raising her majesty's sedan, whispered hurriedly that the life of the king was in danger; for that it had been concerted to send out immediately 15,000 men to invest the Louvre behind, while the palace was attacked from the city. Catherine, however, composedly continued her progress, and arrived in safety at the hôtel de Guise. The humiliating incidents of her passage thither had not disposed the mind of the queen to great amenity of manner; therefore, as soon as she found herself in the presence of Guise, Catherine imperiously commanded the duke to cause at once the removal of the barricades, and to repair in person to confer with his majesty in council at the Louvre. "Madame," responded the duke, coldly, "I have before told you that I have no share in the insurrection of the people, nor have I since promoted the popular turbulence, except in measure as it is necessary for my own safety. My friends are of opinion that I should not at present repair to the Louvre, and expose my life to the mercy of my enemies." Catherine assured the duke that he had nothing to fear, and that Henry was well disposed towards him. The duke, however, continued obdurate, and demanded the royal signature to, and the proclamation of, the articles which he had proposed, before he would use his influence to restore tranquillity, or repair to an audience of his majesty. "The queen-mother," says an eye-witness of the events which he relates, "did all in her power to persuade and to re-assure. M. de Guise, however, would neither listen nor believe; the queen, therefore, sent word to the king of the failure of her negotiation by the secretary Pinart, who had accompanied her." Catherine despatched Pinart, after a brief private interview, under pretext of bringing back unlimited powers from the king, to enable her, as she stated, to conclude the convention demanded by the duke.[1] She then sat down and coolly commenced a discussion upon each clause of the articles drawn at Nancy. The scene which ensued was a rare and notable piece of diplomatic acting; the manner of the queen—insinuating and *empressée*—bland from excess of exquisite complacency that she was outwitting her adversary; the duke, bending with humble words before her majesty, and yet unable altogether to conceal the arrogance of conscious power, that he alone authoritatively wielded the popular impulse, and that, when he gave the signal, the king would become a prisoner in his own capital. Daringly the duke appealed to Catherine to give her co-operation in aiding present events, which, he said, formed part of that great scheme which they had both advocated, for excluding le

[1] Hist. de la Journée des Barricades. MS. Amplifications des Particularités qui se passèrent à Paris. Mém. de la Ligue. Davila, liv. ix.

Béarnnois, and giving the crown to her grandson Henri de Lorraine. He likewise reproached the queen for her lukewarm adherence to the treaty signed at Nemours, despite the reiteration of her good-will and sympathy while at Châlons. Catherine listened; raised frivolous points, and discussed them at length, and with such address and apparent candour and good humour, that Guise, despite his long initiation in the study of the queen's wilesome moods, was completely deceived.

As soon as Catherine quitted the Louvre, Henry abruptly entered the apartment of his consort, and took hasty farewell of her, leaving the queen drowned in tears. The resolution which he had come to seemed to inspire the king with renewed energy. About one o'clock he arrayed himself in the costume which he usually wore when taking recreation in the gardens of the Tuileries. Close at hand were the royal mews, which it had been the habit of the king frequently to visit. Henry, therefore, presently boldly quitted the Louvre, and went on foot to an adjacent gate called La Porte Neuve, of which he exclusively possessed a key, whereby he entered the precincts of the Tuileries. His majesty brandished a light cane in his hand, and was followed by a troop of dogs; his manner was *insouciant*, and he leisurely surveyed the aspect of the streets before him on emerging from the Louvre. Henry then entered Catherine's hôtel, and waited the result of her negotiation, as, in case of a sudden assault on the Louvre, he was there in safety, with a favourable chance of escape, did the worst happen.[1] The king was accompanied by D'O, Bellièvre, the abbé d'Elbène, Rambouillet, and others of the courtiers. He talked and jested with apparent unconcern to Bellièvre, and compared his present predicament and probable evasion

[1] Hist. de la Journée des Barricades—MS. Journal de Henri III.

with his celebrated flight from Cracow, which the former had so ably concerted and aided. The king had scarcely been half an hour at the Tuileries before a messenger arrived, bringing a confidential communication from one of the royal adherents, a tradesman in the city, warning the king of the proposed blockade of the Louvre, and admonishing his majesty to take timely precautions. The envoy had traversed Paris, at the risk of his life, on this errand, aided by the intervention of a captain belonging to one of the city bands, also a concealed foe of the League. This intelligence greatly affected Henry; he, however, resolved to wait for some intimation from Catherine, before taking the decisive measure of leaving the capital. Crillon, meanwhile, withdrew the royal guard and the Swiss companies, and safely marched them out of Paris by the private gate of the Tuileries. This was one great step achieved for the security of the royal person. Meanwhile, alarming rumours pervaded Paris that some great enterprise was meditated against the Louvre. Many nobles hastily quitted their mansions and repaired to the king, whom they followed to the Tuileries; amongst these came the ducs de Montpensier and de Longueville, the chancellor de Cheverny, the comte de Guiche, the comte de St. Paul, the maréchals de Biron and d'Aumont, whose blood was fiercely thirsted for by the Parisian populace. The secretaries of state, Brulard and Villeroy, also presented themselves. The reports brought by these noble personages were not re-assuring: they told of tumultuous assemblages, and of the seditious deportment of the students of the university, who had congregated in arms in the Cloître de St. Severin, where their fury was lashed and kindled in a tenfold degree by the incendiary orations of the curé Lincestre. It was also reported that the hôtel de Guise was besieged by a yelling mob, which demanded that the queen-mother should appear on the balcony, and swear to observe the proposals made by Guise for the pacification of the city. Indeed, the sound of tumultuous turmoil and the clangour of the tocsins of the parishes of St. André, St. Severin, and St. Pierre des Assis, reached the ears of the group of anxious listeners in the Tuileries. The emissaries of madame de Montpensier also had caused it to be bruited abroad that the king had commanded eight pieces of cannon to be taken from the arsenal, to clear the streets in the vicinity of the Louvre. Henry sat overwhelmed and dejected in the halls of the Tuileries, the first monarch of his royal race who quailed beneath that roof—destined afterwards to ring with outrages so atrocious to the descendants of St. Louis—listening with sinking of heart to the cries and distant wrestlings of a Parisian mob.

Henry's suspense was presently relieved by the entrance of Pinart, the secretary of state, who had accompanied the queen in her progress, and whom Catherine sent from the hôtel de Guise. Pinart had met with considerable obstacles on his way to the Tuileries, and had seen indications threatening enough to induce him to urge the king to a prompt departure, before it became publicly known that the queen rejected the conditions proposed by the duke. He, therefore, briefly communicated Catherine's message, which the king received apart. Henry required no stimulant to urge him to a prompt and undignified flight. He made rapid preparations for immediate departure, though in consternation as intense as if he had never contemplated such necessity. The tears of the unfortunate king freely flowed. Whilst his coach was preparing, Henry rested with folded arms on a low wall abutting his stables, whither in his despair and haste to depart he had hurried, and wept the ingratitude of the Parisians, protesting that he had cherished them and their city more even than his own wife.[1] When his horses were harnessed Henry entered his coach, attended by the ducs de Montpensier and Longueville, and rapidly driving out of the courtyard of the palace, he took the road towards Chartres. As the king passed the Tour de Nesle, his suite was fired on by the arquebusiers on guard, and one ball struck his majesty's carriage. As soon as the king's coach drove forth, it was literally *sauve qui peut* with the motley throng whom he left behind in the gardens of the Tuileries. The report of Henry's probable departure had prevailed in the capital before the arrival of Pinart, though it was disbelieved by the majority of persons. The rumour had been spread by two servants appertaining to M. de Biron, who, meeting their master hurrying towards the Louvre, reported everywhere that the king had abandoned his capital. The more ardent of the royalists, however, and many members of the high courts, came flocking to the Louvre and to the Tuileries to ascertain the truth of the report. Many of these persons, when they heard of Henry's flight, fearing that the city would be plundered, prepared to follow his majesty without even returning to their homes; believing that before many hours elapsed La Porte Neuve would be as securely guarded as the other gates of Paris, at which exit was no longer permitted, except by a pass signed by one of the Seize. Horses and conveyances were, therefore, bought or hired at fabulous prices by the terrified courtiers. The road between Paris and Rambouillet exhibited the same grotesque scenes which rendered for ever memorable the flight back to the capital from St. Germain during the conspiracy of Les Jours Gras in the reign of Charles IX. The magnificent and pompous Cheverny, that minister after Catherine's own heart,

[1] MS. Hist. de la Journée des Barricades. F. de Thoisy, Bibl. Imp. Davila. Hist. de la Maison de Guise.

was forced to bestride a wretched hack worth the sum of ten francs, which seems to have bolted every way excepting along the route taken by the royal equipage. Bellièvre, more fortunate apparently, saddled with his own hands a fiery Andalusian charger appertaining to the royal stud, and recently presented to Henry by his brother-in-law, Philip II. of Spain, but which several times threw its rider, who excelled not in equestrian exercises. The secretary Brulart quitted Paris with only two testons in his pocket. The learned and eloquent advocate Espesses procured a mule, upon which to follow the king, but failed to secure a saddle and bridle. The latter he remedied by a contrivance of his own; while madame de Fréluc, state housekeeper to the queen at the hôtel des Tuileries, meantime obligingly manufactured something resembling a pair of spurs from the branches of a tree growing at hand.[1] "It was a spectacle most deplorable," says de Thou, "to see this prince, who a few days previously had been master of one of the greatest and most populous cities in the world, the inhabitants of which he had enriched by his constant residence amongst them and his immense profusions, obliged to flee therefrom to save his life, followed by his servants, dispersed and flying, some on foot, others on miserable baggage-horses, many without mantles or boots." Henry spoke not a word until he reached the hamlet of Châillot. He then rose in the carriage, and fiercely surveying Paris, he uttered, it is said, a malediction upon the turbulent and ungrateful city, vowing with a terrible oath never more to enter it, except over its

[1] De Thou, liv. xc. Hist. de la Journée des Barricades—MS. Nouvelles de Paris, récit véritable comment le duc de Guise est nouvellement arrivé à Paris, et le roy s'est retiré à Chartres, en 4to, 1588.—Allemand.

prostrate walls, and in the guise of a conqueror.[1] The king, after this ebullition of wrath, again relapsed into despondency, from which he was roused by the sight of his superb chancellor, who came ambling up to the coach on his ill-conditioned steed to condole with his majesty. Henry fell back in the carriage in a convulsion of laughter, and from that time his spirits revived. The king halted first at a place called Trapes, where he drank wine, for him an unusual indulgence. He then proceeded to Rambouillet, where he passed the night, the guest of his faithful subject, Nicholas d'Angennes.[2] Guards were posted round the castle, and every precaution taken for the safety of the royal person, in case, as it was apprehended, the people of Paris might pursue the king. The palace of St. Germain had at first been Henry's intended destination; but its contiguity to Paris induced the king, by the advice of Cheverny, to prefer the town of Chartres, of which the chancellor was governor, and its bishop a prelate of the house of de Thou—a family whose attachment to the royal cause was notorious. The king and his counsellors spent the night in drawing up circular letters addressed to the governors of the provinces, prelates, and dignitaries of the realm. His majesty explained the violent proceedings and causes which had induced him to leave the capital, and demeaned himself by entering into a general justification of his conduct. This unfortunate prince, always badly counselled, or else singularly obdurate and tenacious of advice, himself rendered indelible the outrage which had befallen him by the craven-hearted tone of these letters, in which he actually exhorted his subjects "to

[1] Mathieu: Hist. liv. viii. "Je quitte," exclaimed the king, "ces nouveaux rois de Paris!"

[2] De Thou. Cayet: Chronologie Novennaire.

pray God to bring about a prompt reconciliation between himself, the duc de Guise, and the Parisians." "The king," says Mathieu, "dictated and signed letters, not worded with the heart of a prince nor of a great captain, but in the style of a trembling fugitive—a man who dared not defend himself by hand or by heel—who, deeming himself unworthy to command, condescended to beseech and propitiate his subjects."

By daybreak, the following morning, Henry continued his journey to Chartres. He was greeted with enthusiasm by the people. The bishop Nicholas de Thou, went out to meet his majesty at the head of his clergy, to conduct him to the episcopal abode. Loud cries of "Vive le roi!" greeted Henry—an acclamation which at any rate possessed the zest of novelty. His regiment of guards arrived at a later hour on the same day; also the Swiss regiments, which were encamped in the adjacent villages. A numerous court speedily gathered round the king; for most of the nobility either repaired to Chartres or withdrew to their country residences the better to promote the designs of the League—a course adopted by all the great nobles alienated by Henry's unjust partialities and caprice. Amongst the persons who escaped and joined Henry at Chartres was Nicholas Poulain, whose revelations, had they been attended to betimes, might have reversed the respective positions of king Henry and the duc de Guise. The duke once arrested or driven forth from Paris, the crown might then legally have resumed the princely fiefs munificently bestowed on the house of Lorraine by Henry's predecessors, and which had enabled its members to raise the banner of revolt against the sovereign.

Queen Catherine, during the flight of the king, remained closeted with the duc de Guise, and with extraordinary dexterity maintained the conference, ever bringing forward some new and subtle point. The hour was approaching that of six in the evening, when without ceremonial whatever the sieur de Maineville rushed into the apartment where the two were conferring, and, approaching the duke, whispered a few hurried words in his ear. The duke precipitately rose, and exclaimed in a menacing voice, "Madame! you have betrayed me! Whilst your majesty has been dallying with me here, the king has quitted Paris. I am lost; his majesty will be more my enemy than ever!" It was a moment of extreme peril for the queen—alone in the palace of Guise, which was filled with his armed retainers, while without resounded the clamour of a bloodthirsty mob. The intrepid spirit of the queen deserted her not in this emergency. Without change of countenance Catherine calmly rose and replied, "that she did not believe the report, as the king had never communicated to her such intent; nevertheless some sudden intelligence might have occasioned his majesty's determination; she would therefore return immediately to the Louvre." The duke hesitated for a few seconds, then, evidently deeming it more prudent to obey the queen's wish, he escorted her to her sedan.[1] Not a single guarantee of safety—not a man, as an additional escort, did Catherine demand from Guise before trusting herself in the midst of the excited and angry multitudes. The queen stepped smilingly into her sedan, and, attended as before, by her four gentlemen-in-waiting, courageously passed the barricades, still wearing the same affable and courteous demeanour. In many of the streets the people cheered her majesty; in other localities rough questions and admonitions were addressed to the queen, all of which Catherine took in good part, and replied to in suitable terms. At length

[1] Hist. de la Journée des Barricades—MS. Davila. Vie de Catherine de Medici. Brantôme. De Coste: Dames Illustres.

the queen entered the Louvre: most desolate was its aspect. The guards were withdrawn, the courtiers dispersed, and the ladies of the young queen were bemoaning in their mistress's apartment the catastrophe which had befallen the brilliant court. Catherine's presence banished the depression everywhere prevailing; her knowledge and wonderful resources never shone more conspicuously than in an emergency, when affairs depended for their adjustment upon her personal energy. She began by declaring her intent to take up her abode, pending the return of king Henry, at the Louvre; she commanded a guard, and posted sentinels to perform the usual duties around the palace; she visited and comforted queen Louise; and finally, the queen sent to request the presence of the duchesses de Montpensier and de Nemours at the palace. Unhesitatingly her mandates were obeyed; old associations were vivid, and the court and the people feared Catherine's sway rather than that of her son. The queen, moreover, privately despatched a gentleman with a mandate to Crillon and Damville, colonels of the French and Swiss guards, admonishing them to follow the king diligently, and to march night and day, if necessary, until they had rejoined his majesty. The Swiss made some demur about following the king to oppose the duc de Guise, but finally their objections were overruled.

The departure of the king, meanwhile, placed the duc de Guise in the most onerous and embarrassing position. His barricades were now unavailing; and the choice lay distinctly before him, either to fortify himself in Paris, the chief and leader of an absolute rebellion; or spontaneously to make those concessions for the pacification of the capital and the submission of its turbulent populace which he had before refused to the urgent entreaties of queen Catherine. "The two Henrys," to quote from one cf the pamphlets of the day, "showed themselves on this memorable day to be confirmed simpletons, the one for not having during the first day of the barricades, and when, until eleven o'clock, it was in his power, executed the design of his heart against the duc de Guise; and the latter, on the morrow, for having allowed the prey he had so cleverly entrapped to escape from his net."[1] As it was, the duke stood guilty, in the eyes of foreigners and of all loyal Frenchmen, of a most treasonable and scandalous enterprise, in having contributed to compel his sovereign to abandon his capital; the odium was great, but the duke felt his responsibility to be still more oppressive. By this daring act the king was a fugitive; the royal troops had been ejected; the city was barricaded; business and trade of every kind suspended, and the courts of justice remained closed. Neither could the duke positively rely on the municipality of the capital, for two of the sheriffs and other civic dignitaries had followed the king to Chartres. Catherine, moreover, was in the Louvre, a popular princess, as well as an able one, and the duke as yet knew not how far his proceedings might have roused the jealousy of the queen and rendered her hostile. Scarcely had Catherine departed from the hôtel de Guise, when the comte de Brissac arrived to confer with the duke. It was hastily resolved to dismiss and disarm the students of the university who were still enrolled—a menacing band in the suite of Brissac—to silence the tocsins, and to clear and close the churches, which were for the most part filled with rabble listening to and applauding the denunciations of the factious curés. The duc de Guise then mounted on horseback, and attended by his cousin the chevalier d'Aumale, the archbishop of Lyons, and the bishop of Meaux, he proceeded to the Palais de Justice. As he

[1] Journal de Henri III. L'Etoile.

passed along he commanded the people to remove the barricades from all the adjacent streets, that the district might no longer be blockaded and traffic impeded. The duke was promptly obeyed; at his desire the people set to work with so hearty a good-will on the demolition of their street defences, that when he quitted the Palais the way was comparatively cleared. The chevalier d'Aumale was next despatched to visit each of the bridges of the capital, bearing a similar mandate to the insurgent officer in command. The will of the duke here also again proved to be paramount.[1]

The duc de Guise, with the prelates his companions, proceeded next to visit the first president of the parliament of Paris, de Harlay. The latter received the duke with stern reserve of manner; and when Guise commented on the hasty flight of the king, an event greatly to be deplored, and added that it was his intention to request the people to remove their barricades, so that MM. de la Cour could meet to carry on their deliberations, de Harlay replied, "When the majesty of the sovereign has been thus violated, we, his magistrates, have no further right to exercise our functions: nevertheless, he lauded the tardy resolve of monseigneur de Guise." The duke then requested the president to cancel the summons which he had issued requiring the Chambers to meet on the following day, Saturday, May 15th. "I grieve that his majesty has been so badly counselled as to depart from his capital in a rage: nevertheless, as this has been done, we must care for the preservation of our lives and reputations; therefore, I pray you, monsieur, to prorogue the Chambers for to-morrow." De Harlay refused, saying that the notices had been delivered at the houses of the presidents and other influential members, and that it was his resolve

[1] De Thou, liv. xc. Cayet: Chronologie Novennaire. Hist. de la Journée des Barricades. MS.

to discharge the duties of his office subject alone to the king. Guise remained silent for nearly ten minutes; then fixing his eyes steadily on the intrepid magistrate, who thus had the courage to resist his mandate, he said, "At least, then, monsieur, promise that the events of the last two days shall not be discussed." De Harlay complied conditionally, if her majesty approved, and was not pleased to order otherwise. This conversation took place in the long walk in the garden of the Palais.[1] Guise then took his leave, and departed by a postern which opened close upon the Pont Neuf. The duke then visited in rotation the presidents of the criminal courts. He deplored the unfortunate events of the preceding days, the obstinacy of the king and the rancour of his enemies, which, he said, had been the cause of all. Having, then, as he supposed, wound up again the wheels of the state, the duke despatched an officer with a message to the president de Harlay, absolutely prohibiting in very distinct terms the meeting of the Chambers during the following morning, and again commanded him to issue notices rescinding his former summons. De Harlay, though surprised at this fresh notification after his interview with the duke, undauntedly sent back word, "that he should do his duty, and that the chambers would meet, as they recognized only the royal authority and had no affair with the duc de Guise." The duke was with the queen at the Louvre when this message was reported to him; his anger was unrestrained. Catherine, to pacify the duke, then promised to interpose; and, accordingly, she sent a messenger to de Harlay at two o'clock in the morning requesting that the Chambers should not be assembled on that day. De Harlay rose from his bed and returned a respectful reply to

[1] Cayet. Mathieu. Dupleix.

her majesty, promising obedience to her mandate. After some further parley with the queen, Guise returned to his hôtel, traversing the streets on foot, addressing the people with affable language, and cheering them in their task of clearing away the barricades. "M. de Guise," says de Thou, "went himself and posted the guards, conversing familiarly with the insurgents, who were all of the lowest dregs of the populace, and whose vulgar slang offended his ears. He embraced some, smiled on others, and listened to all, without, however, losing his dignity of manner, but always keeping the serene and stately demeanour becoming to his quality."[1]

So well was the duke obeyed that the following morning there was scarcely a barricade to be seen. The council of the Seize then established itself permanently in the Hôtel de Ville, and daringly commenced the reforms so long clamoured for, without reference to the Louvre. During the day the commandant of the Bastille, Laurent Tetu, was summoned to deliver that fortress into the hands of Guise and the Seize. Tetu made a cowardly expostulation; and when he was informed that the people had gone to fetch artillery from the arsenal to batter the fortress, he resigned his charge to Bussy le Clerc, whom the duke nominated as governor in his stead.[2] A quantity of provisions was found stored within the Bastille, also wine. The cannon of the fortress, amounting to sixteen pieces, were loaded and turned upon the city: nothing, in fact, could have been more supine than the conduct of Henry and his ministers. They had a plentiful supply of provisions, an arsenal stored with arms and ammunition, 4,000 troops within Paris, three additional regiments encamped beyond St. Denis—

[1] De Thou, liv. xc.

[2] Hist. des Barricades. MS.

soldiers, all of them, inured to warfare—and yet Henry had suffered himself to be overpowered and disarmed by a mob of demagogues, whose rising had not been one regularly organized. His dread of the hostility of Philip II. ever haunted king Henry; and the most remote or vague apprehension of Spanish intervention seems to have deprived him of every particle of dignity and presence of mind.

Le Clerc no sooner entered upon the functions of governor of the Bastille, than he carried the keys of the fortress and also those of the Porte St. Antoine to the duc de Guise. The latter returned the keys of the Bastille to le Clerc, but refused to receive the keys of the Porte St. Antoine. A scene of entreaty, on the part of the new commandant and his colleagues, and of mock resistance, on that of Guise, ensued; the duke protesting that his honour prevented him from usurping one of the royal prerogatives. Finally, the controversy was adjusted by the keys of the city gate being delivered into the safe keeping of Maineville and Brissac. An order of arrest was next issued against Claude la Perreuse, his majesty's able and zealous prévôt des marchands, who was committed *"pour sa propre sécurité,"* on the sole authority of the duke and the council des Seize to the Bastille.[1] Rapin, prévôt de l'Hôtel de Ville, was also dismissed, and deemed himself in such danger from the animosity of his fellow-citizens, that he sought refuge in the house of the president de Harlay, and took the opportunity of quitting Paris in the suite of the marquis de Villequier, when the latter proceeded to visit the king at Chartres.

1 "On sache certainment que M. le prévôst savoit tout ce qu'on devoit exécuter, même qu'il ne bougeoit d'avec M. d'O, auteur de ce conseil, et auquel M. d'Epernon, allant en Normandie, avoit donné toute créance envers le roy, le priant se fier et reposer sur luy, le substituant en son lieu."—Histoire de la Journée des Barricades.

Further arrests of suspected persons were achieved;[1] domiciliary visits were made in the houses of parties believed to be hostile to the League. The duke issued commands that the private cabinet of king Henry, situated in one of the towers of the Bastille, and which contained the most important of his majesty's papers, should be held inviolate, and a sentry placed before the door. The treasure coffers in the Hôtel de Ville were also sealed with the seal of Lorraine and holden intact. The rich financier Zamet asked permission during the day to convey his most valuable effects to the hôtel de Guise; a favour which the duke granted, and likewise extended his offer of protection to the person of Zamet, whom he invited to become his guest.

The most noble protest, however, which was made against the usurpations of the duc de Guise came from the English ambassador, the earl of Stafford. Early during the morning of Saturday, May 15th, it was mentioned at the council des Seize that the English ambassador was suspected of harbouring the enemies of the League, and of having made a great collection of arms and ammunition of war in his hôtel upon the Quai des Bernardins. The rumour was referred to the duc de Guise, who thereupon commanded Brissac to repair to the abode of the ambassador and ask an interview. He was directed to compliment the earl in the name of the duc de Guise, and to assure him of the protection of the latter, and also to offer that a guard should be mounted before the gates of his hôtel for the better protection of his person. The earl replied, "that had he been a private individual he should have thanked M. de Guise for his courteous attention; but that being the ambassador of her Britannic majesty

[1] The duke, nevertheless, resented any unauthorized *arrests*; two of his soldiers having so transgressed, the duke, in the vehemence of his indignation, drew his sword and severely wounded both.

and accredited to the king, it was not in his power to accept any other protection than that of the king." Brissac replied by observing, "that the duc de Guise had come to Paris without evil designs, that he had only acted on the defensive, for a great conspiracy had been organized against him and the city of Paris: that the Hôtel de Ville was filled with gibbets, upon which the king had resolved to hang many of the most notable citizens, and that M. de Guise urgently prayed the earl to inform queen Elizabeth of these circumstances." The earl responded, "that he should be happy to believe M. de Brissac; but he begged to be permitted to observe that the events of the capital would be most indignantly denounced by all the princes of Christendom; for it was the manifest duty of subjects to remain obedient to their sovereign. If so many gibbets had been prepared, it might be advisable for M. de Guise to exhibit them, to justify, in however slight a degree, the odious and detestable acts committed. That M. de Guise might rely on a faithful record of his proceedings being transmitted to queen Elizabeth; but as to rendering himself the interpreter or apologist of the designs of the League, he must utterly decline such an office." Brissac, finding that the ambassador was not to be intimidated, said "that a guard was necessary to defend the ambassador from the fury of the people, who were bent on avenging the cruel murder of their former queen, Mary Stuart." "Softly, monsieur, the word 'cruel' cannot be applied to a solemn and judicial decree, legitimately pronounced and executed. As for the rest, I do not believe that the people bear me ill-will." "Have you arms in this hôtel, or have you not?" angrily demanded Brissac. "If you were to demand this question of me in the private capacity of having been the intimate friend of your late valiant uncle, M. de Cossé, I probably might reply. But being what I am, you will obtain no answer," replied the earl. "Your hôtel will be attacked and plundered, then, monseigneur; the people believe that you have arms!" The ambassador replied that he should defend himself to the last, and the people at their own risk and peril would violate his abode and the solemn privileges of an ambassador. Brissac then said, "Monseigneur, I pray you urgently, tell me, as your friend, whether you have arms in this your hôtel?" "As you demand the question of me in a private capacity, I reply that, had I been a private individual, I should have provided arms; but, being an ambassador, I have taken to myself no arms other than those of right and public law." With this reply the count departed, and repaired to report his conference with lord Stafford to the duc de Guise.[1] Notwithstanding the stubborn demeanour of the English ambassador, it was felt that his person and property must be defended from outrage; the duke, therefore, mounted a strong guard on the Quai des Bernardins and the adjacent Place Maubert, and himself addressed letters to queen Elizabeth explanatory of his recent proceedings, and protesting that he still remained the obedient servant of Henry III.

In the Palais, meanwhile, a few members of the parliament met, comprehending those whose abodes were too distant to have rendered possible the reception of the counter order prohibiting the assemblage of the Chambers. The president de Harlay, however, was not seated in his tribune, and upon inquiry it was ascertained that he was still in the Sainte Chapelle, where he had gone to perform his morning orisons. Some of the members repaired thither, and persuaded the president to accompany them back to the Salle de St.

[1] Particularités qui se passèrent à Paris Mai, 1588. Lettres de Pasquier.

Louis. Amongst the members present were, the president du Guesle, the attorney-general, the president de Thou, and others. After some conference it was suggested that a deputation ought, during that very day, to wait upon the king to express the extreme regret of the parliament at the events of la Journée des Barricades, and to assure his majesty of its loyal adherence. The president de Thou was commissioned to proceed privately to the Louvre, and consult queen Catherine as to the expediency of the step. Catherine highly approved the decision; she informed de Thou that she was about herself to despatch Pinart to visit the king, and would advertise his majesty of the loyal intentions of his parliament. The same evening the envoys set out; the deputation consisted of the president du Guesle, his son the attorney-general, and of four influential members named Courtin, Brissard, Gillot, and Bonnin.[1]

The day following being Sunday, the most treasonable demonstrations were made in the churches of the capital. The preachers of Paris regaled their hearers with harangues highly seditious and inflammatory. At St. Severin, Jean Prevot expatiated on the glory and the patriotism of the duc de Guise, whom he compared to Cæsar. If the duke could hitherto boast of having experienced the fortune of Cæsar, he certainly had not been endowed with the genius of Cæsar. Boucher, at St. Benôit, delivered an address of almost rabid bitterness against the reigning house. Its crimes, dissensions, tyranny, and pusillanimity, were gloated over with a fierce fanaticism which inspired awe. He compared the triumph of the duc de Guise over the armed hosts of Henri de Valois to that of Joshua, before whom the walls of Jericho fell. At St. André, Jean

1 De Thou. Archives du Royaume, H. 1789. Régistres de l'Hôtel de Ville.

Lincestre, one of the most turbulent churchmen in the capital, moved his auditory to tears and to alternate laughter by the vehemence of his rhetoric, and his coarse allusions to the private scandals of the court. Catherine repaired to hear mass in La Sainte Chapelle, accompanied by queen Louise. The duc de Guise met her majesty at the Palais, and attended her back to the Louvre; the queen, however, was highly indignant at the seizure of the Bastille and the arrest of La Perreuse, the prévôt des marchands, and demonstrated her displeasure so undisguisedly after her return to the Louvre, that Guise deemed it best to offer some conciliatory concession: he, therefore, consented to the liberation of M. la Perreuse. "Madame," said he, "if it be your will, I will go this instant and fetch him; but, believe me, he is safer there where he is than at his own house." Catherine angrily persisted in her demand; the duke, therefore, sent directions accordingly to the Seize, and the ex-provost's liberation was effected during the following day. The queen likewise sharply reproached the duke for the seditious harangues which he suffered in the churches; she also desired that every vestige of a barricade might disappear from all parts of the city by the following morning. The queen was obeyed; the magnitude of his triumph had bewildered the duke; he dared not assume the power, irresponsibility, and freedom of a great revolutionary leader. He wished to test the security of his path, and to carry the queen with him as a skilful coadjutress. Up to a certain point the address and acts of Guise had prevailed; he became a successful agitator and a popular hero: arrived at this elevated summit, his object being undefined even to himself, his policy was a failure. Supreme power insensibly glided from his grasp—for he dared not concentrate it in his own person. After years of intrigue Guise remained in doubt as to the degree in which his designs were supported and sympathized in by the great mass of the people; instead of tenaciousness of purpose, he therefore demonstrated uncertainty.

All the strongholds and the public edifices of Paris were now in the hands of the Seize, yet they deemed themselves insecure while the king's faithful servants remained in possession of the principal forts in the vicinity of the capital. On Monday, therefore, the governor of the castle of Vincennes was summoned to surrender. He quitted the fortress to parley with the commissioners of the Seize, and was treacherously detained. The castle, bereft of its governor, eventually capitulated.[1] Vincennes, during the barricades, had been the abode of the widowed duchesse de Montmorency. Two days after the departure of the king, the duc de Guise wrote to madame de Montmorency, requesting her to receive there the duchesse de Guise, whose state of pregnancy rendered it unsafe for her to remain amid the tumult of Paris. Madame de Montmorency, who felt most lively indignation at the occurrences in Paris, replied by at once vacating the royal apartments within the fortress, and retired to Chantilly a few hours before the arrival of the envoys of the League.

On the afternoon of Monday, May 17th, the duchesse de Guise entered Paris, accompanied by the cardinals de Bourbon and de Vendôme. The prince de Joinville, with a great suite, went out to meet and escort his mother to the hôtel de Guise, where she was received by her husband, by the cardinal de Guise, and by madame de Montpensier. The duchess remained only a few days in Paris, and retired to Vincennes. The old cardinal de Bourbon, however, still the dupe of the

[1] Hist. des Barricades. MS.

duc de Guise, and infatuated as ever with the hope of eventually reigning, took up his abode in the hôtel de Guise.[1]

The transports of the duchesse de Montpensier at the altitude to which her aspiring kinsmen had risen, were fervid and uncontrollable. So indignant was she at the departure of her step-son the duc de Montpensier with the king, that she forthwith quitted his hôtel, which she had continued to occupy after the demise of her husband, and fixed her residence in the hôtel de Montmorency. Queen Catherine one day rebuked the arrogance of the duchess, and remonstrated with her on the impropriety and danger of showing elation so visible. "What will you have, madame?" replied the duchess; "I cannot contain my joy, and feel like a brave soldier whose heart expands with triumph while contemplating the glorious fruition of his own deeds!"[2]

[1] MS. Hist. de la Journée des Barricades. F. de Thoisy.
[2] Journal de Henri III. L'Etoile.

BOOK VI.

CHAPTER I.

1588.

Manifesto issued by Henry III.—Letters of the duc de Guise—Assembly in the Hôtel de Ville—Election of a new municipality and other officers of state—Progress of the revolt—Deportment of king Henry—His political attitude—He grants audience to the deputies from the parliament of Paris—Procession of Penitents—The new municipality of Paris is presented to the king by queen Catherine—The duc d'Epernon—His apparent disgrace, and departure for Angoulême—Negotiations of queen Catherine and M. de Villeroy with the duc de Guise—Edict of Union—Henry receives the duc de Guise—Details of the sojourn of the duke at Chartres—Papal manifesto in favour of the League—Enterprise against the life of Epernon—Henry arrives at Blois—He summarily dismisses his ministers, and appoints a fresh cabinet—The court at Blois—Princesses of Lorraine—Opening of the States-General of 1588.

On the 17th day of May letters-missive, addressed to the provincial courts of the realm, appeared simultaneously from king Henry and the duc de Guise. Henry's address had been concocted at Rambouillet during the panic and excitement of his flight from Paris; and afterwards, it was not thought expedient to make alterations in the style of this document. Henry, as it has been related, therein professed his pacific intentions, and justified his conduct. The manifesto issued by Guise was drawn in bolder and more dictatorial language. The duke repudiated, like his royal master, all hostile intents; he declared his innocence of having promoted the insurrection which had compelled the king to quit Paris; he announced that he had possessed himself of the arsenal, the Bastille, the Châtelet, and other strongholds of the capital, "to restore them again to a *pacific* and *well-counselled* monarch, such as he hoped to render his majesty through the intercession of the pope and other Christian potentates; but that, if evil prevailed, he trusted to be able to defend religion and the orthodox community from the persecution which the allies and confederates of heresy about the person of the sovereign were preparing"—a strong declaration this, and little in accord with the duke's humble protestations of submission. The rest of the document is written in the plausible though dogmatic style of one who is conscious that he needs justification, though appreciating his power; and it concluded by audaciously proclaiming that, had it so pleased the duke, he could easily have arrested the king twenty-four hours before his majesty's flight. These manifestoes provoked numerous replies, nearly all of which were hostile in tone to the royal cause, even when adverse to the designs of the League.[1]

The cardinal de Bourbon, meantime, as first prince of the blood, convened, conjointly with the duc de Guise, a public assembly in the Hôtel de Ville for the election of a new prévôt des marchands in the room of La Perreuse, and of *echevins* to replace the civic functionaries who had fled to Chartres after the king. This meeting was held on Thursday, the 19th of May; the adherents of the League mustered in force, and the duc de Guise was present. The elections were made by ballot, without reference to the pleasure of the king, which in past times had always been ascertained before the nomination of municipal officers. The sieur de Marchemont was elected in the room of La Perreuse, but on his steadily declining the office, that most

[1] Mém. de la Ligue, tome ii. De Thou, tome xc. Mathieu, liv. viii. Cayet: Chronologie Novennaire.

furious of Leaguers, la Chapelle Marteau, master of Requests,[1] was appointed—a man who, having been ruined by the reckless extravagances of his parents, desired to involve every other person and thing in a similar perdition. The new sheriffs were Roland, Compans, a member of the Seize, Cotteblanche, and des Près.[2] The king's attorney-general in the municipal courts was dismissed, and one Brigart elected in his stead. The duke also proceeded to displace Seguier, chief justice of the criminal courts and of the Châtelet, and to nominate la Bruyère, one of the most factious of demagogues, to the vacant office. The new sheriffs were no sooner installed than they dismissed the colonels, captains, and aldermen of the wards, and nominated instead their own partisans. The officers of the minor municipal courts were likewise displaced, until every office was in the hands of the Seize. Loyal attachment or fidelity to the person of the sovereign became the badge for instant dismissal. The duke even attempted to remodel the royal household—an enterprise, however, so sternly resisted by Catherine that Guise dared not proceed in this project. Notice of the new elections was given to her majesty by the duke and the cardinal de Bourbon. Catherine's anger was intense, and she flatly refused to permit the new prévôt la Chapelle and the sheriffs to present themselves, as was customary, before the privy council to take the oaths of allegiance and fidelity. The duke, however, firmly persisted on the necessity of this concession, adding that the people had rightly displaced those unfaithful servants who had badly counselled the king. After much debate, the queen again reiterated a positive re-

1 Michel Marteau, sieur de la Chapelle, familiarly termed la Chapelle Marteau.

2 Extraits des Régistres de l'Hôtel de Ville. Archives du Royaume, lettre H.

fusal to countenance so gross an invasion of the royal authority as to dismiss his majesty's officers, and she haughtily commanded the duke to leave her presence. The deference shown by the duke for the queen-mother was boundless; it is true that he feared the queen, but also he reposed unlimited confidence in Catherine's friendly feeling. Guise, therefore, proposed a compromise—to wit, that the queen should authorize the new provost and other officers to discharge the duties of their functions while application was being made to procure the sanction of the king—to which expedient Catherine agreed.

The League, meanwhile, demanded and received the submission of the commandants of the forts in the neighbourhood of Paris, and also the oath of the chief authorities of the adjacent towns, villages, and hamlets. The pretext assigned for this act of usurpation was, that the king harboured a design to starve the Parisians, he having, while at Trapes and other places between Paris and Chartres, forbidden the transport of provisions to the capital. Saint Cloud, Charenton, Poissy Corbeil, Lagny, Meulan, and Pontoise were thus seized. The towns of Amiens and La Charité sent deputies to the duc de Guise with assurances of good-will; an example imitated by Château Thierry, and even by a section of the inhabitants of the town of Chartres, Henry's temporary abode.

The deputies sent by the parliament of Paris, on their arrival at Chartres, were immediately admitted to audience by the king. His majesty replied to their condolences by a speech of some length. He accepted their protestations, and declared that he knew how to distinguish between his faithful subjects and the factious; he authorized the parliament to continue its sessions, and to deliberate upon the means of restoring tranquillity to the capital. He declared that upon a suitable expression of contrition he was prepared to pardon the people of Paris, but threatened that, if this their acknowledgment of penitence were delayed, he would make them feel the offence which they had committed, so that the memory of their castigation should endure for ever. The king recapitulated the incidents of the Jour des Barricades; he dilated on his legitimate and royal title, and concluded his discourse with these words, "Return, therefore, messieurs, to your duty and offices with good heart; fear nothing, for I your king am on your side. Above all, proclaim abroad all that I have said to you!" After dinner Henry again sent for the envoys, and conversed for some time on the condition of affairs, and promised to send an ambassador to the parliament who should fully advertise them of his final intentions.[1] The manner of the king was languid and slightly sarcastic; he frequently alluded to "mon cousin de Guise," but with that lisping irony of tone which to those conversant with the character of the monarch was indicative of vehement resentment. From the commencement of his sojourn at Chartres, one of those rapid changes often to be observed in the mental constitution of Henry III., had passed over the king. His usual indolent and frivolous pleasures lost their zest. He was reserved with his ministers, and cold towards his favourites. His nights were spent in meditation, and when he arose a feverish irritability replaced Henry's usual good-natured condescension of manner. Far from vouchsafing his approval or manifesting his gratitude towards the queen-mother for her courageous daring in his behalf, and her subsequent skilful management of the duc de Guise, the facts seemed to haunt the mind of the king as confirmatory of the suspicion which he had long entertained of her

[1] Les Propos que le Roy a tenu à Chartres aux Deputez de sa Cour de Parlement—8vo. De Thou.

collusion with the "hero of the barricades." Towards his ministers, Cheverny, Bellièvre, and Villeroy, the ungraciousness of his majesty's manner was observed by many. It was with a smile on the lip and a menace in the eye that he listened to their exhortations that he should intrust the negotiations with Guise to the sole management of Catherine and Villeroy. In short, Henry had taken the resolve never to forgive or to forget the outrage which he had received from the duc de Guise; he was preparing to dissimulate, and to suffer any humiliation to restore an aspect of outward amity to their relations, as tending to hasten the vengeance which he thirsted for. The degradation which had befallen him compelled the king to reflect; and the dastardly concessions which from time to time had been wrung from him, filled him with anger and remorse, and inflamed a bitter hate against those under whose counsels he had acted. The arguments used by the queen-mother, by Bellièvre, Villequier, and Cheverny, in their earnest intercession "that he would not attempt the life of Guise," after the bold disregard shown by the latter to the mandate of his sovereign not to enter Paris, were remembered to their disadvantage at this period. The king, however, resolved to employ the men who had aided in bringing affairs to their present lamentable condition to re-adjust them. When Henry fell into one of these moods, which de Thou calls "*sa bile noire*," he became terrible as his brother Charles IX. Ordinarily the fit had passed away swiftly, for the slothful, laughter-loving monarch soon found that the rôle of a despot was irksome. The lords of the League, however, by abridging the royal recreations, and diminishing his majesty's pecuniary resources, had provided the sharp antidote so long needed; so that when they hoped to find an easy and indifferent monarch, alike oblivious of insult and amenable to control, they found to their consternation a master wily as well as vindictive.

The mean opinion which the magnates of the League entertained relative to the mental capacity of their sovereign, is demonstrated by the procession which left the capital on the afternoon of the 17th of May, ostensibly to entreat the forgiveness of king Henry for the late contumacious rebellion. It seems as if every individual or thing patronized by Henry was eventually destined to combine for his overthrow. The order of Penitents of Notre Dame, established by Henry, and fostered by him with such singular persistency, had been suddenly patronized by the League, and numbers of the partisans of the Seize had enrolled themselves under its banner. It was a religious confederation—one, moreover, well organized, and might, therefore, become a political engine of no despicable power. The return of Henry to Paris was ardently desired by the League; and to promote this object, by acting on the fears of the king, it was resolved to rouse a hostile demonstration within the city of Chartres. The passion of the king for processions was remembered, and made subservient to this design. It was determined that the Penitents should proceed to Chartres to ask the pardon of the king for the late enterprise; so that, under this pretext, an opportunity might be afforded to communicate with the disaffected. To obviate the risk of a refusal on the part of his majesty to admit to his presence members who, if they could chant *misereres* with unction, had also shown that they knew how to fight desperately behind a barricade, the new provost Chapelle Marteau and the president de Neuilly proceeded to the Capuchin monastery and prevailed upon de Bouchage, brother and heir of the late duc de Joyeuse, to lead the procession. Le Père Ange, as the duke was called in his monastic retreat, readily consented, remembering his master's pleasure in such spectacles, without reflecting that his company was probably requested merely as a passport to obtain admission into the town of Chartres for these *soi-disant* Penitents—an oversight for which he was afterwards bitterly reproached by the king. The procession was grotesque and blasphemous; it was intended to represent the scene along the Via Dolorosa which terminated at Calvary. The moral to be conveyed was, "that as Christ pardoned the enemies who had scourged and ill-treated him, so the king was bound to forgive the Parisians the outrage to which he had been subjected." "First walked a man with a long beard, dirty and uncombed, blowing occasional blasts on a cracked trumpet. Then came three other men of ferocious aspect, having each a copper basin on his head instead of a Roman helmet, and wearing over his sackcloth a rusty suit of armour. These persons dragged after them le Père Ange, bound hand and foot, and clad in a white vestment in shape like an alb. On his head was a wig, and upon this a crown of thorns was placed; while drops of blood stood on his cheeks, represented by paint. He carried a large cross, under the weight of which he frequently feigned to stumble and fall. Behind le Père Ange walked four men also wearing armour, holding the ropes with which he was bound, and who at intervals lashed furiously with a scourge upon the cords. On each side of the father walked two young Capuchin monks, personating, one the Virgin Mary, the other St. Mary Magdalene. Their arms were crossed on their breasts, their tearful eyes were raised to heaven, and they prostrated themselves each time that le Père Ange fell to the ground."[1] Afterwards came a long procession of Peni-

[1] Aubigné — Hist. Universelle, tome iii. liv. i. Mémoires de la Ligue. Maimbourg, tome ii.

tents, including Neuilly and the most fanatical leaders of the Seize, consisting of several hundred members.

An order having been previously sent by Henry to admit the Penitents on their arrival at the gates of Chartres, the procession entered the cathedral at vesper hour, amid the hootings and derisive jeers of a mob of people congregated to witness so grotesque a spectacle.[1] The king was in the church, attended by some of the principal personages of his suite, when le Père Ange and his coadjutors poured into the edifice. Beating their breasts and crying *miséricorde!* the majority fell prostrate one over the other before the altar. Some of the spectators laughed, others wept; more, despite the sanctity of the place, joined in ribald outcry with the friars. Henry gazed with displeasure at the blasphemous *travestie;* he desired that the discordant blasts of the trumpet and the frantic shrieks of the Penitents might cease. "I commiserate from the bottom of my heart," said his majesty, "the credulity of M. de Bouchage, who being misled by his monks and deceived by the factious, should have lent himself to such an exhibition, which every one must brand as ludicrous." In his altered mood Henry was now sensible of the odium and indecency of the spectacle, which, however, did not exceed in folly that first memorable exhibition of Penitents in which his majesty had condescended to parade the length and breadth of Paris with his head thrust in a sack! The duc de Montpensier openly ridiculed the exhibition;[2] the maréchal de Biron scoffed at it; while Crillon offered the services of the guard to give the Penitents each a round dozen of stripes, seeing how inefficiently this portion of the performance was enacted.

[1] The procession arrived at Chartres on Tuesday, March 17.

[2] "Tout iroit encore bien n'étoit que la musique est un peu aigre et que l'on fait semblant de fouetter," said the duke.

Henry addressed a few cold words to Père Ange, and quitted the cathedral, declining further conference with the Penitents. The president de Neuilly, however, was afterwards admitted to the royal presence to present an address from the Cour des Aides. The president hypocritically condoled with his majesty, and offered the comforting assurance of his own fidelity. The king, however, knowing that Neuilly was the most intolerant of Leaguers, and having been admonished of the private purport of his visit to Chartres, interrupted his address by saying abruptly, "Hold! poor fool that you are; do you not suppose that, if I bore ill-will against you and your faction, I could long ago have executed my enterprise? No, I have loved the Parisians; therefore go back to your comrades, monsieur, and try to behave yourself as a good subject and citizen in degree as I have proved myself to be your clement sovereign!"[1] The maréchal de Biron, meantime, received advices through one of his friends, a canon of the cathedral, of the secret treachery of Neuilly, who, with others of the Penitents, was present at a midnight assembly of the factious. Biron instantly informed the king, and asked permission to surprise the assemblage and arrest the members, including Neuilly, whom he proposed to hang on the spot. The king declined to follow this advice, stating his intent in a few days to depart from Chartres for the town of Mantes; a step which afterwards greatly offended the loyal inhabitants of the former place.

The king, meantime, despatched Claude Dorron on a mission to the parliament of Paris, according to his promise. His majesty's ambassador made an harangue of great eloquence and learning: in the name of the king he announced that the States-general were to be

[1] Journal de Henri III.

convoked about the end of the year; and that it was the royal resolve to take measures to provide a Roman Catholic successor for the throne of France, selected *from among the princes of the blood royal of France.* His majesty promised to grant an amnesty for the past, provided that the Parisians laid down arms and submitted to the royal authority; it was also intimated that his majesty, desiring to content his subjects on all matters, had seen fit to annul twenty-six financial edicts especially deemed burdensome by the people. The placable manifestations made by the king greatly discomposed the projects of the duc de Guise, who was at Château Thierry, whither he had repaired to receive the submission of the garrison, when the royal envoy entered Paris. In the face of such pacific declarations it was difficult to compel the people of France to believe that the king ever harboured the tyrannical intentions attributed to him, and which had been alleged in excuse for the rising of the capital. Already the royal adherents in the city of Paris ventured to denounce the barricades, and appealed to the benevolence of his majesty's attitude as a full refutation of the atrocious calumnies propagated by the League; a slight reaction, therefore, was visible for the royal cause. The king had promised his subjects an orthodox successor and fiscal relief, and many indications warned the duke that the French people were not prepared to fight in support of his contemplated regal usurpation, apart from the defence of their religion and liberties. Upon the old cardinal de Bourbon the effect of the king's declaration acted promptly; he demanded only that the sceptre of St. Louis should not be desecrated by the grasp of a heretic; his majesty, therefore, having promised this, the cardinal retired from the hôtel de Guise to his abbey of St. Germain, and placed himself in active correspondence with queen Catherine. Though the duke continued to be supported by the approval and counsels of the Spanish ambassador, he derived no material support from Spain. The great Armada was on the point of emerging from the port of Lisbon; and the energy, the wealth, and the statecraft of Philip II. were concentrated on that expedition. Guise, as the puppet of Spain, had opened a pathway for the mighty fleet. Elizabeth of England, having been deprived, by his rebellion, of the alliance of France and Flanders, and of the valiant aid of Henri de Navarre, was esteemed to be already vanquished; while the English islands were regarded as the future head-quarters of the Inquisition.

The duc de Guise, on his return to Paris, feeling the necessity of making some concessions, proceeded to the Hôtel de Ville, and insisted that the new municipal officers and the provost la Chapelle should, without delay, repair to Chartres, and personally ask the king to sanction their election. An address was voted, in which the demands of the League were renewed, and especially the exile of Epernon and his kindred. The king was requested to pardon the late tumults, and to confirm the municipal elections. The same day the duc de Guise addressed a letter to king Henry defending his past conduct, but filled with professions of loyalty. This epistle he despatched to Chartres by the captain St. Paul, the officer of the League who had led back the royal guard to the Louvre on the day of the barricades. St. Paul also announced the approaching arrival of the municipality, and requested his majesty to postpone his departure from Chartres, in order to grant them audience. Henry received and perused the letter of the duke, and dismissed the envoy without an answer during the same day. Amongst other speeches which his majesty made to St. Paul was this ominous one:—"That the duc de Guise when fighting for the faith had always been fortunate; but that if he dared to assail the sacred person of his king and sovereign, he might be assured that God would withdraw his benediction, and that he would miserably perish."

After despatching his envoy to Chartres, the duc de Guise repaired to the Louvre and earnestly besought the queen to present the new municipality to her son. Catherine after some demur consented; she desired to make personal investigation of the temper and designs of the king; also to examine into the truth of the report that the duc d'Epernon was about to rejoin the king at the head of 500 men. The following day, therefore, the queen set out for Chartres, being preceded by the prévôt des marchands la Chapelle, the recently appointed officers, and by deputies from the duc de Guise and the lords of the League then in Paris. Henry bestowed a cool greeting on his mother, and in lieu of the long private conference which Catherine had designed, he demonstrated great haste to grant audience to the deputation that all the personages might return before nightfall to Paris. Henry received the envoys sitting in a chair of state beneath a canopy erected in the hall of the episcopal palace. Catherine stood at the right of the king; at his majesty's left were M. d'O and many of the obnoxious chamberlains, who stood calmly by to hear themselves presently designated by most uncomplimentary epithets. On approaching the dais, the members of the deputation prostrated themselves before the king, and supplicated him to pardon them if, "in their desolation and lamentable mourning, they should utter facts or advices unpalatable to his royal ear." This exordium over, the members rose, when one of them advanced and read the harangue agreed upon, which was authenticated by the autographs of the cardinal de Bourbon, the duc de Guise, Chapelle Marteau, and the sheriffs of Paris.[1] Henry returned precisely the same reply as he had commissioned Dorron to make to the parliament of Paris. Respecting the duc d'Epernon, his majesty said that "that grievance was rather of a stale and private nature; nevertheless, he should always prefer the welfare of the commonwealth to every private consideration." Catherine then asked the king, in the presence of the provost and others, to return to Paris. The courtesy of Henry's tone then changed, and he replied by an abrupt and positive "Non, madame!" The king and his mother then retired, and a conference of some length ensued, at which Villeroy was present. The articles of the convention to be concluded with Guise and his party were the subject of debate. Henry demonstrated a serenity and indifference the most astonishing, and discussed the treasonable demands presented by the duke with the utmost *sang froid*. The conference ended by nothing being resolved, the king engaging to send Villeroy to Paris after his arrival at Mantes, whither he intended to proceed the following day. Catherine, therefore, took leave of her son, and returned to Paris highly dissatisfied with her interview.

The career of the duc d'Epernon in Normandy, meanwhile, had been beset with difficulties. Some of the most important cities of the province refused to acknowledge his authority; which was also fiercely assailed by M. de Villars, governor of Havre, who declined to admit the new governor into that port without an order countersigned by the duc de Guise. Epernon, whose high and valiant spirit chafed at these obstacles, was taking active measures for the reduction of the rebels when the news of the barricades and of

[1] Régistres de l'Hôtel de Ville. Archives du Royaume, H.

the flight of the king to Chartres reached him. The importance of the victory obtained by the League, in relation to his own personal fortunes, arrested the military designs of the duke, and he hurriedly prepared to rejoin his royal master. From the abbé d'Elbène he had received a faithful record of the events of the capital. The duke indignantly protested against the tame surrender of the Swiss and the royal guards, which he averred was the work of queen Catherine, who desired neither that her son nor the duc de Guise should establish paramount authority. In the desperate emergency in which the king was placed, the duke perceived that the royal power must temporarily cease to shield him from the hatred of his enemies. Foremost amongst these was Villeroy, the able, aspiring, and acute secretary of state—Catherine's *protégé*, and, as it was believed, the secret partisan of the duc de Guise. The queen-mother herself, whose power he had defied in the days of his prosperity, vehemently demanded his dismissal. The designs and motives of the king, however, afforded the duke a theme for still more puzzling speculation. From M. d'O and the abbé d'Elbène he heard of his majesty's careless and perfectly cool demeanour, of his clement declarations and gracious reception of the authors of the recent insurrection. He heard of the levy of no troops, nor of the despatch of missives rallying round the royal standard the valiant and loyal of the realm to avenge the foul insult inflicted by the princes of Lorraine. Epernon received, on the contrary, advices from Paris filled with gloomy forebodings, and recounting the sailing forth of the Invincible Armada, everywhere to annihilate heresy and its upholders; and of the amicable negotiations of the queen-mother with the duc de Guise and his sister madame de Montpensier. That his fall was impending Epernon felt no doubt; but he too well knew the disposition of the king to believe that such coercion would not be avenged. His conduct at this crisis, therefore, exhibited address so skilful as to demonstrate that he was not far surpassed by his master as an adept in dissimulation.

On the 22nd day of May the duc d'Epernon arrived at Chartres. The intelligence of his approach had created a great panic and renewed the cabals of the courtiers. The ducs de Montpensier and Longueville and the maréchal d'Aumont waited upon his majesty and announced their resolve to leave the court if Epernon remained, seeing that jealousy of the favourite's power had combined to produce the present deplorable condition of affairs; while, as the duke's dismissal was one of the clauses most insisted upon in the articles demanded by the League, it was clear if he remained no compact could be concluded. Henry replied, to the amazement of all, "that the presence of the duc d'Epernon could not be more disagreeable to any one than to himself." He then publicly instructed the abbé d'Elbène to notify this to Epernon, and to express his desire that the duke should withdraw after having previously resigned the government of Normandy. The abbé d'Elbène was the confidential friend of Epernon, and after the departure of the latter had been the depositary of many of the king's most secret intentions. M. de Bellièvre was subsequently officially commissioned to convey the same notification. The duke, however, appeared not in the least disconcerted at the command, but had continued his journey, travelling leisurely to Chartres. The king apparently gave him a very indifferent reception, and seemed delighted to avenge upon Epernon personally the odium which had resulted from their previous intimacy. If this alienation was not feigned—as there is every appearance to suppose that it was—Epernon and his royal master bore their separation with surprising equanimity. The duke, who formerly was of temper most haughty and intractable, laid down on the instant his command in Normandy without remonstrance, while the king a few hours afterwards bestowed the dignity on the duc de Montpensier. Neither did Epernon resent his almost total exclusion from the royal cabinet and the privy council. The king, moreover, was further induced to issue a mandate commanding the duke to relinquish his government of Angoulême and to restore the fortresses of Loches, Saintes, and Boulogne, of which he was commandant, "his majesty being resolved from henceforth to annihilate the jealousies which had so long convulsed the realm." Epernon, however, suddenly quitted Chartres, and being joined by his brave young duchess, who with difficulty made her escape in disguise from Paris, he journeyed with speed to Angoulême, and, throwing himself into the castle, prepared to defend it by the help of the king of Navarre against his enemies, refusing to relinquish more of his offices. It was afterwards ascertained that the abbé d'Elbène, who accompanied the duke in his flight, spent the greater part of the preceding night in secret conference with the king in his bed-chamber. Henry foreseeing that an accommodation with Guise must be purchased by the sacrifice of Epernon, and also finding that Catherine and his ministers were unanimous in their demand for the duke's exile, probably resolved not to afford his enemies the additional satisfaction of prescribing this concession; while the duc d'Epernon, in concert with his royal master, promoted the deception which was to deliver them both from the toils of faction.

The defiance of the duc d'Epernon, and his refusal to relinquish the government of Angoulême, appeared to inspire the king with furious indignation. Villeroy wrote to command the citizens of Angoulême to eject the duke, while M. de Tagens, commander of the royal forces in the district, received a mandate to intercept and arrest him. Epernon, nevertheless, made such speed that he had seized the fortress of Angoulême and established his authority before the decree arrived; while subsequently the duke conducted himself with such dexterity and courage as greatly to enhance his repute.

The king, meanwhile, departed on the eleventh day of June for Rouen, for the intrigues of the League in Chartres began to occasion him intense apprehension. He was here joined by the comte de Soissons, who offered his majesty his humble services, and made many excuses for having fought against Joyeuse at Coutras. The king of Navarre after that signal triumph had, as it has been related, partially disbanded his army and retired to Pau with the comte de Soissons. Le Béarnnois had not taken the rout of the German legions to heart, especially when a design came to light by which it appeared that the baron de Dhona had been empowered to seize and convey him forcibly into Germany as a hostage for the payment of the vast sums due to the *reiters* from the Huguenots of the realm. The king of Navarre was making a military progress through Poitiers and Saintonge when the news of la Journée des Barricades reached him. The princes immediately retired to La Rochelle; while Henri sanctioned the departure of the comte de Soissons to join the king, offering to follow himself with his valiant army, should his presence be deemed acceptable.

Queen Catherine, during this interval, was absorbed in negotiation. The king, after his arrival at Rouen, sent the comte de Schomberg on a secret mission to Paris, to investigate and report on the designs of the chieftains of the League. Soon afterwards he accredited his first physician Miron to aid the queen in preparing an accommodation. These envoys reported that no pacification could ever be truly achieved unless the ambition of the duc de Guise was primarily satiated; at the same time they forwarded intelligence that the town of Meaux had joined the League, while the cardinal de Guise had rendered himself master of the city of Troyes. The king, therefore, sent for Villeroy, and confided to him the important task, conjointly with Miron, of drawing up a treaty with the League which was to embody the articles of Nemours and Nancy, and satisfy the ambitious aspirations of the duke and his partisans. Catherine was to exercise a paramount authority over the negotiators, who were to be guided by her directions. Villeroy has been accused of playing into the hands of the duc de Guise, and of misusing the powers confided to him, for the gratification of his private resentments. In his Memoirs, however, Villeroy indignantly repudiates the charge, and takes great credit to himself for having granted to the duc de Guise the powers of lieutenant-general only, when the secret instructions of the king authorized him to offer him the dignity of constable of France. The letters-patent elevating Guise to the office of lieutenant-general were, nevertheless, drawn by the pen of Villeroy, and presented by him for the royal signature, and the amplification of the privileges even of a constable conceded in that document is remarkable.

The League openly claimed Villeroy as one of its most able and crafty members. In the celebrated "Instruction" addressed by the archbishop of Lyons at this period to the duc de Guise, and subsequently made public, he is alluded to with commendation, and as one of the men by whose aid the duke might climb to the altitude of power. This document, emanating from the pen of Espinac, is drawn with able plausibility, though its tenor recommends some of the boldest invasions on the royal prerogative that have ever proceeded from the most enterprising of rebels. The dicta of the turbulent prelate were received with reverence by his party, and acted upon as the test and standard of the League. Henry pleasantly declared that the archbishop was "the brain of the League, and the quintessence of faction." Even the duc de Guise condescended to pay a pretended reverence to a document he termed "the Catechism of the League," which embodied ideas that he had acted upon, but as yet never openly avowed. The prelate addresses himself to Guise; he tells him that there are three things indispensably requisite for his future ascendency—the favour of the king, for the which he must *condescend* to conclude a convention; a great state office, such as that of constable; and the devotion of the courtiers, and especially of the secretaries of state, who, either by menaces or by bribes, must be won, so that no affair, great or small, shall be despatched unknown to the duke. He then proceeds to hint that the good-will of the secretary intrusted with the drawing-up of the letters-patent conferring the office to be demanded, must be carefully secured, "for understand, that the adjustment of the words conveying the said power will signify greatly. If M. de Villeroy is not charged with this office, it is of great importance that he should be cognizant of and accessory to the document." "As for the queen-mother," writes Espinac, "you must have perceived that sooner or later her majesty compasses all that she intends, and that those individuals who have attempted to promote discord and variance between the king and herself have always found themselves ruined. The queen is evidently now minded to will what her son wills, and to hold his interests dearest. Nevertheless her majesty has resolved to suffer no rival, nor to permit that another shall exercise greater authority than herself." Espinac, therefore, advises the duke to conciliate Catherine in every way; he cites the example of queen Plectrude, mother of Childeric, in her relations with Charles Martel, Maire du palais, and shows that, notwithstanding the subordination of the latter to the will of that queen, he rose to the rank of duke of France, and established his posterity on the throne; an example well worthy of imitation. The prelate next enters into an argument on the means likely to seduce the fidelity of ministers, and render them devoted to the duke.[1]

The treaty, or edict of Union, of July, 1588, as it was termed, was at length concluded by Catherine, Villeroy, and Miron, for the king; and by Guise, the cardinal de Bourbon, and the lords of the Confederation on behalf of the League. The duchesse de Montpensier was employed by the queen as ambassadress between the Louvre and the hôtel de Guise. Its negotiation was facilitated by the withdrawal from court of the duc d'Epernon; and having tacitly exacted this concession, the duc de Guise magnanimously refrained for the present from molesting the smaller fry of favourites, who still thronged the avenues of the royal bedchamber and cabinet. The articles were precisely similar to those presented by the duke to queen Catherine on the afternoon of la Journée des Barricades. The king pledged his royal word to convoke immediately the States-general, to legislate on the great question of the royal succession. The duc de Guise received the office of lieutenant-general of the armies of France, with power of absolute command wherever the king was not present; and his post of grand-master of the household was confirmed afresh. Henry gave his royal promise to make interest with pope Sixtus V. to bestow the papal legation of Avignon on the cardinal de Guise, and to

[1] Instruction à M. de Guise par l'Archevêque de Lyons après la Paix de Juillet, 1588. Mémoires de Villeroy—Pièces Justificatives.

solicit a cardinal's hat for the archbishop of Lyons. The duc de Nemours was to be gratified with the dignity of governor of the Lyonnois; the duc d'Aumale with that of Picardy. Monsieur de la Chastre was created a marshal; and M. de Maineville, the agent who had been employed by the duc de Guise to inflame the insurrectionary ardour of the people of Paris, was made a councillor of state! All the persons gratified by dignities or pecuniary rewards by the Seize, or on the personal authority of the duc de Guise, were to resign their offices and gratuities in order to receive them again on the following day by warrant of the king.[1] When the patents registering these shameful concessions were laid before his majesty by Villeroy, Henry's tears, it is said, plentifully bedewed these records of his degradation. If the royal tears fell from a sense of bitter compunction for his past follies and misconduct, a responsive feeling of commiseration may be evoked; but the humiliation of his kingly dignity was the just and inevitable castigation of Henry's incorrigible perversity, and for the misery which his vices had inflicted on the nation. The edict was signed by the king at Rouen, and registered by the parliament of Paris on the 21st day of July, 1588. Catherine wrote to her son expressly to insist on the necessity of such concessions, and stating her conviction of the loyal sincerity of the duc de Guise. The Spanish ambassador Mendoza lauded the edict as one necessary and good. All the nobles of the realm tacitly accepted the convention, or made no effort to support the king in its rejection, excepting Montmorency and the malcontent nobles of the south, the duc d'Epernon, and the duc de Nevers — a Gonzaga, who hoping one day that his posterity might reign over Mantua, ever believed him-

[1] Mém. de M. de Villeroy. Mathieu: Hist. de Henri III. Maimbourg: Mém. de la Ligue. Dupleix. Cayet.

self bound to resist encroachments on the royal prerogatives.

Another element of terror also powerfully affected Henry's imagination, and contributed to procure the ratification of the edict. Along the French coast, off Boulogne, Philip's formidable Armada glided in majestic gloom, bearing a terrible commission to depose heretic princes; and laden with chains, racks, and inquisitors for the castigation of those who opposed the supremacy or the faith of the Holy Roman See. It was insinuated to the king that a word from Guise might temporarily divert the destination of this fleet from the shores of England, to aid in confirming an orthodox faith and a faithful dynasty in the realm rendered illustrious by the piety and holiness of St. Louis.

Henry, therefore, intent on his own secret projects, and believing that the meeting of the States would rend from Guise a portion of his usurped power, resigned himself to an act the immediate effect of which was to restore outward obedience to the royal behests, and thus to place within his power the castigation he intended to inflict on his opponents. The idle luxury and repose of life which his majesty led while at Rouen, moreover, had mitigated the vehemence of Henry's resentment. The king passed the greater part of the day on the Seine reposing in his famous gondola, which had been suffered to proceed from Paris up the river to Rouen. The *ennui* and indifference manifested by Henry grieved his faithful adherents, to none of whom did he now impart his secret resolves and meditations.

The king quitted Rouen on the 23rd of July, having previously caused a *Te Deum* to be chanted in the cathedral for the restoration of peace. It was, however, observed that his majesty paid little attention to the service, and conversed nearly the whole time behind a curtain with M. d'O. Henry then proceeded to

Mantes, where he was met by the queens Catherine and Louise, with whom he made a sojourn of two days. Catherine then returned to Paris, having obtained permission for the duc de Guise and other members of his family to present themselves at Chartres during the ensuing week in her *cortège*.

On the 26th day of July the king reluctantly returned to Chartres, there to give the last confirmation to the Edict of Union by receiving the duc de Guise. At the gate of the city called Des Epars, M. Jean de Gauville, chief magistrate of the town, met his majesty with a deputation, about five o'clock in the evening. The coachman inadvertently stopped the royal carriage close upon a piece of ground marshy and partially covered with water. Gauville, therefore, who was arrayed in his magisterial robes of black satin, advanced, and, contrary to the etiquette usually observed, began to address his majesty standing. Henry since his reverses had been peculiarly susceptible of slights; observing this omission of the customary homage, he angrily interrupted the harangue by calling, "On your knees, sir! on your knees, I say!" Gauville, therefore, was compelled to kneel in the mire and compliment the king on his most auspicious arrival.[1] As he passed through the town the king was received with salutes of artillery, and under triumphal arches. Turning to Gauville, the duties of whose office required him to remain in the vicinity of the royal carriage, Henry said, sarcastically, "This will do; you will now be better prepared to do honour to mon cousin de Guise when he enters your town!" The king proceeded to the cathedral, where he was received and presented with holy water by the dean, M. Daubermont. A few days subsequently Catherine, accompanied by the

[1] Extrait de l'Histoire MS. de la Ville de Chartres, faite par Souchet, Chanoine de cette Ville—Bibl. de la Ville de Chartres.

cardinal de Bourbon, the duc de Guise, the cardinal de Guise, the duchesse de Nemours dowager of Guise, the prince de Joinville, and the archbishop of Lyons, arrived at Chartres. The cardinal de Bourbon was attended by fifty archers of his guard, wearing splendid uniforms of crimson velvet and gold. The duc de Guise was followed by a troop of eighty horsemen armed to the teeth. The queen was escorted by a regiment of the royal guard. Henry received these august personages in the hall of the episcopal palace, arrayed in his robes, and sitting under a canopy of state. To the queen he gave most cordial greeting. These salutations over, Catherine, taking the duc de Guise by the hand, led him to the steps of the dais, and presented him to her son as his good and loyal subject. Henry saluted the duke with grave majesty of demeanour—without frankness, and yet affably. The duke bent the knee and kissed the royal hand. Henry then received the other members of the house of Lorraine present, to all of whom he addressed some brief observation. The king's manner was easy and his speech fluent, while it was observed that the duc de Guise suffered under considerable constraint. His reception by the people had, nevertheless, been enthusiastic; from the confines of the town of Chartres to the episcopal palace the acclamations of "Vive Guise!" were unceasing. The duke's abode was in the Cloître St. Martin, in the house of a widow named Olive, whither he repaired after his first brief audience with his sovereign, whom he left about to retire to hold conclave with Catherine and Villeroy, the latter of whom Henry overwhelmed with favours. The presence of Guise in Chartres proved the signal for a general rally of the League. The members secretly met and despatched one of their number to offer the duke a guard, and to assure him that on the slightest peril menacing his life or his liberty they were ready to take up arms in his defence. Guise thanked the members for their zeal, but said "that he relied on the faith and word of the king; besides, as it was his duty as lieutenant-general of the realm to preserve the public peace, he requested them very affectionately not to make hostile demonstration whatever."[1] These proceedings were forthwith reported to Biron by his friend the canon, and came to the royal ears, and, as may be supposed, did not propitiate the king.

The same evening a private prohibition was issued through the duc de Montpensier, forbidding any of the household to visit the duc de Guise at his lodgings, or to pay a similar compliment to any of the recently arrived persons his kinsmen or adherents. Catherine in vain tried to prevent the issue of the order; the king listened with an air of dogged resolve to her remonstrances, and declined to make any reply. It required all what the court had long termed "*l'agréable dissimulation du duc de Guise*" to enable the duke to continue his obsequious deportment amid so many annoyances.

The following day, August 2nd, the king gave a banquet to Guise, during which their reconciliation outwardly seemed complete. The duke demeaned himself with deference, while Henry took dangerous delight in aiming his jests and *bons mots* at his guest, who apparently received them all in good part. "Whom shall we pledge, mon cousin?" asked the king during the repast, taking from the table a cup brimful of red wine. "It is for your majesty to decide," replied the duke. "Well, to our good friends the Huguenots." "'Tis well spoken, sire," hastily responded Guise. "But," resumed the king, "I was going to add also to the health of our fine and worthy barricaders of Paris! Let us not forget them,

[1] De Thou. Hist. du Chanoine Souchet. Journal de l'Etoile.

I pray you!" The duke smiled, but his countenance plainly showed the displeasure he felt at these taunts. During the night the house in which M. d'O lodged, and which was adjacent to the abode of la veuve Olive, took fire and burned fiercely. Instantly throughout Chartres the rumour spread that this was a device on the part of the king, in order that during the confusion he might kill the duc de Guise. The city, therefore, was soon in commotion. Bands of armed men suddenly issued from the lowest suburbs and repaired to the Cloître St. Martin ready to defend their hero. Others placed themselves so as to intercept the progress of the gentlemen of the household to the palace, and amongst those so arrested was M. d'O. The tumult, however, was soon pacified, but as no one in the panic had aided to extinguish the conflagration, the lodging of M. d'O was burned to the ground, and a young girl, the daughter of the hostess, perished in the flames.[1]

The sudden arrival of the Spanish ambassador Mendoza renewed during the few subsequent days the political ferment in Chartres. The ambassador presented himself, as he said, to announce to king Henry that the Spanish fleet had defeated the English in the Channel, and had achieved a safe landing on the coast of England! So elated was Philip's representative at this intelligence that before quitting Paris he drew up a pretended recital of the event—the rumour of which only had reached him, though he chose to assert it as a fact—and deposited the manuscript in the hands of his majesty's printer, commanding him to print and distribute copies to whoever chose to ask for them. On entering the town of Chartres Mendoza proceeded straight to the cathedral, which is dedicated to the Holy Virgin. Prostrating himself before the porch,

[1] Rélation du Chanoine Souchet—Bibl. de Chartres.

over which was a statue of Mary, he audibly returned thanks for the great victory achieved by the Spanish arms. He then repaired to the episcopal palace, and entering the hall, where he found many of the courtiers assembled awaiting the presence of the king, he exclaimed, *Victoria! Victoria! vive el rey Catolico!* and proceeded to recount the success of the great Armada. Whilst Mendoza was thus occupied Henry entered the presence-chamber, attended by the duc de Guise, Villeroy, and others. The ambassador hastened to impart his glorious tidings, to which his majesty listened attentively. The king then glanced round the circle, and observed with dry sarcasm that the ambassador must be labouring under some unhappy delusion, as he had that morning received a despatch from M. de Gourdan, governor of Calais, in which that officer, so far from recording the victory of the Spanish fleet, had forwarded intelligence of a naval combat in which the English armament had disabled twelve Spanish frigates, and killed 5,000 men. Moreover, the immediate object of M. de Gourdan's despatch was to give information that a large vessel, used as a galley-ship by the Spaniards, had grounded on the coast of France.[1] Mendoza retreated abashed at this refutation of his boastful narration, while the king continued to discourse on the subject in the bantering tone which had now become almost habitual. The ambassador, having recovered his presence of mind, then stepped into the circle, and demanded that orders should be issued to deliver up to him the stranded ship and her crew, which, he said, consisted of refractory seamen, Moorish renegades, Turks, and prisoners of war. Henry replied that he would advise with his council. The matter was afterwards hotly debated; the duc de Guise and the ad-

[1] Cayet: Chronologie Novennaire.

herents of the League pressed the king to accede to the demand made by Mendoza; but the duc de Nevers and Biron so strongly represented to his majesty the cruelty of riveting again the chains of those unhappy captives that Henry, following also his own inclinations, peremptorily refused to allow one of them to be molested.

All the letters-patent and other documents connected with the Edict of Union having been signed and sealed, the assembly at Chartres began to disperse. Already the emissaries of the duc de Guise were busily employed canvassing for the approaching election for the States-general convened to meet at Blois during the ensuing month of October. That the misrepresentations of the League might not affect the legitimacy of the elections, the king despatched the president Auguste de Thou, with other notable and learned persons, to make a progress throughout the provinces, in order to explain the origin and issue of the recent troubles, and to admonish the people to make true and dispassionate choice of deputies. Catherine, at the solicitation of the duc de Guise and of the provost la Chapelle, before her departure from Chartres, again made request to the king to return and take up his abode in the Louvre until the assemblage of the States. Her majesty declared that the Parisians would never believe in the clemency of the king, or in the reality of the Edict of Union, until such an act of oblivion and reconciliation should be vouchsafed. "Madame," replied the king, "I will not; you demand in vain." "Ah, mon fils," remonstrated Catherine, "what will be thought of my influence? what respect will, for the future, be paid to me, if you thus refuse my solicitation? Is it possible that you have banished that humane and forgiving spirit which I have ever seen so prompt to pardon injuries?" "It is quite true, madame; it is gone. But what can you expect? That rascal Epernon, as everybody says, has corrupted my mind and spoiled my temper."[1] When Henry took this tone the queen knew from experience that he was impracticable: and fortunate it was that Henry steadily resisted his mother's blandishments; for the duc de Nevers[2] asserts that, had his majesty returned to the capital, a conspiracy existed, unknown to the queen, to seize and confine him in the Capuchin monastery with his former friend Joyeuse, upon an annual pension of 200,000 crowns. When the royal resolve not to return to Paris became known, many towns deputed envoys to invite his majesty to hold his court within their precincts, and amongst others were the towns of Tours, Blois, Amboise, and Lyons. The king courteously thanked his loyal subjects, but announced his intention to remain at Chartres until the 21st of September, when he should proceed to Blois to hold his States.

During this interval the duc de Guise, anxious to impress foreign nations and the people of the realm with a conviction of his loyalty and disinterestedness, studiously refrained from entering Paris, but remained in constant attendance upon the king, returning to Chartres after every expedition which he made for party purposes in the provinces. Henry now frequently entertained the duke in familiar converse, likewise the archbishop of Lyons. He also lauded the services of the comte de Brissac, and commended the zeal of Bassompierre in having so promptly raised levies for the League in the German States. Madame de Montpensier even shared in Henry's courtesies; and his majesty commanded that the duchess should be included amongst the numerous guests to be invited to Blois during the meeting of the States. The duke seems to

[1] Journal de Henri III. Edited by Pierre de l'Etoile, from MSS. in the Bibl. Imp., written by a Bourgeois de Paris. Dupuis, fol. 219.

[2] Mém. du Duc de Nevers.

have been completely deceived as to the real temper of the king, and believed that, with his usual weak *insouciance,* Henry was content to forget the past, and to inaugurate a new era of power for the house of Lorraine. The haughty independence of the duke's actions in the discharge of his functions of lieutenant-général and grand master of the court accordingly increased in a proportionate degree as his awe and dread of his master's retaliation vanished. The king coldly passed by and seemed blind to these various assumptions; and soon, therefore, the majority of courtiers rendered homage as obsequious as the duke could desire. With many the duke's generosity imposed; others inclined before his mien *de grand prince;* those who wanted place or pension naturally looked to the victor of the barricades as the assured channel through which the benefits they desired must flow. The *prestige* of the duke alone wanted the seal of papal commendation to render it above challenge. This sanction did not tarry. Sixtus V., who had so severely reproved the duke de Nevers, and who formerly had written such fierce rebukes to the Gallican prelates for their insubordination to their anointed sovereign, opened the pontifical arms to the successful champion of orthodoxy—a prince who ere long might, as Christian king of France, term himself eldest son of the church. The pope, therefore, addressed letters to the duke, in which he exhorted him to perfect the glorious extirpation of the Huguenots; and likened the family of Lorraine to the holy house of the Maccabees, which of old delivered the children of Israel from their persecutors. The duke caused the pontifical letters to be printed and dispersed over Paris. Henry, though secretly irritated at this insolent *bravade,* made no demonstration of displeasure.

Neither did the king openly resent an audacious enterprise, which occurred at this period, to assassinate the duc d'Epernon at Angoulême, under the pretext of fulfilling the mandate which the king had sent, countersigned by Villeroy, the duke's mortal enemy, interdicting the people from receiving Epernon as their governor. Of all Henry's favourites Epernon was the only one dreaded by the Guisards. The duke was bold, able, and stanch in his attachment to the king. He was, moreover, a link between Henry III. and the king of Navarre, within whose territory of Albret Epernon's duchy was situated. Moreover, the duchesse d'Epernon was the subject born of Henri de Navarre, as well as his near relative; and her vast estates, as heiress of Foix Candale, were within his immediate jurisdiction in Béarn. Many of the early days of the duke, when a poor cadet of la Valette, had been spent at the court of Jeanne d'Albret as the companion of her son Henri. The duke's regard for *le Béarnnois*, therefore, had ever been strong, and to the utmost of his power Epernon maintained the interests of the king of Navarre throughout the stormy interval when the eventual succession of the latter to the crown of France seemed more than doubtful.

On the arrival of the duc d'Epernon at Angoulême after his flight from Chartres, the king of Navarre sent to offer his old companion his support to maintain himself against his foes. The negotiation continued, and was drawing to a satisfactory termination, when the life of Epernon was endangered by one of the most perfidious of conspiracies. The Leaguers had jealously watched the correspondence between the king of Navarre and Epernon; for they disbelieved that Henry III. loathed the society and principles of his former favourite as he averred. To remove the duke, who thus might become the medium of communication between the two Henrys, and perhaps the negotiator of a greater league to overthrow the usurped power of the third Henry, became the subject of their serious anxiety. No plan appeared to the subtle plotters better than to ground their conspiracy on the order signed by Henry, and forwarded by Villeroy; for the deductions resulting therefrom could easily be so perverted as to lodge the odium of the contemplated assassination on the unfortunate king. Thus, even if their blow missed, it was probable that indignation at the treachery of his royal master would produce a permanent alienation between the king and Epernon. Villeroy seems to have lent himself as the agent of the conspiracy; for he received deputies from the intended assassins, and forwarded the requisite instructions to the mayor of Angoulême and the officer, commandant of the royal troops in the town.

On the 10th of August, St. Lawrence's Day, as the duc d'Epernon had just quitted the bath, and was preparing to proceed to mass, a party of conspirators boldly entered the castle armed with pistols and cutlasses, and proceeded to the duke's cabinet, with the intent of accomplishing his assassination. The abbé d'Elbène and the sieur de Marivaux were conversing with the duke; in the ante-chamber of the apartment were several persons, including two of his secretaries and Sorlin surgeon to the king. The report of a pistol accidentally discharged by the mayor of Angoulême, who headed the assassins, all being partisans of the League, fortunately drew attention to the murderous intent of these ruffians. The duke was apprised of his danger by his chaplain, who rushed into the ante-chamber and conjured Epernon to escape. Instantly the brave band rallied round the duke, and succeeded in barricading the doors of an inner chamber, which served the duke as a dressing closet. The assassins passed through the apartments crying, "*Tue! Tue! rendez vous, monsieur!*" and at length entered the adjacent *garde-robe*. A conflict here ensued, during which Sorlin made his escape down to the kitchens, and, *faute de mieux*, marshalled the cooks with their spits to defend their master's life. The day being the Feast of St. Lawrence, the garrison and the majority of the household had gone to attend mass in the cathedral, no one in the castle having the most remote suspicion of a *soulèvement*. The tocsin, meanwhile, sounded in the town, and the inhabitants flew to arms, and rushed towards the castle to join in its assault. The courtyard was seized, and a petard applied to the massive door of the castle to blow it open, that assistance might be afforded to the mayor and his colleagues within. Epernon, who had been surprised at so untimely a moment, hastily dressed, then seizing his sword he presently sallied out upon his assailants, followed by d'Elbène and Marivaux. The fierce aspect of the duke so terrified the cowardly band, already daunted by the resistance it had encountered, that all its members took to their heels, and wildly fleeing for their lives, sought refuge in a small turret chamber at the end of one of the corridors, in which they barricaded themselves. Epernon followed, and was preparing to force the door, when a servant maid rushed past pursued by one of the insurgents with a naked sword, who called out to her master that Souchet, the brother of the captive mayor, and a band were making their way into the castle through a hole in the wall. The duke upon this repaired to the spot indicated, leaving a sufficient guard before the turret portal, and arrived just in time to arrest two persons who had forced their way through the aperture, and to block it effectually. The persons thus arrested were then shot. The people, nevertheless, closely invested the castle, blocking up every avenue, so that the besieged could procure neither provision nor water. Besides the gentlemen of his suite, the duke had only eight soldiers and food sufficient for twelve hours. The most furious assaults were made to batter down the wall, and to gain entrance into the castle. A continuous fire of arquebuses was aimed at the windows; flaming brands were thrown through into the chambers, while the duke was peremptorily ordered to surrender on the king's warrant, and to produce the persons of his prisoners of the turret; one of whom, at the risk of his life, had let himself down into the fosse, by tearing his vestments into strips, which he plaited together.

Meanwhile the duchesse d'Epernon, when the riot commenced, was hearing mass in the Dominican church. At the sound of the tocsin and the tumultuous yells of the populace, the congregation took flight. The duchess, attended by two equerries, also tried to make her way back to the citadel; she was seized, however, by the rioters, who, when her equerries drew their swords to defend their young mistress, barbarously shot them before her eyes. The duchess fainted at the sight, and was carried to a chamber over the Hôtel de Ville, and there strictly guarded. Méré, one of the leaders of the insurgents, presently entered the apartment, and roughly seizing the arm of the duchess threatened to stab her to the heart unless she promised to persuade her husband to surrender the castle. The heroic spirit of Catherine de Foix rallied to spurn the threat, and she declared "that the prospect of death did not appal her, for that she held the fame and honour of her gallant husband dearer than ten thousand lives!" Méré, unmoved by the youth and beauty of the duchess, then fiercely assured her that in case the people were compelled to attack the fortress with artillery, she should be placed in front of one of their gabions. The duchess replied, "that if they led her before the fortress, with her last breath she would implore and exhort her husband not to surrender to such *canaille*; nevertheless she hoped to survive, to make the sieur de Méré one day remember the insolence of his speech to a princess of her quality!"

The following day madame d'Epernon was honourably conducted back to her husband, as the news of the approach of the king of Navarre from the neighbouring town of St. Lazare, to rescue the duc d'Epernon, filled the city with panic; it was rumoured also that Tageus, commandant of the king's forces in the province, was hastening to the succour of the duke. In fact, the comte de la Rochefoucauld, at the head of a detachment of Huguenots, appeared before Angoulême at nightfall, prepared to attack the insurgents on the following morning. The leaders of the expedition, therefore, seeing themselves thus abandoned, requested the bishop of Angoulême to mediate between themselves and the duke; meantime the duchess was conducted to the citadel. As all the doors had been walled up, or otherwise barricaded, a ladder was brought, up which the duchess gallantly ascended, and made her entry into the castle through one of its windows. The surviving prisoners of the turret chamber were set at liberty, and the people gradually retired; thus leaving Epernon victorious over his enemies after a siege of thirty hours, during which the garrison had fasted. When hostilities terminated there remained, moreover, not another round of ammunition to distribute.[1]

The king quitted Chartres at the time he had named without manifesting displeasure or any feeling whatever at this enterprise against the duke; indeed, Villeroy, favoured by the queen-mother and flattered by the duc de Guise, began to indulge in halcyon expectations of the dignities which were to repay the services he was

[1] Conspiration de ceux d'Angoulême contre d'Espernon. Archives Curieuses, tome xii. Davila.

preparing to render at Blois. Henry took a cordial leave of his ministers, Cheverny, Bellièvre, and the secretaries of state Villeroy, Pinart, and Brulart, and gave them *congé* until the first day of October. Escorted by the duc de Guise and a suite of twenty gentlemen, Henry quitted Chartres, and after spending two nights on the road arrived at Blois. No sooner had the king entered the castle than he proceeded to execute a design which created the greatest consternation and alarm. Without taking counsel of the queen-mother or of the duc de Guise, Henry, the morning following his arrival, dismissed his ministers *en masse*, and signed, sealed, and despatched the *lettres de cachet*, which deprived them of their offices and exiled them from court, before he imparted his determination to any, excepting to his private secretary Benoise, who drew up and countersigned the mandates. The most unmitigable resentment actuated the mind of the king against these personages; he regarded them as venal, sold to obey the bidding of the queen-mother, and devoted to the will of Guise. To their counsels and feeble administration he attributed the late catastrophes. Moreover, Henry, being resolved to free himself by any means from his humiliating tutelage to the princes of Lorraine, had determined to raise to power men who should owe their offices to his favour, and who would obey, and neither suggest concessions nor scrutinize his motives. He desired ministers who would zealously serve the royal cause during the approaching parliament, and whose interest it was so to act; and not men—parties to the cabals in the state, and who each acknowledged an authority, residing in the person of queen Catherine or the duc de Guise, superior to that of their royal master. The king could not pardon Bellièvre for the manner in which he had obeyed his mandate to arrest the advance of the duc de Guise; and he jealously watched the *liaison* between the former and Villeroy: the latter the king abominated. The restless, intriguing secretary was accused by his sovereign of treason to the royal cause; nor was it surprising that such was his majesty's impression, for during his journey to Blois Henry had perused the "Instructions" promulgated by the archbishop of Lyons, in which Villeroy was plainly indicated as the stepping-stone which should raise Guise to the summit of power. The devotion of Villeroy to the queen-mother, likewise, was highly offensive to Henry. The two under-secretaries, Brulart and Pinart, were also dependents of Catherine and reported every incident, and in many cases solicited her majesty's consent before despatching mandates. In Henry's frame of mind, and meditating the emancipation which he did, such espionage would have been intolerable and utterly subversive of his designs.

Benoise in person carried the missives, which also forbade their return to court, to the deposed ministers. He first repaired to M. de Villeroy. The rage and consternation of the latter were excessive: he bitterly observed, "that it would have been more agreeable to him to have walked from office by the door, rather than to be thus unceremoniously ejected by the window!" Benoise then proceeded to the castle of Grignon, the abode of Bellièvre. This veteran diplomatist bore his reverse with great equanimity: after reading the mandate, he replied "that his majesty's commands should be obeyed, for that having spent a long life in exhorting others to submission, it would be indeed strange if he failed himself in setting the example of dutiful submission." Cheverny was met by Benoise on his road to Blois, his mansion being only six miles distant from the castle. The announcement fell like a thunder-clap on the chancellor, who deemed his office secured to him for life. His dismissal, he was aware, proceeded not from Catherine, his indulgent patroness, nor from the duc de Guise, who paid Cheverny homage in his double capacity, as a man wealthy and of illustrious rank, and an easy and convenient minister. The court with its pageantries was the scene in which the chancellor revelled, and to be banished therefrom seemed the most cruel of exiles. The king's mandate directed the ex-chancellor to give the great seal into the hands of Benoise. Cheverny, however, being unable to believe in the reality of his dismissal, determined to proceed to Blois and at least receive the fiat from the lips of the queen-mother, who had on that morning accomplished her last journey from Paris to Blois. He therefore requested the secretary to enter his coach, and together they proceeded to the castle. Cheverny modestly descended in the court-yard, and sent to ask admittance to the presence of the queen. He was instantly ushered into her majesty's cabinet, where he found Catherine suffering from a severe attack of gout and in bitter affliction at the resolves of her son. After a conference of two hours, the queen with great difficulty proceeded to seek the king to request him to admit Cheverny to audience. Henry steadily refused, and commanded that the ex-chancellor should leave the castle. Cheverny, therefore, retired in high displeasure to his castle of Eclimont, in the vicinity of Chartres, after resigning the great seal into the hands of the queen, who summoned Benoise to carry it to the king.[1] The secretaries Pinart and Brulart being persons comparatively insignificant, their *lettres de cachet* were transmitted by an ordinary cabinet messenger.

King Henry having thus avenged himself on his late ministers, commenced to nominate others who

[1] Mém. de Cheverny. De Thou. Davila.

should aid him in the perilous task of compassing the overthrow of the more dangerous interloper Guise, who had presumed to exalt himself as co-regent in the realm. The suddenness and vigour of the king's measures disconcerted the duke, and at first he ventured not to interfere; indeed, for a brief interval he believed that the king, to assure his future repose, had resolved to fill all the offices in the state with men professing the orthodox code of politics. The duke, therefore, presented himself before his majesty and demanded the seals for the archbishop of Lyons. Henry smiled sarcastically, but gave no reply. During the afternoon, however, he despatched a courier to Paris to summon Montholon, the attorney-general of the parliament of Paris, whom he had resolved to invest with the high dignity of chancellor—or, rather, with that of keeper of the great seal; for by the fundamental laws of the realm the chancellor of France could never be superseded except upon attainder. The choice made by his majesty was singular: he had no personal knowledge of Montholon, who possessed a high repute for virtue, though he had never mingled in politics, nor had he taken a prominent part in public affairs. Montholon was the son of the chancellor of Francis I., whom that monarch had also called unexpectedly to power on the attainder of the chancellor Poyet. When the new chancellor arrived, in obedience to the royal summons, Henry received him attended by M. de Bellegarde and by the captain of the formidable Quarante-cinq, Lognac. Pasquier[1] states that on entering the royal cabinet Montholon turned, and asked the usher in waiting which of the three cavaliers before him was the king! Despite his want of courtly *savoir*, Montholon took the oaths during the same afternoon, and received the great seal

[1] Pasquier, liv. xiii.

from the king's hands. The pale and studious countenance of Montholon, his simple and retiring manners, and austere speech, formed a great contrast to the demeanour of his opulent and magnificent predecessor. As a magistrate the new chancellor yielded in legal knowledge to none, and the rectitude and integrity of his decisions were universally respected; but he was incompetent to fulfil the varied duties of the high office of chancellor, and stood isolated and friendless in the midst of a court which, in virtue of his dignity, he ought to have ruled. In the room of Villeroy, Henry appointed Martin Ruzé de Beaulieu, in whose loyalty he had the fullest confidence, and who had served the king during his residence in Poland. The colleague of Beaulieu was Louis sieur de Revol. The king also wrote to propose office to Arnault d'Ossat, afterwards the famous cardinal of that name, but then a humble priest resident in Rome, and only known to the king by repute. D'Ossat, however, declined the honour, apprehending the perilous position of affairs, which, he alleged, required to be adjusted by men of age and large experience. Having thus vindicated his authority and installed his new ministers, had Henry possessed either fortitude or resolution all might still have prospered, and the tragedies which ensued have been averted by the unqualified submission of the malcontents, including the duc de Guise himself. But the energy of the king and his assertion of his sovereign dignity lasted only for a brief period: like a hurricane, his wrath had ever raged, annihilating with irresistible fury, to be succeeded, however, by apathy as profound. The king's resentments gnawed and inflamed him to action: his vengeance satiated, he relapsed, exhausted by the effort, into listless torpor, until fresh insult again stung him into retaliation. Meantime, in Henry's unsteady grasp France was perishing; devoured by her internecine feuds and anarchy, the once glorious realm was falling from her rank amid the nations of Europe.

By the beginning of the month of October numerous noble personages had arrived at Blois to be present at the opening of the States-general, and to partake in the approaching marriage festivities of the princess Christine of Lorraine with the grand duke of Tuscany. It was the last gathering of the court of France under a monarch of the house of Valois.

The court assembled; never had it been outwardly more brilliant even during the palmy days of Francis I. The princesses of the house of Guise mustered in an overwhelming majority. There was the consort of the duc de Guise, Catherine de Cleves, who beheld with wonder and amazement the state and power of her husband, "le nonpair du monde," as she called him, herself only eclipsed by the duchesse de Montpensier, who was acknowledged universally as the queen of the League. Madame de Montpensier wandered through the splendid saloons of the *château* in flippant mood, recklessly aiming her censures, and stinging by her satire. The duchess treated the king with unparalleled insolence and contempt, and never spoke of his majesty without appending the prefix of frère Henri, or le Moine Henri. The duchess d'Aumale was the third princess of Lorraine present at Blois, but unlike her relatives, Marie d'Elbœuf mourned and seemed to have lost that brilliant vivacity once so captivating to the king. The mother of the Guises, the duchesse de Nemours, was also present to partake in their triumph. The duchesses de Retz and d'Usez—to the latter of whom the king and Epernon had given the title of madame la Bossue, on account of a slight deformity of the shoulder—mesdemoiselles de Guise and de Mayenne were likewise present. Then there was madame de Noirmoutier,[1] lovely and frail as ever, whom the duc de Guise still served with devotion. There was also madame Duprat, the beautiful wife of Nantouillet, the ex-provost of Paris, whose domestic unhappiness had long afforded a choice subject of scandal for the court. Pale, subdued, and timid, queen Louise moved amongst these brilliant dames, repulsed by the levity of some, and awed by the assumptions of others. Catherine appeared splendidly appareled, broken in health, but moving with her accustomed majesty and inimitable tact; seldom wounding, dexterously gliding over prejudices, and greeted alike by royalist and leaguer with respectful deference. The duchesse de Nevers had promised to pay her *devoirs* to the queen, but upon one pretext or another she continued to delay her arrival, having never pardoned the outrage to which she had been subjected by the king. From this brilliant throng Marguerite de Valois, once the star and cynosure of the courtiers, was absent—forgotten almost as if the triumphs of her beauty, her intrigues, and her hostility to her brother the king, had never afforded subject for public comment. Her disgraceful flight from Agen to Carlat, and her subsequent capture by the marquis de Canillac, governor of Auvergne, had ceased to excite speculation. In the strong fort of Usson, therefore, Marguerite now sojourned, unmolested either by her brother or her husband.

"Le beau ivoire de son bras" had, however, speedily enabled Marguerite to make a captive of her captor, the marquis de Canillac; and soon within the rock-bound fortress of Usson in Auvergne, the abode for centuries of stern warriors, revelries were holden which surpassed even

[1] Madame de Sauve, who had espoused for her second husband the marquis de Noirmoutier, brother of the duc de la Tremouille.

the orgies of l'hôtel du Couture Ste. Catherine.[1] The widowed duchesse de Joyeuse, Marguerite de Lorraine, sister of the queen, also joined the august assemblage. Her tearful depression and disinclination to share in the festivities of the court, rendered the duchess a congenial companion to her sister the queen, and together these royal ladies prayed, wept, and took counsel on the ominous aspect of affairs. The duc and duchesse de Mercœur had been also invited to join the court; but the queen and her sister sent the duke a private admonition to refrain from sharing in the deliberations of the States, at least until the royal intentions should be more amply declared. To this timely notification from his sisters the duke owed his life; for Henry was now especially incensed at his presumption in attempting to establish the pretended claims of his consort Marie, heiress of Penthièvre, to the duchy of Bretagne. Amongst the noblemen inmates of the castle or town of Blois, were the comte de Soissons, the ducs de Guise, d'Aumale, Montpensier, and Nevers; the grand prior of France, illegitimate son of Charles IX.; the cardinals de Bourbon, Vendôme, and Guise; the prince de Joinville; the duc de Nemours; the maréchals de Retz and Aumont; Biron, and the newly-created lord keeper François de Montholon. There was also Amiot, bishop of Auxerre, the elegant classic, and learned translator of Plutarch, ex-tutor of the sons of Catherine de Medici. The old antagonism between the queen-mother and Amiot still rankled. Catherine hated and dreaded every man of genius who owed not his rise to her patronage. Amiot had been the *protégé* and friend of Marguerite d'Angoulême, queen of Navarre, and of her daughter Jeanne d'Albret. The liberal tendencies of Amiot, and a certain unbending rigidity of character,

[1] Brantôme: Vie de Marguerite de Valois. Bazin: Notice sur Marguerite de France. Sully.

greatly displeased the queen; added to which the prelate had unfortunately an irritability of temper, engendered by arduous study, which at times effectually kept both his friends and enemies at bay. Charles IX., however, ever demonstrated great regard for Amiot; and when the office of high almoner of France became vacant, he bestowed that dignity on his preceptor, an appointment certain to be followed by episcopal honours. The indignation of Catherine was extreme. She peremptorily summoned the new dignitary to her cabinet—that apartment within which so many momentous events were transacted, and that had so often rung to the stern menace of its owner. After some ironical compliments, the queen exclaimed, "Ah! M. Amiot, you dare then persist in offering defiance to my will! I have routed the Guises, the Châtillons, the constable, the chancellor, the king of Navarre, and Condé, and now I have you to deal with, little insignificant upstart! If you do not decamp hence within twenty-four hours, and resign your appointments, your life shall pay for your disobedience!" Amiot cowered under the terrible wrath of the queen, and promised the most unqualified submission. Accordingly on leaving her majesty's presence, he made preparation to quit Paris secretly, in order to retire to the monastery from whence the queen of Navarre had rescued him. After the lapse of a few days the king remarked the absence of his almoner, and soon divined the secret cause of his retreat. The rage of Charles IX. was not to be trifled with, and so fiercely did it foam forth that Catherine found herself compelled to recall the almoner. Accordingly a mandate from the queen no less peremptory than the first called Amiot forth from his retreat, to assume episcopal honours as bishop of Auxerre with the dignity of high almoner. From thenceforth the relations between Amiot and Catherine had been the reverse of cordial, and consequently he never possessed the favour of Henry III. Disgusted at the foibles and manners of the court, the acute mind of the bishop of Auxerre had eagerly adopted the code of the League, which represented, as he averred, the cause of order, liberty, and progress.

Nearly all these personages were lodged within the precincts of the royal castle. The cardinals de Bourbon and de Guise took up their abode in the hôtel d'Alluye, in the town of Blois; the former that he might escape the espionage of the queen-mother; the latter, who foresaw the certainty of his election as president of the States, that he might be unfettered in the discharge of that office.

The deputies began to arrive at Blois about the last week in September, 1588. For the ceremony of the opening session, and for a place of general assembly for the three orders, the great hall of the castle was prepared. The hall of the Dominican convent in Blois was chosen for the separate deliberations of the clergy; the Palais de Justice was assigned to the nobles; while the tiers état met in the Hôtel de Ville. As usual, a vexatious dispute relative to precedence inaugurated the deliberations, and which was not finally settled before the 16th day of the ensuing month of October, to which period the opening of the assembly had been postponed. From Paris the provost Chapelle Marteau, the sheriffs Roland and Compans, besides a troop of malcontent preachers and others, arrived, and presenting themselves before his majesty, met with a gracious reception. Henry, meanwhile, assumed a sedate and austere demeanour, and performed his religious devotions with scrupulous regularity. By his majesty's command a solemn fast of three days was proclaimed before the ceremony of the opening of the States, and each member received an injunction to partake of the holy communion. The king, with his courtiers and nobles, communicated in the church of St. Sauveur; while the deputies received the wafer from the cardinal de Bourbon in the church of the Dominicans. His majesty's proclamation was outwardly observed: nevertheless, the most scandalous cabals and compacts were formed, and projects of reform were discussed by the principal chieftains of the League without the slightest reference to the will and good pleasure of the sovereign. The cardinal de Bourbon privately conferred with the clergy, whom Henry tried to propitiate by acknowledging and openly greeting his venerable kinsman as first prince of the blood. The princes of Lorraine caballed to force forward the measures which should settle the question of the succession and exclude le Béarnnois, and in other matters give preponderance to the duc de Guise in the great national council, so that the king might apparently owe every concession to his salutary mediation. The friends of the king, on their side, canvassed the members and invited them to rally round the sacred person of the sovereign. The provost of Paris and his myrmidons intrigued to obtain the exact and literal performance of the Edict of Union, the abolition of the existing system of taxation, the deposition of the king, and the elevation of the Lorraine princes. The king's inexperienced ministers, with Montholon at their head, did nothing but prepare elaborate addresses, and initiate themselves for the conspicuous part they were to perform in the approaching pageants. The king himself, meanwhile, steadily maintained that the adherents of the League formed a very small minority of the States, and were not in any way to be apprehended.

The hall of the palace of Blois on the 16th day of October, 1588, presented a gorgeous spectacle. The members of the States assembled under such ominous circumstances, met at an early hour. There were present 134 ecclesiastical members, 180 nobles, and 192 deputies chosen from the tiers état. The clergy wore their sacerdotal robes, and the peers their mantles. At one end of the hall rose a magnificent *dais,* upon which stood a throne and footstool gorgeously decorated; on each side, one step lower, was a chair of state for the queens Catherine and Louise. On the right of the platform was a bench, covered with cloth of gold, for the cardinal de Vendôme, the comte de Soissons, and the duc de Montpensier: behind these royal personages a similar bench was placed for the occupation of the ducs de Nemours, de Nevers, and de Retz. On the left of the throne places were provided for the cardinals de Guise, de Lenoncourt, and de Gondy. The duc de Guise, as lord high steward, occupied a chair in front of the throne, sitting with his back to the king and facing the deputies. A little to the right of the duke sat the lord keeper Montholon. At the foot of the royal *dais,* which gradually sloped to the centre of the hall, stood a square table, at which sat the secretaries of state Beaulieu and Revol. A staircase led from an upper apartment in the castle down to the platform of state, and by this his majesty was to present himself to the assembly. When all was prepared the duc de Guise rose, and attended by the 200 gentlemen of the chamber armed with their battle-axes, quitted the assembly to escort thither the king. The deputies of the three orders rose and stood bareheaded as his majesty appeared. Henry was attended by a superb *cortége* of princes and nobles. He bowed graciously to the assembly and saluted gallantly the ladies of the court, who occupied a gallery opposite to the throne. The countenance of the king, however, was grave and anxious as he looked round on the faces of the men whose mission it was to decide and solve difficulties of such vital moment to his dynasty. Queen Catherine entered next, attended by a great suite of ladies; she bowed to the king as she passed the throne, and took her seat in the chair of state to the right. The reigning queen followed, accompanied by the duchesse de Joyeuse. Louise looked pale and sad; the hostile attitude of her kinsmen of Lorraine greatly embittered her position, for she sympathized not in their dangerous ambition. The king then rose and addressed the assemblage in a speech of great eloquence and plausibility. To have judged by the fluent majesty of his words and the nobleness of the sentiments he enunciated, Henry might have been the most valiant and best of princes. He commenced by vindicating his policy, conduct, and sovereign dignity. He avowed his resolve to die for the defence of the holy Roman orthodox faith, and declared in a figure of speech that he claimed no mausoleum more superb and honourable than one reared on the ruins of heresy. He deplored the prevalence of blasphemy, simony, and malversations. He gave his royal pledge to abolish the practice of granting donations of survivorships to offices of state. The king then launched forth an eloquent eulogium on the virtues and talents of the queen-mother, to whom, he said, he was indebted for his life, his throne, and whatever knowledge he possessed; and that it was owing to her majesty's advice that he had convoked the States. "Some of the greatest princes of my realm," said his majesty, "have entered into unlawful leagues and associations; but in the exercise of my accustomed clemency I desire to obliterate the memory of the past; and for this reason, and to relieve the natural fear which assails many of my loving subjects, that after my demise they may fall under the dominion of a heretic prince, I have caused this august assembly to be convoked to remedy this evil, and to restore order, justice, and submission to the laws throughout my kingdom." Henry then again solemnly accepted the Edict of Union; and, for its better confirmation, his majesty invited the members to present themselves on the following Tuesday, when all might again swear solemnly to observe the edict, and to witness its recognition and acceptance by himself as a fundamental law of the monarchy.[1] Henry pronounced this oration with great animation of manner and distinctness of speech. The lord keeper then rose and delivered an harangue, in which he entered into the details of the various topics touched upon by his majesty. The archbishop of Bourges replied on behalf of the clergy, the baron de Senecy for the nobility, and Chapelle Marteau for the tiers état. Their harangues were complimentary, assuring the king of their loyalty and devotion to his crown, and of their allegiance to the faith.

Thus the first session of the States passed smoothly enough. The royal protestations, however, and the eagerness with which the king had lauded an edict known to be odious to him, were interpreted by the deputies into an admission of weakness, and as a deprecation of their menaced hostility. The paragraph in the royal harangue beginning with the words, "some of the greatest princes of my realm," was deeply offensive to the duc de Guise and the chiefs of the League. It insinuated that they had been guilty of treason, which his majesty, in the plenitude of his benevolence, was pleased to overlook. It was the design of the duke that his enterprises, both present and to come, should be esteemed by his countrymen and by foreign potentates as patriotic, and the result of his great zeal for the welfare and repute of his sovereign. Henry's allusions, therefore, were calculated to dissipate this opinion, and to expose the princes of the League to the

[1] De Thou. Pasquier, liv. xiii. Cayet. Mathieu: Hist. de Henri III.

censure of Europe as traitors and rebels. As soon, therefore, as the session terminated, the duc de Guise repaired to the apartment of the cardinal de Bourbon, who had been prevented by indisposition from being present at the ceremonial, and related to him the mischievous tenor of the royal speech. They were presently joined by the archbishop of Lyons, and together the three departed for the abode of the cardinal de Guise. An anxious conference ensued, in which it was resolved that the passage in question should be erased from the royal speech before it was printed and dispersed over the realm. The difficulty of this undertaking was acknowledged not to be slight, considering the present humour of the king. The provost la Chapelle accompanied by several brawling preachers of Paris, next presented himself to confer on the same subject with the cardinal de Guise. They entered, exasperated to the last degree by the royal harangue, which they declared branded the clergy and municipality of Paris with the foul epithet of "traitors." It was, therefore, resolved that the duc de Guise should return to the castle, and commence proceedings by asking immediate audience of the queen-mother. "Monsieur, if you had believed me, who never do things by halves, we should not now be placed in this said serious predicament," exclaimed the cardinal de Guise to his brother. The queen, however, declined to interfere, and recommended the duke to offer a respectful remonstrance and a request to his majesty to modify his expressions through the lord-keeper Montholon. This counsel was rejected; and the following morning the archbishop of Lyons was deputed to wait upon the king, and insist on the emendations required. The duc de Guise and the members of the Seize present in Blois had, moreover, the temerity to issue a prohibition to his majesty's printer, forbidding him to dispose of any copies of the royal harangue. The archbishop entered the royal cabinet with the address in his hand. He then boldly demanded the erasure of certain passages which, he said, reflected grossly on the loyalty of his majesty's faithful servants; who, though they might be content to become in the presence of their colleagues the object of his majesty's sarcasm, yet they could not consent to allow such comments on their conduct to go forth throughout the realm. The king kept his eyes steadily fixed on the fire, and made no reply. The archbishop then recommenced his objurgations. The king then referred the princes to his ministers, adding, "that he had spoken as it became him to do; and that, if anything more was said on the subject, he should believe that treasonable violence was intended." The audacious prelate replied "that the king might think as he chose, but if the erasures demanded were not conceded by his majesty, the majority of deputies would quit Blois, including the princes of Guise and himself." Henry then waved his hand in token of dismissal, and the archbishop retired in furious indignation to report the contumacy of the king to his colleagues. Nothing further was transacted during the day; an ominous gloom overshadowed all; the contest had commenced in good earnest between the sovereign and the States, which Henry had hoped to lull into submission.

The following day, Tuesday, October 18th, the king again met the States, clad in his royal robes. The Edict of Union was then read aloud, and solemnly subscribed and sworn to by the king, his nobles, and prelates, and by the deputies of the people. Henry made an address declaratory of his resolve to maintain the edict, and commanded the assembly to repeat the oath after the archbishop of Bourges—the prelates folding their hands on their breasts, and the deputies raising their right hand towards heaven. This his majesty's behest was obeyed. The archbishop then addressed a pacific exhortation to the members; after which they proceeded in procession, headed by the king, to assist at a solemn Te Deum chanted in the church of St. Sauveur, which edifice was situated in the courtyard of the castle. Henry was afterwards escorted back to his own apartments by the deputies, who regaled him with loud shouts of Vive le roi.[1] The king took this opportunity to assure the turbulent provost Chapelle Marteau that he had forgotten the occurrences in Paris; and that, provided the Parisians remained faithful, he never intended to recall or avenge the enterprise of la Journée des Barricades. The same day Henry conferred the command of his army of Poitou on the duc de Nevers; and directed the secretary of state Beaulieu to draw up a special patent dispensing the duke from relinquishing his office to the duc de Guise, or being in any way in military subjection to the latter in his capacity of lieutenant-general of the armies of France. The king thus thought to secure, at least, the loyal and disinterested services of one general, and of one of the great divisions of his army; the design was politic, and eventually proved of vast importance to the royal cause. This act, however, was bitterly resented by the duc de Guise, who loudly protested against so manifest an infringement of the privileges of his office; but his discontent failed to move the resolve of the king. The natural cunning of Henry's disposition was sharpened by his perilous position. Fear effectually roused him from his sloth, and rendered him watchful, acute, and in a degree laborious.

Meantime the duc de Guise continued his clamorous

[1] Journal de Henri III. par l'Etoile. Cayet: Chronologie Novennaire.

agitation for the suppression of certain passages in the royal speech. At length Catherine proceeded cautiously to confer with her son on the subject, and made earnest representation, beseeching him to condescend to the demand of the princes of Lorraine. Henry's fury was excessive, when he heard of the prohibition they had issued to the printer to suspend the publication of the harangue. For long his majesty resisted, but after a period given to meditation Henry suddenly declared himself willing to sanction the erasures demanded. This unexpected mutation of will was viewed with the greatest suspicion by many; by others, including the duc de Guise, it was deemed but as the ordinary concession of a will essentially weak and unstable. The king, therefore, summoned the duc de Guise, his brother the cardinal, and the archbishop of Lyons, and in their presence he took a pen and drew it through the obnoxious passage without observation whatever. During the audience a fog, which had partially subsisted throughout the day, became so dense that a light was requisite. By the flickering rays of a single wax taper, hastily brought by the page in waiting, Henry signed the retractation, and dismissed his unwelcome guests, after having himself significantly handed the document to the duc de Guise.[1]

[1] Pièces et Extraits servant à l'Histoire depuis l'an 1550, jusqu'en 1594, en fol. Bibl. St. Magloire, iv.—Bibl. Imp. MS.

CHAPTER II.

1588.

Seizure of the marquisate of Saluzzo by the duke of Savoy—Political consequences—Intrigues of the duc de Guise—His treasonable enterprises—Proposal of the States to declare the king of Navarre deposed from his rank of heir-presumptive of France—Henry declines to sanction the edict—Factious deportment of the members—Their cabals, and submission to the authority of the duc de Guise—Catherine receives repeated warnings respecting the designs of Guise—She sends for the duc de Mayenne—His quarrel with the duc de Guise—Assassination of madame Duprat—Marriage festivities of Christine de Lorraine and the grand duke Ferdinand of Tuscany—Emeute amongst the pages in waiting—Departure from Blois of the duchesses de Guise and de Montpensier—The assembly decrees the reduction of the existing taxation—Distress and opposition of the king—His interviews with the archbishop of Lyons, and with M. Bernard, orator of the Tiers Etat—Henry is compelled to sanction the edict—He is present at a Te Deum sung in the church of St. Sauveur—The king resolves the arrest or assassination of the duc de Guise—His counsellors—The death of Guise is determined—Interviews of the duke with Henry III.—The duchesse d'Aumale—She warns Henry of his danger—Measures of the king—Death of the duc de Guise—Circumstances connected with that event—Arrest of the cardinal de Bourbon, and of the princes and princesses of Lorraine, inmates of the castle of Blois—Arrest of Chapelle Marteau, and of various deputies of the States—Interview between the king and his mother Catherine de Medici—Council of state—Assassination of the cardinal de Guise is resolved—Death of the cardinal—Subsequent measures adopted by Henry III.

The day following that upon which king Henry had suffered his oration from the throne to be revised and modelled at the dictation of the princes of Lorraine, the news arrived of the seizure of the marquisate of

Saluzzo by the duke of Savoy. This territory, the last that remained to France of her conquests beyond the Alps, had during the last ten years been a source of contention and the subject of endless negotiations. The duke of Savoy had recently married Doña Catalina, youngest daughter of Philip II. This alliance contracted, the duke, forgetful of the benefits which his ancestors had received from the crown of France, perfidiously adopted the policy of Spain, and espoused the party of the League. Accordingly after the barricades the duke caused overtures to be made to Guise, promising to co-operate in his designs, provided that on the contemplated accession of the house of Lorraine to supreme power, the territories of Provence, Dauphiny, and Saluzzo should be ceded to Savoy. The duke declined the proposal, adding "that the vintage must ripen before grapes could be gathered." The duke upon this rebuff ungenerously commanded his ambassador, the sieur des Alines, to reveal the designs of the princes of Guise to king Henry; and also earnestly to pray his majesty to cede to him the marquisate of Saluzzo, or to confer its government on the duc de Nemours or the marquis de St. Sorlin, the brother of the latter, as the only method of arresting the foul contagion of heresy from spreading over the frontiers of Provence into Italy. This proposal was highly displeasing to Henry, who returned one of his sarcastic refusals. Having succeeded no better in this second negotiation, the duke prepared to take forcible possession of the marquisate, protesting at the same time the purity of his intentions and his willingness to cede the government to a prince of the orthodox house of Nemours.

Through the intervention of the duc de Nemours, half brother of Guise, a second negotiation with the League was entered into by the duke of Savoy, when his projects were neither positively agreed to nor yet censured by the duc de Guise, who wished, before closing with the alliance, to test the disposition of the States. Meantime the duke of Savoy despatched the marquis de St. Sorlin[1] to take possession of the marquisate; a campaign which was easily achieved, military discipline being lax in the strongholds of Saluzzo as it was everywhere else throughout the realm. The news reached Blois on the second day of November. This usurpation greatly incensed the king, who rightly attributed it to the intrigues of the duke, especially as the invading army marched under the banner of his half brother St. Sorlin. His majesty, therefore, sent a message to the States, desiring them to vote men and money for the recovery of the territory usurped. A hope animated the king that this foreign campaign might divert the fury of faction from his realm; the delusion lasted, however, but a brief instant. The intelligence of the seizure of Saluzzo roused malignant animosity; angry and seditious debates ensued, inflamed by the suggestions of Guise, who dreaded nothing more than a foreign campaign. The deputies accused the king of collusion with the duke of Savoy, in order to put an end to the war waging against the king of Navarre, which his majesty had unwillingly undertaken. They insisted that no fresh war should be entered into until heresy had been extirpated from the realm. The king

[1] Anne d'Este, duchesse de Guise and de Nemours, had two sons, the duc de Nemours and the marquis de St. Sorlin, by her second alliance. The duc de Nemours, her husband, died in 1585. Henry, marquis de St. Sorlin, became duc de Nemours on the demise of his elder brother, in 1595. He married Anne de Lorraine, only daughter and heiress of the duc d'Aumale. Claude Amedée, duc de Nemours, 1651, married Elizabeth de Vendôme, by whom he had two daughters, coheiresses, Maria queen of Portugal consort of Alphonso VI. and of Peter II. kings of Portugal, and Jeanne, who married Charles Emmanuel, duke of Savoy.

in vain remonstrated, and represented the infamy of allowing so flagrant a usurpation to remain unpunished. The more Henry entreated, the greater was the obduracy shown by the clergy and the members of the Tiers Etat, who were all devoted to the princes of the League. The nobles, meantime, inspirited by the pleadings and eloquent orations of d'Angennes, sieur de Maintenon, at length boldly avowed their resolve to support the king in his quarrel against Savoy with their estates and their swords. They petitioned the king to declare war against the duke of Savoy, despite the opposition of the commons, and promised to support that step, as they were in honour bound, as the special privilege of their order. The town of Blois resounded with angry clamour, "Shall the king for the recovery of a petty Italian territory, which he has consented to lose, delude us so that the great objects of the Union may be frustrated, and the Béarnnois be able finally to domineer over us?" asked the partisans of the League. A division disastrous to the cause of the Union seemed about to occur in the States; yet the ministers of the king gazed around in helpless vacuity. Unfitted by their previous avocation for the eminence of their present position, they retreated, deafened by the clamour, and disconcerted by the sharp ordeal which awaited them when in the presence of the representatives of the people. They prevaricated when they ought to have firmly maintained the royal prerogative. At this juncture the duc de Guise presented himself to enact again his favourite *rôle* of mediator, and to arbitrate for the settlement of the difficulties which he himself had provoked—all which tended to exalt and render conspicuous the power he possessed. Accordingly he caused a message to be conveyed to the king to the effect, "That this turmoil would never have happened had his majesty deigned, in the first instance, to consult him.

That he witnessed with grief his majesty's alienation; and that although he had reason to be aggrieved that the king had not condescended to ask his services, nevertheless he would work for the accomplishment of the royal desire relative to the declaration of war against Savoy." The duke, accordingly, privately sent the cardinal de Guise to admonish the clergy that it would be prudent no longer to oppose the will of the king in the affair of Saluzzo, but he prayed them to unite outwardly with the nobles in assuring his majesty of their loyal co-operation: he added, that their assent would be a mere form, for he had resolved that the war against le Béarnnois and his heretics should precede every other campaign; but that it was necessary to make the concession, otherwise many of the chief nobles would forsake the cause of the League. The same message was conveyed to Chapelle Marteau, and communicated to the Tiers Etat. At the same time the duke secretly imparted his message to the ambassadors of Spain and Savoy, and requested them to assure their respective cabinets that no foreign war would in reality be entered upon. The effect of the duke's communication to the States acted with instantaneous effect; the war against the duke of Savoy was presently unanimously voted, and a deputation, headed by the archbishop of Bourges, obtained an audience of his majesty to communicate the resolution.[1] This tardy concession had the effect of still more exasperating the king, who was well aware of the proceedings of Guise. The seizure of Saluzzo, Henry regarded as the first overt attempt on the part of the duke to despoil him of his crown. He beheld also with indignation the influence possessed by the duke over the national assembly; and the last lingering hope which, through

[1] De Thou, liv. xciii.

all his humiliations, had animated the mind of the king, that by the aid of the States he might wrest from his presumptuous subject the power he had usurped, vanished. The king was daily advertised of the secret councils holden in the hôtel Alluye, where the chiefs of the League and the partisans of the Seize met to discuss, propose, and decide on the measures to be brought before the assembly. The treasonable nature of the intimations made by the duke to the ambassadors of foreign powers was communicated to the king by the English ambassador, at the express command of queen Elizabeth. In his very presence Henry heard his audacious competitor addressed by the title of "Notre Grand!" as the duke moved loftily amongst the crowd of courtiers, feeling more truly a king than the royal master whom he oppressed and insulted.. Several intercepted letters, written by members of the States, gave the duke the same lofty appellation.

On the 4th day of November the deputies of the clergy framed a resolution in which they declared the king of Navarre "excommunicate, accursed, and incapable of succeeding to the crown of France." The king was desired to confiscate his duchies, marquisates, and lordships; to dismiss him from the government of Guyenne, and to banish him from the realm. It was further resolved that the king should be petitioned to proclaim this the degradation of Henri de Bourbon, *soi-disant* king of Navarre, in the full assembly of the States with solemn formalities, and to be pleased to notify the same to the ambassadors of foreign powers resident at the court of France.[1] The resolution was sent the same day for the assent of the nobles and Tiers Ftat, who ratified it by majorities without discussion. The States then elected twelve members from

[1] Recueil des Pièces Originales concernant la Tenue des Etats-Généraux, 1588, tome iv. p. 179.

each order to carry the resolution to the king, and to ask for the formal assent and ratification of the sovereign. The archbishop d'Embrun was appointed chief of the deputation—a prelate devoted to the house of Lorraine, bigoted and turbulent.[1] Henry listened patiently to the harangue pronounced by the prelate, and replied by observing that the act of the States was invalid and illegal, inasmuch as the assembly had not previously fulfilled the indispensable formality of summoning the king of Navarre to return into the bosom of the church; and that he could not, therefore, now give the assent demanded from him. The archbishop replied, "Sire, the prince is a withered and accursed branch, excommunicate, and not in any fashion to be recognised by your faithful subjects." Henry, nevertheless, persisted in his refusal, and commanded the archbishop to return to the assembly and report his reply. The assembly thereupon, after taking counsel with Guise, met the following day, when the royal objection was overruled by an immense majority. The archbishop then returned to inform the king "that the States had deliberated, but that the members declined to act upon his majesty's suggestion, whom they urgently prayed to ratify their decree." Henry dissimulated his dissatisfaction, and again observed that in a judicial act of such great importance every formality ought to be observed. "If your consciences are so tender that you fear to communicate with an outcast from the fold of the church, seek absolution and dispensation from monseigneur le legat here in our court. Nevertheless, do not think that I wish the said Henri de Bourbon to be cited hither, that means may be contrived to render him capable of aspiring to my crown. If God continues to withhold from me the blessing of off-

1 "L'archevêque d'Embrun (Guillaume Avanson) homme livré bassement au duc de Guise," says M. de Thou.

spring of my own, I will take good heed that no prince having even the taint of apostasy shall succeed me!" "Sire," responded the archbishop, "the States do not deem it expedient to address summons whatever to this said Henri de Bourbon Vendôme." "We will then take early counsel on the petition of the States-general," abruptly replied Henry.[1] The deputation of members then retired, highly discontented with the reply of the king. Henry, however, who perceived that the degradation of the king of Navarre would speedily place the duc de Guise in the position of heir-presumptive, resolutely refused to sanction the decree of the assembly, and addressed some sharp taunts to Guise on the subject. The cabals which from thenceforth raged within the palace and the town of Blois disconcerted even the queen-mother, inured as Catherine had been throughout a long life to the violent demonstrations of faction. Sorrowful were the queen's reminiscences; while her future loomed dreary and menacing. She beheld at length the designs of the duc de Guise revealed in their true aim and proportions; and she awoke from the delusion that one of the chief designs of the holy League was to wrest from the heretic king of Navarre his lawful heritage of the crown to bestow it upon her grandson. Her health was failing, her political influence gone with the king her son, her power over the duc de Guise diminishing as he found himself nearer to the attainment of his ambitious aspirations. The insolent and disrespectful deportment of the princesses of Guise was also a source of serious disquietude to Catherine. It was true that in her presence their demeanour seldom transgressed the rules of courtly etiquette; but the language of the duchesse de Montpensier, as reported to the queen, was treasonable

[1] Journal de Bernard aux Etats de Blois, 1588. Précis Verbal du Tiers Etat.

and disaffected; while her treatment of queen Louise had deeply wounded the dignity and the feelings of the latter. Madame de Montpensier carried a pair of golden scissors pendent from a *chatelaine* at her girdle, which she often displayed before the court, observing, "that she carried those scissors to give the king the *tonsure* when he had abdicated; as he was unworthy to wear the crown, and would speedily be made to cede it to a prince able and valiant, capable of defending the realm from the poison of heresy. As for the king, he was ruining everything by his dissimulation and villanous cowardice!"

The position of the duc de Guise, meanwhile, was precarious almost as that of his royal master. His success and apparent triumph had greatly alienated the princes of his house. The duc d'Aumale from his government of Picardy frequently warned the queen of the dangerous designs of his cousin on the crown; and the duchess had in vain implored the king to grant her a secret audience. But the memory of the past had now little influence over the king. He had ceased to view madame d'Aumale as the sprightly and fascinating beauty at whose feet he would once willingly have laid his crown; and Henry now regarding her as a princess the consort of one of his most rebellious subjects, steadily refused to grant her prayer. The duc de Mayenne also wrote to the queen-mother deprecating the treasonable designs of his brother; and declaring that though a partisan of the holy League he remained his majesty's faithful subject, and would become the mortal enemy of any man who presumed to lay his hand on the crown. Queen Catherine during the month of November sent for the duc de Mayenne, hoping probably that his counsels and disapprobation might check the enterprises of his brother. The duke obeyed her majesty's summons. A quarrel, however, immediately arose between the brothers relative to madame de Noirmoutier, both having unfortunately mistaken the hour of their appointment and met in the apartment of that lady. Hot words ensued, swords were drawn, and a hostile meeting arranged. The brothers met at dawn on the open plot of ground at the end of the great avenue of the castle. The duc de Mayenne, however, then refused to combat, not presuming, as he said, to assail the life of his elder brother and chief. An outward reconciliation ensued; but the duc de Mayenne immediately departed, still more alienated from his brother, and disposed to oppose his projects. Catherine herself solemnly warned the duc de Guise to beware of exasperating the king, whose present mood she acknowledged herself unable to fathom; and she advised him to retire to Joinville. The princess Christine of Lorraine also sent for the duke her kinsman, and emphatically adjured him to desist from treasonable cabals,[1] and to put an end to the private conferences at the hôtel of the cardinal de Guise. She, moreover, expressed her conviction that, unless the duke made such concessions and reconciled himself to his royal master, a catastrophe fatal to his life or liberty must ensue. "*Madame,*" replied the duke, sharply, "*on n'oserait !*" The States, meanwhile, at the suggestion of the duc de Guise, passed a resolution and carried it to the king for confirmation, to the effect that the measures agreed upon in the full assembly of the States should be sanctioned without delay by his majesty, and be at once acted upon as part of the law of the land. The custom was, that after a measure had

[1] Le duc n'oubliait rien pour fortifier son parti; il prenoit la défense de ceux qui lui étoient attachés, gagnoit les autres par les caresses, se rendoit affable à chaque particulier, promettoit des emplois, des dignités, des charges, des gouvernements aux plus intéressés, comme s'il eut été déjà le maître; mettoit enfin tout en usage pour s'attirer l'amitié de tout le monde"—Vie de Jacques Auguste de Thou, tome i.

been proposed, and sanctioned by the States-general, it was submitted for revision to the council of state, so that by this formality its promulgation could be indefinitely postponed. After the dissolution of the States of Blois in 1577, the Code Henri thus went through the ordeal of a tedious probation, and had been at last published only to appease the clamour of the people for reform. The duc de Guise foresaw that the clause of attainder against the king of Navarre would remain a dead letter, even if the royal sanction were eventually extorted, if this privilege of revision still remained to the king. Henry, descrying the duke's intent, positively declined to sanction any innovations on the ordinary method of issuing edicts.

During these enterprises the duke remained his majesty's guest, and daily presented himself to serve the king at his evening repast in his capacity of grand master. His equipage was magnificent, and the pages and gentlemen of M. de Guise fairly rivalled in number those of the king. His demeanour was condescending and affable: he made splendid gifts to the ladies of the court, especially to madame de Noirmoutier, and sought by every means to propitiate the favour of the queen-mother.

The grand festival of the court at this period was esteemed to be the approaching marriage of the princess Christine with Ferdinand, grand duke of Tuscany —its heroine another princess of Lorraine, as Henry bitterly observed. The most splendid preparations were made for this ceremony—the last courtly revel of the Valois. Never was wedding, however, celebrated under more gloomy auspices, whether as regarded the circumstances under which it was contracted or the bridegroom chosen. The old castle of Louis XII. echoed the turmoil of contention; the stealthy step of the assassin glided through its noble corridors; the wail of faction resounded where in days of yore all had been peace and loyal veneration. The court of Louis XII. and of Francis I., so brilliant and chivalrous, was extinct; but a dark and dreary abyss separated as yet the men of the old dynasty from the new one about to be inaugurated over France.

Neither was the history of Christine's royal bridegroom encouraging. Ferdinand, grand duke of Tuscany, a priest and cardinal, had just received dispensation from his vows, with permission to marry from the Holy See. He had been appointed to succeed to the ducal throne by his brother Francis, duke of Tuscany, who died suddenly, October 9th, 1587, without leaving legitimate male heirs. Francis had first espoused Jeanne, archduchess of Austria;[1] and, secondly, the celebrated Bianca Capello, the adopted daughter of the Venetian Senate, whom, nevertheless, he had entertained as his mistress during the life of his imperial consort. The duchess Blanche died five hours after her consort, assailed by mysterious symptoms and convulsions; and the universal supposition was that both the duke and his consort expired from poison administered, if not directly by the cardinal Ferdinand, at least with his connivance. No sooner, therefore, had Ferdinand ascended the Tuscan throne than he despatched Nicholas Tornabuoni, bishop of Santo Sepulchro, on an ambassage to Rome, to solicit dispensation from his ecclesiastical vows. At the same time he addressed his kinswoman queen Catherine, praying that the hand of her granddaughter Christine might be given him. Both these missions were attended with a fortunate result; and the grand duke, therefore, had accredited Horace Rucellai to Blois to deliver letters procuratory into the hands of queen Catherine; also, a

[1] Daughter of the emperor Ferdinand I., and of Anne heiress of Hungary.

private missive praying her majesty to select whom she would as a proxy to espouse the princess in his name. Catherine, therefore, fixed upon the youthful prince Charles d'Angoulême, grand prior of France,[1] to represent the duke of Tuscany in the approaching ceremonial, which, in homage to the Medici, was to be solemnized with the utmost splendour.

On the eve of the nuptials of the young princess, however, a terrible crime spread dismay throughout the royal castle, and shed a deeper gloom over its inmates. Madame Duprat,[2] the wife of the provost Duprat, sieur de Nantouillet—whose alliance the king, when duc d'Anjou, had tried to procure for mademoiselle de Châteauneuf—was a pretty, frivolous woman, of luxurious habits, and whose profuse expenditure had made itself felt even on the well-filled coffers of the wealthy financier. The extravagance of his wife had first disturbed the domestic felicity of the provost. Her husband's remonstrances madame Duprat retaliated by a levity of demeanour highly reprehensible. Her beauty and simpering manner brought to her feet a crowd of admirers; she was well received by the queen at the Louvre, and had contrived to ingratiate herself with the queen-mother, who gave her the appointment of lady of the bedchamber. Soon the provost's obdurate wife became one of the most influential ladies of the capital, while her aggrieved husband, who was considerably her senior, retired to his castle of Nantouillet apparently resigned to his fate and her neglect. Nantouillet, however, had two nephews—men ferocious and outlawed for their numerous crimes. One of these

[1] Son of Charles IX. and Marie Touchet, born April 23, 1573, in the castle of Le Fayet, in Dauphiny. He espoused Charlotte de Montmorency, comtesse d'Alais, eldest daughter of the constable Henri and Antoinette de la Marck.

[2] Anne de Barbançon, daughter of François seigneur de Cany.

nephews, the baron de Viteaux, stabbed the marquis du Guast at the bidding of Marguerite de Valois. The second had committed a notable theft on the coffers of his uncle the provost. To propitiate the latter these relatives feigned to espouse his quarrel against his wife, and undertook to avenge Nantouillet for her infidelity. It has never been ascertained whether the provost was cognizant of their bloody purpose. A few days before the ceremony of the marriage of Christine de Lorraine, madame Duprat, between the hours of five and six in the afternoon, was attiring herself for the queen's evening reception, attended by two women, who were combing her hair before the fire in her apartment, when the door was suddenly forced open, and three assassins rushed upon the unfortunate lady and stabbed her in the throat. With a cry of agony madame Duprat fell, and immediately expired in the arms of her women. The palace guard was called out and the most rigorous search instituted; but no traces could be discovered of the assassins, who had entered the palace unseen, and escaped thence undetected. The provost Duprat, when apprized of the catastrophe, exhibited the greatest grief, and vehemently denied all knowledge of or participation in the crime. No subsequent investigations elucidated the mystery; though the general belief implicated Nantouillet as the chief instigator of this foul assassination.

The marriage of mademoiselle de Lorraine quickly followed this tragical event. The ceremony was performed on Sunday, the 28th day of November, in the chapel of the palace at vesper hour. The king gave away the bride; and the ceremony was graced by the presence of the two queens, the duc de Guise, and by that of all the noble and illustrious personages assembled at Blois. Henry celebrated the event by a grand banquet in the evening, after which there was a comedy and ballet. The castle was illuminated, also all the principal edifices of Blois, and salutes of cannon were fired at intervals. The following day Henry gave a second sumptuous banquet to the foreign ambassadors resident in France. During the evening a serious *émeute* occurred amongst the pages and gentlemen in waiting on the royal guests. The pages, to the number of several hundreds, had assembled, as was the custom, in the court of the castle and on the grand staircase which conducted to the state apartments. As a diversion they presently divided into bands, part declaring themselves Royalists, and the others Guisards. The pastime went smoothly enough for a time; at length their ardour becoming inflamed, they began to dispute in good earnest. From words they came to blows, and a sanguinary fight ensued, the uproar of which reached the town. The gates of the castle were closed, and a messenger despatched to ask instructions from his majesty. The duc de Guise was with the queen-mother when Catherine received information of the fray. According to some relations of the event, the duke smiled and continued his discourse, and refused to interfere when requested to do so by her majesty, lest it should be reported that he had attempted the king's life. Madame de Montpensier, meantime, entered the cabinet and entreated her brother with her usual vivacity of expression to escape for his life; for the tumult, she said, had evidently been concerted to compass his destruction. The duke, however, refused to leave the presence of the queen, though he fixed his eyes searchingly on her majesty's countenance. Another account states that, on hearing of the tumult, the duke fled to his chamber and barricaded the door with coffers, being resolved to sell his life dearly. Meantime madame de Montpensier despatched a secret emissary to notify their supposed danger to the cardinal de Guise. The town, however, was already in commotion, and troops of people besieged the gates of the château, eager to rescue their champion. Others armed themselves to defend the king, whose life they supposed, on the contrary, to be assailed. During this interval, however, Crillon, captain of the guards, having vainly waited for directions, took upon himself to quell the tumult with his regiment, which good office he speedily performed. The gates of the castle were then thrown open, and the people entered to survey the prostrate and, in many instances, lifeless bodies of the combatants, who had fought with desperate fury.[1] It was ascertained that the pages of the cardinal de Bourbon had commenced the fray by attacking the pages of the duc de Guise. "Truly the pages of M. de Bourbon show more wit than their master," exclaimed the king, when informed of this circumstance; "they know how to defend the house which shelters them, while M. le cardinal aids to pull it about his ears!"

After the conclusion of the nuptial festivities of the grand-duchess Christine, the duchesse de Guise quitted Blois and proceeded to Paris for her accouchement. She was accompanied by madame de Montpensier, whose violent conduct had greatly offended queen Catherine. Many of the great nobles also, foreseeing the disasters at hand, took leave of their sovereign, and retiring to their respective castles, waited the event. The most intense resentment agitated Henry, and projects of vengeance occupied his mind to the exclusion almost of any other affairs. The last drop, however, which caused the already brimming cup of wrath to overflow had yet to gather. Thus far no definite concession had been obtained from the king likely to pro-

[1] Cayet. De Thou, liv. xciii. Davila.

mote the designs harboured by Guise. Henry had, however, guaranteed by every sacred solemnity the Edict of Union—to obtain the promulgation of which had been the ostensible cause of the rising previous to the treaty of Nemours, and of the subsequent revolt of Paris. So far the League had prevailed. The king, however, showed a manifest unwillingness to proceed against the king of Navarre. He had rejected the proposal made to render at once valid as law any resolution passed by a majority of the three orders. He had also privately, yet firmly, expressed his royal wish that the much-mooted question of the reception of the canons of Trent should not be discussed, as it was his intention to retain intact the Concordat of Francis I. It was evident, therefore, that Henry still felt himself a king. Despite the bitter humiliation which he had endured, he dared still to assert his authority, and was far as ever from becoming the puppet of the prince who had brought shame on his royal dignity. Deeper degradation and embarrassment, therefore, the duc de Guise and his followers perceived would be requisite before Frère Henri would resign himself meekly to the tutelage of his oppressors—before he could be induced to acknowledge the favour and protection of Guise to be his palladium. The tenor of the Edict of Union bound the king to continue the war against the heretics; but in order to fulfil this condition money was needful to support the vast cost of three armies in the field. The duc de Guise, therefore, resolved to attack the king through the medium of finance—to raise a clamour for the war, and yet, at the same time, to withhold the funds requisite for its prosecution; and even more, under pretext of the king's past prodigalities, to diminish the rate of the taxes levied by his predecessors. By this ungenerous device the duke hoped to bring his sovereign to his feet. Voluntarily the duke perceived that Henry would never sanction or confer upon him that pre-eminent position at court, which the archbishop of Lyons, in his "Instructions," had pointed out as the only path leading to the throne. The enthusiasm of the people, his power over the national assembly, and the apparent listless inaction of the king had lately roused dangerous and ambitious aspirings in the breast of Guise. What if the king, wearied of the harassing contest, and panting to return to his sloth, his luxury, and his pleasures, should be driven to a voluntary abdication! The old cardinal, whom the duke termed to his intimates *un véritable boutefeu*, would offer but a feeble obstacle to his designs. Moreover, the duke was becoming weary of the *rôle* of a popular hero; he shrunk from the coarse familiarity of his plebeian partisans, and shuddered when compelled to grasp the dingy hands extended to him in token of fellowship and good-will.

Accordingly, on the 2nd day of December, the States decreed that as the people ought to be relieved from the excessive taxations of the late years, the sum of 2,066,000 crowns should be immediately deducted from the existing imposts. The measure was proposed in each of the three chambers by notorious partisans of the princes. During the discussion, which lasted two days, Henry in vain tried to divert the storm. The proposal threw the king into alternate paroxysms of fury and despair. His private domain was mortgaged, his debts were immense, war was clamoured for, and instead of granting fresh subsidies, it was proposed to diminish the existing taxation! The unhappy monarch descried the snare in which it was sought to envelope him. As usual, he first cowered beneath the blow, to rise, however, when driven to extremity, and take savage vengeance on the traitors who thus sought to betray him. On the 3rd day of December, 1588, the king sent for Bernard, orator of the tiers état, the archbishop of Lyons, and the president de Neuilly. He then addressed to them a pathetic remonstrance most unworthy of his royal dignity. His majesty said "that it was his intention to reform his household, so that if the States-general deemed two capons to be a too prodigal supply for his table, he would be content with one. That he experienced great regret for his past prodigalities; but that to propose to reduce the taxes to the standard of the imposts of the year 1576 would be the ruin of his kingdom and dynasty. That the expense of the war against the heretics which he had engaged to make must be considered; for without funds no military enterprises could be undertaken. That he would risk his life in the prosecution of this holy war. "May God so requite me if I fail! The money, when voted, may remain in the hands of certain able burgesses whom we will name. In this I know well that I am acting contrary to the advice of my council, who tell me that my realm will become democratic like that of the duke of Venice. But, nevertheless, I will do it." Henry continued his piteous wail in these words: "I have no intention, messieurs, to give profusely as heretofore. Assure the States of this. I have not now a single sou; and it is a scandal and a shame for my ministers to tolerate such a state of things. I swear on my salvation that since the month of May last I have not given 4,000 francs." The archbishop of Lyons made his majesty a few soothing speeches; the president de Neuilly, who had always tears at his command, blubbered like a child; while the able and sententious Bernard mentally took note of the interview to transcribe it entire in his admirable journal of the "States of Blois."[1] Notwithstanding Henry's deprecation, the

[1] Journal de Bernard aux Etats de Blois, tome v. p. 120—Recueil du Sieur Barrois—Mathieu: Hist. de Henri III.

measure passed with scarcely a dissentient voice, so entire was the sway of the princes of Guise over the assembly, and hostile the feeling towards the king and his ministers. Every expostulation made by the chancellor Montholon was derided; and, strong in their unanimity, the States deputed the archbishop of Bourges to carry the bill to his majesty and demand his assent to the measure. Henry positively refused his sanction, unmoved by the specious address of the prelate, who, however, could not refrain from commiserating the position of his royal master. Three times during the same day, nevertheless, did the archbishop return to wait upon the king, by command of the assembly, to insist on the measure. At length, weary and browbeaten, the king, by the advice of his mother, affixed his signature to the document so pertinaciously demanded. The following day a Te Deum was chanted in the church of St. Sauveur, which the king was solicited to attend. Severely now were Henry's crimes and errors visited upon him; the complete degradation of the royal majesty would not have been deemed perfect had the king been spared the fierce and seditious harangue, prepared for the occasion by one Brisson, a prebend of the cathedral of Senlis. To the face of the king this demagogue poured forth the most foul insults; he assailed the personages employed about the person of his sovereign; "Those wretched harpies! those thieves! those accursed counsellors, let them be banished with contumely!" The preacher next descended to coarse jests, and to indecent allusions respecting various high personages of the realm absent from Blois. A laugh, imperfectly suppressed, convulsed the assemblage. Henry sat beneath his canopy of state, his head bowed in his hands; at the conclusion he rose, and with that majesty of demeanour which under the most trying circumstances never forspok him, he quitted the church, followed by the deputies, who attended him to the castle, uttering mocking, though vehement shouts of Vive le roy.[1]

From thenceforth the fate of Guise was decided; a vindictive craving for the blood of that most audacious of traitors racked the mind of the king. It had been forgotten that the weak, prodigal, faithless, and effeminate king, *l'homme-femme,* as his subjects, the deputies of Blois, loved to term their sovereign, was also the prince who had planned the massacre of the Protestants, the murder of Coligny, and who, throughout his reign, had been the perfidious slayer of the reputations of all who had ventured to thwart his designs. The security and boldness manifested by the duc de Guise cannot be explained, aware as was the duke of his recent narrow escape from assassination in the chamber of queen Louise. He disregarded the countless intimations which reached him from all quarters, and the urgent prayer of his consort and sister, that he would retire betimes from Blois, leaving there the cardinal de Guise. "The liberty of M. de Damville saved the life of his brother, the maréchal de Montmorency," significantly observed madame de Montpensier. Confident in the success of his intrigues, the duke precipitated himself beneath the dagger of the assassin; intoxicated by his power, and relying on the cowardice and indolence of his sovereign, the conduct of the duke presents a singular mixture of courage, audacity, and imprudence. A great revolutionary leader would have projected able measures for the safety of himself and his adherents; a mere demagogue would not have ventured on the perilous enterprises concerted by Guise; but the duke, neither a great nor yet an insignificant agitator, and being but partially supported by his own order, fell the instant that his sovereign gave the signal for his overthrow.

[1] Journal de Bernard. De Thou, liv. xciii.

During the afternoon of the 5th of December, the archbishop of Lyons again presented himself in the royal closet with an insolent message from Chapelle Marteau and the tiers état, to the effect that, as his majesty appeared so greatly in need of supplies for his private treasury, the provost was ready to propose to the chambers a vote of 120,000 crowns. "The tiers état," says Bernard, "rejoiced at seeing the king come to the 'wallet and the bowl,' decided to oblige him by the offer of 120,000 crowns." Espinac was also commissioned to admonish the king to dismiss his favourites, M. d'O, the two brothers de Rambouillet, his chief physician Miron, Ornano, the maréchal d'Aumont, and M. de Lognac, captain of the Quarante-cinq, and other persons of minor note. He also intimated that the States were about to petition his majesty to dismiss the Quarante-cinq, as guards obnoxious to the people and of no public utility, as his majesty still retained his regiments of *gardes du corps.*

The royal answer to these intimations is not on record, if it be not indeed contained in the first act performed by the king after the departure of the archbishop. Henry then summoned the obnoxious personages mentioned above, and mockingly commanded them all instantly to proceed to the apartment of the duc de Guise, and ask his pardon if they had been unfortunate enough to offend him; and afterwards to solicit his permission to retain their offices in the household. The duc de Guise actually had the presumption to believe that his sovereign was in earnest in authorizing this humble ambassage, and gravely gave his absolution, with the assurance, "that if the conduct of the officers in question agreed with their protestations, that they should experience no further molestation."[1]

Meantime the duchesse d'Aumale continued perseveringly to demand audience from the king, and employed Ornano as a mediator: Henry, blindly persisting in his resentment, declared that whatever the duchess had to communicate might be transmitted through the queen-mother, or by the lips of Ornano. An extraordinary scene was then witnessed in the saloon of queen Louise. The duchess d'Aumale one morning entered attired in mourning robes, and throwing herself on her knees in the middle of the chamber, soon appeared to be absorbed in prayer. Several ladies, after contemplating the spectacle in mute surprise, approached madame d'Aumale, and inquired why she made choice of such a locality to recite her orisons? The duchess raised her tearful eyes, and replied, "Mesdames, I have great and momentous things to confide to the king, and I am praying for the succour of Heaven, so that the heart of his majesty may be softened to admit me to his presence!" The same day the duchess saw the king privately in the oratory of queen Louise. She informed his majesty "that the designs of the duc de Guise had become pernicious, and that the king, if he wished to preserve his crown, must take precautionary measures. That the States to a man would support the duke, and that they designed to proclaim him constable of France; but she prayed his majesty to believe that the duc d'Aumale, and the other princes of his house, would aid the king in any measures for the defence and safety of his crown and person."[1] During the same afternoon the king had a severe personal altercation with the duc de Guise respecting the town of Orléans, a place in those days esteemed only second in importance to Paris. The king wished to create M. d'Entragues governor of Orléans. This appointment had been made in consequence of a private understanding between Entragues

[1] De Thou, liv. cxiii.

and the king, the former of whom, in consideration of receiving this office, vacant by the dismissal of the chancellor Cheverny, pledged himself to adhere to the interests of the king, to forsake utterly his old colleagues of the Union, and to renounce his friendship for the duc de Guise. When the royal intent was communicated to the duc de Guise, he maintained that Orléans, being one of the places which his majesty had engaged to cede to the League by the recent Edict of Union, the appointment to the important office of governor was vested solely in himself and his colleagues. The king warmly denied ever having relinquished so important a city, and asserted that the duke had mistaken the town of Dourlens for that of Orléans, the former of which he acknowledged to have given to the League. The duke still asserting to the contrary, the king in great wrath sent a gentleman to summon the queen-mother, who had negotiated the treaty, that her testimony might confute that of the duke. Catherine was carried in a chair to the royal cabinet, but when the question was put by the king, she answered evasively, "that her memory failed her; but that she was of advice that the ex-secretaries of state Villeroy and Pinart should be summoned, who might previously consult their minutes of the various conferences." The king, nevertheless, still persisting in his determination to confer the appointment on Entragues, the duke forgot himself so far as to rise in a rage, saying, "that of a truth the king had ceded the town of Orléans, and that he knew well how to preserve it!" At vespers, the king, who had always his eye on the duke, observed that, instead of joining in the service, the latter was attentively perusing a small pamphlet. "Mon cousin, you are always so very devout," said the king, sarcastically, on quitting the chapel. "Excuse me, sire," responded the duke, "I have been reading a pamphlet composed by a Huguenot on the condition of France. Believe me, he is a pleasant babbler. I counsel you to read it yourself, sire!" The king coldly declined. The book was a virulent libel on the person and government of the king; but Henry understood, and parried what the courtiers termed *"l'agréable malice de M. de Guise."*[1] "The king at this time," says the royal physician Miron, in his relation of these events, "pretended to be greatly absorbed by his devotional exercises, especially as he perceived that M. de Guise was lulled into security thereby. He therefore, about this time, commanded that a number of small cells should be constructed over his apartment, for the accommodation of certain Capuchin friars, much in his majesty's confidence; and for some days he seemed so indifferent and absorbed, that outwardly his majesty appeared to have lost even animation and feeling."

Advices, meanwhile, came from the duc d'Epernon, admonishing his royal master to be on his guard, as it was reported that a notable conspiracy had been concocted in Blois against his life and person. The same warning was again forwarded by the duc de Mayenne. At the same time the maréchal d'Aumont, whose wife was the aunt of the duchesse d'Elbœuf, revealed to the king the overtures which had been lately made to him by the duc de Guise, who, as the price of the marshal's co-operation, had offered to procure for him the government of Normandy by compelling the duc de Montpensier to resign that lucrative post. In test of the sincerity of his proposal, the marshal stated that the duke had bared his arm to perforate a vein, that he might sign the engagement with his blood. "The duc de Guise, sire, skilful as was his sophistry, did not, as you perceive, succeed in seducing me from my alle-

1 Cayet: Chronologie Novennaire. De Thou, liv. xciii.

giance; nevertheless such offers are likely to dazzle and mislead our young nobles. Already, sire, is every effort thus made by the duke and his partisans, who employ flattery, promises, and menaces to accomplish their purpose."[1]

What "this purpose" absolutely was, it is difficult to decide, amidst the immense mass of documents, manuscript and printed, relating to this stormy period. Most of these records vary in their statements relative to the projects then agitating the mind of Guise, though they all unanimously agree in ascribing to him treasonable and even regicidal designs. The duke had not found it so easy as he expected to compass the attainder of the king of Navarre, despite the papal excommunication, and the zealous support of the orders of the clergy and the tiers état. The destruction of the Spanish Armada had crippled the resources of Philip II., and infused new life and fresh vigour into the counsels of the king of Navarre. In La Rochelle, by the provident care and friendship of queen Elizabeth, arms, provisions, and money were amassing for the support of the Protestant cause. The heroes of Coutras had gathered round their valiant chieftain. Montmorency, the first Christian baron of France, uniting his banner to that of Bourbon, reigned over the fair south with despotic sway. The Angoumois was holden by Epernon; Dauphiny by Lesdiguières; the Lyonnais by the duc de Nemours, whose fidelity Guise mistrusted. A triumph over this formidable opposition must be the reward of several successful military campaigns; for until the king of Navarre was disarmed and his territory confiscated, any fiat of the States against him virtually remained in abeyance. But, meantime, while Guise was securing his future succession to the throne, the king might escape from vassal-

[1] De Thou, who gives at length the address of the maréchal d'Aumont.

age. Taking these adverse circumstances into consideration, the duc de Guise perceived that at the present time, if ever, his designs upon the throne must be matured. If the king could be terrified or cajoled into making voluntary abdication, the duke might now assume the sceptre with the assent of the national assembly, and consolidate his power during the lifetime of king Henry. A perilous interregnum would thus be avoided. The States-general appeared willing to abet his usurpation; Paris troubled, and perhaps fearful, stretched forth her arms to the hero of the barricades; the queen-mother Catherine enfeebled, and already stricken by the hand of death, could oppose but an ineffectual opposition. Already it had been secretly agreed in the councils of l'hôtel d'Alluye, that the assembly should declare its session indissoluble, if the slightest disposition were perceived on the part of the king to dissolve or even to prorogue the States.

In the cabinet of king Henry also ominous debates pended, their issue being decisive of the death or arrest of the traitor whose hand was lifted to grasp the diadem. That vengeance, from the Day of the Barricades, had Henry steadily pursued; he thirsted for the perdition of him who had humiliated his dignity and despoiled life of that which, to the king, was sweetest. It does not appear that Henry fully opened his schemes to the queen-mother. Nevertheless, Catherine knew that some great blow was meditated; neither was she so taken by surprise at the subsequent catastrophe as has been generally believed. "Monsieur, mon fils, you must hasten your measures; you will ruin all by delay; but I pray you, take good heed to establish such good order that you are not again deceived as you were at the barricades of Paris," was the mysterious counsel which Catherine gave to her son at a conference between them at this period. Neither did Henry confide in his ministers; he was aware of their incompetence, and had expressly chosen them that no controlling voice but his own might be heard in the cabinet.

About the 19th day of December Henry summoned the maréchal d'Aumont, Nicholas d'Angennes sieur de Rambouillet, and Antoine de Brechanteau sieur de Beauvais-Nangis to a nocturnal conference. He then ably laid before these noblemen the position of affairs, avowed that he had resolved to execute summary vengeance on Guise or to effect his arrest, and requested that they would each one give him their counsel on the matter. The king recapitulated the humiliating insults which he had received since the opening of the States; and he declared that the deputies, as a first step, were about to confer upon Guise the dignity of Captain General of France. "I shudder with horror and amaze," exclaimed his majesty, "when I also represent to myself what must be the condition of France, when aliens presume to dispute for this the first crown in the world with its legitimate heir!" The noblemen listened with respectful commiseration, and demanded a day to consider the important question proposed. Henry assented, and desired them to meet at the same place and hour on the morrow, his majesty adding, "that he should greatly prefer, if possible, to proceed against the duke by the ordinary channels of justice." The following day the marshal and his colleagues repaired to the royal cabinet, accompanied by Louis de Rambouillet sieur de Maintenon, whom his majesty had instructed d'Aumont to initiate. The marshal spoke first, and advised the king to arrest the duc de Guise and all the princes of his house, and bring them to trial before the parliament of Paris. "It is impossible! no judge would be bold enough to condemn them! The people of Paris would rise and rescue them!" exclaimed the king. The royal assertion was not to be gainsaid; for to such a lamentable condition had Henry's past misrule and profligacy reduced him. His army was under the command of princes of the house of Lorraine; the judges of his criminal courts had been nominated by them; the capital, with its municipality, was at their devotion; the Bastille, Vincennes, and other important forts, were in the hands of their partisans; the States-general, that august court of appeal and arbitration between the sovereign and his people, had forgotten its functions, and a mob of turbulent democrats presided in an assembly which was adorned only a few years previously by the eloquence of a Montluc, and guided by the virtuous moderation of de l'Hopital. It was too true the king had no redress but one against the treason of his powerful competitor, and that one resource Henry shrunk from proposing. The armies of the king of Navarre and Montmorency, reinforced perhaps by the stalwart soldiers of the English queen, could alone have restored the royal supremacy, and have enabled the king legally to bring to condign punishment those who had conspired against his person and dignity. His ancient detestation of the Huguenots, his fear of Spanish vengeance and invasion, and the shades of the massacred of St. Bartholomew's Day, stood between the king and his reconciliation with Henri de Navarre. The two brothers de Rambouillet and the sieur de Beauvais-Nangis, however, presently broke the spell by counselling their royal master to rid himself summarily of so factious a subject, whose treason was manifest in the eyes of all men. Henry needed but a word to confirm him in the decision he had previously formed—to take the life of the duke. It was, therefore, decided that the fiat should be executed at the first convenient opportunity, and the persons of the cardinal de Bourbon, the prince de Joinville, the cardinal de Guise, the duc de

Nemours, the duc d'Elbœuf, and the archbishop of Lyons secured.[1]

The difficulty, however, lay in devising the opportunity. The duke never approached the royal apartment unattended by a great suite of gentlemen. The king's closet was entered through a large apartment in which Henry dined in public, and which was also occasionally used as a council chamber. When this saloon was empty the noblemen visiting the king were suffered there to leave their attendants; but on the days when a council sat, those having the privilege of *entrée* were obliged to dismiss their suite at the foot of the staircase leading to the hall of council from the courtyard of the castle. The duke had boasted of the impossibility of any successful attempt being made on his person when accompanied by his gentlemen; it was, therefore, resolved that the design should be executed during the session of a council, to which the duc de Guise was to be summoned by the king, when he would be thus compelled to dispense with the attendance of his suite. The duke, who had long excused himself from being present at the councils of his sovereign, was not aware, it is said, of the arrangement relative to the saloon.

On Wednesday, the 22nd, the duc de Guise after vespers accompanied the king in his evening promenade on the terrace of the castle. Henry, probably with the intent of eliciting for the last time the

[1] De Thou, liv. xciii. Davila. Mathieu. Two writers, Davila and Papon, Hist. de Provence, assert that Henry proposed to Louis de Berton de Crillon to assassinate the duc de Guise. The brave de Crillon declined with indignation *cette office de bourreau*, and warmly rebuked his sovereign for the proposal. The account further states that Henry replied, "C'est assez ; je vous connois, et vous pardonne un refus que je ne dois qu'à votre scrupuleuse délicatesse!" Crillon offered to challenge the duke, and kill him in legal combat. The story, however, is little probable.

true designs of Guise, commenced to discourse on various political subjects. His majesty expressed his grave displeasure that, notwithstanding his prohibition, the matter of the recognition of the council of Trent had been mooted in the national assembly. He also desired the duke to effect the withdrawal of a proposition about to be introduced before the assembly by the cardinal de Guise, to deprive the maréchal de Matignon of his command in Guyenne. The king also spoke at length on the informality and injustice of the decree rendered against the king of Navarre. The duke cut the king short on all these matters, and refused to reply. He then said that he availed himself of this opportunity to speak to his majesty in private; for, perceiving that affairs were daily growing more desperate, and the king's alienation more visible, despite his promises and engagements, he had taken the resolution to resign his office of lieutenant-general, and to supplicate his majesty to permit him to retire to Joinville. "No, no!" ironically exclaimed the king. "Think, I beseech you, monseigneur, twice before you do this. A night will inspire you with greater wisdom." "Sire," replied Guise, "I have resolved, and do resign my offices, with the exception of those of grand-master and governor of Champagne, the which I pray your majesty to confirm afterwards to my son." "He only made this resignation," said the king, angrily, on re-entering his apartment, "because the States have resolved, despite my will and sanction, to proclaim him constable. I am aware of his devices!" The king then refused to accept the duke's offered resignation, and put an end to the conference by returning to the palace, confirmed more than ever in his sanguinary resolves.

On the return of the duc de Guise to his apartments, he found on his table several anonymous billets containing emphatic warnings. One enclosed the words,

"Be on your guard; a dangerous attempt is about to be made on your life." The duke took a pencil, wrote the words "*On n'oserait*" beneath the lines, and contemptuously tossed the note under the table.[1] Nevertheless, he rose the following morning depressed and uneasy, and quitted the palace early to hold conference with the Seize in the apartments of the cardinal de Guise. There the duke met MM. de Lyons and de Guise, Chapelle Marteau, Maineville, and the president de Neuilly. He related his interview with the king, the royal anger, and the subsequent warnings he had received; and for the first time the duke seemed inclined to adopt the prudent counsel so often given him and retire to Orléans. His colleagues, however, now vehemently dissuaded him. "*Monsieur, monsieur; qui quitte la partie la perd,*" said the archbishop of Lyons. "We are strongest—let us disarm the tyrant!" exclaimed Chapelle Marteau. The president shed copious tears, and tried to console and encourage his companions. "The king is a fool, a tyrant, and mad; and we treat him as if we feared him!" shouted M. de Maineville. It was resolved, therefore, that for the present the duke should remain at Blois.

At dinner the duke found another slip of paper concealed under his plate. "*Ce ne seroit jamais fait si je voulois m'arrester à tous ces avis. Il n'oserait!*" again repeated he. About nine o'clock in the evening Guise repaired to the apartment of madame de Noirmoutier.[2] Before his departure, Jenne, his surgeon, saw no less than five epistles delivered to the duke, all containing advices to hold himself prepared for a sudden enter-

[1] Cayet: Chronologie Novennaire. Etienne Pasquier, liv. vi., lettre 13. Journal de Henri III., année 1588.

[2] Madame de Sauve took for her second husband François, marquis de Noirmoutier, a cadet of the princely house of la Tremouille. She died in Paris in the year 1617, aged sixty-six.

prise against his person on the part of the king. His good genius in the shape of these mysterious notifications even pursued the duke to the apartment of his mistress. He thrust them, however, under the pillow of the couch, exclaiming "*Dormons!*" and refused to take any precautionary measures.

The king, whom no man throughout his dominions could match in dissimulation, passed the day with his accustomed tranquil indifference. During the morning his majesty issued a programme for the devout celebration of Christmas week. He also announced that it was his intention to proceed on the afternoon of the following day to Notre Dame des Noyers, a small house in the park of Blois, and there celebrate in retirement the approaching festival. In the afternoon Henry presided at his council, and despatched a number of mandates in order, as he said, that his devotional exercises during the ensuing week might not be interrupted. There were two important affairs pending before the council; one was the case of la Motte Serrant, a notable brigand and murderer in the province of Anjou, who waylaid Huguenot travellers, and either killed them or carried them to his castle, where they were detained in captivity until they paid a large ransom. The process of this criminal had been commenced in the courts of Angers, when la Motte petitioned that letters of evocation might be granted him, transferring his case from the Angevine courts to the council of state—a prayer supported by the duc de Guise. The second cause was a petition from the town of Langres against the oppression of the bishop. The people of Langres, who were devoted royalists, fearing that their town might fall into the hands of the League, demolished a fortified wall of communication between the episcopal palace and the fortifications of the town, suspecting that the bishop intended to betray the place to the duc de Guise. The bishop immediately addressed a petition to the privy council, praying that the townspeople might be condemned to rebuild this wall at their cost, the demolition of which he furiously resented. This demand had been also laid before the council by the duc de Guise in person. Henry, therefore, announced that it was his will to expedite both these mandates before his departure. He therefore commanded the clerk of the council, M. de Marle, to send summonses to the duc de Guise, the cardinal his brother, and the archbishop of Lyons, to repair to the council chamber by seven o'clock the following morning, as he intended to leave the castle before the hour of eight. At nine o'clock in the evening—the hour at which Guise repaired to the apartment of madame de Noirmoutier—the king sent for Larchant, captain of the Scotch guards, and without explaining his design, commanded that by seven in the morning the men of the regiment should be drawn up in the courtyard of the castle, in order to petition the duc de Guise as he passed to the council that the arrears of their pay might be granted. After the duke should have passed into the castle, Larchant received a command to guard the door, and upon no pretext to allow any person to enter or to depart. The king also directed that a guard of twenty men should be posted at the entrance opening into the Galerie des Cerfs, which communicated with the wing of the castle forming the royal residence. His majesty then casually observed that he wished to perform an act of royal favour towards the poor soldiers of his guard at this holy season, and knew no one at whose intercession he would more willingly grant such than that of *son cousin de Guise.* In the hearing of Larchant the king sent directions to M. de Liancourt, his equerry, to have his coach ready at the portal opening from the Galerie des Cerfs at eight o'clock precisely. In the apartment, in attendance on the king, were the maréchal d'Aumont, the two brothers de Rambouillet, M. d'O, Ornano, Lognac, captain of the Quarante-cinq, and M. de Bellegarde. These gentlemen received his majesty's commands to present themselves in his cabinet at six o'clock the following morning, and to bring with them the two secretaries of state Beaulieu and Revol. Lognac and his band of Gascons were directed to attend at five o'clock, in order, as his majesty said in the presence of several of the body, to escort him to Notre Dame des Noyers. Henry then significantly dismissed these personages without uttering a word relative to the tragedy which his preparations were to inaugurate, though all were in the secret; but his majesty admonished them, on taking leave for the night, "to be good men and true." The king then retired to his private cabinet with M. de Bellegarde, chief gentleman of the chamber, and who upon this night alone disrobed his majesty. The king remained until midnight in conversation with Bellegarde, who then lighted him to the door of the queen's apartment. "Good night, my son," said his majesty; "desire du Halde to awake me at four o'clock, and be ready yourself at that hour!"[1]

The apartments of the queen-mother were beneath those of her son; for Catherine's infirmity from gout and corpulence was now so great that she was compelled to occupy a chamber on the ground floor of the castle. On this eventful night her majesty retired early, being greatly indisposed from the painful swelling of her feet and from impeded respiration. It is agreed by all narrators of these events that Catherine was not

[1] Rélation de la Mort de Messieurs les Duc et Cardinal de Guise, par le Sieur Miron, Médecin du Henri III., 1588. Discours de ce que est arrivé à Blois jusques au Mort du Duc et du Cardinal de Guise. Satyre Ménipée reimprimé parmi les Pièces Justificatives, 1726.

aware of the precise nature of the enterprise which her son had resolved to execute; neither did she know the place in which it was to be consummated. One of Henry's especial injunctions to his confederates was above all to tread softly, lest the unusual noise might arouse the queen his mother, who would then interpose to save the life of the duke.

Obedient to the order he had received, du Halde, first valet-de-chambre, rose at four o'clock, and proceeded to knock at the door of their majesties' apartment. Madame de Piolant, a waiting-woman to queen Louise, answered by inquiring who the intruder was at that untimely hour? "It is du Halde. Tell the king that it is four o'clock." "His majesty sleeps, and the queen also; I cannot disturb them," answered madame de Piolant. "Rouse the king, or I will knock so loud that it shall awake their majesties on the instant," was the peremptory reply. "Piolant," exclaimed the king, in a feeble voice, from the inner chamber, "what is it?" "Sire, it is M. du Halde, who says that it is four o'clock." "Ah! hand me my slippers, my dressing-gown, and my taper."[1] So saying, the king rose, and refusing to reply to the questions addressed to him by the queen, entered his cabinet, where Bellegarde waited: first, however, his majesty desiring du Halde to follow, conducted him to one of the little chambers over his apartment, destined, as it was said, for the reception of Capuchin monks, and, bidding him enter, locked the door. Du Halde afterwards declared he had never felt so troubled in his life, not knowing what this treatment presaged.

It was nearly five o'clock before the king was attired. The gentlemen of Lognac's band began then to arrive by a back staircase, as they had been commanded, all

[1] Rélation de la Mort de Messieurs le Duc et Cardinal de Guise—par le Sieur Miron.

in ignorance of the deed required of them. As they entered singly the king appeared, and desiring each man to follow him, conducted him with stealthy step to a large cell adjacent to that in which du Halde was confined, and carefully locked the door. Thus Henry speedily had the greater part of his band of trusty Gascons under lock and key; and so safely stowed as to insure their silence, and to excite no suspicion at the number of persons assembled at so early an hour in his chamber. By the time that this was accomplished the lords, whom the king had on the previous evening invited, were assembled. Henry, therefore, entered his cabinet, which was lighted by wax tapers. The faces of all were pale, and wore an anxious and constrained expression; the king alone seemed easy, and even cheerful, though his movements indicated restlessness and a certain degree of agitation, which he resolutely tried to repress. Without the rain poured in torrents; and it was about as cold and dismal a morning as ever dawned during the month of December. Henry then made a short harangue to the nobles present, in which he recapitulated the treasonable enterprises of Guise, and his consequent resolve to take his life during that very morning. "This said duke has driven me to extremity by his enterprises on my crown and on my life, and it has come to this strait that either I must die or he. Will you not unanimously aid your king to defend his life and realm?" All the nobles present unanimously declared that the king had spoken well, and offered him their lives and their swords.[1] The king then proceeded to the chamber in which he had locked up the gentlemen of his body-guard. To them also he made a moving oration, describing all that he had suffered from the duc de Guise, and especially dwelling on the fact that their disband-

[1] De Thou, liv. xciii.

ment and dispersion had been proposed to the States by the duke. "This day, mes braves," said his majesty, "is destined to be the last of my life or of that of the said duc de Guise; it is for you to decide whether he shall perish or your king and master become his victim. I am, as you have long perceived, a prisoner in my own castle; a hardy stroke can alone deliver me from my shameful fetters, and it is from your valour alone that I can escape my enemies. Will you not then promise to serve me, and to avenge my wrongs by depriving this said traitor of life?" A shout of assent responded to the appeal.[1] The king, placing his finger on his lip to enjoin silence, for fear, as he observed, of awaking the queen-mother, then said, "Well! which of you have poniards?" Eight of these weapons only being produced, the king said that poniards and pistols should be supplied to those who had come unarmed. Henry then led his Gascons forth from the chamber, and himself assigned to each his task in the approaching tragedy. Twelve of his assassins he posted in the outer cabinet looking on the courtyard of the castle, which he intended to be the scene of the murder, and in which stood the king's bed. Lognac here took the command armed with a rapier, and ranged his men close to the velvet *portière* by which the cabinet was entered from the ante-chamber, opening into the hall where the council sat. Eight Gascon gentlemen were led by the king and stationed in this ante-chamber, and the rest he placed at intervals along la Galerie des Cerfs, which communicated with the royal closet,[2] and at the end of which there was a door opening into the courtyard. Henry then returned to his private cabinet, and eagerly waited for the news of the arrival of each privy councillor

[1] "Cap de Dion, sire! ion lou vous rendis mort!" replied they, in Gascon dialect.

[2] Rélation de Miron.

as the hour of assembly approached. The most terrible agitation then seized the king; his face became pallid, and he walked rapidly about the room, every now and then raising the tapestry screen which divided the chamber from the one without, exhorting the men to remember the power and valour of M. de Guise, and "to take heed not to allow themselves to be wounded." "*J'en serois marry!*" said the king, whose language had become almost drivelling in his terror and suspense. Loguac, however, sat with folded arms opposite to the door on a coffer, stern and composed; while his twelve Gascons showed on their side no sign of being likely to subject themselves to the casualty which the king affected to apprehend.

Meanwhile, the cardinal de Guise and the archbishop of Lyons received the royal summons, and immediately rose and repaired to the council-chamber at the hour specified. They found there assembled the maréchals d'Aumont and de Retz, M. d'O, the cardinal de Gondi, M. de Rambouillet, and the cardinal de Vendôme. The duc de Guise quitted the chamber of madame de Noirmoutier at three o'clock in the morning, and retired to bed in his own apartments. It afterwards appeared that he had come to the decision of quitting Blois the same day, and so announced his resolve to madame de Noirmoutier. On entering his chamber the duke was surprised to find there his uncle the duc d'Elbœuf, who had crept furtively in the dark from his apartment to warn his nephew of the sinister rumours current. Again the duke, being fatally confident, derided the supposition that the king dared to attempt aught against his life, "which," he said, "would involve his realm in rebellion and perdition from north to south." The duke then slept with a slumber so profound that his gentlemen refused to arouse him until nearly eight o'clock, despite the royal missive, which had been duly received. Guise, when informed that the king desired his presence, rose in haste, and arraying himself in a doublet of gray satin, and throwing his cloak over his arm, he sallied from his apartment. The sight of Larchant and the guard, drawn up in the great court in weather so inclement, seemed for a moment to arouse the duke's suspicion. "Why are you here, my friends?" asked he; "it has never been the custom to mount a guard on days when the council meets." "Monseigneur," replied Larchant, boldly, "we are here to petition that you will cause the arrears of our pay to be distributed. We are reduced to such extremity that we must ere long sell our horses." The duke gravely promised his interposition, and suspecting nothing, passed into the castle. Every outlet and avenue was then seized, according to Henry's command. A brief inspiration of prudence induced the duke to turn from the narrow passage and staircase to the right leading to the council-chamber, and enter the ante-room of Catherine's apartments. There he found the lords of Lanssac and de l'Aubespine, but on being informed that the queen was sleeping, the duke, after leaving his commendations for her majesty, proceeded on his way. The passage and staircase were then immediately occupied—Rouvré and Espinette, lieutenants of the guard, and Hamilton, ensign of the Scotch archers, taking their stand with drawn swords at the door of the council-chamber.

When the duc de Guise entered the chamber, the lords present were dispersed about conversing; there being no sign of the formalities usual on such occasions. The archbishop of Lyons, whose suspicion was strongly roused, approached the duke, and asked, "Where the king was going on such an inclement day?" "He is going into retreat, as usual," replied Guise, indifferently.[1] Presently it was observed that the duke

[1] Information des Massacres commis à Blois. Histoire des Cardinaux—

turned pale, a qualm came over him, and he complained of cold and sickness. At his desire a fire was kindled; he then felt in his pocket for a handkerchief, as the eye injured by the arquebuse shot at Château Thierry began to give him pain. The duke finding that he had forgotten his handkerchief, requested Hotman, clerk of the treasury, to go to the door and see if any of his people waited without. The king's *valet-de-chambre* St. Prix, apprized by d'Aumont of the duke's request, promptly presented a handkerchief from the royal wardrobe. The uneasy sensation and sickness of which the duke complained still continuing, he opened his *bonbonnière*, but finding it empty, asked the sieur de Morfontaine to request St. Prix to send him some dried sweetmeats, such as Damascus raisins or conserve of roses. The latter sent a paper full of prunes de Brignoles, one of which the duke ate, and the rest he put in his silver *bonbonnière*. His nose then began to bleed profusely, and he rose and approached the fire; but the duke spoke jestingly of his indisposition, which he attributed to the inclemency of the weather, and because in his haste he had quitted his chamber without breaking his fast.

The alarm, meantime, had been given to the servants and adherents of the duke in the castle; and but for the wily precautions taken by Henry the enterprise must have failed. Hotman had communicated the duke's command to an usher named Guéroult, who in his turn then advertised the duke's private secretary Pericard of his master's request for a handkerchief. Pericard promptly obtained one, and was proceeding to the council-chamber, when he was stopped by armed sentinels. Apprehending therefore that his master was in peril of his

Aubery, tome v. Information faite par MM. Michon et Courtin. Déposition de Messire Pierre Espinac, Archevêque et Comte de Lyons, Primat des Gaules—signé par ce Prélat.

life, Pericard rushed across the quadrangle, and entering the chamber of the duchesse de Nemours, called out that her son's life was in jeopardy, and entreated her to rise and proceed to the apartment of the queen-mother. Scarcely had the words left his lips when twelve Swiss soldiers and an officer came up, and unceremoniously turning the active secretary into the court, placed the duchess in arrest in her apartment. Pericard then went himself to the chamber of the queen-mother; he found that no person might have access to her majesty, and that the outer room was filled with officers and guards.[1]

The king, meanwhile, sent a command that prayers might be offered up by his chaplain in ordinary, Dourgain, for the success of his design in an oratory close to his chamber. All being now prepared for the act which he had resolved, Henry commanded Revol to summon the duc de Guise. "Revol, go and ask M. de Guise to come and speak to me in the old cabinet of audience!" The secretary obeyed, but came back to inform the king that the sieur de Nambre, one of the Quarante-cinq, refused him permission to pass through into the ante-chamber. "Revol! mon Dieu qu'avez vous! how pale you look! Rub your cheeks, Revol; rub your cheeks; you will spoil everything!" exclaimed the king. Henry then lifted the tapestry portal, and desired M. de Nambre to allow the secretary to pass.

The nobles in the council chamber sat round the table listening, while Petremol, superintendent of finance, read aloud from a paper. Revol approached the duke, and said in a low voice, that the king asked for him. The duke rose, and taking his handkerchief and comfit-case in one hand, and holding his cloak in the other,

[1] Rélation et Déposition de Jean Pericard, Conseiller et Secrétaire de Finance, et Secrétaire de feu M. de Guise. Hist. des Cardinaux. De Thou. Rélation de Miron.

he bowed graciously to the cardinal de Vendôme, and passed into the ante-room, the door of which was closed after him by Nambre. The duke affably saluted the occupants of the room, and approaching the tapestry *portière* he raised it, to pass into the small apartment called the old cabinet of audience. In doing so he turned to survey these persons, whose sullen mien seemed suddenly to strike him with apprehension. On observing this momentary hesitation, the Gascon Montferry, thinking that Guise was about to draw his sword, suddenly rushed forward and struck his poniard into the duke's breast, exclaiming, "Traitor! thus shalt thou die!" The sieur des Effrenats then seized the duke round the legs to drag him to the ground, while St. Malines dealt him another mortal wound from behind in the throat. Lognac then struck the unfortunate prince a blow in the groin. So sudden had been the attack that the duke only feebly uttered, "*Ah mes amis! O quelle trahison! Miséricorde!*" before a flow of blood from the mouth rendered him speechless; yet such was his great strength, that though embarrassed by his cloak and having his limbs fettered by the ruthless grasp of his assassins, the duke dragged them across the apartment. Lognac seeing him advance with outstretched arms, blinded by the blood which poured down his face from a wound across the forehead, held forth the scabbard of his sword, over which the duke stumbled and fell to the ground at the foot of the king's bed, faintly breathing forth the words, "*Mon Dieu! mon Dieu! ayez pitié de moi!*"[1] All was over in less than five minutes.

[1] Miron: Rélation de la Mort des Duc et Cardinal de Guise. Discours sur la Mort des Duc et Cardinal de Guise. Advis de ceux qui ont étés à Blois, 1588, 8vo. Rélation et Déposition de Olphan du Gast, one of the Quarante-cinq, and a participant in the murder. De Thou. Pasquier. Martyre des deux Frères.

Upon it being reported to him that his enemy lay in his death gasp, Henry slowly raised the tapestry screen and came forth to gloat over the spectacle. The most savage exultation gleamed in the king's eyes, as he viewed the prostrate form of Guise. After silently surveying the still breathing body for some instants, the king exclaimed, "*Mon Dieu! qu'il est grand!*" and slowly retreated back to his inner chamber. Revol then, by command of his royal master, approached to search the person of the duke, and carry any papers to his majesty. Around the duke's arm was a gold chain riveted, having a small key attached; in his pocket was a purse containing twelve gold crowns, also a slip of paper, upon which were written the words, "To entertain a war in France it is necessary to expend seven hundred thousand livres a month." A diamond ring, in the shape of a heart, was taken from the duke's finger, and appropriated by d'Entragues. As Revol was making his search, a spasm convulsed the body of the expiring prince. "Monseigneur! I beseech you ask, while there is yet time, the pardon of the Almighty and that of the king!" said the secretary, earnestly. The lips of the duke moved and the words "*mes péchés*" were audible; he then heaved a sigh and expired.

In the council-chamber the fate of the duke had been divined—the noise, the groans, the trampling of feet, and the confusion which ensued immediately on the closing of the door after the exit of Guise, afforded too fatal a testimony. The archbishop of Lyons, brave and impetuous in all his actions, rushed towards the door of the ante-chamber, and tried to open it, but in vain. The cardinal de Guise rose so precipitately as to overturn his chair, exclaiming "*l'on outrage mon frère!*" but directed his flight towards the opposite door leading from the chamber. "*La France est perdue!*" exclaimed the archbishop in despair, as, on retreating from the door he perceived that the room was filled with armed soldiers, who had already seized the cardinal, and were approaching to effect his own arrest. The maréchal d'Aumont then drew his sword, and commanded that every member should resume the place he had before occupied; which being done, he commenced an harangue, exhorting the captive princes to patience and submission. A few minutes passed in this suspense, when the door leading into the royal apartments was violently flung open, and Lognac entered, holding his sword, the blade of which was still red with the blood of Guise.[1] The sleeves of Lognac's habit were turned back, his collar was loose, and his shirt open at the breast. The king's voice was then heard within saying, in an imperious tone, "Open the doors!—Remove the hangings, that all may enter!" Lognac then addressed the cardinal de Vendôme, and said that the king required his presence and that of messieurs of the council. The mandate was obeyed, Lognac remaining standing by the two prisoners until relieved by Rouvré and a second detachment of soldiers. The king, when the council entered, stood in the middle of the room, with a face inflamed with fury, near to the body of the duke, which was now partially covered with a Turkey rug. "At last, I am a king!" exclaimed Henry, sternly, addressing the cardinal de Vendôme; "the duc de Guise is dead. Those rebels, who made boast of their zeal for religion, will now no longer dare to arrest my designs for the pacification of the realm; nevertheless, know and behold, monseigneur, what he may expect who presumes in future to usurp or infringe upon my authority!"[2] The cardinal made no reply. The king then addressing

[1] Rélation et Déposition de M. Pierre d'Espinac, Archevêque de Lyons. De Thou, liv. xciii. Pasquier.

[2] Ibid. Brantôme: Capitaines Illustres. Hilarion de Coste: Dames Illustres.

d'Aumont and M. d'O, gave some directions in a low voice respecting the cardinal de Guise and the archbishop, who were then conveyed closely guarded from the council chamber.

The cardinal de Bourbon, meantime, had been arrested in his bed. Shaking with affright, the old prelate was hastily arrayed by his attendants, and conveyed, weeping like a child, into the presence of the king. The sight of the titular king of the League seemed to kindle afresh the fury of the king. He upbraided the terrified prelate in the most outrageous and indecent manner. "Fool! knave! and puppet! do you recognise that?" asked his majesty, pointing to the body of Guise. "But for your age, old imbecile, I would treat you the same. Even now I am undecided! What! you aspired to become the second person in my kingdom! Mort de Dieu! I will make you so little, that the least in my realm shall be greater than you!"[1] Henry then turned away, and entered the inner cabinet, commanding that the cardinal de Bourbon should be conveyed under a guard to his chamber.

The arrest during this interval had been successfully executed of the ducs de Nemours and d'Elbœuf, the prince de Joinville, and the duchesse de Nemours, mother of the Guises, and of the duchesse d'Aumale. Specially fortunate did the duchesse de Montpensier esteem herself to have taken her departure so opportunely; for Henry was heard to declare that, if madame de Montpensier had been in the castle, to a certainty he would have taken her life, so malignant and abominable did he deem her treason. Pericard, the secretary of the duc de Guise, was arrested; but not before he had managed to return to the apartments of his late master

[1] Histoire au vrai du Meurtre et Assassinat du Duc de Guise. Paris, [illegible]. Bibl. Imp. 2284, MS. Thevet: Hommes Illustres. Dictionnaire de Bayle, art. "Henri III."

and burn a box of papers. During the afternoon of the same day Pericard was taken into the presence of the king, and subjected to a rigorous examination by the secretaries of state, Beaulieu and Revol.[1] Bernardin, chief valet-de-chambre of the deceased duke, was arrested; even madame de Noirmoutier was compelled to submit to a severe interrogatory before the secretary Beaulieu, as she had been the last to hold familiar converse with the duke. Nothing new, however, was elicited by any of these examinations.

Meantime, the provost-marshal, Duplessis Richelieu,[2] had been introduced into the king's closet; when, having received the orders of his majesty, which were given energetically and without a symptom of hesitation, he proceeded at a quarter to nine o'clock with a guard of soldiers to the Hôtel de Ville, where the commons assembled. The town of Blois was in commotion; the most sinister rumours had already spread from house to house; the castle gates were closed; the drums of the Swiss beat to arms; and 400 troops formed in the great quadrangle, besides the men of the two companies of the French *gardes de corps* under Larchant; and that while rain descended in torrents. Chapelle Marteau, the president of the tiers état, alarmed by these rumours, had repaired to the quarters of the duc de Guise about half-past eight. He was not suffered, however, to enter the precincts of the castle, but beheld preparations ominous enough to fill him with ter-

[1] "Le dit déposant étant entré dans le dit cabinet, trouva le roy et ceux de son conseil debout prest à sortir pour aller à la masse."—Déposition de Jean Pericard, secrétaire du feu Duc de Guise.

[2] The father of the cardinal de Richelieu. François Duplessis Richelieu, grand provost, married Susanne de la Porte. He died in 1590, so impoverished by the wars, that his collar of the Order was pawned to furnish funds for his funeral. Madame de Richelieu, an admirable mother and heroine, re-established her son's pecuniary affairs. She had three sons and two daughters.

ror. The commons, meanwhile, had met at an early hour to receive a report from the archbishop of Lyons on the debate before the privy council relative to the publication of the edict for the diminution of existing imposts. Marteau, therefore, on his arrival at the Hôtel de Ville, found most of the members assembled. A great panic, however, prevailed; and many of the deputies who had made themselves peculiarly obnoxious proposed to withdraw whilst still in their power to escape. When their factious proceedings had fairly roused the fury of their sovereign, the members then remembered with dread the wily irascibility of his majesty's temper. La Chapelle Marteau wisely attempted to check this disposition to flight, by representing "that if death were to be the lot of any in the assembly, there could not be a more glorious place of martyrdom than that in which they had met." The words had scarcely left the mouth of the provost, when the folding-doors of the hall were burst open with a violent shock, and on the threshold the members beheld the stalwart form of the provost-marshal Richelieu, and behind him a throng of soldiers with spears and lighted matches. "Let no one stir! Messieurs, a foul conspiracy has been concocted against the life of our sovereign lord the king!" exclaimed Richelieu, drawing his sword. Upon this many of the deputies rose in confusion, and Chapelle Marteau descended from his tribune. "Tue! tue! Mort Dieu! Tue! Let no one stir on his life!" again exclaimed Richelieu. On a sign from the provost-marshal the soldiers then rushed into the hall, holding their spears breast high, to the consternation of the deputies, many of whom received severe wounds, or were otherwise hurt, in trying to regain their places. Richelieu presently advanced into the centre of the hall; when Marteau, from his tribune, prayed that less violence might be used, as the deputies humbly submitted themselves to the will of the king. Upon this the provost-marshal directed the soldiers to ground their arms, and drawing a roll from his pocket, he read, addressing la Chapelle Marteau, "You are first accused as being cognizant of this conspiracy to slay and dethrone the king—I say you, M. le président Marteau. Also you, M. le président Neuilly, you M. Compans, M. d'Orléans, le président de Tour, MM. le Roy and Cotteblanche, stand forth! All of you, follow me." The soldiers then surrounded these personages and hurried them away, without permitting them to take their hats or cloaks. "When we reached the castle," says Chapelle Marteau, in his vivid relation of these events,[1] "we found the great gates closed, and were commanded to pass on to the private wicket. This done, we ascended the great staircase, at the foot of which we met M. de Dunes, booted and spurred, who passed us disdainfully without the slightest token of recognition. When we entered the chamber in which the council sat, we came upon some of the gentlemen of the guard called les Quarante-cinq, who were standing together near the door, lounging, laughing, and jesting. We passed through this chamber, conducted by the grand provost and his archers. Many noblemen of the privy council were conversing together, all of them having their faces blanched with terror and consternation. When we arrived at the door leading into the king's cabinet, M. de Richelieu commanded us to halt. Whilst we waited the pleasure of his majesty, we perceived two large streams of blood which issued from under the portal of the royal cabinet. M. de Neuilly, upon this, exclaimed, 'Oh, my God! my God! what disaster is this!' and whilst we gazed, stupefied with horror, a *valet-de-garderobe* came with a vessel

[1] Rélation et Déposition de Messire Michel Marteau de la Chapelle, Conseiller en la Chambre des Comptes, Prévôst des Marchands de cette Ville de Paris.

of water and a brush, and effaced the stains." M. de Mauvissière then approached, and asked the deputies whether they had seen the body of M. de Guise? "How! is he dead?" asked the provost of Paris. "Oh, what a disastrous and perfidious deed!" Mauvissière significantly placed his finger on his lips, and at that moment Larchant, captain of the Scotch guard, came from the king, and calling Hamilton, the ensign of his company, directed him to take charge of the provost and deputies arrested, and conduct them into a chamber in one of the towers of the castle. The order was promptly obeyed, and before the clock struck the hour of ten, the turbulent provost of Paris and his myrmidons of the League found themselves prisoners in a small turret chamber, twelve feet square, and lighted by a single loophole strongly grated. The king, meantime, had caused the comte de Brissac to be arrested by Larchant; also, M. de Bois-Dauphin, a notable leader during the barricades, and the proposer of many recent measures deemed by his majesty to be peculiarly obnoxious. Strict search was likewise made to find the bishop of Comminges, the canon of Senlis (preacher of the seditious oration in the church of St. Sauveur), and the bishops of Rhodes and Boulogne. These ecclesiastics, however, secured their safety by a precipitate flight.

The king, during these transactions, which were accomplished within the space of two hours, continued to grant audiences and to despatch the missives indispensably requisite after the deed he had perpetrated. First, he sent a secretary of state to impart the death of the duc de Guise to the legate Morosini, and to request the nuncio to meet him at mass in the church of St. Sauveur at midday. Henry then despatched M. de Dunes, brother of Entragues, to take possession of the citadel of Orléans; while he sent Ornano on the same mission to Lyons, with a warrant to arrest the duc de Mayenne. Afterwards the king arrayed himself to hear mass, intending to visit the queen his mother before he proceeded to the church. As Henry passed through the chamber where the body of the duke still lay, he turned to the crowd of noblemen, who on the rumour of the catastrophe had thronged to the royal apartment, and fiercely said, "*Voilà, messeigneurs, comme je punirai à l'advenir ceux qui ne me seront fidèles !*"

Catherine was in bed when her son entered. Her agitation was excessive, and her lips trembled as she replied to his salutation. The cardinal bishop of Paris, Gondy, sat by the bedside of the queen, and had been reading to her majesty from his breviary. "Madame," said the king, "I have no longer a compeer! I have caused Guise to be slain! To-day, I reign!" continued he, in a triumphant tone. "M. mon fils, may God grant that your anticipations may be realized! Lose no time, I beseech you, in putting your affairs in order, as you have so acted and so resolved." The king replied that he had lost no time. "Right, my son; I pray God fervently that this your act may prosper in its results. Again, I say, God grant that this resolution may not leave you king of nothing!"[1] Henry replied "that he had taken every precaution." Catherine then seemed disinclined to discourse; she was suffering from a paroxysm of pain in the chest, and spoke slowly and with difficulty. Henry then kissed the hand of his mother and took leave, after first requesting the cardinal de Gondy to repair to the lodging of the legate and accompany the latter to St. Sauveur. The king showed the most intense anxiety

[1] Davila, liv. ix. Riguccio Galluzzi: Istoria del Granducato di Toscana, liv. v. De Thou, liv. xciii. Particularités Notables concernants l'Assassinat de MM. de Guise, Paris, 1589. Lettres de Pasquier.

to meet the legate; indeed, the apprehended censures of the Church for the unscrupulous deed he had perpetrated seemed alone to diminish his exultation. As Henry proceeded to the church, he assumed an easy and even jocund deportment to those around; when, however, his majesty's eye fell upon any of the late friends and adherents of the deceased duke amid the throng of courtiers, the menace of his glance grew ominous. During his progress Henry encountered one of the supporters of la Motte Serrant, the robber-chief of Anjou. "The pardon of la Motte is revoked; his cause shall be tried by the ordinary courts, who will pronounce sentence. The king is again supreme!" said his majesty, drily. The bishop of Langres, who had appeared at Blois personally to defend his cause, tried to evade the royal notice; but Henry, perceiving the prelate, called him forth and said, "Three weeks ago you obtained an order in council against my faithful people of Langres, without deigning to suffer their defence respecting the wall to be heard. To-day I annul that process. Depart to your diocese, and live in peace with your flock!"

Before the porch of St. Sauveur the legate Morosini waited, accompanied by Gondy, cardinal-bishop of Paris, and other prelates, and by the Venetian ambassador. Henry took the nuncio apart, and conversed with him for some time in most cordial fashion. Henry assured the prelate that he was resolved as ever to pursue the war against the heretics of his realm; and that the death of the duke had been resolved for purely secular causes, principally for his treasonable enterprises upon the crown and his relations with foreign powers. Morosini, as yet uncertain how to act, assented, and seemed convinced by the royal sophistry. He, moreover, promised to send a courier to Rome to relate the matter to his Holiness, and especially to impart the stringent causes which had induced his majesty to have recourse to so desperate a measure. Had the king been satisfied with the revenge he had taken, all might have prospered, as far as his relations with the Holy See were concerned. But the lenient view taken by the legate emboldened Henry to enterprise yet farther, and to brave the ban of the Church by the murder of one of her chief prelates. The nuncio entreated his majesty that no harm, other than temporary captivity, might befall the cardinal de Guise and the archbishop of Lyons. The king returned an evasive reply: the legate[1] persisted and admonished his majesty to observe in the case of the prelates all legal formalities for their arraignment, did he deem them worthy of extreme penalties.

Meantime, during the king's absence, the *valets du garderobe* cleansed the royal cabinet from its pollution of blood. Many of the more humble friends of the duke took this opportunity to visit and lament over his remains by dint of bribing the officials. Portail, surgeon-major to the king, placed his hand on the cold lips of the corpse, and on the heart, to satisfy himself that life was indeed extinct. It was ascertained that the duke had received six mortal wounds—of these two stabs perforated the lungs, and one beneath the right eyebrow penetrated to the brain. The king's chaplain, Etienne Dourguin, also entered the chamber, and recited the psalm *De Profundis* over the body.[2] He then proceeded charitably to visit the heart-broken mother of the duke, madame de Nemours, who had not been suffered to quit her chamber, though apprized of the

1 "Le cardinal François Morosini était un prélat d'une esprit equitable, et très bien inténtionné pour le roy, auquel il avoit obligation du chapeau."—De Thou: Vie.

2 Déposition d'Etienne Dourguin, et de Claude de Bulles, Chaplain and Almoner to the King—Hist. des Cardinaux. Cayet: Chronologie Novennaire.

assassination of her son. The body of the duke was then wrapped in a cloth of green serge, and deposited in a large unfurnished chamber near to the chapel of St. Calais, within the castle, according to the command given by his majesty.

During the afternoon a council was holden, before which Brissac and other deputies of the *noblesse* were brought. Henry pronounced a plausible discourse, assuring his auditors of his orthodoxy, and announced his resolve, notwithstanding the provocations he had received, not to prorogue the States, but, on the contrary, to grant all reasonable petitions for the relief of his people and the better government of his realm. Brissac then made humble petition to the king, protesting his innocence and requesting his liberation, which Henry was pleased partially to grant; and also that of the greater culprit, M. de Bois-Dauphin. The latter, on receiving his liberty, departed as quickly as possible from Blois. Brissac, more courageous and politic, remained at his post, as president of the chamber of peers, until the closing of the assembly.

The fate of the cardinal de Guise and the archbishop of Lyons was then discussed. The council was composed of the bitter foes of the princes of Lorraine. The king himself still thirsted for further vengeance. There were present in the council those who advised his majesty to extirpate the rebellious race, root and branch, now that he had made so successful a commencement. The crimes of the cardinal were industriously paraded; his seizure of Troyes, his appropriation of the treasure in the castle of Château Thierry, formerly appertaining to the deceased duc d'Alençon, his coarse abuse of the king, and, above all, a speech heard by many present which he had been imprudent to make only on the day preceding—to wit, "that he should not die content until he had grasped between his feet the head of the tyrant, whilst a barber conferred upon him a Capuchin's crown."[1] It was, moreover, represented to his majesty that while the other princes of Lorraine—the ducs de Mayenne, Aumale, and Elbœuf—had made pacific overtures to the king, and had even warned him of his danger, the cardinal had taken every opportunity to demonstrate hostility; and if liberated would, doubtless, persuade his kinsmen to avenge the death of Guise, and himself become the instigator of countless leagues and conspiracies. It was a perilous venture to take the life of a prince of the Church—the cardinal-dean, moreover, of the Sacred College. For long Henry hesitated: but his unprincipled favourites urged him to the deed, exclaiming that else the blood of Guise had been shed in vain! Reports were also brought to the king of the violent deportment of the cardinal after his arrest on being told of the death of his brother; and of the oath he had solemnly sworn to avenge the treacherous deed. Finally Henry assented to the bloody fiat; animosity, fear, and the elation which he felt at his freedom from the controlling power under which he had so long chafed—all concurred to inspire this decision. The king, however, gave strict order that execution should not be done on the cardinal until the decree had been again submitted to him on his rising the following morning.

The cardinal de Guise and his fellow-prisoner, the archbishop of Lyons, had been first conducted into a small chamber situated in the Tour du Château Regnaud, lighted by three oval panes of glass close to the ceiling, at the door of which four of the king's Gascon gentlemen kept guard. About four o'clock in the afternoon they were removed to a lower chamber, vaulted, and having a window closed by a grate. Food was then brought to them for the first time, consisting

[1] Cayet: Chronologie Novennaire.

of eggs and bread, and wine; and a wood fire was kindled.[1] The prelates then sent to petition Larchant, captain of the Scotch body-guard, that they might have their breviaries, also beds, and their night-gear. The cardinal seemed much depressed, and ate scarcely a morsel; he sat silently by the fire, and murmured sorrowful words at intervals, as if communing with himself. The archbishop of Lyons, still sustained by his bold and quenchless spirit, presently proposed to say vespers. About eleven o'clock two coarse mattresses were brought for the prelates to repose upon; while several soldiers of the guard, to the great relief of the prisoners, were withdrawn from within the chamber. The prelates, before seeking repose, confessed, and mutually gave each other absolution. At three o'clock they rose in the dark and recited prayers, in which act of devotion they continued until eight o'clock. The door of the prison then opened, and a *valet-de-chambre* entered, carrying a flambeau, followed by Louis du Guast, a captain of the body-guard. Du Guast approached, and making a profound obeisance, said, addressing the cardinal de Guise, "Monseigneur, the king requires your presence." The cardinal turned pale on the utterance of these ominous words, but rose with dignity and prepared to follow du Guast. The archbishop of Lyons, foreseeing the fatal catastrophe about to happen, pressed the hand of the cardinal, and whispered in his ear, "Monsieur, commend your soul to God." "My father, embrace me and give me your benediction," exclaimed the cardinal, casting himself on his knees before the prelate. The archbishop then, for the first

[1] Rélation et Déposition de Monseigneur l'Archevêque de Lyons. Another account states that the prelates were deprived of bed, table, and chairs, and that no food was given them but raw fish, sent by the express order of the king. This relation is a manifest error, for the archbishop of Lyons, one of the prisoners, affords a very different testimony. Archives Curieuses, tome xii. Hist. des Cardinaux.

time, became deeply affected, with difficulty pronouncing the formula. The cardinal rose, and was then led away.

As soon as the door closed, du Guast turned to his captive and roughly said, "*Cardinal, il faut mourir!*" In a small gallery adjacent four soldiers waited for their victim. Du Guast there took leave of the cardinal and retired, desiring the soldiers to do their duty. The cardinal calmly prepared himself for death, and asked for a few moments to commend his soul to God. Kneeling with his face turned towards a recess in the wall, the prelate commenced to pray with devotion. While he was so engaged, one of the soldiers plunged his sword into the body of the cardinal, who, turning reproachfully, covered his face with his mantle, and sank to the ground. Thrusts from daggers and halberds then fell swiftly on the prostrate body of the prelate, which was so mutilated by the savage violence of his assassins that his friends could scarcely recognise his remains. The body was suffered to lie for an hour on the spot where it had fallen; it was then wrapped in coarse sacking and deposited by the side of that of the duc de Guise. The order for the death of the cardinal had been given by the king at daybreak, on being informed by the bishop of Mans, brother of Nicholas and Louis de Rambouillet, that the deputies of the clergy had resolved to petition him in person during the day for the release of the cardinal de Guise, who was their president. Henry answered in a rage, "Let the said cardinal die; I am weary of his name!" The gentlemen of the Quarante-cinq, however, declined to peril their souls by assassinating a cardinal;[1] and

[1] The king, it is asserted, applied first to Larchant to undertake the assassination of the cardinal; then to his provost Richelieu. Loignac flatly refused, but introduced du Guast, a necessitous soldier, who promised to see that his majesty's fiat was accomplished. Du Guast, in his deposition made by order of the parliament of Paris, stated that the

Loguac even tried to divert the king from so perilous an enterprise.

While this tragedy was enacting, Henry was attending matins in St. Calais, the private chapel of the castle. As he quitted the edifice the baron de Luxe, brother-in-law of the captive archbishop of Lyons, threw himself at the feet of the king, and besought his majesty to spare the life of that prelate. Henry commented severely on the past misconduct of the archbishop, whom he called "a turbulent churchman, the quintessence of the League," but said that in his royal clemency he had that morning made a solemn vow to shed no more blood; "therefore, monsieur, go to your said brother-in-law, and assure him that at your intercession I commute the just penalty of death, which he deserves, into that of perpetual captivity."

Another suppliant waited the presence of the king in the chamber of the queen-mother, to which Henry repaired. By the bed of the queen stood Anne d'Este, duchesse de Nemours, the mother of the Guises. The duchess was arrayed in mourning robes; her face was pale, and wore an expression of intense agony. She had just heard of the slaughter of her second son from the lips of Catherine, who had implored the king to permit her thus to mitigate, if possible, the anguish of the unhappy mother. The queen predicted that terrible era of subsequent vengeance, as she looked upon the tearless face of the duchess, and listened to the vows which unconsciously escaped her lips. The duchess fiercely upbraided the king for his perfidious cruelty, and said "that she had always predicted evil to her sons from the notorious treachery of the king's character, and that with her consent they had never presented

king said it was his resolve to exterminate the race of Lorraine Guise, "jusques à l'enfant qui étoit au ventre de la mère."

themselves at Blois." "Madame," sneeringly replied Henry, "you ought, on the contrary, to rejoice that your excellent sons perished both of them like Julius Cæsar, being slain in the midst of the assembled senate."[1] The duchess then asked for the bodies of her sons that she might cause them to be interred. The king abruptly refused to grant the request; and left the apartment, giving orders that madame de Nemours should be reconducted to her chamber and suffered to communicate with no one.

The same night, whilst the king attended the midnight mass which ushered in the festival of Christmas-day, 1588, the bodies of the deceased princes were lowered by ropes from the windows of the council-chamber into the court-yard by the provost-marshal Richelieu and his archers. They were then carried into a small room beneath the hall of council, and which opened on to the terrace leading to the castle pleasaunce. A large fire of pine wood had been kindled in this chamber to consume the remains of the illustrious victims. The heads of the duke and his brother were first struck off and thrown on the blazing pile. Some writers state that the bodies were burned in the wide chimney of the adjacent Salle des Etats, where the king had opened the session of the States, and the ashes scattered to the wind.[2] The provost Chapelle Marteau, however, who was afterwards incarcerated in the room beneath the council-chamber, states in his deposition that when he was first conducted there he could distinctly trace on the floor of the chamber, from which the blood had not been washed, the outlines of the stalwart form of the duc de Guise. De Thou gives a different version of the disposal of the bodies. He

[1] Advis de ceux qui ont été à Blois. Paris, 1588. 8vo.
[2] Cayet. Pasquier. Mathieu. Cheverny. Davila, &c.

simply states that, by the advice of his surgeon, Henry caused the remains of the duke and his brother to be buried in quick-lime, so that not a relic of them might remain to excite the compassion or the veneration of the multitude. Richelieu afterwards waited on the duchesse de Nemours, and assured her with many oaths that the bodies of her sons had been deposited in consecrated ground in his presence.

CHAPTER III.

1588—1589.

Tumults in Paris—Announcement of the death of the duc de Guise—Anguish of madame de Guise—Frantic grief of the duchesse de Montpensier—She swears to avenge the murder of her brothers—Hostile measures adopted in the capital—Frenzy of the populace—Reply of Henry III. to the deputation sent to Blois by the town of Orléans—Supine indifference manifested by the king—Interview of Henry's ambassadors with pope Sixtus V.—Demands made by the pontiff—Illness of queen Catherine—Her last days—Demise of the queen—Her will and funeral obsequies—Illness of Henry III.—Arrival of Diane duchesse d'Angoulême—Condition of affairs—Revolts throughout France—Escape of the duc de Nemours—Henry conducts his prisoners to the castle of Amboise—He dissolves the States-general—Exploits of the king of Navarre—He offers to advance to the rescue of the king—Progress of the revolt in Paris—Arrest of the first president of the parliament Achille de Harlay, and of various members deemed to be hostile to the League—They are incarcerated in the Bastille—Ferocious violence of the populace—Madame de Montpensier appears in the public processions—Conspiracy of M. du Guast—Henry conducts his prisoners back to Blois—He gives liberty to the duchesse de Nemours—Correspondence of Henry III. with Epernon—He is counselled to enter into alliance with the king of Navarre—Madame d'Angoulême undertakes the negotiation—Military measures adopted—Mission of Sancy and Schomberg to raise levies in Switzerland and Germany—Departure of the king for Tours—His prisoners—The parliament is translated from Paris to Tours—Entry into Paris of the duc de Mayenne—His reluctance to accept the office of chief of the League—The council of Forty—Negotiation of Duplessis Mornay with Henry III.—Treaty between the two Henrys—Advance of the duc de Mayenne and the army of the League into Beausse—Intervention of the legate Morosini to promote a reconciliation between Henry III. and the duc de Mayenne.

The assassination of the duc de Guise was known in Paris on the day following its perpetration. While Richelieu and his archers were lighting the funeral pile of the unfortunate princes, the mob of Paris had risen to avenge their death. One Verdereau, a humble adherent of the house of Lorraine, contrived to slip outside the gates of Blois before the order was issued prohibiting any to pass without an order signed by the king. In the same manner most of Henry's precautions were frustrated: the friends of the princes of Lorraine showed themselves more ardent and alert than the subjects of the king. In Lyons the royal design of seizing the person of the duc de Mayenne, and that of securing the adherence of the important city of Orléans were likewise circumvented. M. de Rossieux, a gentleman appertaining to the household of Mayenne, quitted Blois at the same hour as did M. d'Entragues. The newly-elected royal governor and the emissary of the League entered Orléans precisely at the same time. D'Entragues quietly took possession of the citadel, an edifice which had been recently erected in one of the principal suburbs without the gates; while Rossieux repaired to the Hôtel de Ville, and boldly addressing the people, recounted the tragedies at Blois. His eloquence roused the people to paroxysms of alternate fury and despair. The gates of the town were seized by the municipal authorities, and a courier despatched to notify the event to the duc de Mayenne. A deputation of eight citizens was forthwith elected to proceed to Blois to supplicate the king to remove Entragues, whom the city refused to receive as its governor; and to pray that the captive prince de Joinville, now duc de Guise, might be invested with that office. If Henry had had the spirit and policy immediately after the death of Guise to place himself at the head of his troops and advance upon Orléans, and from thence have proceeded to Paris, so great at first was the panic and consternation that the royal cause would doubtless have gained a permanent ascendency. Instead of which politic measure, the king, idly exulting in his supposed victory, and relying on the pacific intimations aforetime sent to him by the princes of Lorraine, and on the dread which his late acts would inspire, amused himself by retaliating the past arrogance of the deputies, and in writing useless edicts and letters.

The energy that had carried Henry through the past episode was fast expiring: his raging vengeance satiated, fears, regrets, indecision, and weariness followed. The hand of the king and his minions had effectually indeed struck the blow—but the great general and statesman, whose valour and address might alone have enabled Henry to grasp and triumph over the momentous events ensuing therefrom, he had not at command. So great was the confusion at Blois, and so badly concerted were the after-measures indispensably requisite for the safety of the realm, that the duc de Nevers, general of the army of Poitou—the only military chieftain whom the king of his free will had lately nominated—received advices of the death of the duc de Guise and his brother from M. de la Châtre, hitherto the warm adherent of the princes of Lorraine; who fortunately, instead of seeking to excite the mutinous resentment of the army, assured Nevers of his loyal co-operation. La Châtre, however, acted from the persuasion that the king, having resorted to so desperate and exasperating an expedient, had taken every subsequent precaution to insure the royal supremacy. A few days, nevertheless, undeceived him as to this supposition, and materially altered the tenor of M. de la Châtre's consequent proceedings.

As soon as the news reached Paris, on Christmas Eve, of the death of the duc de Guise, the duc d'Aumale and his brother the chevalier d'Aumale, met the members of the Seize at the Hôtel de Ville; but believing the report to be fictitious, they despatched an envoy to Orléans to inquire. "This weak, cowardly prince of ours would not dare!" said they.

Fresh intelligence confirmatory of the assertion of Verdereau, but still silent on the death of the cardinal de Guise, reached the capital, however, before nine in the evening. The consequent confusion and panic in the city had never been surpassed. Guards were hastily posted at the gates, and watch-fires lighted in the principal squares. The people assembled and listened with groans and tears to the relation of the catastrophe. The duchesse de Guise and madame de Montpensier resided together at the hôtel de Montmorency. Thither, during the night, the people and the principal officers of the municipality proceeded, joined by the crowds pouring from the churches of the capital, in which the midnight mass had been celebrated. The condition of the duchesse de Guise was pitiable. On the first rumour of the death of her consort she had fallen into a swoon, and being in the eighth month of her pregnancy her state soon became perilous. Nevertheless, the populace in front of the hôtel clamoured and insisted on her appearance in the balcony. Supported in the arms of her women, the unhappy duchess appeared for a few seconds, and was carried back to her apartment insensible. The duchesse de Montpensier was indisposed, being confined to her couch from a swelling of the ankles, to which she was subject. When informed of the assassination of her brother, her ungovernable passion nearly destroyed her life. Her face became for a few minutes vividly suffused, then she lay motionless and livid. After an interval her cries of despair, horror, and rage resounded through the *enceinte* of the vast hôtel. She tore her hair, and in words of appalling purport cursed the tyrant.

The duchess then made a vain effort to rise from her couch to go through the streets of Paris and denounce the deed; but her limbs refused her support, and she sank back into the arms of her women. The news that the chief members of the council of Seize awaited in the hôtel for audience at length restored the duchess to comparative composure, and she desired that they might be immediately conducted to her couch. The duchess then vehemently harangued the Seize. She exhorted them to rise and avenge the cruel perfidy of the king, to whom she applied epithets the most degrading and ignominious. Raising her hands aloft, the duchess then vowed that henceforth her own life should be devoted to revenge. She advised the Seize to confer the chief command on the duc d'Aumale, who, she ironically said, might be found at the Carthusian monastery at his devotions, pending the arrival of that valiant and wise prince, her brother, M. de Mayenne.

The following day being Christmas Day, the most incendiary harangues were delivered in the churches against the king, while the "martyred duke" was eulogized, and his loss lamented with frantic expressions of grief. In some of the churches the congregation rose, and joined audibly in the laments of the preachers, exclaiming, "*Nous n'avons pas de roy! Maudit soit le tyran!*" During the afternoon the chevalier d'Aumale quitted Paris with fifty or sixty horse, for the succour of the people of Orléans. Madame de Montpensier also addressed letters to her brother M. de Mayenne, imploring him to repair to the capital, and giving the duke assurance that the Parisians would greet his presence with acclamations.

The duc de Mayenne, however, never acted but after

mature reflection. He possessed no gifts of eloquence like his deceased brother, nor had he that gracious and affable address and princely bearing which conduced so greatly to the duke's popularity; he was, on the contrary, dry, phlegmatic, and practical. He vehemently resented the death of his brothers; but yet, before declaring himself the mortal foe of his sovereign, Mayenne desired to ascertain whether that course would be most conducive to his interests. He remembered the secret advices that he sent to the king, in which he had himself stigmatized the actions of his brother as treasonable. Moreover, the duc de Mayenne had much to lose by embarking in civil war. His pecuniary affairs were flourishing, and he owed no man anything. Too proud and reserved to enact the *rôle* of a popular hero, Mayenne lavished nothing in useless prodigality. The father of these princes the great duc de Guise, who perished before Orléans, predicted that of all his sons Charles duc de Mayenne would be the stay and the oracle of his family. "My elder son Henry," said the duke, "dazzled by the position which he must inherit as chief of the Catholics of the realm, will surely fall through his ambitious aspirations." The duc de Mayenne, however, felt a chivalrous affection and veneration for his brother the duke, and sincerely mourned his untimely fate. It is doubtful, however, whether Mayenne would have accepted the office of Chief of the League, had it not been for the passionate entreaties and clamour of madame de Montpensier, who aggravated the duke's displeasure and suspicion by reminding him of the notorious fact, that Henry had despatched Ornano to effect his arrest. It was, moreover, felt by his warmest partisans, that the brother of Guise might now alone with honour approach the court at the special call of his sovereign, to defend the crown, to uphold the sceptre, and magnanimously to restore peace to the realm. The royal confidence, however, was already pre-eminently bestowed on the ducs de Nevers and Epernon; Mayenne, therefore, could not present himself at Blois, still the prison of his mother and his nearest kindred, as a subordinate. The duke, therefore, still undecided as to his eventual course, leisurely advanced to Maçon; and from thence, accompanied by his duchess,[1] he journeyed to Chalons.

On Monday, the 26th of December, an assembly was convened in the Hôtel de Ville, to consider the critical condition of affairs, and to provide for the defence of Paris. The duc d'Aumale was appointed governor, pending the hoped for arrival of Mayenne; Drouart and Crucé were nominated to fill the offices of Chapelle Marteau, Compans and Cotteblanche, the provost and sheriffs of Paris, until the happy liberation of the latter had been effected. It was resolved to arrest the most noted royalists in Paris; and to despatch missives to every city, village, and hamlet in membership with the League, to notify that the capital city no longer recognized the authority of the king. The assembly, likewise, unanimously voted that the municipal dignitaries should wait upon the duchesse de Guise to express their condolence at her bereavement, and to assure her that Paris adopted her fatherless children; in pledge of which, if God should be pleased presently to bestow upon her a son, that the city would present the prince at the baptismal font. The deputation waited upon madame de Guise during the same afternoon; the duchess received the members in her darkened chamber, reposing under a canopy draped with black. She

[1] Henriette de Savoye Villars, only daughter and heiress of Honorat de Savoye, marquis de Villars, marshal and admiral of France. Henriette was the widow of M. de Montpezat, by whom she had six children. Her wealth was great, and her marriage with the duc de Mayenne was solemnized August 6, 1576.

thanked the city for its participation in her woe, and accepted the proposal.[1]

A few hours later the news reached Paris of the assassination of the cardinal de Guise, and the arrest of the archbishop of Lyons. The excitement of the people burst forth with renewed madness. The curés of Paris anathematized the king; groans and execrations were heard in the streets of the capital, and several persons are stated to have expired of grief and rage. The statues of the king were overthrown and rolled in the gutters; his effigy was everywhere effaced, and the royal arms torn down. The people, mad for vengeance, rushed to the great Augustinian monastery, and tore to shreds two magnificent pictures decorating one side of the chapel, representing the first installation of the Knights du St. Esprit. One preacher Lincestre, on the last day of the year, preached a sermon in the church dedicated to St. Bartholomew, opposite the Palais, which so excited his hearers that the congregation rose and pulled down the arms and cyphers of the king which decorated the church; and having thus satiated their fury, sat down to listen to the remainder of the discourse. Lincestre told the people that he had discovered an anagram in the words, "Henri de Valois," which he said made "Vilain Herode;" a name which this seditious demagogue ever after applied to his sovereign. The president le Maitre and others were on this day delegated to proceed to Blois, to demand the liberation of the prisoners. The envoys took the precaution to make their wills before they trusted themselves in the clutches of the "execrable traitor and perjurer."[2]

At Blois during these transactions, when the utmost vigour and resolution should have been displayed, no

[1] Journal de Paris. [2] Ibid.

affair was despatched. Henry's incompetent ministers trembled before the wrath of the League. The chief nobles who still adhered to the royal cause, caring nothing personally for the king, had departed, foreseeing the events which had come to pass; those that remained quarrelled and distracted the weak and irritable mind of their master by the diversity of the counsels which they tendered. His captives Henry guarded with the utmost vigilance, as if he believed that the pacification of the country depended on their safe prison. The duchesses de Nemours and d'Aumale were not suffered to leave their apartments, or to see the queen-mother, who besought her son to liberate her old friend madame de Nemours. A commission had been appointed to interrogate the archbishop of Lyons, who, however, now relieved from fear of losing his life, resolutely refused to answer, pleading his privileges as a churchman. No threat nor persuasion could induce Espinac to criminate his late friends and allies, the duc de Guise and the cardinal. Henry, meantime, dismissed the deputation sent to him from Orléans with harsh words: "I command you to receive and obey M. d'Entragues as your governor," said his majesty. "If you do it not willingly, I will soon compel your obedience." In confirmation of his threat, Henry despatched the maréchal d'Aumont with the Swiss troops and some companies of the regiment of *gardes de corps*, to support d'Entragues, who was already besieged in the citadel.

The deliberations of the States at Blois, meanwhile, ostensibly continued; many members who had first sought safety in flight, returned—but nothing of moment was discussed. Resolutions were proposed by Henry's partisans; and received instant confirmation. The freedom and spirit of the assembly was broken. Abroad the deputies beheld innumerable risings; whilst half the principal towns of the kingdom rejected the royal authority: legislation, therefore, had become useless. In this peril Henry still temporized, distracted by calamities which each successive day rendered more menacing. Rambouillet, the most able of the men who now surrounded the king, urged Henry to send for his army under Nevers, and to march at its head upon Orléans; secondly, to enter into a treaty with the Protestant Cantons of Switzerland, and to recruit for troops, to form the nucleus of an army to invest Paris. The counsels of the maréchal de Retz induced the infatuated king to discard this wholesome advice. De Retz represented that his subjects would rise to a man if the army under Nevers, destined for the destruction of heresy, was turned against the king's Catholic liegemen; and that the enlistment of heretics would cause every orthodox trooper in the royal service to desert. The king pretended to ridicule the opposition which he encountered, and spoke rashly upon the ultimate vengeance he had determined to exact—threats which, before the fall of Guise, would have been treated with contemptuous indifference. Henry laughed at the fury of the Parisian populace, and said, "that he knew those said demagogues of Paris better than any man in the realm, and that after a little bravado and lament for their Roy Guisard, they would fall at his feet, when he should well know how to make them repent for their present follies! As for M. de Mayenne, he will have some trouble to keep his head above water within his own government, and will not be such a fool as to embarrass himself with the Parisians," observed his majesty.[1] It was also reported to the king that M. de Mayenne, on receiving the news of the murder of his brothers, rode bareheaded, brandishing a naked sword, into the

[1] Mémoires Secrets d'un Politique, Janvier, 1589. Archives Curieuses.

principal square of Lyons, and publicly swore to avenge their death by shedding the blood of their assassin. Henry declared his disbelief of the fact asserted; and wrote to Mayenne, commanding him to repair to Blois, and vindicating his late measures on the advices sent to him by the ducs de Mayenne and d'Aumale.

Neither was the news from Rome more reassuring. The legate Morosini, in his despatch to Sixtus V., represented the king as having been guilty of the most heinous perfidy. On the arrival of the intelligence the pope, however, appeared to take a lenient view of the proceeding, his Holiness declaring, as he sat down to dinner, "that MM. de Guise should have taken precautions, and, as they had not had the wit to take care of their own safety, that nothing could be said; that he had several times warned them of their danger, and that those who knew not how to defend themselves, when forewarned, were unworthy of commiseration."[1] The indignation of the temporal prince at the daring enterprises of the Guises had momentarily overpowered the horror and abhorrence with which the traditional policy of the Holy See required Sixtus to denounce the treacherous assassination of a member of the Sacred College. The Spanish ambassador, however, had secret audience of his Holiness on the evening of Friday, January 8th, and succeeded in arousing the pontifical wrath, especially after Sixtus had perused the missive sent to him by Morosini. The following morning, therefore, Henry's special envoy, the cardinal de Joyeuse, on repairing to the Vatican was received with gloomy formality, and the pope severely censured the "perfidious treachery" of the king. "The king," said his

[1] Lettre du Cardinal de Joyeuse à Henri III., Janvier, 1589. François de Joyeuse, cardinal-bishop of Narbonne, special envoy to the Holy See, brother of the deceased duc de Joyeuse. This letter, it is believed, was revised by the learned Arnaud d'Ossat, afterwards cardinal d'Ossat.

Holiness, "has committed an execrable deed, deserving the extreme censure of the Church. It was not thus that personages so august ought to have been brought to death, after your king had sworn solemnly that no harm should happen to them. The duc de Guise, if his majesty had complaint against him, ought to have been arrested and put upon a legal trial; while his Eminence his brother should have been sent to me. No one will in future trust the king; his affairs will never prosper. It is an unheard-of crime to have so put a cardinal to death." Joyeuse then slyly recalled to the memory of his Holiness the expressions which Sixtus had used on learning the unauthorized arrival of the duc de Guise in Paris—to wit, that the pope had observed, "if Guise had been his subject he would have had him thrown on the instant from the windows of the palace." "As for the death of the duc de Guise," continued the undaunted envoy, "the king has no account to render to you; but for the doom of the cardinal his brother, a prince and member of the Sacred College, and a prelate owing canonical obedience to your Holiness, the king humbly requests absolution." "Let the king write to me to supplicate absolution for his crimes, meantime I will consult my cardinals," replied the pope abruptly. Joyeuse replied, "that the king had applied for absolution through his regular ambassador, M. de Pisani,[1] and by himself; and that his majesty wished that none might be privy to the affair except his Holiness." Sixtus, however, gloomily persevered—first, in demanding the immediate release of the cardinal de Bourbon and the archbishop of Lyons; and secondly, that the king, having committed so heinous a crime, should make humble confession under his own hand

[1] Charles de Vivonne—the correspondence between Henry and M. de Pisani and the cardinal de Joyeuse is contained in Bibl. Imp. MS. Dupuy, 29 et seq.

and seal. "As for the rest," said the pope, "the affair shall in a few days be amply discussed in Consistory." He then dismissed the cardinal de Joyeuse, and declined to admit to his presence any envoy from king Henry until his majesty had made Christian confession of his errors; and had released the prelates still in captivity at Blois.

Meanwhile, a more heavy misfortune befel the king than any that might result from the aggregate outpourings of papal wrath. The master-spirit which had so long guided the counsels of France—the genius, alternately used for the glory and for the misfortune of the realm, and from the influence of which Henry had in vain sought emancipation, was about to be withdrawn from earth. Catherine de Medici, at the moment when her energy, her astuteness, and her unrivalled powers of conciliation were needed to deliver her son from the abyss into which his furious passions had plunged him, lay on the bed of death. From the fatal 24th of December her strength had rapidly given way. Her real sorrow at the death of the duc de Guise, her indignation at the perfidy with which, despite the nature of the provocation given, the king had violated his word and her own—without the support of which Henry's asseverations would have been treated with derision—and her consternation at the desperate condition of affairs, pressed with fatal effect on the already stricken frame of the queen. Her matured experience at once revealed to Catherine the lamentable consequences of the late catastrophe. She had lived to witness the son, once loved by herself with absorbing affection, hated and reviled. Aware of his incapacity, and of his untoward temper at once fanatical and puerile, she mourned the approaching overthrow of the royal race of Valois; she mourned at beholding the son for whom she had sacrificed so much laden with opprobrium, and dishonoured by his vices. More than this, Catherine predicted the eventual triumph of her detested son-in-law, le Béarnnois: while she acknowledged that now the salvation of her son depended on his prompt reconciliation with the son of Jeanne d'Albret, and the consequent recognition of Henri de Navarre, heretic as he was, as Henry's legitimate successor. Another conviction embittered the dying hour of the queen. In her zeal to erase from the royal lineage and succession the name of Henri de Navarre and to substitute that of her grandson, Catherine had countenanced and even upheld the revolutionary and ambitious designs of the princes of Guise; for without her secret support they must have fallen long ago before the hate of the king and his favourites. This reflection weighed heavily on the mind of Catherine.

But amid the prevailing desolation, the panic, and the woe, the queen was dying. The life that during its course had presented so unparalleled a combination of grandeur and adversity, political triumph and reverses, was about to be extinguished—and it was difficult for the king and his courtiers to realize the momentous fact.

For many months previously Catherine had been a severe sufferer from gout, which attacked her arms and feet, and at times her head. The queen suffered also from dropsy. The anxiety and fatigue which Catherine had undergone during the barricades of Paris, and subsequently, increased the worst symptoms of her malady. After her arrival at Blois sadness and melancholy greatly oppressed her spirit; she seemed to have lost her zest for those subtle political combinations in which she had excelled. The dismissal of Cheverny had also greatly affected Catherine; while the subsequent *tracasseries* between the king and the duc de Guise, and the unbending contumacy of the latter, inspired her with the keenest disquietude. Often during the silent hours of the night she paced her chamber in solitude; for the queen refused to tolerate the presence of watchers by her couch. Strong was the wrestling of that proud and determined spirit against the approach of death. As the transactions of the twenty-nine years during which the queen had wielded almost despotic power passed in review, tremendous must have been the retrospect. A profound believer in astrology and portents, Catherine in silent agony also noted what she believed to be the signs and omens of her approaching dissolution.

On Christmas Day Catherine was too exhausted to rise, and mass was celebrated in her apartment by Gondy, cardinal-bishop of Paris. During the following week she rose during a portion of every day, and appeared at times nearly convalescent. The queen, however, studiously refrained from interfering in politics, probably feeling herself too weak to contend with the catastrophes she felt to be impending. She, however, interceded for the prisoners, and Henry, at his mother's intercession, liberated the duchesse d'Aumale,[1] and permitted her to return with le Maitre and the deputies sent by the Parisians, on the solemn promise made by the young duchess that she would do all in her power to induce her husband to quit the League. For her old friend, the cardinal de Bourbon, Catherine could obtain no alleviation, excepting a reluctant permission from the king granting her license to pay the cardinal a visit in his prison-chamber. On New Year's Day Catherine was carried thither in a chair. The interview between the queen and her aged relative was deeply affecting. The cardinal, in his transports at

[1] "Ce maudit tyran de roy renvoya madame d'Aumale, et lui promit monts et merveilles, afin qu'elle détourna son mari du gouvernement de cette ville de Paris, ce que le dit seigneur ne voulut pas faire, comme sage et avisé qu'il étoit."—Journal de Paris.

seeing the queen, threw himself on his knees at her feet, kissing and clasping her hands, while he wept like a child. Responsive tears were likewise shed by Catherine, and she in vain strove to utter cheering words. The mood of the cardinal, however, changed. While commenting on his precarious position he flew into one of his accustomed fits of puerile rage, and reproached the queen for having contributed by her persuasions to induce them all to trust the protestations of the king her son. He was even so far carried away by excitement as to accuse the queen of having intentionally decoyed them to Blois. Catherine tried to calm his vehemence by her denials and expostulations; but the aged prelate was too excited to listen. "Hearken, monseigneur," said the queen, "I am innocent of having contrived your present position; and may God visit me with his eternal damnation if I devised that which you reproach me with, or if I assented to it!" "Oh, madame, madame!" persisted the cardinal, vehemently, "this is your doing! this is your device! Oh, madame, it is you who have slain us all!" The excitement of the interview was now more than the enfeebled frame of Catherine could endure. She turned pale, and exclaimed, "O God, this is too much! take me away; I have no strength left!" Her attendants then carried Catherine back to her chamber, and laid her immediately on the bed from which she never again rose. She continued to grow gradually worse; until a heavy stupor coming on, her pains were somewhat alleviated. The king remained constantly in her chamber, as did also queen Louise and Christine, grand-duchess of Tuscany. On the following day, Monday, January 2nd, the queen made her will with admirable presence of mind, bequeathing legacies to all her old friends and adherents. She gave her large hereditary possessions in Auvergne, first to Diane,[1] illegitimate daughter of her deceased husband, to revert to Charles de Valois, duc d'Angoulême, natural son of Charles IX. and Marie Touchet; disinheriting her daughter Marguerite de Valois, whose infamous life had brought disgrace on the royal house of Valois. To madame de Montmorency and to Christine, grand duchess of Tuscany, the queen also left a considerable sum in jewels.[2] The king immediately ratified the will, expressing his perfect approval of the dispositions which her majesty had made. A long and private conference then ensued between Catherine and her son, during which, some contemporary historians assert that the queen urgently counselled the policy which Henry afterwards pursued—his reconciliation with the king of Navarre, and his union with the latter to put down the formidable factions of the realm. She prayed the king to treat his sister Marguerite with lenity, and to provide adequately for her royal rank. During her last hours the queen was assisted by Julien de St. Germain, abbé de Charlieu, confessor to the king, a man of great virtue and piety, and a distinguished theologian. The selection of this ecclesiastic gave a seeming confirmation to the prediction of one of Catherine's astrologers, who warned her "to beware of St. Germain," as that name was destined to exercise a fatal influence over her destiny. Consequently the queen,

[1] Diane de France, the legitimated daughter of Henry II. and Philippe Duc, a beautiful Savoyarde. Diane married, 1st, Horatio Farnese, killed before Hesdin, 1553. 2nd, the maréchal de Montmorency, in 1557, who died in 1579. Madame de Montmorency assumed the title of duchesse d'Angoulême after the decease of queen Catherine. She died in December, 1618, at the age of eighty years. "Elle étoit," says de Thou," "une princesse de haute entendement, sage, et vertueuse."

[2] Testament de Catherine de Medici, MS. Bibl. Imp. Dupuy, 137.

who was superstitious to excess, had long carefully avoided the palace of St. Germain, and had even vacated her apartments in the Louvre, which was situated in the parish of St. Germain l'Auxerrois. Why the abbé de Charlieu was selected to minister to the dying hours of the queen it is impossible to divine. There were many prelates then in Blois; the cardinal-bishop of Paris had been previously in attendance by the couch of the queen; besides, in apartments within the palace, close at hand, were the cardinal de Bourbon, the archbishop of Lyons, and the king's private chaplain the bishop of Mans. The assertion, therefore, is untenable, that the spiritual aid of the abbé de Charlieu was resorted to because all the prelates had fled from Blois, some incensed at, and others being alarmed by the fate of the cardinal de Guise. During the whole of Wednesday, January 4th, the queen lay insensible; but in the night her sufferings became again intense. From this period she gradually sank, and died about one o'clock on Thursday, January 5th, in the arms of the king her son, apparently without pain, though from the night of the preceding Tuesday she had lost the power of speech.[1] A surgical examination of the cause of the decease of queen Catherine was made on the evening of the day of her demise. The king, who eagerly followed every morbid impulse, was present at the autopsy—a circumstance which afforded his enemies the Leaguers of Paris fresh subject for malicious comment.[2]

The remains of the deceased queen were then arrayed in royal robes, and deposited beneath a magnificent

[1] De Thou, liv. xciv. Brantôme: Vie de Catherine de Medici. De Coste: Dames Illustres. Mathieu: Hist. du Règne de Henri III. Cayet: Chronologie Novennaire. Ste Marthe: Hist. Généalogique de la Royale Maison de France. Hist. of the House of Medici.

[2] Ibid. Pasquier: Lettre 8, liv. xiii. Journal de l'Etoile.

catafalque in the apartment in which she resigned her life. Brantôme states that the robes and mortuary garments used at the interment of queen Anne de Bretagne were brought from the sacristy of St. Sauveur and appropriated for the ceremony, as no aid could be derived from Paris. Afterwards the body was deposited in a leaden coffin, and carried with most pompous ceremonial to the church of St. Sauveur, where it was deposited in an open niche close to the altar until the condition of the country should permit of its transport to St. Denis for interment in the superb chapelle de Valois.[1] The king attended the funeral ceremonies attired in violet robes; and queen Louise and the ladies of the court wore mourning cloaks of tan-coloured velvet. The members of the States attended the solemnities. Awe and misgiving were imprinted on the countenances of all as the orator Bertaut expatiated on the genius and resources of the queen, and deplored that at this dread crisis France should find herself bereft of the wisdom and consummate ability of a princess whose reputation had caused her to be appealed to as the refuge and arbiter of all classes of his majesty's subjects. The orator apostrophized the queen in verse: she was, said he,

> L'oracle de nos jours,
> En qui seule vivoit l'art d'enchanter l'orage
> Par les charmes divines d'un esprit docte et sage!

The heralds, after announcing the royal titles of the august deceased, proclaimed her consort of a king, and

[1] Catherine de Medici was born in Florence April 13, 1519; she died January 5, 1589, in her seventieth year. After the accession of Henri IV. Marguerite de Valois disputed her mother's will, and claimed all the vast property bequeathed to Diane de France, and to Charles duc d'Angoulême. The queen gained her suit, and immediately settled the wealth so recovered on the Dauphin, eldest son of Henri IV. and of Marie de Medici.

the mother of three kings and two queens. The body of the queen having been imperfectly embalmed, from the impossibility of obtaining the requisite materials, was removed three weeks subsequently from the niche close to the altar and secretly interred during the night in one of the side aisles of the church. There the remains of the "great queen, the mother of kings," rested in a lowly grave until after the assassination of Henri IV., when queen Marie de Medici caused the body of Catherine to be exhumed and transported to St. Denis, and deposited in the same vault in which her husband Henry II. reposed. Her heart was enclosed in the urn which contained that of Henry II. deposited in the chapelle d'Orléans, of the Celestine Convent, Quartier St. Paul. This urn is the work of the sculptor Germain Pilon; it is adorned by three exquisite figures representing Faith, Hope, and Charity, and is still to be seen in the halls of the Louvre.

The people of Paris showed no sympathy or regret at the decease of Catherine de Medici, who, until lately, had been the most popular personage in the realm. It was believed that the queen had connived at, and even prompted the massacre of the Guises. The Parisians had formed so contemptuous an opinion of their sovereign, that they believed it had required the more vigorous brain and cooler daring of his mother to conceive and execute so unscrupulous a deed. The people threatened if the funeral *cortége* passed through Paris, *en route* for St. Denis, to seize the body of the queen and to throw it into the Seine. All Catherine's rich effects and the furniture of her sumptuous palaces in Paris were sold by auction to pay the enormous debts which she owed to various merchants and traders of the capital. As the sums thus derived proved inadequate to liquidate the claims made against the deceased queen, a portion of her vast domains in

Auvergne was eventually sold during the reign of Henri IV. to acquit these debts, which had been incurred by the magnificent state which Catherine ever maintained at all her numerous palaces.[1] On Sunday, January 8th, the preacher Lincestre, referring to the demise of the queen-mother, said, "This princess has done much good and much ill; the latter, I fear, predominates. The difficulty is now to decide whether the orthodox ought to pray for the soul of a princess who so often made league with heresy. It is said, however, that she made an exemplary end, and was not a consenting party to the death of our good princes. Therefore I say, give her the advantage of at least one pater and one ave, and much benefit may they do her. Nevertheless, follow your own devisings."

Round the neck of the queen, after her decease, was found her celebrated talisman or medal, of which with his own hand the king took possession. It was said to be formed of several metals fused together under astrological combinations having relation to the date of the queen's nativity, mingled with human blood and with the blood of a hart. The medal was covered with effigies of hideous demons, and with various magical symbols and letters. The possession of the talisman was supposed to confer the power of divination, and to enable its bearer to rule with arbitrary sway. A few days after Catherine's death, the charm was broken by order of the king. The fragments, however, were carefully preserved, and came eventually into the possession of the abbé Fauval, who caused the talisman to be repaired and engraved. A fac-simile of this curious relic[2] is now to be seen amongst the treasures of the Bibliothèque

[1] De Thou, liv. xciv. Bibl. Imp. Residu St. Germain, tome iii. p. 18ème.

[2] There is also a prayer extant said to have been used daily by the queen; and which was likewise found on her body after death, the skin upon which it was written being stained with her blood.

Impériale; but the original, against which for so many years the ambitious heart of Catherine de Medici throbbed, has long been destroyed. The mourning worn by the courtiers at Blois was of the most elaborate and exaggerated description, and closely resembled the "sacks" of the Penitents of Notre Dame. The king caused the apartments to be draped with black cloth beset with silver tears; his own chambers, however, including the cabinet in which the duc de Guise was assassinated, assumed the most lugubrious aspect. Heavy draperies of black cloth were drawn across from the corners of the room, so as to give to each apartment the appearance of a *chapelle ardente.*

After the disaster of his mother's death, all Henry's fortitude and energy forsook him. The reaction came which his enemies so surely looked for; and thoroughly depressed and unnerved, the king took to his bed, where he remained several days, suffering at intervals from a malady not of a dangerous character, with which he was occasionally afflicted. Queen Louise, totally overwhelmed with the late catastrophe and by the open revolt of her kindred of Lorraine, also retired to her bed, and from no feigned necessity, for soon her majesty was declared to be alarmingly ill. To represent the majesty of France at Blois, therefore, there remained only the young grand-duchess of Tuscany, herself in deep affliction for the death of her grandmother queen Catherine, to whom she was greatly attached; and for the assassination of her kinsmen of Guise; also because the unsettled condition of the realm rendered it necessary that her journey to Florence, to join her newly-espoused lord, should be postponed. Henry, therefore, sent for his sister Diane de France, duchesse de Montmorency and d'Angoulême. "Ma sœur, have I not done well to rid my realm of these tyrants?" asked Henry, when madame d'Angoulême appeared at his bedside. "You have done too much, sire, and not enough!" answered the duchess, significantly. In Diane de France Henry found a counsellor prudent, moderate, and able. "This estimable princess," says Brantôme, "as soon as she heard of the great necessity of the king her brother, set off from her château of l'Isle Adam in haste, amid manifold dangers, and brought him 50,000 crowns, the which came in a most acceptable time—for which succour the king bore her such good-will and gratitude, that had he lived he would have made a most notable demonstration."[1]

The king, meanwhile, maintained a secret correspondence with the duc d'Epernon, but refrained from recalling him to court in the vain hope of propitiating his enemies; and because madame d'Angoulême stated her belief that the presence of the former favourite would prevent many of his majesty's faithful nobles from repairing to Blois. Henry was at length roused from his apathy by the necessity of receiving the reports of the States; and by the intelligence that the duc de Mayenne, without deigning to answer the summons sent by his sovereign, had at length determined to proceed to Paris, having repaired with that intention to Dijon, where madame de Montpensier met him. As his majesty deemed the castle of Blois, under these circumstances, to be unfitted for the safe keeping of his prisoners, he determined to transport them to the stronger fortress of Amboise. The dread lest these unfortunate princes might escape perpetually haunted the king, and he took the most extraordinary precautions to ensure their vigilant guard. The old cardinal de Bourbon, exhausted by the severity of the tribulations which he had endured, and profoundly afflicted at the death of the queen-mother, had taken to his bed; the duc

1 Vie de Madame Diane de France, Duchesse de Castro, Montmorency, and Angoulême—Dames Illustres.

d'Elbœuf, totally overwhelmed by his prison, sank into such despondency that he would neither eat nor change his raiment; the duchesse de Nemours spent her hours in prayer and fasting for the repose of the souls of her deceased sons; the duc de Nemours, young and active, alone consoled himself by devising all manner of plans for his evasion. These illustrious prisoners were all superbly lodged in the apartments which they had originally occupied on their arrival at Blois. The archbishop of Lyons, with courage undiminished, still occupied the vaulted chamber, the threshold of which was stained by the blood of the cardinal de Guise. The prelate whiled away his leisure in writing fiery appeals to the justice of the king, and in inditing letters to his beautiful sister, madame de Luxe, towards whom his enemies accused him of manifesting too tender a regard. The provost Chapelle Marteau, and the *échevins* Cotteblanche and Compans, were in the most lamentable plight, they having been conducted back again into the small apartment within the wide hearth of which a portion of the bodies of the unfortunate duke and his brother had been consumed.[1] After much cogitation Henry resolved to remove the governor of Amboise M. de Billy, an old and faithful servant of the crown, and to substitute in his room the Gascon du Guast, who had undertaken the assassination of the cardinal de Guise. Henry believed that he could not choose a more vigilant jailer than du Guast, or one more interested in the safe-keeping of the prisoners. His decision was highly commended by Lognac captain of the Quarante-cinq, and by the duc d'Epernon. This appointment having relieved the royal mind from a great weight of solicitude, Henry himself resolved to undertake the ignoble office of transporting the captive princes to Amboise, so fearful

[1] Relation de Chapelle Marteau, Prévôt des Marchands.

was he of their rescue *en route.* On the eve of the 13th of January, the day appointed for the removal of the princes, the duc de Nemours escaped from Blois, and evading pursuit reached Paris in safety. The duke's flight was accomplished with the utmost skill and *sang froid.* He was attended in his prison by his principal maître-d'hôtel and by a valet; the latter placed himself in his master's bed, while the duke, enveloping himself in the cloak of his valet, boldly followed the maître d'hôtel from the chamber. The *ruse* was not discovered until the following morning, as the guards suffered the two domestics, as they supposed, of the duke to pass unchallenged, as had been their usual habit. The duc de Nemours fled to Dourdans, a castle which appertained to his mother, and from thence he proceeded to Paris, and entered the capital escorted by the duc d'Aumale.[1]

Henry's consternation was excessive at the escape of M. de Nemours, and this event increased his anxiety to effect the safe transfer of the rest of his captives to the fortress of Amboise. By the counsel of his ministers Henry had resolved on the following day to restore the duchesse de Nemours to liberty, trusting that her loyalty to the descendants of Louis XII. might induce her to exhort her son, the duc de Mayenne, to renounce his engagements with the League; while her influence would perhaps mitigate the furious zeal of madame de Montpensier, who ever showed her mother exemplary respect. The flight of M. de Nemours changed Henry's placable intent, and he resolved that the duchess should share the same fate as the remainder of his captives.

At mid-day on the 13th of January the royal barge was prepared, and the prisoners brought out under a strong guard. Before madame de Nemours stepped into the boat she turned, and, raising her arms aloft,

[1] Journal de Paris. De Thou.

invoked the statue of Louis XII. which decorated the grand portal of the castle. *"Ah! grand roi!* exclaimed she, *"jamais n'avez vous fait construire cette maison vostre, pour servoir de forest ny de massacre à vos petits-enfants!"*[1] The duchess having entered the barge, king Henry appeared, and, with a countenance of sullen dissatisfaction, took his seat beneath a fringed canopy, and addressed not a word to his prisoners during their progress on the river. At Amboise he consigned them to the safe keeping of du Guast, who had previously received commands to subject the captives to a much more rigorous system of espionage.

Henry remained at Amboise two days, when having, as he believed, satisfactorily accomplished his designs, he returned to Blois, where he was anxiously expected by the deputies of the States-general, who had meantime prepared a memorial demanding the dissolution of the assembly, on the ground "that their debates were useless, and that the presence of the members was necessary in their various provinces to support his majesty's dominion." Henry was pleased to comply with their prayer, because the fact was obvious that the deputies were departing of their own accord, and that soon none would remain. Accordingly the ceremony of the prorogation of the assembly was performed with great pomp on the 16th day of January. The harangue for the nobles was pronounced by Brissac, to whom the king now gave entire liberty. The archbishop of Bourges was the orator of the clergy, and Bernard officiated for the tiers état in room of the captive provost, Marteau. Never were addresses of a more plausible nature pronounced; no allusion was made to the troubled condition of the realm, or to the recent events. Suggestions for a new system of taxation,

[1] Mathieu, liv. vii.—Hist. du Règne de Henri III. Le Martyre des deux Frères.

and for sundry laws, were submitted to the king, and were as gravely accepted. "Never," says de Thou,[1] "had been heard more elaborate and sonorous discourses; never had orators recourse to more subtle argument, or to a more polished eloquence. Never had the king assisted with greater outward tranquillity at any public ceremonial. Callous to the fact that the majority of his subjects had risen in arms against his authority, the king's demeanour was easy and unconcerned as if he had been participating in some national jubilee." The deputies finally quitted Blois on the 20th of the month, the king taking affectionate farewell of each member as he left the church of St. Sauveur, where divine service had been performed, during which the Edict of Union was again solemnly confirmed by the oath of all present. The king restored M. de Bois-Dauphin to liberty, and released the inferior deputies arrested by Richelieu. His majesty also granted the abolition of several grievances complained of; and voluntarily relieved his subjects from the payment of a third of the sum due to the current revenue.

Every hour, meanwhile, brought news of fresh disasters. The cause of the king momentarily seemed to become more desperate. The maréchal d'Aumont and d'Entragues were driven out of the citadel of Orléans by the townsmen, and upon the advance of a body of the soldiers of the League under Mayenne, they prudently retreated. D'Aumont had relied on receiving timely succour from the duc de Nevers, who had just achieved, by the capture of La Ganache from the Protestants, the solitary success which signalized the royal arms at this disastrous period. The soldiers of Nevers, however, were all, with the exception of a few companies, secretly pledged to the League; and con-

[1] Liv. xciv. p. 503.

sequently they broke out into mutinous defiance of their royalist leaders, and fled, some to Paris, others to join the army of the duc de Mayenne. In Bretagne the duc de Mercœur, brother of queen Louise, revolted and carried that important province to the League. The state jewels of his sister the queen had been left in the Louvre on the departure of the court for Blois; these were seized by the duc d'Aumale, and actually sent to Mercœur to raise money upon for the prosecution of the war. Simultaneously news arrived of the defection of the towns of Dreux, Crespy, Senlis, Clermont, Sainte Maixence, Amiens, Abbeville, Rouen, le Mans; and of every place in Normandy excepting Dieppe, Caen, and Pont de l'Arche. Toulouse revolted, and the mob, instigated by the bishop of Comminges, slew the first president of the parliament, Etienne Duranté, under circumstances of atrocious violence. Lyons elected the duc de Nemours for its governor, and renounced its allegiance to king Henry. In the south Montmorency and Lesdiguières captured many places; while the king of Navarre took Maran and the then important town of Niort. Throughout the realm frightful violence reigned; murders, rapine, treacherous surprises and horrid profligacy prevailed. No man's life was secure; families became divided, some fighting for the king, others for the League. Church lands were seized, abbeys rifled, and benefices confiscated for the benefit of private individuals. Knavery and violence alone prospered; those who had nothing to lose were the sole gainers; the rich were despoiled, the honest poor man oppressed. Amongst those most miserable, during this season of anarchy and woe, was the king. He beheld himself deserted by all—a few towns on the Loire being his sole cities of refuge, and even these he held by the precarious tenure of the fidelity of their several commandants. The nobles of the realm nominally devoted to the royal cause held aloof in dismay at the course of events, which seemed to doom all partisans of the sovereign to ruin, to exile, or to death. The Spanish ambassador, don Bernardin Mendoza, still remained at Blois, and though Henry was aware of his incessant intrigues to induce the inhabitants of the town to rise and invest the castle, yet the king dared not command his departure. Already many about the person of the king, and especially Diane de France duchesse d'Angoulême, timidly pronounced the name of Henri de Navarre as the prince and warrior who, by being called at the same time to defend his own eventual rights, could alone preserve the crown.[1] Throughout this crisis queen Elizabeth proved the stanch friend of Henry III. The queen sent him an admonition through her ambassador, lord Stafford, to continue at any cost or discouragement "that which he had at first purported to achieve; for that she promised, on the word of a queen, in case he came to a downfal, that she would aid him to rise again."[2] The ambassador strongly advocated the immediate coalition of the king with Henri de Navarre. The humiliation of being at length compelled to seek aid from the strong arm of le Béarnnois; his fear of the thunders of the Vatican; and the supplications of the legate Morosini—who promised, if the worst to be apprehended came to pass, that he would interpose authoritatively in the name of the Holy See be-

[1] Amongst other noble personages were MM. de Château-Vieux, Schomberg, d'O, Balzac, du Plessis Liancourt, and Larchant, captain of the body-guard. When the king of Navarre was informed of the death of the princes of Guise, he said, "J'avois toujours prévu et dit que MM. de Guise n'estoient capables de remuer l'enterprise qu'ils avoient mise en leurs entendements, et en venir à fin, sans le péril de leurs vies!"—Cayet.

[2] Mémoires d'un Politique, Janvier, 1589.

tween the duc de Mayenne and his majesty, and moreover appease the ire of the supreme pontiff—still encouraged Henry to temporize.

On the 16th day of January, while Henry pompously closed the States-general of 1588-9, a scene of lawless violence was enacting in Paris. At the time when his majesty dismissed the national deputies, the League presumed to suspend the venerable and time-honoured parliament of Paris. The coincidence was deemed strange and ominous. The chambers had assembled as usual; the members appearing to condole with one another on the prevalent anarchy rather than to engage in legislation. Suddenly the doors of la Chambre Dorée were burst open, and, in strict imitation of the forms observed at the arrest of Chapelle Marteau and his fellow-prisoners at Blois, Bussy le Clerc, captain of the Bastille, strode forward with drawn sword and commanded the first president de Harlay, and the presidents de Thou and de Potier, besides several minor members, to follow him. "Follow me, messieurs! To the Hôtel de Ville!" De Harlay demanded on whose authority the summons was sent? Bussy replied by desiring the members whom he had named to follow him without cavil, or he should be compelled to put forth the powers intrusted to him. The presidents complied, for resistance would have been vain. They were, however, followed by fifty or sixty members who rose to attend the first president, scorning, as they said, to abandon their leader when in peril. The august procession passed sadly along the Pont au Change and the Place de Grève. The streets were crowded with people, who jeered and mocked as the members passed. When they arrived before the Hôtel de Ville the president de Harlay approached the portal to enter—but the doors were barred; and with a savage menace Bussy commanded the members to "pass on."

They were conducted straight to the Bastille. Those deemed malignant enemies of the League, and who were named in Bussy's roll, were confined in cells; the rest of the members who had voluntarily followed were set at liberty, after receiving an admonition.[1] "Never," says a contemporary, "had the high court of parliament received such a blow as that of Monday, January 16th." The following day the parliament was summoned to meet as usual, and the president Brisson was nominated by the Seize to fill the office of first president, in the room of Achille de Harlay, then a prisoner in the Bastille. Brisson, not daring to resist this mandate, made a secret protest before a notary that he had accepted the post under compulsion. Of the 180 members of which the parliament of Paris was then composed, 126 members presently took oath to remain faithful to the League, to administer justice in the name of the supreme council, and to avenge the death of the Guises. All the subordinate officers of the high courts, and ultimately the advocates and attorneys, signed the same oath. The Sorbonne, meantime, issued a decree in answer to a formal application from the Seize, absolving the people from their oath of allegiance "to Henry de Valois, formerly their king," and erasing his name from the prayers and litanies of the church: they also declared it not only legitimate, but the bounden duty of all good Catholics to take up arms against the king, to exterminate, to blast, and to destroy.[2]

The preachers of Paris continued their invectives, and personally addressed any noted personage amongst their congregations with the utmost effrontery. On

[1] Journal de Paris. De Thou. "Le roy fut ebahit quand il entendit ces nouvelles. Puis ayant quelque peu ruminé cela, il se tourna vers M. d'O et luy dit ces mots quasi en le menaçant, 'Ce sont vos jeux d'O, vous voyez maintenant que vous me perdez!'"—Mémoires d'un Politique.

[2] The decree is dated January 7, 1589. Régistres de l'Hôtel de Ville. De Thou.

New Year's Day, when the parliament of Paris attended mass, as was customary, in the parish church of St: Bartholomew, Lincestre, after exhorting his hearers to revenge the assassination of the princes, had called on the president de Harlay to swear to contribute all in his power to this vengeance. "Raise your hand on high, M. le premier président! raise it aloft, high, that the people may see and register your oath!" De Harlay was compelled to comply, or the mob in its frenzy would have slain on the instant his colleagues and himself. The king was grossly abused by the clergy in language befitting the vilest localities; and foul charges were made respecting his amours which scandalized even the most reckless of their crew of applauders. Day and night processions of penitents perambulated the streets; delicate women, barefooted, and wrapped only in sheets or in loose robes of canvas, walked in these processions at the frantic summons of the preachers, not daring to refuse. Madame de Montpensier herself set the example of this "great expiation," as it was termed. Clad only in a loose robe of lace, barefooted, with her hair streaming over her shoulders, Catherine de Lorraine, the daughter and sister of the Guises, showed herself to the people. Her beauty and the fierce vehemence of her gestures excited the bystanders to frenzy. The processions thenceforth for more than a month were ceaseless; people, as if seized with a sudden delirium, sometimes rose from their beds in the middle of the night and paraded the streets with torches, singing dirges and blasphemous songs. During the day processions of young boys organized by the clergy perambulated from church to church carrying torches, which at stated intervals they extinguished, with frantic cries of "Dies iræ;" then dashing the brand on the pavement, they trampled out the flame—emblematic, it was said, of the sudden and swift extinction which had befallen king Henry. Abominable excesses attended these midnight processions, in which women took part; soon they were joined by the most profligate of both sexes; and scenes of horrible licence occurred within the very sanctuaries of the capital. La Dame de Ste. Beuve, a beautiful young widow of noble birth,[1] though the mistress of the chevalier d'Aumale, rendered herself conspicuous in these processions by her unblushing profligacy. Yet, next to madame de Montpensier, the Nemesis of the League, this woman exercised the greatest degree of influence. It was at the instigation of madame de Ste. Beuve, who was called in derision la Sainte Veuve, that the people entered the church of St. Paul and overthrew the magnificent mausoleum which the king had there erected over his three favourites St. Maigrin, Quélus, and Maugiron. The tomb was rifled, and the ashes of the minions thrown into the Seine. The chevalier d'Aumale, at the suggestion of his mistress, also undertook an expedition with Crucé and others to pillage the wealthy monastic establishment of Minimes, in the neighbourhood of Vincennes. A great booty was found in the convent chapel in vessels and candlesticks of gold, and in sumptuous robes of brocade and lace, which was carried to Paris. Henry, in the indulgence of his morbid whimsicalities, had decorated the high altar of the chapel in a style so as rather to resemble a bacchanalian board than a table set apart for the celebration of solemn mysteries. Gigantic satyrs held the wax tapers on either side of the altar. A crowned Bacchus supported the missal; the gold patens were engraved with amorous scenes taken from the Iliad of Homer, and with other mythological subjects little cal-

[1] Madame de Ste. Beuve was the daughter of André de Hacqueville, premier-président du grand conseil, and of Anne Hennequin.

culated to promote ascetic devotion.[1] These articles were carried in triumph and exhibited; the satyrs were declared to be the demons to which Henry sacrificed. The preacher Lincestre thundered from the pulpit in St. Bartholomew's against the depravity and *diableries* of the execrable tyrant. Engravings of the "discoveries at the Minimes of Vincennes" were distributed, and soon were to be found in the hand of every ragged urchin of the capital.

On Monday, January 30th, a grand requiem was performed in Notre Dame for the duc de Guise and his brother. The churches of the capital were hung with black; and for this day Paris remained prostrate, fasting and weeping the demise of her hero of the Barricades. The bishop of Rennes, the uncle of la Sainte Veuve, officiated at the altar; while the funeral oration was delivered by a learned doctor of the League, one Messire François Pigenat.[2] All the persons who assisted at the ceremony presented themselves attired in black. Madame de Montpensier and the duc d'Aumale appeared in great state; but the widowed duchesse de Guise was not present. The following day a procession of half-clad penitents of both sexes paraded the streets of Paris; but as the weather was rigorous in the extreme a great number of individuals lost their lives through exposure to the cold, which had the fortunate effect of diminishing the fervour for these displays.

The supreme council of the Seize, during these transactions, found the government which it had usurped to be a charge of almost insuperable difficulty.

[1] Cayet: Chronologie Novennaire. The recital of this foray at the Minimes of Vincennes is given with point in that stinging satire, entitled "Sorcelleries de Henri de Valois." "Le roy et Epernon font batir un lieu à l'écart dans le Marché à Chevaux, et là ils commencèrent en un jardin à faire leur exorcismes; mais Henri de Valois eut peür un jour."—La Vie et Faits Notables de Henri de Valois.

[2] François Pigenat, curé de St. Nicholas des Champs.

The parliament of Paris, nevertheless, ratified all that was demanded from it. The new president Brisson, though one of the most able men in the realm, was so intimidated that he proposed, accepted, and confirmed all things on oath at the dictation of the League. The most violent dissensions rent the council. As no one consented to be subordinate, affairs were soon brought to a stand. The duchesse de Montpensier wished to rule as a queen during the absence of her brother Mayenne; the duc d'Aumale, obtuse and self-sufficient, vehemently asserted his authority, which, however, no one seemed to acknowledge and regard. Madame de Montpensier, the chevalier d'Aumale, and la Sainte Veuve, were the ruling deities of the Parisian populace. The turbulent curés, therefore, pending the squabbles of the chiefs of the League, held during the entire month of January almost undisputed sway. The duchess, since her memorable progress through the streets of Paris *en habit de Pénitente*, had again suffered severely from the swelling of her ankles. Perceiving, however, that the disorganized condition of the capital offered the best chance for the eventual triumph of the royal cause, she bravely rose from her bed and proceeded, as has been related, to join the duc and duchesse de Mayenne at Dijon, resolved to escort the former into Paris and proclaim him king.

When king Henry heard of the imprisonment of the first president Achille de Harlay, he fell into a profound fit of musing. "My Parisians were fools, but now they are madmen," at length said his majesty, with a sigh. Treachery, however, again encompassed the unfortunate king, and threatened at this time to drive him to straits still more deplorable. But his necessity again roused the spirit of the king; and once more his foes, even in Paris itself, trembled before the wrath of their outraged sovereign.

After the death of the duc de Guise, the presence and society of Lognac captain of the Quarante-cinq, had become hateful to the king. Henry, therefore, according to his usual custom, took the first opportunity summarily to disgrace and exile him from court. Lognac, in revenge, repaired to Amboise, and informed du Guast that the king intended to sacrifice him to the manes of the cardinal de Guise, and that already his majesty had publicly declared that he never commanded the murder of the said cardinal, which du Guast had perpetrated from private motives. The fury of the bold Gascon trooper was so greatly excited at the report, that he immediately set all the prisoners at liberty within the castle; and commenced negotiations with the Seize for their ransom, and for the surrender of the fortress. The cardinal de Bourbon was forthwith treated as king by his fellow-prisoners; while du Guast, now exposed to the full brunt of the dexterous flattery of M. de Lyons, implicitly obeyed the latter in most things. Henry luckily received timely notice of the defection of du Guast—it is supposed through one Gotz, a lieutenant in the company of the latter, and his boon companion. The king, therefore, without hesitation repaired to Amboise, and at first could scarcely obtain admittance within his own fortress. Du Guast for long showed himself inexorable to the command or to the abject entreaties of his sovereign, who having no means of effecting his arrest or the recapture of the castle, was compelled to submit to a humiliating negotiation, in which Gotz acted as mediator. It was finally agreed that du Guast should deliver to the king the cardinal de Bourbon, the duchesse de Nemours, and the ducs d'Elbœuf and de Guise, on receiving the sum of 30,000 crowns. The archbishop of Lyons, Chapelle Marteau, Neuilly, and the sheriffs, were, on the contrary, to be left in the hands of du Guast, who was empowered by his majesty to detain them until a satisfactory ransom was offered for their liberation.[1] This disgraceful compact ratified, Henry ordered out his barge, and conducted the prisoners back to Blois, where they were confined in the same apartments which they had formerly occupied. Before quitting Amboise, Henry gave madame de Nemours her freedom, with permission to retire whither she would, exhorting her to restore tranquillity to the realm by her good and pacific counsels. This humiliating expedition inflicted immense injury on the royal cause. Du Guast, at liberty to treat for the ransom of the prisoners in his hands, sent his brother to Paris modestly offering to release them all on the payment of 300,000 crowns and his nomination to the chief command in the town of Châlons sur Saône.

After the return of the king to Blois, the Spanish ambassador took leave of the court, and established himself in his hôtel in Paris, where he remained throughout the subsequent troubles the active agent of the king of Spain; whose intrigues were now aimed at procuring the recognition of his daughter the infanta Isabel, daughter of Elizabeth de Valois, eldest sister of Henry III., as the future sovereign of France.

By the end of the month of January, 1589, the condition of the king could not be more forlorn; he was without money, without servants, without friends—ill, a prey to the darkest depression, alienated from his wife, and despoiled of the ensigns of that royal pomp which was the joy and delight of his eyes. From thi. point, however, the king's situation began to improve. The violence of the League, the gross tyranny and cruelty of its officers, the extortion practised everywhere, caused the hearts of many to incline again

[1] Pasquier. Maimbourg. Hist. de la Ligue. Journal de Paris.

towards the rule of their legitimate sovereign. Many nobles arrived at Blois, including the duc de Montpensier and his son the prince de Dombes, the prince de Conty, the duc de Nevers, monsieur Damville the heir of Montmorency, and the cardinal de Lenoncourt. The members of the parliament of Paris who had refused to take oath to the League, also presented themselves, with other official personages. Again the court of Henry began to assume something of its wonted brilliancy. The king now showed himself active, energetic, and disposed to take vigorous measures to crush the rebellion. Manifestoes were issued against the ducs de Mayenne and Aumale, and the chevalier d'Aumale, by which—unless they made their submission by the first day of the ensuing month of March—they were declared traitors, whom it was lawful for any one to capture and put to death. The king also issued a manifesto against the city of Paris, commanding the citizens to lay down arms on or before the 14th day of the ensuing month of March, under pain of incurring the penalties of high treason, with the abrogation of their charters and municipal privileges. The king also wrote to the duc d'Epernon, cancelling his decree of banishment, and commanding him to send 800 soldiers to garrison the town and castle of Blois; he also conferred upon the duke the title of governor of Blois. The most important decision of all was his majesty's tardy resolve to send Nicholas Harlay sieur de Sancy, on a mission to the Protestant princes of Germany and to the Swiss Cantons, empowered to raise loans of money, and to recruit men for the service of the state. Unlimited authority was given to Sancy to conclude the necessary treaties and conventions,[1] without reference to the council of state. Sancy departed on this

[1] Lettre de Henri III au Comte de Montbelliard, 1589. MS. Bibl. Imp. Dupuy, 137.

important ambassage about the beginning of February, and safely arrived at Geneva on the 14th day of the same month. It was next determined that the king should quit the castle of Blois, which being not fortified was in danger of capture by the Leaguers. The town of Bourges was first selected for the head-quarters of the king; subsequently the ancient city of Tours was decided upon as being better adapted for the royal abode.

The decision taken to appeal to the great Protestant powers of Europe for succour in the extremity to which the royal party was reduced, rendered the reconsideration of the question applicable and timely—whether the king should not avail himself of the aid of the chief and captain of the continental Huguenots, Henri king of Navarre, his own kinsman and vassal? The duc de Nevers obstinately opposed the step; the legate Morosini went into transports of indignation at the bare surmise of a calamity so dire. Queen Louise wept and offered prayers in her oratory to avert so heinous a sacrilege. The duchesse d'Angoulême, however, wise as well as patriotic, strongly counselled the king unhesitatingly to adopt the measure, and offered herself to negotiate the alliance. The king of Navarre showed the most marked sympathy for the position of the king, and proclaimed his willingness to serve his majesty against their united enemies. Nevertheless he steadily continued his conquests; for as long as Nevers and the army of Poitou menaced his dominions, he was, he said, bound to defend them. After the capture of Niort, the king of Navarre, profiting by the disturbed state of the realm, possessed himself of the towns of Loudun, Monars, Montreuil, and Châtelleraud. These exploits achieved, the king of Navarre, though just recovering from a severe attack of sickness with which he had been seized at a village called St. Père, generously advanced to the assistance of the royal garrison of Argenton in Berry, besieged by a general of the League, which he succoured. Such was the ignominious position of Henry III. between two victorious armies on his own territories, himself without a regiment which he could rely upon, and liable any day to be quietly captured by Navarre and the Huguenots, or by Mayenne and the Holy League. There seemed to be no resource for the king but to vacate the realm, or to justify the prediction made by Sixtus V. at the period of the peace of Nemours. The fiery old pontiff spoke thus to the duc de Nevers: "If this pardon and reconciliation are not sincere between the king and MM. de Lorraine, we shall see the king of France driven to treat the Catholics as his deadly foes. We shall behold him recruiting troops from Germany, England, and other Protestant states, to maintain a preponderance in his own realm. We shall see him forced into concluding shameful treaties with the king of Navarre, with Condé; so that France will be inundated with Lutherans and Calvinists. You see, monseigneur," said the pope, furiously, "what all these your fine associations and leagues will lead to!" Having so clear an insight into future events, Sixtus certainly did not demean himself at this juncture with the prudence and moderation which might have been expected. To hasten the affair of his absolution, the king had sent the bishop of Mans to Rome, the bearer of the letter under his own hand, which had been prescribed by the pope. At the same time the League sent the abbé d'Orbais to oppose the royal shrift, and to pray his Holiness to launch a sentence of excommunication and interdict upon the person and the abode of the "execrable tyrant." The most indecent scenes often occurred from the uncontrollable temper of the pope. The bishop of Mans was also empowered to demand the abrogation of the decree of the Sorbonne which had pronounced Henry deposed and accursed. At the first audience the bishop presented Henry's letter, and throwing himself on his knees before the pontifical footstool, he said, "Most holy father, in the name of the very Christian king, I pray for absolution, with all the respect and submission which the supreme head of the Church has the right to demand from the most humble and obedient of his sons. I supplicate your Holiness to confer upon the said king your holy benediction, and to re-establish him in your favour, and in all the privileges and immunities which the said monarch and his ancestors have so long enjoyed!"[1] Sixtus smiled grimly at hearing himself addressed in so humble a strain by the representative of a once potent monarch; he extended his hand to the venerable prelate and bade him sit by his side. The pope then commenced a series of observations, the gist of which was that king Henry should send the cardinal de Bourbon and the archbishop of Lyons to be judged in Rome, but evaded any direct reply to the supplication addressed to him. The cardinal de Joyeuse, in an admirable letter written to the king, expatiates on the indecision shown by the papal court, and recounts the various modes of penance suggested by members of the Sacred College as suitable for the king's heinous guilt. Some of the cardinals proposed that the reception of the canons of Trent by the Gallican church might be deemed sufficient penance; others the introduction of the Inquisition throughout the realm; while some prelates, deeming a personal castigation more wholesome, suggested that Henry should leave his palace, clad in his shirt, carrying a lighted taper, and in such guise assist at high mass. The king, in his reply to this letter, observes with proper dignity, "You will inform

[1] De Thou, liv. xciv. and xcv.

his Holiness that I am still disposed earnestly to ask absolution, relying, however, that such a mark of submission rendered to the Holy See will be deemed sufficient. You had better make it to be comprehended at once, that if it be intended to press for ceremonies and formalities contrary to my honour and dignity, that I shall at once reject and eschew such !"[1] The whole of the month of February passed in these agitations. The king at length authorized the duchesse d'Angoulême to open negotiations with the king of Navarre, and himself prepared to quit Blois for Tours.

On the 18th of March a brilliant cavalcade issued from the portals of the venerable castle. On that day Henry took leave of his niece Christine, grand-duchess of Tuscany, and, attended by his court, escorted her half a league on her road to Lyons. The young duchess bade farewell to her uncle with tears; but she was departing to a splendid destiny—to share the honours of the Medici, her maternal kindred—and her sorrow soon became appeased. At Lyons, however, a great danger menaced her. The hand of Christine de Lorraine had once been ardently sought by the duc de Nemours, whose suit queen Catherine encouraged until the grander destiny of consort of Ferdinand de Medici was presented for the acceptance of the young princess. Catherine hesitated not a moment; the charms of Florence and the traditions of her aspiring kindred ever roused the queen's enthusiasm. The duc de Nemours was consequently dismissed, and Christine affianced to the grand duke. The people of Lyons, therefore, whose governor the duke was, entered into a conspiracy to arrest the young princess and deliver her into the power of her discarded suitor. One of the boldest amongst the plotters, however, prudently proposed to send and advertise

[1] Lettre du Roi au Cardinal de Joyeuse. Archives Curieuses.

the duc de Nemours of the scheme, and obtain his assent. The duke honourably forbade the violence; and sent a gentleman of his household to reassure the princess, who had purposely been informed of the design when without the district which owned the royal sway. Christine, thereupon, owing to the interposition of the duke, passed in all safety and honour through Lyons, and on to Marseilles, where she found the grand ducal fleet at anchor, ready to convey her to Genoa.[1]

The king quitted Blois a few days subsequently, leaving in the castle a strong garrison from the army levied by Epernon, whose influence over his master was rapidly rising to its wonted ascendency, though the sovereign and his old favourite had not yet met. The king's unfortunate prisoners followed in his train to Montrichard, where Henry halted for a day; his majesty then caused the princes to be conveyed to the fortress of Azáy le Rideau, pending his decision as to their ultimate and separate destinations. In a letter written by the aged cardinal de Bourbon to the cardinal de Vendôme, it seems that the announcement of their removal from Blois was only made to the prisoners late on the preceding evening. The cardinal rose, and at midnight indited a most sorrowful epistle to Vendôme. He wrote: "M. de Menon has just presented himself to announce that we are to hold ourselves in readiness to depart early to-morrow morning for a certain castle, the which will be declared to us on our road. We have heard that it is probably the château of Azáy, which I once visited with the queen and Monsieur. Should such be the case, I find myself reduced to the miserable strait of falling into the hands of the

1 Chronologie Novennaire. The duchess Christine became a widow 1608. She survived, living in great state and honour, until the year 1638.

Huguenots, who hold that neighbourhood, as no river separates Azáy from l'Isle Bouchard.[1] This apprehension gives me intense affliction, so that I cannot recover myself. I implore and conjure you, therefore, by the friendship and respect which you owe me as your uncle, to intercede with the king to avert such a calamity.'[2] The residence of the cardinal in the castle of Azáy being very brief, he was soon relieved from his disquietudes. He was conducted to Chinon, and there straitly guarded by its governor, M. dé Chavigny, a devoted adherent of the royal cause. The duc d'Elbœuf was imprisoned in Loches—the king delivering him up to the custody of the duc d'Epernon as a hostage in case Mayenne and the League assailed the castle of Blois, to which the duke had repaired on its being vacated by the court. The young duc de Guise was confined in the citadel of Tours, from whence he ultimately succeeded in making his escape.

The duchesse d'Angoulême, meantime, proceeded to Chatelleraud, where she had an interview with the king of Navarre, who was encamped in the neighbourhood of l'Isle Bouchard. Henri readily accepted her overtures for his reconciliation with king Henry; and promised, on the granting of suitable conditions to his party, to repair to Tours and assume the command of the royal army. The king of Navarre, moreover, expressed his special acknowledgments for the firmness with which king Henry had maintained his rights when actually assailed by the League; and chivalrously declared he deemed it an incident to be proud of in his career, that he should be called upon, with his band of heroic followers, to defend the person and the crown of his sovereign! The king of Navarre therefore

[1] The king of Navarre was encamped at l'Isle Bouchard.

[2] Lettre du Cardinal de Bourbon au Cardinal de Vendôme. MS. Bibl. Imp. Béth. vol. 8866.

despatched M. Duplessis Mornay, the stanch Huguenot and able statesman, to Tours to negotiate the terms of alliance. Duplessis repaired privately to the house of Gaspard maréchal de Schomberg, his friend and kinsman. On the same night that Henry arrived at Tours M. de Mornay was secretly conducted by Diane de France to the cabinet of the king. Then and there a truce of one year, commencing from the ensuing third day of April, was signed; moreover, a secret article was agreed upon—to wit, that the king of Navarre should bring a succour to the royal army of 1,200 horse and 2,000 arquebusiers, and in return Henry agreed to cede one important town on the Loire. Saumur being eventually offered, was accepted by the king of Návarre. This important place was therefore evacuated by the secretary of state Beaulieu—on whom the king had conferred the command—and occupied by Duplessis Mornay and a strong Huguenot garrison.[1] The next act performed by king Henry was to issue a proclamation summoning the parliament to meet in his ancient town of Tours. This edict, translating the parliament from Paris, is dated April 22nd. In obedience to the royal summons all the members faithful to their allegiance appeared in Tours. The learned advocate Jacques Faye d'Espesses was appointed first president, after that dignity had been offered to and declined by Jacques Auguste de Thou, the famous historian. The post of attorney-general, resigned by Espesses, was given to Louis Servin, a young man of brilliant acquirements, a great orator, and devoted to the royal cause. The king held his first bed of justice in Tours[2]

[1] Hist. de la Vie de Philippe de Mornay, Seigneur Duplessis Mornay, p. 129, et suiv.

[2] The parliament held its assemblies while in Tours in the hall of the Convent of St. Julien. MS. Bibl. Imp.: Etablissement du Parlement en la Ville de Tours. Suppl. fr. 9566.

on the 23rd day of April. His majesty, as usual, gained great applause by his eloquence: he detailed the measures taken for the subjugation of his enemies, but was silent respecting the convention which he had concluded with the king of Navarre. He bemoaned the rebellion of his subjects, the contumacy and treason of the Gallican clergy, the diminished numbers of his faithful parliament, and the prison of their illustrious chief de Harlay.

In Paris, meanwhile, affairs were involved in anarchy still more hopeless. The Seize, busied in preparing an extended scheme of government, to consist of a council of forty members, to present to Mayenne on his entrance into the capital, fought and menaced each other over their council-board in the Hôtel de Ville. Every one who had applied himself, in however humble a capacity, in forwarding the designs of the League, demanded to have his name placed on the list of the chosen forty. The curés of the capital, who had enacted so prominent and seditious a part, on the other hand, expected that the clerical members should be exclusively chosen from their body, and the lay members from lists furnished by themselves. The duchesse de Montpensier insisted that no name should be enrolled whose owner was not prepared to elevate Mayenne to the throne, which she had chosen to proclaim vacant. A system of terrorism prevailed. All suspected of favouring royalty were committed to the Bastille. Those who refrained from sharing in the processions were subjected to shameful espionage; and many persons convicted of having eaten meat in the Lenten season were committed to the diocesan prison. One family was arrested because a servant-maid deposed that her mistress had been merry on Shrove Tuesday; "for," as the tyrants of the capital averred, "laughter and mirth at a period of national mourning was a misdemeanour and to be punished accordingly."

On the seventh day of February, 1589, the duchesse de Guise gave birth to a son. The infant came into the world, it was stated, with hands clasped in supplication and with eyes raised to heaven. The people adopted the myth, and raged the more fiercely on receiving so palpable an indication of the sympathy of Heaven. The baptism of the young prince was celebrated with extraordinary displays of zeal on Tuesday, February 8th. Processions, illuminations, meetings—which the most fanatic attended, with Lincestre and Prevost at their head, to anathematize the tyrant assassin—addresses and presents to madame de Guise, followed in rapid succession. The ceremony was performed in the church of St. Jean en Grève: the child was named Alexandre Paris. It was conveyed to the church enveloped in a mantle of black crape, and was carried by M. de Maineville. Roland, being the principal *échevin* of Paris, represented the city in the absence of its provost, Chapelle Marteau. The duchesse d'Aumale was compelled, much against her desire, to officiate as godmother. The city bands were present; and the baptismal procession was escorted with military pomp to the church.[1] The excitement attending this event had scarcely subsided, when the duc and duchesse de Mayenne and madame de Montpensier entered Paris. All the cities devoted to the League had opened their gates and greeted the duke with rapturous acclamations, following the example of Orléans, which place Mayenne had visited shortly after the retreat of the royal army. At Chartres, where the royal cause at last had fallen, Mayenne was saluted with shouts of "*Vivent les princes Lorraine!*" Nevertheless, the duke reluctantly em-

[1] Journal de Paris.

barked in the war; his temperament was peaceful, and even lethargic. He hated turmoil; he beheld his house prosperous and wealthy. Mayenne had shown little sympathy with the political projects of his brother the duc de Guise; but was known to have deprecated his ambition. The duke, moreover, openly declared that far from supporting the practices and pursuing the projects of his deceased brothers, had the king contented himself with their arrest, he would have drawn his sword for the support of the royal authority. The perfidy of the king, the impossibility of relying on his word, and the ascendency of Nevers and Epernon, were vividly portrayed by the duchesse de Montpensier. Her impassioned pleadings for vengeance, and her frantic denunciations, at length wrought upon the mind of Mayenne, until he believed himself bound to unsheath the avenging sword. As for the duchesse de Mayenne, her equable and matter-of-fact temperament was shaken almost into stupor before the hurricanes of wrath in which her sister-in-law indulged. Devoted to the education of her daughters and to works of pious charity, madame de Mayenne had no ambition to ascend the altitudes to which the duchess pointed. There was also only one previous instance on record when the duc de Mayenne had been betrayed into a crime by vehemence of passion. The son of the chancellor de Birague had the presumption to solicit from the duke the hand of one of his daughters, acknowledging, at the same time, that he held in his possession a written promise of marriage from the young princess. The duke, without reply, drew his sword and plunged it through the body of the unfortunate young cavalier.

The duc de Mayenne entered Paris on Sunday, February 12th. He was met outside the city by the municipality, the members of the supreme council, and by the principal citizens, who escorted him with extraordinary pomp to the hôtel de Montmorency, where he was received by his consort and by madame de Montpensier—these princesses having preceded him—and by the duchesses de Nemours, de Guise, and d'Aumale. Madame de Montpensier brought back three prisoners in her train—Louis de Rambouillet sieur de Maintenon, M. de Poigny, and César de Balsac seigneur de Gié; these noblemen, the king's devoted servants, she caused to be conducted to the Bastille. The duc de Mayenne immediately entered on the arduous task of organizing a government. His anticipations of the difficulty and odium of the undertaking were more than realized. The Seize, though outwardly deferential, caballed for the confirmation of their past acts and future projects. Mayenne, who had been called to remodel the government and to create a system to supersede the old *régime*, found himself as much the slave of the factions as the humblest denizen of the capital. The duke, therefore, to avoid further schisms, deemed it prudent for the present to accept the nominations for the council of Forty which the provisional government had selected. This famous list comprehends five of the curés[1] of the capital, the bishops of Meaux, Senlis, and Agen, the marquis de Canillac (the nobleman who had been so highly favoured by queen Marguerite), the sieurs de Maineville, de St. Paul, and others. The tiers état was represented, as may be imagined, by a motley crew of demagogues, of which Crucé, la Bruière, Neuilly, Drouait, and Sesnant, were the most conspicuous members. This last-mentioned person, Pierre Sesnant, was also secretary of the council, and soon set at defiance every other will but his own, even presuming to treat the duc de Mayenne with disrespect.

[1] Prevost, curé of St. Severin; Boucher, curé of St. Benoit; Aubry, curé of St. André; Pelletier, curé of St. Jacques; Pigenat, curé of St. Nicholas.

ful freedom. When any deliberation was taking a turn which he deemed adverse, this Sesnant would rise and exclaim, "*Doucement, messieurs, je proteste au nom de quarante mille hommes!*" Mayenne, after installing this heterogeneous assembly, next took the oaths as Lieutenant-Général de l'état et couronne de France. The duke had wisdom enough to perceive how untenable were the designs of madame de Montpensier on the crown. Scarcely would the tumultuous assemblage of the Hôtel de Ville render him homage as its own elected president; and as for the nobles of the League, they made it clearly apparent that, while willing to obey the duke as their peer, their complaisance would extend no farther. The oaths were administered to the duke by the president Brisson on the 7th day of March, 1589. New seals were cut, having on one side the usual *fleurs-de-lis*; on the reverse a vacant throne, with the words "Le Scel du Royaume de France."

The first act of the new government was to commute the existing taxation to the amount of one-third. The king, however, had made this concession on the closing of the States-general. The people, therefore, clamoured for further innovation and exemptions. The clergy also demanded release from their financial engagements—their guarantee for the payment of the interest on the city debt—which they had contracted at the States assembled at Poissy, 1561. The payment of these *rentes de l'Hôtel de Ville* had long been a tax peculiarly odious to the church; it was therefore proposed and agreed to relieve the clergy from their responsibilities. This decree brought ruin to numberless families of the middle class of citizens, whose chief means of subsistence had been derived from the punctual payment of these dividends. Another notable expedient was then devised to pacify the clamours of the lower classes of Paris. A petition was addressed to the council complaining of the high rate of rentals in the capital—a state of affairs declared to be an intolerable oppression. The supreme council, therefore, issued an *ordonnance* arbitrarily diminishing the rentals of houses and apartments throughout the capital to the amount of one-third, calculated on the rate of rent as existing at the time when the edict was issued. At the same time the forty members voted themselves an ample provision of one hundred crowns a month each for support while engaged in the duties of legislation. The Parisian *bourgeoisie* thus beheld itself ruined; the clergy, the populace, and the members of the supreme council alone held jubilee. The impoverishment of the middle classes, however, was soon felt by the poor of the capital. The shops were closed, the manufacturer dismissed his workmen, the small householder could no longer afford the luxury of servants. The absence of the court, the breaking-up of the establishments of the nobles, and the dismissal of their splendid retinues, increased the prevalent penury. The people began at length to discover that the fanatical ravings of the priests of Paris would not feed them; and that the parading of the shrines of their patron saints was toilsome work indeed when they possessed no roof to shelter them on the conclusion of the ceremonials of each day. It was the utter misery of the populace of the large cities throughout France, and the loyal union of the middle classes with the nobles, that eventually saved the realm from dismemberment.

The insubordination of the supreme council of Union and its subserviency to private influences at length compelled Mayenne to make the attempt of introducing fifteen fresh members chosen by himself, whose votes might balance, and in some measure restrain, the lawless independence of their colleagues. After much cajolery and some intimidation the duke succeeded in his object, in which he was supported by the ducs de Nemours and d'Aumale, the chevalier d'Aumale, Henri de Lorraine comte de Chaligny, Roland, and Desprez. Amongst the new members of the council were the ex-secretary of state Villeroy and his father, the presidents l'Huillier, Janin, Vetus, le Maître and others, besides two dignitaries of the church, the bishop of Rouen and the abbé de Lenoncourt. The partisans of Guise trusted that these nominations would subdue the ultra-democratic tendencies of the existing government, and gradually pave the way for the assumption by Mayenne of supreme power. The duke nominated the duc d'Aumale as president of the Supreme Conseil de l'Union. He then quitted Paris to take command of the army of the League, assembling in the county of Beausse, to take the field for the rescue of the captives of Amboise, and the reduction of the loyal towns on the Loire. Mayenne proceeded to Châteaudun to organize, in the first instance, an attack upon the towns of Tours and Blois, in the confident hope that the capture of the person of the king must speedily accomplish the aspiring designs of his party.

The overtures made by king Henry to the king of Navarre, though not as yet publicly acknowledged, were known to the legate Morosini, and consequently to the prelates faithful to the royal cause. This unhallowed union, as it was termed, created the greatest scandal. Not one of Henry's ecclesiastical subjects, however, dare protest openly against it. The rapid revolt of town after town, and the advance of the duc de Mayenne from Paris, plainly showed that its alternative must be the captivity of the king and his enforced abdication. The utter repudiation of all authority, and the lawless independence manifested by both the clergy and laity, members of the holy League, amazed and irritated the legate. The Sorbonne, without reference whatever to the Holy See, had excommunicated and deposed the king; by the same authority the royal name had been erased from the litanies of the Church, and a different form of prayer inserted. Scandalous scenes of violence ensued in the churches, which were used rather as places for the tumultuous assemblage of the disaffected than for the purposes of prayer. In the most disturbed districts, two large pictures, painted in white on black cloth, were affixed in the churches on each side of the altar, the one representing the murder of the duc de Guise, the other that of the cardinal; the inscription at the foot of the portraits gave to the former the title of 'Prince de Force,' to the latter that of 'Prince de Patience.' The legate, therefore, proposed that through his mediation an attempt should be made to reconcile the grievances of Royalist and Leaguer. He affectionately admonished Henry that such concession was his bounden duty, after the outrages he had perpetrated at Blois. "Sire, make one more attempt at conciliation before you incur the anathema of our Holy Mother Church by your blasphemous league with princes accursed, alien, and heretic. Remember your solemn oath to maintain the Edict of Union, and to pursue and annihilate heresy!" The remonstrances of the legate produced a great effect upon the mind of the king, and for the first time in his life Henry's conscience upbraided him for his meditated violation of a pledge solemnly given, after having invoked the malediction of Heaven if he attempted its infringement. Moreover, it was a bitter humiliation—the appeal to the chivalry of Henri de Navarre, and the admission that his safety depended on the gallant devotion of those heroes whom his troops had combated at Coutras. The king, therefore, gave cordial assent to Morosini's proposal, and thus again committed a virtual perfidy against the king of Navarre; for an agreement with Mayenne and the League would necessarily annihilate his recent convention with the Huguenots. Henry intrusted the legate with a minute containing the concessions he was prepared to make; a copy of which he secretly sent by courier to the duc de Lorraine, with a letter requesting the interest of the latter with his kindred in procuring the reception of the conditions offered. The king proposed to set his prisoners at liberty; to confirm the princes of the League in their respective governments; to give them certain towns as security for his pacific intents; and to grant a general amnesty for the past. "The king," says Davila, "offered the duc de Lorraine the cities of Metz, Toul, and Verdun, and agreed to get mademoiselle the duchesse de Bouillon for his son M. de Vaudemont. He proposed to leave the duc de Mayenne in possession of the government of Burgundy, and to give him 100,000 crowns of ready money. He tendered the governments of Champagne, St. Dizier, and Rocroy to the duc de Guise, with a pension of 20,000 crowns; to the duc de Nevers the government of Lyons, with 10,000 crowns of pension; to the duc d'Aumale a town and the same amount of pension; to the duc d'Elbœuf the town of Poictiers and 10,000 crowns of pension; finally, to the chevalier d'Aumale the postof general-in-chief of infantry, and a pension of 20,000 francs."

In executing the above articles his majesty proposed that disputed questions should be submitted to the arbitration of the pope, the dukes of Tuscany, Lorraine, and Ferrara, and the signory of Venice. Content, as he might well be, with such amazing and cowardly concessions, Morosini took leave of the king, and proceeded to visit the duc de Mayenne at Châteaudun, where the latter had just arrived. The duke, however, steadily rejected all compromise short of the abdication of the king. "I cannot, nor will I, conclude any convention apart from the lords of the Confederation. What trust can we put in the word of a miscreant prince who has just committed so detestable a crime! Deposed from his kingly dignity, what right can Henry put forth now to sign a treaty? Even if I accepted these propositions, his Holiness could never induce me to render him personally the duty and homage of a subject. I will die a thousand deaths rather than submit!" Astonished and much disconcerted, Morosini, after repeatedly attempting to bend the inflexible resolution of the duc de Mayenne, took his leave, and retired to Lyons, in obedience to instructions previously received from Rome, foreseeing that the proclamation of the alliance between the kings of France and Navarre was now inevitable. The legate sent immediate notice to Henry of the failure of his negotiation: "Your majesty will now find it requisite to take the best counsel you can on your affairs," wrote Morosini.[1] "I am grieved that I can do nothing with M. de Mayenne; I have taken leave of him, and intend to pursue my road through Orléans to Lyons, where I wait the commands of his Holiness." It had been with difficulty that madame de Montpensier succeeded in stirring up the frigid and cautious Mayenne to avenge the death of his brothers; but having been once roused, the duke persisted with characteristic obstinacy in accomplishing that design.

About this period the king, being informed of the seditious enterprises of madame de Montpensier in Paris, sent a gentleman of his chamber to the duchess to deliver a mandate commanding her to refrain from such treasonable proceedings, and retire from Paris; "otherwise, when he entered the capital he would cause her to be burned alive!" The duchess undauntedly replied on the spot, using epithets too vehement to ad-

[1] Cayet: Chronologie Novennaire. Davila.

mit of a literal transcription, and ended by observing, "The death by fire, monsieur, with which you presume to menace me, would be the just doom of that perfidious monster, once by Divine wrath our king. Be assured, however, that I will do all in my power to prevent the return of the said tyrant into this our good city of Paris!"[1]

[1] Journal de Henri III.

CHAPTER IV.

1589.

Proceedings of the court at Tours—The maréchal de Retz—Edicts promulgated by the parliament—Interview between Henry III. and the king of Navarre—Enthusiastic reception of the latter by king Henry and the royalists at Tours—Enterprise of the duc de Mayenne on the town of Tours—Danger of the king—Assault of the suburb St. Symphorien—Retreat of the army of the League—Position of affairs in Paris—Tumults and licence of the mob—The two Henrys place themselves at the head of an army to assault Paris—Intervening military operations—Negotiations with Rome—Excommunication of Henry III.—Reception of the bull in France—Repulse of the duc d'Aumale from before Senlis by a royalist division under the duc de Longueville—Entry into France of the foreign levies—Jacques Clement—The duchesse de Montpensier and the chieftains of the League conspire the assassination of Henry III.—Arrival of the royal army at St. Cloud—Siege of Paris—Departure of Clement for the camp—Assassination of Henry III.—His letter to queen Louise—Demise of the king—Proclamation of Henri Quatre—The duchesse de Montpensier—Her transports and the rejoicings in Paris over the death of the king—Defection of the nobles from the cause of Henri IV.—Henry raises the siege of Paris—He deposits the body of the deceased king at Compiègne—Incidents connected with the interment of the king—Benefactions of Henry III.—Anguish of queen Louise at the decease of Henry III.—She endeavours to avenge his murder—Her life of seclusion and beneficence—Demise of queen Louise—Device and motto of Henry III.

The refusal of the duc de Mayenne to enter into negotiation with king Henry, and the demand peremptorily enforced by Sixtus V. that the captive prelates should be conducted to Rome before he absolved the king from the ecclesiastical censures which he had incurred, left no alternative but the speedy proclamation of the convention concluded with the king of Navarre. The maréchal d'Aumont at this season displayed energy and ability of no ordinary kind. He it was who now presided at the council of state, and gave vigour and purpose to the fitful resolves of the king. The duc de Nevers, finding that his remonstrances were ineffectual to prevent the proclamation of the alliance he deprecated, retired from Tours to his castle in the town of Nevers, and assumed the neutral attitude of a mediator. The maréchal de Retz, deeming the destruction of the king inevitable, basely abandoned his benefactor, under pretext that his health was so impaired that his only chance of six months longer of life was a sojourn at the baths of Lucca. Henry reluctantly gave the marshal permission to depart, scornfully advising him to take heed lest even then he fell not into the power of the League. The marshal put on a disguise, and took extraordinary precautions; but while traversing Berri he was arrested by M. de Neuvy, lieutenant of the duc de Nemours. Mayenne was transported with delight when he heard of the capture of de Retz, and exclaimed, "There is a good 50,000 crowns of ransom!" Henry laughed derisively, and forthwith wrote a letter of condolence to the imprisoned marshal, in which he maliciously deplored "that he had only so brief a space of existence left; nevertheless, that reflection ought to console the marshal for his afflictive detention."[1]

[1] De Retz was compelled to pay 50,000 crowns for his liberty. He then sailed for Spain, and after an interview with Philip II., he retired to Lucca. From Lucca M. de Retz entered a monastery in Florence, when so cowardly were his fears of losing life and fortune in the contest pending in France, that he counterfeited decrepitude, and even insanity, to procure the undisturbed enjoyment of his retreat. For three years the duke was served by one footman and two peasant women; while his accomplished consort managed his vast revenues. On the

The maréchal d'Aumont, after causing public proclamation to be made of the treaty concluded between the two kings, advised his royal master to send to the king of Navarre inviting him to an interview at Tours, that their reconciliation might be complete. He also counselled the king to summon Epernon. This was a step which the king intensely desired, but had refrained from on account of the precarious condition of affairs; especially as a bitter quarrel existed between d'Aumont and the duke, and that madame d'Angoulême had warned him not to attempt the recall of Epernon to court. In a few days, therefore, the duc d'Epernon arrived from Blois. Henry received his favourite with enthusiastic transports. So penetrated was the duke with the chivalrous forgetfulness of his own grievances displayed by d'Aumont, that on leaving his royal master Epernon at once repaired to visit the marshal. "M. le maréchal," said Epernon, "I am here to thank you, and to offer you my humble services. So noble has been your generous forgetfulness of our personal quarrels, that I am proud to acknowledge you as my superior in rank and virtue." D'Aumont was affected to tears. "Monseigneur," said he, "I demand no thanks—only your able services for the king our master. I accept in such fashion your professions and friendship, and give you mine in return with all the sincerity and honour of a Frenchman and a soldier!"[1] The same evening the maréchal d'Aumont and the duc d'Epernon appeared arm-in-arm at the royal reception. In the space of a few days Epernon dominated as ever over the council and in the royal cabinet. His arrival and ad-

success of the arms of Henri IV. being assured, the duke emerged in 1594 from his monastery, and, miraculously, as he said, recovering the use of his limbs, entered France at the head of a body of Swiss, which he had enlisted to serve the cause of the king.

[1] De Thou, liv. xcv. Giraud: Vie du Duc d'Epernon.

vice greatly confirmed the royal resolve to conclude a cordial and complete alliance with le Béarnnois and his Huguenots.

Some important edicts were immediately promulgated. The parliament declared the ducs de Mayenne, Aumale, and Nemours guilty of high treason; it confiscated their lands, proclaimed them deprived of their dignities, and set a price upon their heads. Henry also wrote private letters, countersigned, however, by his ministers, to the duchesses de Nemours, Guise, Montpensier, and d'Aumale, commanding them to retire from Paris to one of his castles on the Loire, under pain of incurring capital penalties. Queen Louise also addressed her kindred, and appealed especially to madame de Nemours, mother of the princes of Guise. The king then despatched an ambassador to the emperor Rodolph II., praying his imperial majesty to give all countenance and aid towards the embodiment of the levies raising by Sancy. The enthusiasm for the royal cause in Switzerland, after Henry's convention with the Huguenots, surpassed the expectation of all. Under the banner of Sancy 10,000 Swiss troops were already enlisted. The comte de Schomberg had also success in recruiting for the service of the king in the Protestant states of Germany, and soon succeeded in raising 10,000 *reiters*, and a formidable body of 16,000 landsknechts, with which he immediately prepared to enter France. The king of Navarre brought 5,000 infantry, 500 arquebusiers, besides a body of 500 gentlemen, the *élite* of his nobles, all valiant and able soldiers. The duc d'Epernon, whose wealth and resources seemed inexhaustible, placed a body of 4,000 troops at the disposal of his sovereign. Moreover, the grand duke of Tuscany secretly sent the king a loan of 200,000 gold crowns; the duc de Nevers also, in proof of his good-will and loyalty, sent his royal master a further sum of 30,000 gold crowns.[1] An ambassage was despatched to Madrid to request the neutrality of Philip II., and to explain to his Catholic majesty how hopeless ultimately was the revolt of the League against the legitimate and orthodox monarch. To his steady friend queen Elizabeth Henry also sent an envoy, to pray for the continued co-operation of her fleets on the coasts of France, and her armies in the Low Countries, so as to divert in measure the mischievous attention of Philip II. from the affairs of France. Excellent nominations of personages were next made by Henry for the internal administration of the realm. The comte de Soissons was made governor of Bretagne; the duc de Montpensier of Normandy; Matignon over Guyenne; Montmorency in Languedoc; la Valette, elder brother of the duc d'Epernon, over Provence; Ornano in Dauphiny; Tavannes in Burgundy; and the duc de Longueville over Picardy. The maréchal d'Aumont received the government of Champagne; the comte de Sourdis that of La Beausse; and d'Entragues the command over the Orléannois. All these governors had the difficult and important task intrusted to them of reconquering the numerous towns in alliance with the League situated within their respective governments. The appointments were rapturously received by the king's loyal subjects, as the commencement of a new and enlightened era of government.

The king of Navarre, meanwhile, lay encamped at Maillé, six miles from the town of Tours. Some friendly interchange of messages had taken place between the sovereigns through the good offices of

[1] De Thou, liv. xcv. De Thou relates that a fanatical preacher ascended the pulpit in the cathedral of Nevers, and preached a sermon redolent of the foulest abuse against the king. The duke sat the sermon out, and then sent for the monk and compelled him to reascend the pulpit and contradict each of his previous assertions, showing good cause wherefore.

madame d'Angoulême and Châtillon, eldest son of the late admiral de Coligny—who at this crisis set the example of reconciliation and the forgetfulness of injuries by proceeding to Tours to offer his homage to king Henry. On Sunday, the last day of April, 1589, Henry, on repairing to hear mass in the abbey of Marmoustier, sent one of his chamberlains to compliment the king of Navarre and to express his desire to see him at Plessis-les-Tours. The king of Navarre replied by promising to be, an hour thence, on the bridge of La Motte, between Maillé and Tours. The majority of Henri's officers strongly dissuaded their master from trusting himself alone with the king of France. "Remember la St. Barthélemy, sire! Remember that no more acceptable holocaust could be offered to quench the wrath of Rome and the League, than your blood and that of your brave Huguenot nobles! M. de Châtillon, like his father was, is deceived by the court: the persuasions of M. l'amiral led your august mother and her nobles to the slaughter in Paris. Take heed, therefore, not to follow a similar advice from the lips of the son."[1] The king of Navarre, however, was not to be deterred; he had consulted Châtillon, Epernon, and d'Aumont, and, above all, Duplessis Mornay and Sully. These personages all inclined to the interview; the first three noblemen strongly insisted on its necessity. Duplessis and Sully, the immediate subjects of the king of Navarre, showed less enthusiasm; though when Henri of himself decided to repair to Plessis, Mornay wrote from Tours: "You have done your duty, sire; a duty, however,

[1] François de Châtillon born April 28th, 1559. He married Marie d'Ailly de Picquiny, who bore him four sons, all killed in an action fought near to Saintes. Châtillon's third son left a daughter, married to Jacques Chabot, marquis de Mirabeau, and one son. François de Châtillon died October 8th, 1591, at the age of 32.

which it was not legitimate for any of your own subjects to prescribe."[1] At le Pont de la Motte the king of Navarre was met by the maréchal d'Aumont and by the ducs d'Epernon and Montbazon, sent by the king to conduct him to Plessis. "M. le maréchal," said Henri, "I repair to Plessis confiding in your word and in your honour."[2] A suite of nobles and a company of guards accompanied the king, who, out of respect for the opinion of the minority of his council and a due precaution for his own safety, had determined to leave these soldiers at one of the gates of the town under the command of captain Vignoles. The roads were thronged with spectators—the park of Plessis being completely occupied, even to the trees, by people eager to witness the meeting and reconciliation of two great kings under circumstances so unwonted. The gallant bearing of the king of Navarre, and the good-humoured merriment expressed by his countenance, caused him to be loudly cheered by the concourse. He alone of his troop wore a cloak or a plume; all, however, were girt with the white scarf, the badge of their party. Henri was arrayed in a scarlet cloak, and wore a grey cap surmounted by his celebrated white *panache*, which was fastened by a medal of gold; his doublet and *haut de chausses* were of olive green velvet. King Henry being apprized of the arrival of the king of Navarre, quitted the monastery chapel, and proceeded through the tennis-court towards the *château* amidst an incredible shouting of "*Vivent les rois!*" The king of Navarre descended the flight of steps leading from the terrace of the castle to the lawn—along which king Henry slowly advanced—and was there received by the comte d'Auvergne and by MM. de Sourdis and de Liancour. The archers on guard in

[1] Vie de Duplessis Mornay, p. 134.

[2] Ibid. Cayet: Chronologie Novennaire. De Thou, liv. xcv.

vain proclaimed "*Place! place! voici le Roy!*" the multitudes rushed forward and took possession of the space reserved for the interview—those from the extreme limits of the park impelling onwards the more fortunate spectators. "The crush was so great," writes a spectator,[1] "that their majesties remained for the space of a quarter of an hour within four yards of each other without being able to embrace. Their salutations and greetings were at length achieved with a marvellous demonstration of gladness. The people were so transported at the sight that they continued their acclamations of '*Vive le roy et le roy de Navarre!*' without intermission for the space of half an hour." The maréchal d'Aumont at length, relates de Thou, contrived to separate the crowd so that their majesties might meet. The king of Navarre then threw himself at the feet of the king, saying, "that he looked upon this day as the happiest of his life, as he was blessed with the sight of his good master and king, and was permitted to offer him service!" Henry, much affected, stooped and raised the king, embracing him very affectionately; and, taking him under the arm, their majesties entered the palace to confer.

It was at this interview that Henry poured forth to his long-alienated kinsman the history of his wrongs, and asserted his own personal preference for the king of Navarre, as manifested by the protection he had formerly accorded him while resident at the court of France, and during the subsequent machinations of the deceased queen Catherine, and of the League to defraud him of his rights as first prince of the blood and heir-presumptive. "Mon frère," said

[1] Divers Evènemens arrivés depuis le 28 Avril jusqu'au premier jour de Mai. Maimbourg: Hist. de la Ligue. Mathieu: Hist. du Règne de Henri III. Cayet, de Thou, &c.

Henry III.,[1] "I have yielded the palm to none of my predecessors in attachment to my people. I have hated warfare, and have avoided every occasion likely to disturb the tranquillity of the realm. The town which I have most patronized has been the first to revolt. I have done unheard-of things to promote its embellishment, tranquillity, and glory. I have filled the universities of Paris with learned men. I have respected the Sorbonne, honoured her parliament, adorned her public edifices, and augmented her commerce. I have lived in Paris rather as a citizen than as her king. In return her clergy have degraded my honour and repute by monstrous calumny; her preachers have clamoured and hunted down my good name; the Sorbonne has pretended to release all my subjects from their oath of allegiance. The Parisian people have revolted, stolen my treasures, suborned my officers, killed my Swiss, attacked my body-guard, broken my seals, burned the escutcheons of my arms, defaced my effigies, and now they have seized my artillery to turn it against myself. Behold, therefore, mon frère, those who under detestable pretexts have rebelled against their anointed prince, and have rendered themselves amenable to the judgments of man and of God! It is against such, mon frère, that I have invoked your aid; it is to repair my honour which they trample under foot; it is to drive forth from France—even as they have driven me from Paris—these accursed traitors that I have summoned you! It is to defend this noble crown, of which you are the legitimate and lawful heir if I die childless; it is to save both me and yourself that I now command you to join your forces to mine, so that, with the sword which God has placed

[1] Mathieu, tome i., liv. viii., p. 781.

in my hand, we may deliver this people and vindicate our sacred rights! Mon frère, will you not participate in this glorious mission?" Le Béarnnois had tender feelings, and was soon affected. Tears rolled down his manly cheeks while he listened to this appeal from his sovereign and his king. Drawing that victorious sword so terrible in battle, Henri threw it ringing at the king's feet, and on his knees swore an oath to avenge his sovereign and never to rest until the king sat once more supreme in the halls of the Louvre. Further conference then ensued, and it was not until after the expiration of two hours that the sovereigns showed themselves again to the people. As soon as the white *panache* was perceived in the distance, again vehement acclamations burst forth. The kings then mounted on horseback and proceeded to the bridge dedicated to Ste. Anne in the Fauxbourg de la Riche. As they passed the gate at which the king of Navarre had left his guard, the king, on perceiving a band of strange soldiers in battle array, drew back in astonishment. Henri, whose wit was ever ready, spurred his horse forwards, and sharply reprimanded his men for presuming to maintain such an attitude within the territory of France. The king upon this came forward, and saying that the men had done their duty, he prayed that they might be excused for so zealous a proof of their devotion. The king of Navarre then took leave of his majesty, and, passing the river, he took up his lodging for the night in the Fauxbourg St. Simphorien, the most extensive of the five fauxbourgs which extended round the city of Tours.

Early the following morning the king of Navarre rose, and without revealing his intention, again crossed the river and paid a visit to king Henry, attended only by one page. An earnest consultation ensued, in which some of the principal features of the forthcoming campaign, and especially the siege of Paris, were discussed and resolved. At the hour when the king attended mass the king of Navarre paid a visit to Françoise d'Orléans, dowager princess of Condé, and to the princess de Conti, and afterwards repaired to the apartments of queen Louise and madame d'Angoulême—a lady whom he highly venerated for her consistency and wisdom of conduct. During the afternoon another council was holden; the king then appeared in public with the king of Navarre, who accompanied his majesty to the portal of the abbey of Marmoutier, and while the king devoutly attended vespers, Henri and the young cavaliers of the court indulged in a game of rackets.[1]

While these important events were passing at Tours, the duc de Mayenne quitted Châteaudun and advanced to Vendôme, which had been treacherously betrayed to the League by its governor the sieur de Maillé. This capture exposed the court to imminent danger, as the distance between Tours and Vendôme is little more than thirty miles, and no town or fort then existed capable of checking the advance of the enemy. Mayenne, however, on receiving advices that the duc d'Epernon had left Blois to join the king at Tours, took the bold resolution of marching suddenly upon the former place—the chiefs of the League having taken oath to raze the castle, the scene of the martyrdom of their heroes. The duke defeated a body of troops at St. Ouyn, near to Amboise, under the comte de Brienne, brother-in-law of Epernon, and took the latter prisoner. After this victory the army of the League, however, retired to Château Regnaud, the duke having ascertained that the garrison of Blois was strong and not likely to be taken by surprise; more-

[1] Mém. de la Ligue. Chronologie Novennaire. Mém. de Sully, Dupleix. Perefixe.

over, he likewise found that the duc d'Epernon had unexpectedly returned to resume his command. At Château Regnaud a design of the greatest audacity was consequently conceived and attempted by Mayenne. The League had many adherents in the town of Tours, who kept the duke fully informed as to the royal proceedings. Through these relations he learned that the king of Navarre departed on the 3rd of May for Chinon, for the purpose of assembling his army and superintending the advance of his artillery. The duc d'Epernon, at the same time, bade farewell to the king and returned to Blois, also for the purpose of leading a considerable part of the Gascons under his command to join the army of Navarre. The king, therefore, though nominally at the head of a powerful army, would remain, until these succours arrived, as defenceless and exposed to attack as during the earliest time of his sojourn in Tours. Mayenne, seeing his opportunity, resolved to attempt an enterprise upon Tours, and by the seizure of the person of the king, at once to secure the ultimate triumph of his faction.

The king, however, was attended by a great train of nobles; while the fauxbourgs of Tours were guarded by small detachments of troops. The regiment of the Swiss guards was quartered in the Fauxbourg St. Pierre; and in the populous Fauxbourg St. Simphorien, by the advice of the king of Navarre, Henry had only the day previously stationed three regiments, respectively commanded by Rubempré, Jersay, and Moncassin, trusty and skilful officers.

During the night of the 7th of May Mayenne dislodged from Château Regnaud, and by eight o'clock the following morning his vanguard was in sight of Tours, having performed a march of thirty miles. These troops, conducted by the chevalier d'Aumale, placed themselves in ambuscade, hoping to surprise and capture the king after his majesty's usual morning visit to the abbey de Marmoutier, which was situated in the Fauxbourg St. Simphorien. The morning rose fresh and brilliant. Henry, therefore, according to his custom, proceeded to hear matins in the abbey chapel, and afterwards proposed to continue his promenade on horseback for a mile or two along the open country. His majesty was passing the last barrier from the fauxbourg when a countryman, whose avocations had called him from the town, rushed forwards, and seizing the reins of the king's horse, exclaimed, "Sire, the cavaliers of the League! save yourself!" These words were scarcely uttered when twenty or thirty men rose from behind a small copse which skirted the road and ran with their arquebuses levelled at the king. Henry made rapid retreat, and the barrier of the fauxbourg was just closed behind him when the chevalier d'Aumale and his men came up and shot the officer in command, one la Fontaine, a captain of light horse. Within an hour the main army under Mayenne appeared before Tours. The duke concentrated his attacks on the fauxbourg. A most sanguinary conflict raged until four o'clock in the afternoon, the result of which was the capture of the suburb by the League. Châtillon, Rumbempré, and Jersay distinguished themselves by notable acts of valour, as did also Crillon; who received a severe wound through the body. The disparity in numbers of the royal troops, however, was too great to admit of the repulse of Mayenne.[1] During the conflict the king contributed by his presence of mind and courage to preserve tranquillity in the town. He caused the gates to be closed and strongly guarded, and forbade a single officer or soldier to join in the conflict without his express permission. He caused his regiment of

[1] Cayet: Chronologie Novennaire. De Thou.

Swiss to enter Tours; and placed guards at all the principal avenues of the streets, with orders not to allow the egress therefrom of a single inhabitant, whatever might be his rank, without a permit. By these judicious measures no persons were able to hold intelligences with the enemy, and no one presumed to stir from the quarter in which his abode was situated. The king next despatched messengers to the king of Navarre and to the duc d'Epernon, bidding them advance to his rescue. He then mounted his horse, and attended by the maréchals d'Aumont and Schomberg, and by the duc de Montbazon, approached the scene of conflict. The fauxbourg, despite the valiant defence made by the royal troops, was carried by assault. A scene of horrible pillage and violence ensued; the houses were sacked, and the inhabitants slaughtered without mercy.

Whilst the conquerors gave themselves up during the night to the vilest excesses, Henry and his nobles, in safety within the walls of Tours, waited in suspense for the arrival of the timely succour which was to deliver them from the assault of the town on the morrow. About nine in the evening the advance of a body of troops was descried. For some time it remained doubtful whether the detachment was not a division of the besieging army. The heart of every royalist within the city of Tours beat with suspense and foreboding. At length, with unutterable joy and thankfulness, the watchers from the towers beheld the white scarfs of Henri's Huguenot troopers. "Les écharpes blanches! les écharpes blanches!" echoed triumphantly from street to street until it reached the cabinet of the king. Henry, it is said, fell on his knees and thanked God for his great deliverance. Fifteen hundred Huguenot troops of Châtillon's band had silently made their way from Maillé and taken a position on a small islet of the Loire, close to the Fauxbourg St. Simphorien.

Châtillon instantly left the city and placed himself at their head. Another band of Gascon troopers entered the Fauxbourg de la Riche; whilst before dawn several hundred soldiers sent by Epernon arrived and occupied the place vacated by the Swiss regiment in the Fauxbourg St. Pierre. Never was monarch more enthusiastically or more efficiently succoured. The acclamations were heard by the outposts of the League; and the duc de Mayenne was roused from his debauch, which he was holding in a church, by the intelligence that the invincible legions of Coutras were at hand. Mayenne and the chevalier d'Aumale immediately made a *reconnaissance,* and then returned to their quarters to hold council. The sentinels of the League, meantime, hailed the Huguenots on the islet, and commenced violently to abuse the king. "Have you forgotten la St. Barthélemy? Retire, Châtillon, retire! we have no quarrel with you; we fight only against the murderers of your father! Retire, we say!" The brave troopers of le Béarnnois, however, bade their opponents leave them in peace. "You are traitors, all of you, to fight against your king. Women abuse each other, soldiers fight. To-morrow we shall see whether your deeds are valiant as your words!" But the military *prestige* of the king of Navarre had alone sufficed to daunt the ardour of Mayenne's army. It was hastily resolved not to risk the existence of the chief army of the League in a combat with the Huguenots, during which the duc de Mayenne might be slain or captured. The signal for retreat, therefore, was given; the troops defiled away as silently as they had approached Tours, the outposts confronting the Huguenot infantry being last withdrawn. The retreat of Mayenne was ascertained at six o'clock in the morning of May 9th by the blazing of the houses of the fauxbourg, which the troops fired before their departure. When king Henry was informed at his *levée* by Châtillon that no obstacle existed to prevent him from repairing as usual to Marmoutier to hear matins, great was his amazement. Followed by his suite, the king first returned thanks publicly for his great deliverance from peril in the cathedral of Tours; and then inspected the suburb the scene of the late conflict. The fires had been promptly extinguished; but the desolation around, and the wailing of those ruined by the catastrophe, and whose abodes had been pillaged and their daughters outraged, greatly moved the royal compassion. Henry distributed money to the sufferers, and commanded temporary abodes to be prepared for the houseless. He then returned to the castle, and ordered M. de Rouvré to maintain stricter guard over the person and actions of the young duc de Guise, who was there incarcerated, believing that the latter had found means to communicate with his uncle the duc de Mayenne. At midday the king of Navarre arrived; he presented himself in the royal cabinet booted, spurred, and covered with mud. The king had been on horseback from break of day, and now entered Tours at the head of another body of troops. Le Béarnnois was chagrined beyond measure at the disappearance of the foe. "Ventre St. Gris!" exclaimed he, bluntly, on entering the presence, "if I had been here, he (Mayenne) should have decamped in very different plight!" The king cordially embraced the king of Navarre, and thanked him for his prompt succour, but steadily refused to permit pursuit to be made after the retreating army of Mayenne. "No, no," said his majesty, "our army is not yet assembled; it would be folly to hazard a double Henri in exchange for a beggarly Carolus."[1]

[1] The king alluded to the current coinage: a Henri was a piece of gold, a Carolus a copper coin of trivial value. Cayet. Mathieu: Règne

The duc de Mayenne retreated to the town of Mons. After making a sojourn of a few days, he advanced and laid siege to Alençon. The king's affairs, meantime, greatly improved; the check received by the army of the League caused the adherents of the royal cause to muster throughout the provinces. Many nobles, hitherto passive and waiting the turn of events, now flocked to the standard of the king; other powerful lords, previously inclined to the League, suddenly deserted the cause and repaired to Tours. Henry received all these laggards with the utmost condescension, but required of them all to demonstrate the same obsequiousness towards the king of Navarre, "son compagnon," as his majesty now designated the latter. The king of Navarre was formally declared by the king to be invested with supreme command over military affairs; and the Huguenot army, by his majesty's command, encamped at Boisgency, preparatory to an attack upon Orléans. His majesty then, with his own hand, delivered the powers of supreme governor over Bretagne to the comte de Soissons, brother of the deceased prince de Condé, and authorized the arrest of the duc and duchesse de Mercœur—the latter of whom, especially, had taken a prominent part in the rebellion of that important duchy. The king, then placing himself at the head of a detachment, advanced upon Poitiers, which had recently declared for the League, principally out of jealousy because Henry had not given that town the preference over Tours for the residence of his court and parliament. Had all these expeditions been successful—that of the king of Navarre on Orléans, the royal summons to the people of Poitiers, and the mission of the comte de Soissons in Bre-

de Henri III., tome viii. Davila, tome ii., liv. xc. Journal de l'Etoile. The name of the duc de Mayenne was Charles de Lorraine.

tagne—the League must have received its *coup-de-grace.*

In Paris the intelligence of the reconciliation of Henry III. with the king of Navarre, and the union of the two sovereigns as brothers in arms, was received with execrations and transports of the wildest rage. Epithets sufficiently expressive of abhorrence for the "execrable tyrant Henri Dévalé"—a new name coined by some wit amongst the factious—and of their detestation for his perjury after having three times confirmed by oath the Edict of Union against the heretics, failed the preachers of Paris. Every ignominious device was adopted to testify their hate, if indeed any new method of obloquy could be discovered.[1] Again the city swarmed with penitential processions, in one of which, persuaded by the furious zeal of her daughter, the duchesse de Nemours condescended to exhibit herself. The relics of the saints were paraded; and the treasures of the Sainte Chapelle and of St. Denis exposed in the churches to the adoration of the frenzied multitudes. To testify their horror of the unholy alliance between Catholic and heretic, three poor Huguenot women were burned in the Place de Grève by command of the council of Forty. The priests of the capital, moreover, withheld absolution from persons who refused previously to make open renunciation of their allegiance to the king. The nearer the downfall of their faction approached, the more extravagant became the excesses of these ecclesiastics. Paris, however, harboured its "valiant Judith," who should yet present the head of Holofernes; the city still bowed at the

[1] "Le Mercredi, 5 Juillet, les Cordeliers otèrent la tête à la figure du roy, qui étoit peint à genoux priant Dieu auprès de sa femme au dessous du maître autel de leur église. Les Jacobins barbouillèrent tout le visage d'une pareille figure du roy en leur cloître."—Journal de l'Etoile.

feet of madame de Montpensier, the fierceness of whose wrath surpassed that of the most rabid of demagogues.

The duchesse de Guise, during these transactions, attended by the princes and princesses of the house of Lorraine, proceeded in state to the Chambre Dorée, and presented a petition to the recusant parliament, praying that processes might be instituted against the slayers of Henri de Lorraine, duc de Guise, her dearly beloved consort, and of Louis de Lorraine, cardinal archbishop, her brother-in-law, and their abettors. The parliament was pleased to grant the petition of the "illustrious widow," and commissioners were forthwith appointed to commence proceedings for a criminal suit against "Henri de Valois, ci-devant Roi de France et de Pologne."[1] Envoys were also accredited to Rome to protest a third time against absolution being accorded to the king, in the name of the family of the deceased princes; each member, including the princesses, sending written instructions to that effect, which were to be laid before his Holiness.

Sixtus V. from this period seems to have been inoculated with the frenzy of the Parisian democracy. His fury, when informed of the alliance between the kings—though he had himself predicted the probability of such event—nearly cost him his life. The envoys of Henry III. dared no longer approach the Vatican, for their very presence appeared to threaten the return of the fit or convulsion into which his Holiness fell after reading the despatch sent by cardinal Morosini containing the intelligence. The cardinal de Joyeuse and the marquis Pisani, therefore, retired from Rome to Venice, and there awaited the event. The Spanish ambassador and the envoy of Savoy adjured the pope to withhold absolution from so flagrant a criminal as Henri de

[1] De Thou, liv. xciv.

Valois; and they maintained that the actions and designs of the League were just and laudable. Sixtus, therefore, assembled a consistory, May 5, and published a monitory against the king, "commanding, warning, and admonishing him to liberate the cardinal de Bourbon and the archbishop of Lyons within ten days after the reception of the bull, and within thirty days afterwards to forward to the Holy See an authentic document detailing his act of submission;" in default of which the pope declared Henri de Valois, *ci-devant* king, excommunicated and accursed, deposed and banished from communion with the faithful.[1] The same sentence was launched against those who had shared in the sacrilegious deed, either by act or counsel, unless they appeared to give account of their crimes before the tribunal of the Holy See within sixty days after the publication of the monitory. The supreme pontiff reserved to himself alone the power of releasing from these ecclesiastical censures when once incurred, excepting at the hour of death, when even then absolution was to be preceded by a solemn declaration of penitence and submission to the behests of the Church in case of recovery. No sooner was this bull made public than the grand-duke of Tuscany, the seigniory of Venice, and the duke of Mantua, sent envoys to Rome to protest against its purport—a sentence which they boldly designated as unjust and arbitrary. They, moreover, declared that in case the king should hereafter think proper to enter Italy at the head of an army to obtain that absolution so arbitrarily withholden at the instigation of the enemies of the Christian king, they should decline to aid the Holy See either by their arms or by their counsels. The princes also despatched a secret envoy to king Henry, who was then before Poitiers, advertising him of the fulmination issued. The grand-duke Ferdinand

[1] De Thou, liv. xcv. Davila. Hist. de la Ligue.

counselled Henry to reply, by promptly assuring Sixtus of his obedience and his willingness to appear before the papal tribunal, which he would do all in his power to contrive at the head of an army within the current year; and, moreover, to take possession of Avignon and the adjacent countship of Venaissin. The duke of Tuscany also offered the king the loan of 1,200,000 gold crowns, provided that his majesty would deliver the town of Marseilles by way of security. In case of the dismemberment of the realm, the Tuscan government coveted that wealthy and populous port, and intended to procure its annexation to the duchy; while if the king, as was now most probable, prevailed, the duke would gain the merit and gratitude of having been one of his most stanch and loyal allies. The young duchesse Christine de Lorraine, mindful of the gratitude which she owed to the king her uncle, unexpectedly used all the influence which she possessed over her newly-espoused consort to induce him to help king Henry to vanquish the League, to the great indignation of her father and his kindred.

Though the royal arms failed before Poitiers; and Orléans still continued obdurate despite the challenge and remonstrances of the king of Navarre, favourable advices from other parts of the kingdom cheered the spirit of the king. Henry, at the head of 600 cavalry, appeared before Poitiers on the 17th day of May. The inhabitants refused to open their gates at the royal summons, though they sent deputies to excuse the act, and to supplicate the king not to assault their town. Henry, thereupon, retired to Châtelleraud, where he was joined by the king of Navarre, who rallied him from his depression, and urged his majesty to advance to the assault of Paris. Troops daily arrived to join the royal standard; and expressions of sympathy and promised aid reached the king from most of the potentates of Europe. Even the duc de Nevers seemed to relent, and for an interval hesitated whether he should not join the royal army. Henry, however, had a bitter and irreconcilable enemy in the duchesse de Nevers, who counselled her husband to maintain his neutral attitude, so that he might neither offend his conscience, nor fight against his sovereign. The generals of the League were reduced to great straits for money and for levies. Several of the Catholic states of Germany prudently declined to sanction the crime of overt rebellion by permitting the officers of the League to recruit within their dominions; while the people of the Protestant territories and the Swiss Cantons enthusiastically espoused the cause for which Henri de Navarre fought. Spain could now do little more for the League than agitate; the interposition of the queen of England in the Low Countries, and the presence there of her lieutenant the earl of Leicester, kept the cabinet of Madrid in a ferment of apprehension.

The landing of the English in Gallicia, under Drake and Norreys, increased the consternation of the Spanish court, which, therefore, until after the demise of Henry III., gave little aid to its late allies. From Rome even, the princes of the League derived no succour. Sixtus absolutely refused to dispense to them either his spiritual or temporal treasures; and irritably declined to grant the duc de Mayenne a loan of 1,400,000 gold crowns, though the acceptance and recognition of the council of Trent throughout the realm was tendered as the equivalent. The jewels of the princesses of the League had long been absorbed into the treasury; while madame de Nemours sacrificed the superb diamonds which she inherited from her mother, Renée de France, which had once appertained to queen Anne de Bretagne.

Before the king departed from Tours he established

a permanent council, to which all affairs connected with the internal administration of the realm were to be referred. The members were, the cardinal de Vendôme, the cardinal de Lenoncourt, Montholon keeper of the seals, and the secretaries Revol and Beaulieu. His majesty then took leave of the queen, who was escorted by the two kings to the castle of Chinon, where she was to reside during the campaign. The queen was accompanied by the duchesse d'Angoulême, and by several of her favourite ladies. On the terrace of Chinon, which commands one of the fairest landscapes of France, Henry and Louise bade each other farewell—a farewell they were destined never more to exchange.

This ancient castle of the Plantagenets was a secure retreat for the queen during the perilous contest about to ensue. The town of Chinon is seated on the river Vienne, about ten leagues from Tours, and the castle was strongly fortified and built on a precipitous rock. In the highest tower, called La Tour d'Argenton, the cardinal de Bourbon was incarcerated. After the arrival of the queen he was often permitted her society, which proved a great consolation to both parties; for the deepest melancholy oppressed Louise, which partly might be ascribed to the depressing malady under which she suffered. The affliction of the queen was great on taking leave of her husband; for the vicissitudes of the last few months seem to have brought the royal pair into companionship more intimate than while they enjoyed the undiminished splendours of their regal state.

Henry then quitted Tours and advanced with the king of Navarre to Blois. They next captured the towns of Gergeau, Pluviers, Estampes, and laid siege to Pontoise. In Normandy the duc de Montpensier made important conquests, and defeated Brissac and a body of 6,000 men, at the village of Pierrefitte, in the vicinity of Falaise. In the county of La Beausse, Châtillon gained a complete victory over two noted generals of the League, the sieurs de Savcuse and de Brosse, who were on their way to join Mayenne with 200 lances, leaving them slain on the field of conflict.

A still more eminent success attended the royal arms during the siege of Pontoise. The town of Senlis had originally given in its adherence to the League, when the remonstrances of M. de Thoré, to whom the place appertained, son of the late constable de Montmorency, induced the principal inhabitants to return to their allegiance to king Henry. The duc d'Aumale, therefore, who commanded in Paris during the absence of Mayenne, piqued by the sarcasms of madame de Montpensier, resolved to attempt the reduction of Senlis. Accordingly Aumale sallied forth from Paris at the head of 6,000 men, 2,000 of whom consisted of the trained bands of Paris; the rest being brought by Balagny commandant in Cambray for queen Catherine, and who since the death of that princess had caused himself to be proclaimed prince of Cambray. With these troops Aumale laid siege to Senlis, and invested the town so closely that articles of capitulation had been agreed upon and a day fixed for the surrender of M. de Thoré. It so happened that the duc de Longueville and la Noue made *rendezvous* for their troops at Compiègne, in order to meet the succours being brought by Sancy; afterwards intending to join the main army commanded by the kings in person. This little army consisted of 2,000 men, officered by some of the noblest cavaliers of France. It was, therefore, gallantly proposed to relieve Senlis, and send the citizen troops of the League flying back to Paris. The attack was made with the greatest vigour and success: the militia bands of the League, unable to stand the onslaught, gave way, and fled in confusion. The rout was soon complete; Mainville and several other leaders fell, while the duc d'Aumale himself fled, pursued by the valiant royalist soldiers to St. Denis, where he found refuge, while Balagny continued his flight to Paris. The victorious army then continued its march, and, as it defiled past the gates of Paris, fired a volley upon the rebel city.[1]

The affright and terror of the Parisians at the successes of the king caused seditious gatherings in several of the public squares. Madame de Montpensier harangued the people; and assuring them of ultimate triumph, she despatched messengers, and amongst others Bernardin, *valet-de-chambre* of the deceased duc de Guise, to the camp before Alençon, imploring the duc de Mayenne to return to the capital. The comments of the duchess on the rout before Senlis and the flight of Aumale were characteristic, and greatly incensed the latter when these letters fell into his hands. Bernardin was arrested by a detachment of Huguenot troopers, and his papers taken from him. "Mon frère," wrote the duchess to Mayenne, "return! else it is all up with us and our cause. What can we hope from a general who, like M. d'Aumale, has committed so cowardly and detestable a fault? Can we expect that he will be endowed either with skill or bravery to repair it, or deliver us?" The king of Navarre first sent the letters to be perused by the king; he then sealed them up and despatched them by an envoy to the duc d'Aumale, with a humorous billet offering to

[1] Cayet: Chronologie Novennaire. De Thou. Davila. Etoile. Mathieu. A piece was composed on the subject of the retreat of Aumale, one verse of which ran as follows:—

"Ce vaillant prince d'Aumale
Pour avoir bien couru,
Quoiqu'il ait perdu sa malle,
N'a pas la mort encouru!"

Madame de Montpensier caused this verse to be posted on the walls of Paris.

stand as the duke's second in case he felt inclined to avenge the affront.[1] Great, however, as was the dismay and weakness of the League, which could only muster 3,000 men to garrison Paris, the pope had placed deadly weapons in the hands of the chieftains—resources which madame de Montpensier hailed as her sole escape from the certain doom which awaited her crimes, did the cause of the king triumph. The papal monitory had been posted on the doors of the basilica of St. Peter's of Rome, and on those of the church of St. John Lateran, on the 24th day of May. The thirty days of grace, during which king Henry was directed to execute the required concessions, having elapsed, a formal bull of excommunication was sent into France, which was read at the portals of the cathedral of Meaux by the bishops of Digne and d'Agen; the same ceremony being performed in Paris and Chartres. The assassination of the king from that day forwards was not only declared lawful and expedient by the preachers of Paris, but acceptable to God. "The death of Henry is the annihilation of heresy and tyranny!" exclaimed they. Crowds listened trembling to these denunciations; the people feared the crime, but they cowered also beneath the anticipated wrath of their outraged king when Paris should lie prostrate. Fanaticism, meantime, silently lighted her torch. A poniard driven to the heart of the accursed, the outcast of the monarchs of Europe, it was averred, would vindicate religion as well as deliver the people from the sanguinary vengeance of a tyrant. Assent too often follows that which it is our interest to believe.

The preachers of Paris announced from their pulpits that very meritorious in the sight of Heaven would he be who should execute the behests of Sixtus the Vice-

[1] De Thou, liv. xcv.

gerent of God. Madame de Montpensier thereupon fell into ecstatic transports, and publicly prayed that the Almighty would raise such a Joshua for their deliverance. Amongst the most assiduous frequenters of the churches was one Jacques Clement, a priest of the Dominican monastery, Rue St. Jacques,[1] and a native of the village of Sorbonne, close to Sens. This Clement had once been a soldier; but, being favoured, as he asserted, by heavenly visions, he obtained his discharge from the ranks and entered a monastery in Sens. There he astonished the provincial brotherhood by his ascetic piety and pretended revelations. The prior, believing that a great light had risen in the order, sent the young monk to study for a season at the great Dominican monastery of the Rue St. Jacques. In Paris Jacques Clement discarded that decorum of conduct which had so edified his superiors; and though his prophetic transports augmented, his life was licentious, and he became a principal actor in the scenes which had disgraced the capital. "This Clement," says de Thou, "came from the Dominicans of Sens. He was a young man about twenty-two years old, ignorant, licentious, indolent, and finding his pastime amongst the lowest of the populace." The gesticulations and cadaverous features of this fanatic attracted the notice of the duchesse de Montpensier, ever on the alert to pounce upon agents likely to serve her projects. She sent for Clement, and for some time admitted him to frequent audience. The beauty of the duchess, and her frenzied appeals, roused the passions of the young monk. This impression the duchess took every means to heighten and to excite. She spoke of the exaltation of the person who might be chosen as the august instrument to execute the fiat of the Church and deliver

[1] The Dominicans were also called Jacobins from the situation of their monastery in the Rue St. Jacques, Quartier de St. Benoît.

the people of Paris; she appealed to his visions in proof that he was destined to accomplish some great achievement, of the exact nature of which she professed to be ignorant; while she plunged him into delirious transports by the excess of her condescensions. Jacques Clement implicitly believed the professions of the duchess: neither did he deem his hopes extravagant, inasmuch as he had been a witness of that famous procession, in which the great grand-daughter of Louis XII. had shown herself to the people, and traversed the streets of Paris without other raiment than a tunic of lace! To merit the favour of his sibyl, therefore, the young monk assiduously dreamed his dreams, denounced the tyrant Henri de Valois, and advocated his assassination. Madame de Montpensier and her colleagues in the conspiracy, meantime, had recourse to Bourgoing, prior of the Dominicans of Paris, a furious Leaguer, to aid in kindling the zeal of the infatuated monk. Clement at length applied to his superiors, and asked them whether "he might kill the king?" They replied by falling at his feet transported at the contemplation, as they declared, of the holy and chosen instrument of Divine vengeance. The brain of Clement appears to have given way under the terrible excitements to which he was subjected. Mysterious voices whispered in his ears at night when alone in his cell, adjuring him to avenge the oppressed people. He was assured that, as soon as the decisive blow had been struck, angels would bear him away from the scene of his crime; and that his body, invisible to mortal eyes, would be miraculously borne back to his convent. Mundane advantages were not forgotten; madame de Montpensier promised him wealth and dignities, and, as de Thou insinuates, bound herself before his departure on his sacred mission to obligations which must for ever consign her name to infamy.

Having thus chosen and imparted the needful temper to her weapon, Catherine de Lorraine beheld with composure the advance of the great besieging army to invest Paris. Pontoise capitulated to the royal arms on the 25th of July. The kings then marched to Estampes, and proceeded to Châtillon-sur-Seine, where they were joined by the duc de Longueville and his troops, the victors of Senlis. From thence the royal army proceeded to Conflans, where Sancy waited at the head of 12,000 troops, levied in Switzerland and elsewhere by his incomparable zeal and address. The kings, at the head of a force exceeding 38,000 men, well furnished with artillery, and accompanied by the most illustrious of the nobles of France, who were now fully roused from the dangerous fallacies of the League, encamped at St. Cloud on the last day of July. The traitorous city trembled as, from its ramparts, it beheld the ranks of soldiery arrayed to overthrow its pride, and to lead its turbulent citizens bound to the footstool of their sovereign. Henry took up his abode in a house appertaining to the cardinal de Gondy, which Catherine de Medici had presented to the father of the latter, Jerome Gondy, the financier—a mansion surrounded by delicious gardens.[1] The quarters of the king of Navarre were at Meudon, and his army extended from thence to the Pont de Charenton. That of the king occupied the ground between St. Cloud and Neuilly.

The duc de Mayenne had caused strong entrench-

[1] The mansion and park of St. Cloud were purchased by Catherine de Medici in 1577. In the year 1574 they appertained to a bourgeois of Paris, one Chappellier; so that the story relative to the massacre of St. Bartholomew's day having been concocted in the room in which Henry was assassinated is manifestly untrue. Queen Catherine bought the mansion with the intent of building a superb palace; but finding the premises too small for her purpose, she presented the house and grounds to Jerome Gondy and his wife. The mansion was inherited by their third son Gondy, cardinal-bishop of Paris.

ments to be constructed along the fauxbourgs St. Germain, St. Jacques, St. Marcel, St. Honoré, and St. Denis, the defence of which he committed to la Châtre. The army with which he had hastily marched to Paris after the capture of Montereau consisted barely, when united to the garrison of Paris, of 10,000 men. The duc de Nemours was, however, on his way to the capital with an additional 10,000 soldiers; while the duc de Lorraine had promised a succour of 3,000 troops.

The same day (Sunday, July 31st) that the king arrived at St. Cloud he received a mysterious intimation from a lady resident in Paris, the demoiselle de Bon Lieu, to hold himself on his guard against treachery and to admit no strangers to his presence. During the afternoon the duchesse de Retz came to visit the king. Henry mentioned the warning he had just received. "Sire," said the duchess, "you should then take better guard for your preservation. Remember, I implore you, that upon your life depends the prosperity, and even the existence, of your loyal subjects!" "Madame," replied Henry, "I trust in God, who will preserve my life so long as He sees it to be necessary for the welfare of my people!" The king passed the remainder of the day in conferences with the king of Navarre and the comte d'Auvergne, the young son of Charles IX. and Marie Touchet, to whom he was much attached.[1] In the evening his majesty took exercise in the gardens attached to the mansion, attended by Biron and d'Entragues.[2] The assassin, nevertheless, against whom Henry had been warned, had arrived at St. Cloud and waited the opportunity to perform his errand.

The approach of the royal army kindled the fanatic fervour of frère Jacques Clement, and he proclaimed

[1] Pasquier, liv. xiv., lettre i.

[2] Mém. de Charles de Valois, Duc d'Angoulême. Hist. des Derniers Troubles, liv. v.

himself ready to go forth and encounter "the tyrant," and arrest his diabolical purpose. Clement, therefore, placed himself in communication with the chiefs of the League cognizant of his design. The duc d'Aumale is vindicated from entertaining any relations with Clement —the duke was then in great odium with the League on account of the flight from Senlis; while his wife had been always treated with reserve as a concealed partisan of the royal cause. On Saturday, July 30th, Clement, through the influence of madame de Montpensier, obtained admittance to the comte de Brienne, who, since his capture at St. Ouyn, had remained a prisoner in the Louvre, and to the first president of the parliament of Paris, Achille de Harlay, still a captive in the Bastille. To both these faithful servants of the king Clement asserted that he was in possession of a secret of the last importance to his majesty, which he wished to impart, provided that he could obtain credentials to pass the outposts of the royal army. Nothing can be more surprising than that both these personages were caught in the snare; and forthwith gave Clement the letters he asked, without previously reflecting how unlikely it was that an obscure Dominican should possess influence enough to penetrate without suspicious patronage from the powers in the ascendant into the prisons of the state. Clement then repaired to the hôtel of madame de Montpensier, and from thence proceeded to hold a midnight interview with the provost Chapelle Marteau, who a few days previously had regained his liberty, at the Carthusians. From thence he proceeded to the monastery of St. Lazare, Fauxbourg St. Antoine, where the duc de Mayenne conferred with him for some time.[1] Clement being now well primed for the enterprise, returned to his monastery, and spent the night and some

[1] De Thou, liv. xcvi.

hours of the following day in prayer and fasting. At dawn between 200 and 300 citizens, suspected of favouring the cause of the king, were arrested and thrown into the prisons, at the suit of the duchesse de Montpensier, who had promised Jacques Clement that their lives should answer for his, in case he was arrested after accomplishing his mission. It is believed that the duchess further instructed Clement, if put to the torture, to confess that he had been bribed to murder the king by the comte de Soissons; for by this means she trusted, if her more heinous design failed, to sow disunion between the princes.[1]

Clement quitted Paris about one o'clock on Sunday, July 31st, and took the road towards St. Cloud. On the way he was overtaken by M. la Guesle, attorney-general, who, with his brother, was proceeding from his house at Vanvres to visit the king. Seeing a monk on the road walking between two soldiers, la Guesle asked whether the priest was their prisoner. They replied in the negative; when Clement, addressing la Guesle, stated that he was bound for St. Cloud, on a mission of great moment to his majesty. The attorney-general replied that it was impossible that he could see the king, and desired him to communicate to himself the revelation he wished to make. This, however, Clement declined, but said that he was proceeding to St. Cloud under a safe-conduct from MM. de Brienne and de Harlay, and with great presence of mind he drew from his robe the letters. With such credentials la Guesle began to treat the Dominican with greater consideration; and at length, fearing that he might be induced to betray this communication, he desired him to mount on horseback behind his brother, by whom he was accompanied. On the road Clement was submitted to

[1] Journal de L'Estoile. Maimbourg: Mém. de la Ligue. Cayet. Dupleix.

a severe cross-examination by la Guesle, but he never prevaricated or flinched from his primary assertions. He admitted, however, that his errand was from some of the principal royalists of the capital, who had agreed during the first assault to open one of the gates to the king's troops. The simplicity and apparent candour of these answers deceived la Guesle: he conducted the monk to his house, and promised to obtain him speedy audience of his majesty. La Guesle, however, took the precaution of examining the letter stated to have been given by the first president, with whose writing he was familiar. The letter was found to be in due form; but still desirous of testing the truth, la Guesle asked Clement how he had procured permission to enter the Bastille? The latter replied, "Through Portail, the son of the king's first surgeon, whom he frequently visited in the Bastille, and who had procured him an interview with M. de Harlay."[1] Upon this M. la Guesle repaired to the king's lodging and informed his majesty. Henry, whom nothing so greatly regaled as the sight of a monk, readily consented to receive the communication, and desired la Guesle to bring the ecclesiastic at his *levée* on the following morning.[2] Meantime Clement remained with the retainers of the attorney-general, and made a hearty supper in their company, cutting his bread with the knife he had brought to perpetrate the assassination which he contemplated. He then strolled out to reconnoitre, and found himself in a court of the royal mansion called la Demie Lune. There he met the grand prior comte d'Auvergne, who had quitted the royal apartment to summon musicians to lull his

[1] Lettre d'un des Premiers Officiers de la Cour de Parlement (la Guesle) sur le sujet de la Mort du Roi. Journal de l'Etoile.

[2] "Histoire au Vray de la Victoire obtenue par Frère Jacques Clement, lequel tua Henri de Valois, 1 Aoust, 1589."—MS. Bibl. Imp. Suppl. Français, 2273.

majesty to sleep. Clement boldly advanced, and asked to be conducted into the presence of the sovereign, as his business was imminent. The comte d'Auvergne, who was a boy of sixteen, rushed hastily onwards, exclaiming, "that the monk must be mad, as his majesty had gone to repose." Thus circumvented Clement returned to the lodging provided for him, and retired to bed and slept soundly.

At seven the following morning la Guesle, followed by Clement, proceeded to attend the royal *levée*. Henry, however, having passed a disturbed night, had not yet risen. The two, therefore, went into the pleasaunce until summoned about eight o'clock to the king's chamber. When in the garden Portail, the king's first surgeon, accosted the monk, and put many pertinent questions relative to his son, with whom Clement had professed to be intimate, all which the latter answered so satisfactorily as further to convince his hearers that his mission was genuine. On re-entering the mansion, the officer on guard committed the negligent oversight of permitting Clement to pass into the royal cabinet without searching his person, as was the universal custom in these perilous times. La Guesle, after greeting the gentlemen-in-waiting in the ante-chamber, passed on, followed by the monk, to the door of the king's private closet and opened it. He then made a gesture to his companion to wait at the threshold, as he perceived that the king, having just risen, was not yet sufficiently attired to grant audience. La Guesle, however, entered, and presented the credentials brought by Clement to his majesty, who ordered that he might be instantly introduced. The king was attended by his first gentleman, M. de Bellegarde, and by du Halde, principal valet-de-chambre. Clement approached and prostrated himself at the feet of the king. "Mon frère," said the king, "you are welcome. What is the news in Paris?"

"Sire, M. le Premier Président is well, and craves permission to kiss your hand." Clement then turned to M. la Guesle and requested permission to speak privately to his majesty. The latter bluntly refused, desiring him to proceed boldly, as none were present but the king's faithful servants. Clement still pretended to hesitate, when Henry, desiring Bellegarde to retire from his side, gave the same order to la Guesle, and sharply commanded the monk to impart that which he had to declare. Clement handed a letter to his majesty, and while Henry glanced at its contents, he suddenly drew a long knife from the sleeve of his habit, and plunged it to the hilt into the abdomen of the king, just below the girdle. *"Ah! mon Dieu! ce malheureux m'a blessé!"* exclaimed the king. Snatching the knife from the wound, Henry struck the assassin twice on the face, who fled with a loud cry and crouched between the beds occupied by his majesty and the gentlemen who slept in the royal chamber.[1] The cabinet, meantime, was soon filled by gentlemen from the adjoining apartment. Two of the Quarante-cinq, Montpezat and Mirepoix, with la Guesle, seized the wretched miscreant, and, dragging him forth, plunged their swords through his body, and hurled it from the windows of the apartment into the court below. The king, meantime, had fallen into the arms of Bellegarde, who laid him on his bed, and despatched du Halde for the surgeons Portail and Lefebre. *"Ah, miserable! que l'avois-je fait?"* moaned the unfortunate monarch. Henry then addressed la Guesle, who had fallen in an agony

[1] Mathieu: Hist. du Règne de Henri III., liv. viii. p. 772. De Thou, liv. xcv. MS. Bibl. Imp. Suppl. Français, 2273. Portrait du Jacobin—MS. Bibl. Imp. Suppl. Français, 2273. Lettres d'Etienne Pasquier, liv. xiv., Mém. de Cheverny, de Charles de Valois, Duc d'Angoulême, etc. Lettre de la Guesle, Procureur-Général. Journal de l'Étoile. Le Martyre de Jacques Clement, 1589. Paris: Chez Fiselier, 1589, en 8vo.

of despair at the foot of the king's bed, protesting that he was the most unhappy man living to have introduced the foul assassin into his majesty's presence. Two of the king's gentlemen, Savary and Bonrepas, after inquiring who had introduced the monk, drew their swords to slay la Guesle, but were arrested in their design by Bellegarde on a signal from the king. The agitation of this scene causing the blood to flow more profusely from the wound, Bellegarde desired many of the personages present to retire into the adjacent chamber. Portail presently arrived, accompanied by his two assistant-surgeons, Pigre and Lefebre. The king reclined on his bed, but complained of no pain, which at first gave hope that the wound might be trifling.[1] Whilst under the hands of his surgeons, however, the king fainted. Meantime the young comte d'Auvergne was hastily summoned; also the duc d'Epernon and M. d'O. The former ran precipitately to the royal apartment, but unable to command his feelings at the sight he there beheld, he fell on his knees by the bed and sobbed aloud. The king had ever treated Henri d'Angoulême with the affection of a parent, and the sight of his tears deeply affected his majesty. He laid his hand on the boy's head, and said, "Mon fils, mon fils! do not grieve! They have tried to kill me, but, by God's mercy, they have not succeeded. This will be nothing; I shall soon be better!" The duc d'Epernon then took M. d'Auvergne by the arm and led him to a distant window, and entreated him not to agitate the king. He still remained weeping bitterly at the window when Portail came up, after having probed and bandaged the wound. "Monseigneur," said he, confidentially addressing the young count, "look to yourself. I fear it will not be

[1] The bowels protruded from the wound, it appears, from the *procè verbal* of the king's death.

possible to save the king." Upon this Epernon and M. d'O came up and insisted upon hearing what Portail had communicated to the comte d'Auvergne. The other surgeons, however, expressed more hope; the king had rallied from his exhaustion; he complained of little pain, and his speech was firm and clear as before the infliction of the wound. An opinion concurrent with the declaration of the majority, therefore, was given to the king, when he steadily asked the question, "Whether it would not be advisable for him to receive the last sacraments of the church?" Henry then caused mass to be celebrated by his private chaplain, Louis de Parade, at a temporary altar placed at the foot of his bed. Afterwards he related to all present the circumstances preceding his wound, and desired that la Guesle should not be molested, as he was not in fault. He then commanded that letters should be despatched, addressed to the governors of the provinces, that a true account of his accident might go forth; also, that the surgeons judged favourably of the wound. It was about ten o'clock when the king gave these directions. He was lying in bed, supported by Bellegarde, while the young comte d'Auvergne, as his majesty complained of cold and numbness, chafed his feet. Henry also desired that the king of Navarre should be summoned, and sent for his secretary that he might dictate a letter to queen Louise, apprizing her majesty of the catastrophe. Henry's last letter to his consort is as follows:—

HENRY III. KING OF FRANCE TO QUEEN LOUISE DE LORRAINE.

M'Amye,—My enemies perceiving that all their artifices and rebellion were fruitless; and that their only hope of safety lay in my death, aware of my zeal and fidelity for the holy Roman Apostolic Faith, and that it was my custom never to refuse audience to ecclesiastics, they decided that no more feasible method existed of executing their accursed design than to hide it under the monastic mantle and cowl—thus outraging all laws human and divine, and violating the sanctity of the priestly habit.

This morning while I was alone in my cabinet with the sieur de Bellegarde, my attorney-general brought to me by my commandment, a young Dominican, who stated that he had letters from the first president of my parliament, and declared he had a message to deliver from the said president. After presenting me with letters from the first president, the said monk, pretending that he had some secret communication to make, I desired the said Bellegarde and my attorney-general to retire a little. This wicked wretch then gave me a stab with a knife, thinking to kill me; but the Almighty, who is the Guardian of kings, willed not that His humble servant should perish for the reverence he has shown to those who declared themselves specially devoted to His service. God by his mercy so directed the blow, that the wound is slight; and I hope in a few days to recover my accustomed health, in which trust I am encouraged, first, by my own sensations; secondly, by the opinion of my surgeons and physicians, who believe that no danger exists. I have thought it wise to advertize you of my true condition, that you may not be alarmed by false and contrary reports.

The above letter was written by Megret the king's secretary, under his majesty's dictation. The following postscript, however, was added by Henry with his own hand:—

M'Amye,—I hope soon to be well. Pray God for me, and do not leave the place where you now are!

Au Pont de St. Cloud, this first day of August, 1589.

HENRY.[1]

This letter, however, and whatever consolation it might have imparted, was long before it reached the hand of the queen. In the consequent confusion which ensued after the decease of the king, it was given to a messenger, who, intent upon his own fortunes, detained the missive for a year, and at length only delivered it up to the queen upon her urgent and reiterated demand.

[1] MS. Bibl. Imp. Béth. 8966, fol. 66.

The intelligence of the precarious condition of the king soon spread throughout the camp, and occasioned the greatest panic and consternation. A strong guard, under Duplessis Richelieu, was placed round the mansion in which the king lay, and all the principal officers of the armies repaired to the royal lodging—some remaining without on the terrace, others being admitted to visit their wounded sovereign. Henry slept composedly during the day for some hours; on awaking, however, excruciating pains, attended with fever and restlessness, came on, and the king vomited a quantity of blood. For two hours his majesty's sufferings were intense; when somewhat relieved, the king declared that he knew his hours were numbered, and eagerly requested the sacraments of the church. Before the rites were administered, Henry addressed his assembled nobles, showing a courage and constancy deemed admirable by all. He exhorted his subjects to union, and advised them to acknowledge the king of Navarre as their legitimate sovereign, and commanded them to refrain from avenging his death; he prayed them to forgive his errors of government, assuring them that he had had always the welfare of the people at heart. The king of Navarre entering his apartment at this moment, the king stretched out his hand towards him. "You see, my brother, how my subjects have treated me! beware, therefore, and take good heed for your own safety." Henry presently continued; addressing the king of Navarre, he said, "It is now for you, my brother, to possess that crown which I have striven to preserve for you; justice and the principle of legitimacy demand that you should succeed me in this realm. You will experience many calamities, unless you resolve to change your religion. I exhort you to do so, as much for the welfare of your soul as for your temporal interests. May my crown flourish on your head, and may your reign be prosperous as that of Charlemagne our puissant ancestor! I have commanded all the great officers of the crown to take the oath of allegiance to you." Emotion kept the king of Navarre silent; he took the king's hands and kissed them respectfully. Henry in a low voice, being much exhausted, here commanded the nobles present to approach his bed. He then requested them to give him the comfort of witnessing their oath of fidelity and recognition of the king of Navarre as their sovereign; being faithful to the last in the opinion which he had always expressed, that the king of Navarre was his only legitimate and rightful successor. All the nobles present then knelt round the bed of their dying monarch, and vowed fidelity to the king of Navarre as the lawful inheritor of the crown. Henry then gave the king of Navarre his benediction, and prayed him to protect and favour the young comte d'Auvergne and M. de Bellegarde. He, moreover, directed the duc de la Tremouille to announce his approaching demise to the division of the army under his command, and to exhort the men to be faithful to his successor. The same command his majesty gave to Saucy, and to the maréchal d'Aumont, the respective commanders of the Swiss and German levies. "This done," says a chronicler,[1] "the king requested to be left alone. The king of Navarre retired weeping, and the princes and nobles; so that in the death chamber there only remained the officers of the wardrobe and his majesty's almoner, chaplain, and surgeon." Bellegarde and Epernon continued to support their royal master, who presently fell into an uneasy slumber. About two o'clock in the morning of August 2nd, Henry woke with a start, and eagerly

[1] Cayet: Chronologie Novennaire. Mathieu: Hist. du Règne de Henri III. Sommaire récit des Choses Mémorables advenues en France sous le Règne de Henri IV. Mém. de Cheverny. Pasquier.

asked for his confessor. "The hour is at hand," said he, "when God will be pleased to manifest his will. Pray for me!" The signal was given, and Boulogne chaplain in chief to the king entered alone from an adjacent chamber, where, with a train of priests, he waited the summons. Henry was left for a brief interval with his confessor. The prayers for the dying were then recited, and the priests bore the Host to the bedside of the dying monarch, who feebly raised his hands in the act of adoration. Before the wafer touched the king's lips, Boulogne said, "Sire, his Holiness has issued a monitory against your majesty for the events which lately occurred at the States of Blois. I exhort you, therefore, to fulfil the behests of our most holy father, otherwise I may not pronounce you absolved." Henry feebly replied, "that it was his will and his intention to satisfy his Holiness on every point." Upon this declaration, which was witnessed by a great throng of nobles, who had been admitted according to custom by Epernon to witness the last moments of their royal master, Boulogne administered the sacred rites. At four o'clock on the morning of Tuesday, August 2nd, Henry III. ceased to exist.[1] A post-mortem examination was immediately made as to the cause of death, several of the surgeons asserting their belief that the knife was poisoned with which the wound had been inflicted. It was found, however, that the intestines were perforated; and that the immediate cause of the king's decease was syncope from internal bleeding. The royal remains were embalmed as tho-

[1] Discours véritable de l'étrange et subite Mort de Henri de Valois. Certificat de plusieurs Seigneurs de Qualité qui assistèrent le Roy depuis qu'il fut blessé jusques à sa mort. This document is signed—Epernon, d'O, Bellegarde, Charles de Valois, grand prior, Balzac, Manon, Duplessis, Louis de Paradles, confessor, Etienne de Boulogne, almoner. Also MS. Bibl. Imp. Dupuy, 137: Attestation des Seigneurs présents à la Mort de Henri III., 1589.

roughly as circumstances permitted, and deposited immediately in a coffin of lead.

D'Aubigné graphically describes the scene which ensued after Henry had breathed his last. "Henry IV.," says he, "found himself king sooner than he desired. Instead of acclamations of 'Vive le roy!' he beheld before him the corpse of his predecessor, at the feet of which knelt two monks of the order of Minimes, holding torches and reciting litanies. Clermont d'Entragues held the jaw of the deceased, while others wept, throwing themselves on the ground mumbling vows, prayers, or protests. Some in this confusion fell on their knees and asked pardon for offences committed against the new king. To these a certain duke (Epernon) replied, 'Hold your tongues; you chatter like women!' M. d'O, his brother Manon, Entragues, and Châteauvieux exclaimed quite close to the king's ear, 'that they would rather suffer ten thousand kinds of death than submit to a heretic prince!' The king, troubled at this spectacle, soon withdrew, taking with him the maréchal de Biron."[1]

Thus miserably perished Henry III., "a prince," says de Thou, "liberal, clement, of majestic presence, zealous for his religion, and a lover of equity." These qualities, however, were counterbalanced by a love of dissipation, by profligacy, indolence, and by an effeminacy of deportment which rendered him despicable in the eyes of his subjects. Never did any prince seem more worthy to ascend a throne than Henry in the opinion of his orthodox subjects, and never did a monarch more thoroughly disappoint such expectations. The reputation which Henry acquired by the victories of Jarnac and Montcontour—at which, however, despite the eulogiums of his flatterers, he acted only a part

[1] Histoire, liv. xi. p. 183, edit in fol.

subordinate to Tavannes and Biron—rendered the contrast with his subsequent inglorious career more conspicuous. France imagined her king to be a hero, and found him imbecile. Henry's prodigality impoverished the state; and the misconduct of his band of minions rendered his court notorious for scandalous brawls and outrages upon the lives and property of the citizens. In matters of religion the vacillating conduct of the king produced lamentable discord. He several times solemnly took oath to extirpate heresy, and formed conventions for the purpose; but, to the indignation of the orthodox, his majesty shortly afterwards entered into voluntary and amicable relation with those whom he had publicly declared to be under the ban of his royal displeasure. Whether such conduct resulted, as the admirers of this prince allege, from a scheme of vengeance more subtle and certain than that to be derived by open warfare, the fact—that few placed faith either in the word or the profession of the king—nobody felt it possible to dispute. The savage ferocity of Henry's temper, when effectually roused, caused his enemies, from pure dread and distrust, to proceed farther in their hostile designs than they probably would have done under a prince moderate, and on whose sincerity they could have relied. The share which Henry took in the murder of Coligny and Lignerolles; and his almost actual perpetration of the assassination of the Guises, must ever leave an indelible stain on his memory. On the other hand, Henry III. was generous, affable, and ordinarily an indulgent master. He was accomplished; and in eloquence of speech was surpassed by none in the realm. In all exercises which then distinguished a finished cavalier, he excelled. He passionately loved music; and in dancing none of the courtiers could compete with their sovereign. He spoke Latin and Italian fluently, and understood the English language. He was clever in the composition of devices and mottoes, and in divining enigmas. In his attire Henry III. exhibited the utmost magnificence; and in all matters connected with personal adornment or the embellishment of his palaces, he showed himself pre-eminent. His tastes, however, were puerile, and his designs fantastic. His religion modelled itself on delusions; incapable of realizing its sublime promptings, Henry adored the frippery, the creation of his own ingenuity with which he surrounded his worship. Nothing conduced to degrade Henry in the eyes of his subjects more than his extraordinary and unkingly *escapades* with his Penitents; such exhibitions were greeted by all classes of his subjects with scorn and laughter. "The unfortunate weakness which the king showed for his minions—his indolent indifference to the murmurs of his people, which first alienated M. d'Alençon and disgusted the duc de Guise; and his solitary egotism—were the causes which chiefly prevented this prince from becoming the idol of his subjects, the dread of his enemies, and the ornament and paragon of the monarchs of his time," says a contemporary historian[1] well versed in the history of the court of this last sovereign of the house of Valois.

The remains of the deceased king were laid in state in the chamber in which he died. The ceremony was brief; the nobles, captains, and minor officers passed in file before the *catafalque*, and sprinkled the coffin with holy water. The king Henri Quatre performed this sad office last. The palace was then vacated by all but the household officers of the late king, and his chaplains and almoners. The new king took up his abode in the hôtel of M. de Tilly close at hand.

The mutilated body of the regicide Jacques Clement,

[1] Mathieu; Hist. du Règne de Henri III.

meanwhile, was drawn on a sledge to the Place in front of the church of St. Cloud, and, after having been torn asunder by horses, was burned on the spot, and the ashes scattered to the wind. A few days afterwards the prior of the Dominican convent Bourgoing, who had aided madame de Montpensier in inciting Clement to commit the crime, was arrested in an attack on a fauxbourg of Paris by two Huguenot troopers. Henri IV. sent him to Tours, where the same sentence was executed on the prior as had been performed on the dead body of his accomplice.

The death of the king was known in Paris a few hours after it occurred: the intelligence was hailed with savage transports. The duchesse de Montpensier demeaned herself like one possessed: it is recorded that she wept, screamed, prayed, and laughed in the delirium of her triumph. The person who first rushed to her hôtel with the news that her dire vengeance had been satiated was a man from the dregs of the populace. "Ah, mon ami," exclaimed madame de Montpensier, throwing her arms round the neck of her informant, "welcome, welcome! Is it indeed true? Are you very sure of the fact? That wicked, perfidious tyrant, can he be dead? Mon Dieu! what joy! what triumph! The only drawback to my content is, that he knew not before he died that it was from my hand the blow came!" Turning to her ladies, the duchess said, "Well, mesdames, what is now your opinion? My head seems to me to adhere more firmly on my shoulders than it did a few hours ago! Do you not agree with me?"[1] If madame de Montpensier in reality uttered words so horrible as the above, which, however, are recorded by most contemporary historians in their works whether published or manuscript, who will ven-

[1] Chronologie Novennaire. Journal de Henri III., etc.

ture to deny the possibility that she had recourse to all the criminal methods attributed to her to inflame the fanatic zeal of Jacques Clement? In after years madame de Montpensier vindicated her violence by the words, "It was my life or the king's life"—meaning that her decapitation would have surely followed the surrender of Paris.

The same afternoon madame de Montpensier, accompanied by her mother the duchesse de Nemours, traversed the streets of Paris in an open car drawn by six horses. The duchess wore a green scarf, and distributed others on her route. The principal lords and leaders of the League, after the decease of the duc de Guise and his brother, had always appeared in public girt with a scarf of black cloth. Whenever the duchess, during her progress, saw several persons assembled together, she rose and exclaimed, "*Bonnes nouvelles, mes amis! bonnes nouvelles! Le tyran est mort! Il n'y a plus de Henri de Valois en France!*" The princesses alighted at the great Franciscan convent where the deceased king loved to retire, and in the chapel of which he often held his chapters of the Order of St. Esprit. The duchesse de Nemours ascended the steps of the high altar and made an harangue to the people, who by the command of madame de Montpensier had been admitted into the chapel. A fresh distribution was also here made of green scarfs. Afterwards, amidst enthusiastic cheers, the duchesses returned to the hôtel de Montmorency.[1] Paris was, indeed, raging in an access of that frenzied madness to which, even up to the present era, it seems her fate to be periodically subject. "Nothing was heard in Paris," says an author contemporary with these events,[2] "but songs

[1] Cayet. Davila. Mathieu.

[2] Sommaire récit des Choses Mémorables advenues en France sous le Règne de Henri IV. jusqu'en 1598, pp. 9, 10, 11.

and ribaldry. The duc de Mayenne and his followers assumed green scarfs, and discarded the black scarf which they had worn since the massacre of Blois. Banquets, masquerades, and shows were devised, during which the name of the deceased king was laden with horrible maledictions. The effigy of the "assassin martyr" was carved in wood, and painted on canvas, and sold to decorate the houses of the Leaguers. He was regarded as canonized, and invoked by many as a new saint and martyr. His relatives were enriched by donations and public contributions. The royalists, on the contrary, detested the name of the assassin; and it was discovered that his name, Jacques Clement, formed the anagram '*c'est l'enfer qui m'a créé;*' and certes, afterwards it seemed as if all the furies of hell were let loose to overwhelm our unhappy France." To one other personage, also, the day of the king's death was a jubilee; and few exulted more in the catastrophe than his sister Marguerite, now queen of France and Navarre—safe on her impregnable rock of Usson from the perils of civil conflict.

Suspense and division also reigned throughout the ranks of the vast army encamped before Paris. The proud nobles of France, whose ancestors had served under the banner of the canonized king Saint Louis—converts many of them also from the League—at length beheld at their head a Huguenot king. During the last hours of the late king several councils had been holden by the king of Navarre in his quarters at Meudon, and by some of the principal nobles at St. Cloud; but the consternation was too great to permit of serious discussion. The calamity which had happened had dissolved the bonds which linked together that army, composed of men of divers nationalities and interests. The Swiss levies appeared inclined to depart; the German troops positively announced their resolve to return. The favourites of the late king apprehended lest they might be deprived of their commands, or disgraced for their proceedings during the late reign. The nobles generally shrunk from acknowledging a heretic prince for their sovereign; while the Huguenot lords watched with intense suspicion lest their gallant monarch, dazzled by his present altitude, and impressed with the expediency of conciliating his new subjects, might renounce his faith and profess the religion of the majority. On the evening of the decease of the king the nobles deputed the duc de Longueville to wait upon Henry, and to declare that the title of "Very Christian, being one of the attributes of the king of France, he could not assume the title without demonstrating its reality." During the night of the 3rd of August Henry held council with some of his most attached servants, such as Guitry, Beauvais-Nangis, and Ségur; the orthodox nobles on their side held assembly in the house of the duc de Piney. It was there resolved to acknowledge Henry's royal title, and to permit his proclamation in the camp, on the following conditions: 1. That within six months he would cause himself to be instructed in the Catholic and apostolic faith. 2. That during this interval he should bind himself to nominate no Huguenot to any state office. 3. That he would permit the nobles to send an ambassage to Rome to explain to his Holiness the weighty reasons that had induced them to recognize his sovereignty. Henry frankly granted these conditions, excepting the second; but in lieu offered to restore the exercise of the Romish faith throughout those districts where it had been suppressed. At this critical moment Sancy prevailed on the Swiss captains and their levies to enroll themselves under the banner of Henri IV. Moved with zeal for the righteous cause of his sovereign, Sancy harangued the assembled legions with fervour, and by a timely pecuniary gift brought them over to a man. This formidable accession to the Huguenot army—consisting of 12,000 men, besides the Germans, who presently also offered their services to the new king—hastened Henry's recognition. The king solemnly promised to confirm the privileges of the nobles, to respect their faith, and to avenge the perfidious slaughter of the deceased king. On the 4th day of August an act of recognition was signed by all the great nobles in camp, excepting the duc d'Epernon, who declined, under pretext that the privilege had been given to the maréchals de Biron and d'Aumont, as commanders-in-chief, to place their signature next to that of the royal princes —a concession which Epernon stated would, if he affixed his signature, for ever derogate from the dignity pre-eminently granted to him by the late king as a duke and peer of France.[1] Epernon, therefore, requested permission to withdraw to his government. The causes of the duke's cold adherence to the interests of the prince, whose firm friend he had been on many occasions during the past reign, can only be surmised. It was known, however, that Epernon had jealously resented the partiality lately displayed by Henry III. towards the king of Navarre, and consequently there had been grave dissensions between them. The duke, however, asserted his loyalty; but owned to some scruples in serving a heretic prince. He added that he had previously solicited leave of absence to visit his young consort from the late king, which had been granted.[2] But the example of Epernon was

[1] The duke's patent gave him precedence after the royal princes, the duc de Joyeuse, and all peers not deriving their descent from sovereign houses.

[2] The peerage of Epernon, duc de Candale and de la Valétte, Captal de Buch, became soon extinct in the direct line. The duke had one son, Bernard Nogaret de la Valette, who espoused Gabrielle, daughter of Henri IV. and the marquise de Verneuil, but died without issue,

infectious, and many of the principal nobles suddenly found themselves compelled to depart to their governments. The king granted permission to retire to all those who sought it without remark or remonstrance. Henry, however, ever bore the duc d'Epernon great resentment for this untimely defection. The ducs de Montpensier and Longueville, the maréchal d'Aumont, the prince de Conti, the young comte d'Auvergne, Biron, Montmorenci sieur de Damville faithfully adhered to the fortunes of their sovereign.

After the solemn recognition of his kingly rights by the great majority of the nobles and other illustrious personages present in the camp of St. Cloud, Henry IV. resolved reluctantly to raise the siege of Paris and retreat into Normandy, the greater part of which province had submitted to the duc de Montpensier, who had acknowledged his authority. The funeral solemnities of the deceased king had yet to be performed; the League held St. Denis; while the hate demonstrated by the Parisians towards their late sovereign rendered it impolitic to deposit his body in the church of St. Cloud. The heart of king Henry, however, was enclosed in a coffer of lead,[1] and secretly interred on one side of the high altar in the church of St. Cloud. Benoise, the faithful and attached secretary of Henry III., superintended the ceremony. After the pacification of the troubles of France, Benoise erected a magnificent mausoleum or small chapel inlaid with rare marbles over the spot where he had deposited the coffer, and for which he composed the following inscription :—

July, 1661. The title passed to the house of Montespan, which became extinct in 1727, when the duchy of Epernon reverted to the house of Noailles by the favour of the king Louis XV.

[1] The leaden pipes and the basins of the fountains which adorned the gardens of St. Cloud were taken to make the royal coffin.

D. O. M.

Æternæ Memoriæ Henrici III. Galliæ et Poloniæ Regis.

Adsta, viator, et dole Regum vicem.
Cor Regis isto conditum est sub marmore,
Qui jura Gallis, Sarmatis jura dedit,
Tectus cucullo hunc sustulit sicarius,
Abi, viator, et dole Regum vicem
Quod ei optaveris tibi eveniat.

C. Benoise, Scriba Regius, et Magister Rationum, Domino suo beneficentissimo, meritiss.

P. A. 1594.

When this ceremony was concluded an authentic act was drawn to be forwarded to Rome, stating that king Henry before his decease had made submission to the Holy See, and had therefore been absolved by Etienne Boulogne, who administered the last sacraments of the Church. The document was signed by all the Roman Catholic peers present at the king's decease. It was noted, however, that Henry III. left no evidence of his repentance by commanding the liberation of the cardinal de Bourbon and the archbishop of Lyons. The intelligence of the assassination of the king had been received with transport in Rome. Sixtus V. ascended the pulpit before the Consistory holden in the Vatican, September 11th, 1589, and lauded the deed of the regicide, exalting his act above the exploits of Judith and Eleazer;[1] "for," said his Holiness, the universal Father of Christendom, "such a holy, glorious, and pious act could only have been inspired and executed by the admirable and immediate interposition of Almighty God. God, our Almighty Lord, in thus saving miraculously the city of Paris, punished also the iniquities committed by deceased monarchs of France. To Him, therefore, be ascribed glory and

[1] Harangue du Saint Père Sixte V. prononcée en plein Consistoire le 2 Septembre, 1589, en Latin et en Français, en 8vo. Paris, 1589.

honour, and to the sainted martyr Clement our tribute of veneration!" Such is a specimen of the blasphemous oration publicly pronounced by Sixtus V. The funeral services performed in the papal city by command of his Holiness were for the repose of the soul of the traitor, and not for that of his victim.

On the 5th day of August king Henry decamped from before Paris, taking with him the body of the late king, which he had resolved to deposit in the abbey church of St. Corneille of Compiègne, until more peaceful times permitted of its transfer to the Chapelle de Valois in the church of St. Denis. The funeral *cortége* was attended by the prince de Conti, the duc de Montpensier, Charles bastard of France, the maréchal de Biron, and the eldest son of the duc de Montmorenci. On the road to Compiègne king Henry assaulted and took the towns of Meulan and Clermont, the body of the deceased king, meantime, being placed under a pavilion and guarded by a company of the guards. On the 24th day of August the procession reached the abbey of St. Corneille. The coffin of the king was placed under a *chapelle ardente* erected on one side of the high altar, with few ceremonies, as its rest there was deemed temporary.

The body of Henry III. remained at St. Corneille until after the assassination of his successor Henri Quatre, who likewise died in the arms of the duc d'Epernon. Marie de Medici, the widow of Henry IV., caused the coffin of Henry III. to be transported from St. Corneille, June 16th, 1610, and that of queen Catherine de Medici from the church of St. Sauveur de Blois to St. Denis, where one ceremonial finally consigned the remains of the three princes—Henry IV., Henry III., and Catherine de Medici—who had played so conspicuous a part in the events of the sixteenth century, to the tomb.[1] The bishop of Séez pronounced the funeral oration of Henry III.

Henry III., the last male representative of the august line of Valois, died at St. Cloud, August 2nd, 1589, aged thirty-eight years, after a troublous reign of fifteen years and two months.

King Henry was a bountiful benefactor to the monastic establishments of his reign. He founded superb monasteries at Vincennes and in the Fauxbourg St. Honoré of Paris. He also repaired and magnificently adorned the chapel of Notre Dame de Cléry, and the tomb of St. Martin in the cathedral church of Tours. During the reign of Henry III. the Pont Neuf was commenced under the famous architect Jacques du Cerceau, to the construction of which the king munificently contributed. Many beautiful architectural works were completed during this reign. The Sainte Chapelle at Champigny, the magnificent palace of the ducs de Montpensier, was embellished with numerous works of art, and by a superb window of painted glass representing the history of St. Louis.

After the intelligence reached queen Louise of the fatal catastrophe of St. Cloud, she retired from the castle of Chinon to Chenonceau, the beautiful château which had appertained to the deceased queen Catherine de Medici, once also the abode of Diane de Poitiers. Louise mourned the untimely death of Henry III., and was constant in her endeavours to avenge it. From that period she completely broke off all relations with her own kindred of Lorraine, and sincerely embraced the cause of Henry IV. Of the duchesse de Montpensier[2]

[1] Hist. de la Mère et du Fils—Mezeray. St. Marthe. Hist. Généalogique de la Royale Maison de France. Art. Henri III.

[2] Catherine de Lorraine died May 6, 1597, at the age of 45. She married the duc de Montpensier August 28th, 1561. Her dowry amounted to 300,000 livres. The duchess was buried in the nunnery of Les Filles Dieu in Paris.

the queen could never speak without shuddering, deeming her, as she said, "the assassin of her deceased lord." At Chenonceau the queen passed her forlorn widowhood in the practice of rigid austerities. Mournful notes of solemn *requiems* for the departed perpetually echoed through those apartments once dedicated to the profligate revels of the court of Catherine de Medici. The queen's apartments consisted of two chambers contiguous to the chapel, hung with black cloth. The ceilings and wainscots were painted black, and embossed with cornucopias and silver tears. There is still extant an eloquent appeal from the pen of Louise to Henry IV., asking for justice on the murderers of her husband, written in elegant French.[1] She was indefatigable in this her pursuit; and in the year 1593 the queen journeyed from Chenonceau to Mantes to ask audience of the king. Henry received her publicly in the church of Notre Dame. There, falling at the king's feet, Louise implored him to avenge the cruel murder of her dear lord and husband; and, moreover, to cause the body of the late king to be removed for interment at St. Denis. Henry raised the queen, and promised to comply with her petition at some future time, when affairs of state and the fortune of war should have placed the culprits within reach of "la justice du roi." The following day Louise returned to Chenonceau, and spent a melancholy interval of seven years in the strictest seclusion. As an alleviation to her grief, the queen invited and provided lodging at Chenonceau for

[1] Queen Louise writes in a transport of grief in her first letter addressed to Henry IV., dated September 6th. She says: "Cette plus que barbare assassinat me fait croire M. mon frère tout aide et support de vous en la justice que vous en demande la desolée veuve qu'il a laissée, de cette enorme et exécrable méchanceté; ne desirant plus de vie que pour voir la punition faite de ceux qui me le rende si misérable."—MC. Bibl. Imp. Béth. 9129, fol. 1. Also for documents relating to Louise see MSS. Dupuy, 137, 579.

a number of Capuchin nuns. In her will she left the sum of 20,000 crowns in trust to her sister-in-law, the duchesse de Mercœur, to build and endow a convent for the reception of these ladies at Bourges. For some unknown reason, however, the duchess, by the advice of the king, chose to transgress the directions of the foundress as to the locality of the convent, and caused a site to be purchased in the Rue St. Honoré, Paris. On the 18th of June, 1606, the Capucines took possession of their house, which was the first nunnery of the order established in France.

In the year 1600 queen Louise, whose health suffered greatly from the damp atmosphere of Chenonceau, removed to the castle of Moulins, leaving her beloved château to the sole occupation of the Capucines. She sank, however, and died of dropsy and general decline, at Moulins, on the 29th day of January, 1601, at the age of 47.

A poet of the day composed the following lines to the memory of Louise, in which allusion is made to the nature of her last malady:—

> Celle là dont le nom remplissoit tout le monde
> Par sa dernier adieu le remplit tout de deuil;
> Son âme emplit le ciel de sa gloire féconde;
> Son corps ne peut emplir de sa cendre un cercueil!

Queen Louise was interred before the high altar in the chapel of her Capuchin nuns.[1] The nuns removed the body of their foundress in 1688, when they took possession of more spacious premises in the Rue Neuve des Petits Champs. In 1806 the Capucine convent was demolished, with its rich and beautiful chapel; and the Rue de la Paix now extends over the entire site, including the extensive pleasure-grounds attached. The

[1] The funeral oration of the queen was preached by le Père Thomas d'Avignon, Capuchin; and a life of Louise was published, entitled "Le Miroir des Veuves." The author was Nicholas Gazet, Cordelier.

jaspar tomb of queen Louise was then conveyed to the Musée des Monuments Français, and her ashes were deposited in a vault at St. Denis.

It appertains not to this history to detail the glorious exploits by which Henry IV. finally won the crown of his ancestors. The assassination of Henry III. was never avenged. The length of time which had elapsed since the commission of the deed; the difficulties which beset the early years of Henry's government, and the clemency of his disposition, combined to frustrate the demands of justice. On the capitulation of Paris, 1594, the king, on the evening succeeding his entry, visited the duchesses de Nemours and Montpensier, and confirmed his previous promises of immunity from the retribution which the latter especially merited. In 1596, the duc de Mayenne made his submission, when in the articles of accommodation it was specially provided that no inquiries or pursuit of justice should be made concerning the death of the late king; but a pardon under the great seal was granted to all personages suspected, or proved to have participated in that crime. The words "princes et princesses" were inserted in the act of amnesty, on account of the duchesse de Montpensier. The parliament of Paris was prohibited by edict from receiving petitions respecting the assassination of Henry III. There was only one individual in France sufficiently courageous to appeal against this amnesty—Diane de France, duchesse d'Angoulême, wrote with her own hand a protest, to which she procured the signature of queen Louise, and in person presented the document to the Chambers.

Henry III. assumed for his device three crowns, one of which appeared to descend from a heaven beset with stars, with the motto—Manet ultima Cœlo.

THE END.

CPSIA information can be obtained
at www.ICGtesting.com
Printed in the USA
LVHW042037300123
738241LV00002B/317

9 783375 138868